FINAL DESTINY

A John Decker Novel

ANTHONY M.STRONG

 WEST STREET

ALSO BY ANTHONY M. STRONG

THE JOHN DECKER SUPERNATURAL THRILLER SERIES

Soul Catcher (prequel) • What Vengeance Comes • Cold Sanctuary

Crimson Deep • Grendel's Labyrinth • Whitechapel Rising

Black Tide • Ghost Canyon • Cryptic Quest • Last Resort

Dark Force • A Ghost of Christmas Past • Deadly Crossing

Final Destiny

THE CUSP FILES

Deadly Truth

THE REMNANTS SERIES

The Remnants of Yesterday • The Silence of Tomorrow

STANDALONE BOOKS

The Haunting of Willow House • Crow Song

AS A.M. STRONG WITH SONYA SARGENT

Patterson Blake FBI Mystery Series

FINAL
DESTINY

West Street Publishing

Cover art and interior design by Bad Dog Media, LLC.

ISBN: 978-1-942207-48-1

To Sonya

FINAL
DESTINY

ONE

ELISE FELDER STOPPED AND STARED, awed by the spectacle ahead of her. Beyond a roughhewn stone entrance that looked more like the mouth to a cave than the doorway to an underground world beneath one of the world's busiest cities lay a grotto of sorts, lit in a warm yellow glow by sconces at intervals along its granite and brick walls. But if this was a grotto, it was bigger than any Elise could imagine. A cavernous chamber that stretched as far as she could see. And on both sides, rows of wine vaults, each one stacked floor to ceiling with fine French champagnes, brandies, and liqueurs.

In the main chamber, a hundred or more revelers danced in sweeping turns to the quick tempo of a stirring Viennese waltz, while even more partygoers sipped champagne, enjoyed hors d'oeuvres served by waiters carrying silver trays, and gushed excitedly about the unusual setting of the soirée.

The dazzling sight took Elise's breath away.

"It's incredible," she whispered, as much to herself as her companion and beau of three weeks, Wallace Alden.

"I thought you'd like it." Wallace escorted her through the door, then stopped and glanced up at the vaulted ceiling soaring fifty feet over their heads. "Just think of what's above us. The streets of New York, bustling with cabs and trolleys and pedestrians going about their business with no idea of what's happening right beneath their feet."

"How is this place even here?" Elise asked, noticing the chamber's more intricate details for the first time. A fresco adorned the far wall. A vineyard scene with rows of grapevines in front of a turreted château framed by distant mountains painted with such exquisite skill that if it were a religious scene, it might have graced the walls of an Old-World cathedral. Each side vault bore a title. Avenue Regoud. Avenue Les Deux Oefs. Avenue Sichel Bordeaux. And painted on the brickwork between, the names of champagne manufacturers.

Wallace smiled, clearly enjoying his companion's delight. "These tunnels and vaulted rooms were built back in 1876, when the anchorages for the New York and Brooklyn Bridge were under construction. Behind these walls, hidden from view, are massive slabs of stone heavier than you could ever imagine that secure the steel cables used to support the bridge and tension them. It's really quite incredible to think that without these cellars and the anchorages that made them possible, the bridge would simply collapse into the East River."

"That's hardly comforting," said Elise, shuddering at the thought of the mighty bridge, thousands of tons of steel trusses and decking, tumbling into the frigid river and taking with it any soul unfortunate enough to be crossing at the time.

"Oh, don't worry. It's quite safe." Wallace was distracted now. He was scanning the crowded taproom, as the wine cellar's main concourse was called, and craning his neck. "Look. There. That's the writer, Max Eastman."

"Oh. Really?" Elise didn't want to admit that she had no idea who Max Eastman was and didn't care.

"And beside him is the political activist, Emma Goldman." The excitement in Wallace's voice rang like a bell. "I'll have to introduce you to them later."

"I can't wait," Elise did her best to look interested. She flicked a strand of blonde hair away from her face, then she asked, "Who are you looking for?"

"Why Clarence, of course. He was kind enough to throw this soiree for us all, so it's only fair that we wish him many happy returns."

He invited you, not me, Elise thought bitterly. Clarence Rothman was the younger brother of Howard Rothman III, a shipping magnate who had taken over the family company upon their father's death, Clarence refused to enter the business and instead lived a bohemian life in Greenwich Village thanks to his fat trust fund. Elise had only met the man once many years before and hadn't liked him. She didn't see the man now, which was good, because her attention at that moment was focused on Wallace, which was why she took his hand and said, "Let's dance."

"There will be plenty of time for dancing after dinner." Wallace extricated his hand and stepped further into the room. "Clarence is serving Chicken a la Maryland. That's a chicken breast topped with sauteed bananas. It's supposed to be quite delicious."

"Dinner won't be served for another hour. If we can't dance, then at least get me a glass of champagne." Elise swallowed a flicker of annoyance. She found Wallace infuriating at times.

"Very well, my love." Wallace studied the room one more time, a slight smile touching his lips. "I'll be right back."

Elise watched him go. She smoothed a crease from her dress and waited, listening to the music, and watching the revelers spin around the dance floor. She became so engrossed that she failed to notice Wallace returning with a pair of champagne flutes until he was almost upon her. But he was not alone. A tall man with thick dark hair, a firm jaw, and iridescent blue eyes accompanied him. Clarence Rothman. Elise groaned inwardly. She had plans for the evening with Wallace. Now they would have to wait.

"Well, hello, my lovely," Clarence cooed, closing the gap between them. There was a martini glass in his hand and a smile on his lips. "I must say, I was rather hoping that Wallace would bring you with him tonight. He's told me so much about you."

"Not too much, I hope."

"We shall see." Clarence let his gaze wander over her. "You look familiar, have we met before?"

"I rather doubt it." Elise lied, plucking one of the champagne flutes from Wallace's grasp and raised it to her lips, sipping the golden liquid. "Many happy returns."

"Why, thank you."

Elise lifted her glass. "And *thank you* for the champagne. Pol Roger if I'm not mistaken."

"You are not. All the way from the Vallée d'Épernay. This is a particularly nice vintage of which my brother received several cases only last week."

"Ah, yes. Wallace tells me that your family has entered the wine business."

"Indeed. It was all Howard's idea. Since we already ship to and from Europe, it only made sense. Of course, I have no interest in any of that." Clarence raised his glass. "I prefer to simply drink the profits. In this case, a rather wonderful vermouth."

Elise took another sip of her champagne. "I suppose it is our good fortune that your brother was willing to part with so much fine wine on the occasion of your birthday."

"I'll let you in on a secret." Clarence leaned close with an impish smile. "He only let me use the wine cellars because he doesn't want my bohemian friends traipsing around the family mansion. He and his fiancée couldn't even be bothered to show up for this party, so I switched out the second grade hooch he put aside for us in favor of a more palatable selection. I'm sure he'll be furious when he realizes how much of his newly imported vintages have found their way down the throats of the Greenwich Village crowd he so despises, especially since he lost a sizable cargo of expensive wine in the hold of that ocean liner that sank a few days ago."

"The Titanic?"

"Indeed. Hundreds of bottles lying on the ocean floor out of my brother's reach forever. Such a shame. And I intend to deplete his stock even more. It's devilish of me, I know, but I simply can't help myself."

"In that case, I shall become a co-conspirator and drink as much Pol Roger as humanly possible." Elise downed the last of her drink.

"Not before you do me the honor of a dance." Clarence grabbed Elise's hand and tugged her toward the middle of the room. "Assuming your beau has no objections, of course."

"Absolutely none, old boy. Just promise you'll bring her back to me when you're done."

"I will promise no such thing." Clarence grinned.

"Maybe later," Elise said, hoping Clarence would lose interest and move on to other guests. And it wasn't just that he had a reputation with the women, and not a good one. She wanted to focus on Wallace. But it was too late. He was already dragging her onto the dance floor and slipping an arm around her waist, or more accurately, a little lower than her waist. And then he was whirling her around even as he held her close. While at the edge of the room, she saw Wallace slip a silver cigarette case from his pocket and start toward one of the wine cellars without giving her a backward glance.

TWO

JOHN DECKER STOOD on the RMS Carpathia's Promenade Deck and peered over the rail at the choppy waters of the North Atlantic below, lost in thought.

It had been two days since the Titanic's deadly encounter with an iceberg and Decker's last sighting of the ancient Egyptian vampire brought aboard by Ignatius Faucher. The latter, Decker knew, was dead even before the Titanic went down, ripped apart by Amenmosep. Of the vampire himself, there had been no sign since the surviving passengers and crew of the doomed ocean liner were picked up by the Carpathia.

But Decker was not fool enough to believe Amenmosep had perished when the Titanic slipped beneath the waves. The vampire was alive and kicking in the moments prior to the tragedy, and having survived thousands of years buried in the Valley of the Kings, he was hardly going to let a little freezing water stop him.

This troubled Decker. The Carpathia was only a few days from docking in New York, where the Titanic survivors would be offloaded before the ocean liner once again set sail for the Mediterranean seaport of Fiume in Austria-Hungary. If Amenmosep reached the United States, he would soon disappear into the bustling metropolis and be free to kill with impunity, extending his own life even further with each additional victim. And without the Order of St. George's resources, it would be impossible to stop him.

"I thought I'd find you out here," said a female voice to Decker's rear.

He turned to find Mina lingering a few feet away, her arms wrapped around her chest against the biting cold and a blanket over her shoulders. "I took another turn around the deck to see if I could find him," he said, by way of explanation.

"It's been two days and we've seen neither hide nor hair of Amenmosep, despite searching the ship from top to bottom more than once."

"I know."

"There's every chance he went down with the Titanic."

"And just as much chance he didn't." Decker turned away from the rail as a rumbling peal of thunder echoed overhead. The weather had been dreadful since the morning after their rescue, with violent storms and thick fog slowing the Carpathia's progress to New York, piling further misery onto the already exhausted survivors of what Decker knew would come to be viewed as one of the worst maritime tragedies in history. "We can't allow him to reach New York."

"If that creature was on board the ship, I would have sensed him."

"Unless you haven't gotten close enough," Decker said. Thanks to her encounter with Abraham Turner, Mina was forever changed. She had absorbed Turner's life force and memories, and with them, some of his abilities. She was now a gestalt consciousness. Neither wholly human nor vampire, but something new. And with this transformation came the ability to sense other nearby vampires.

"The only way I wouldn't be able to detect him is if he were not in the public areas of the ship and beyond the range of my senses."

"Which could be the case. Maybe he killed a crew member and is hiding in an area off-limits to us."

"It's doubtful. The Carpathia is much smaller than the Titanic and therefore has a small crew. If someone didn't show up for their shift, they would be missed."

"Perhaps, but I'll still feel better if we keep looking for as long as possible. The stakes for not doing so are too high."

"I know you don't want to hear this, but unless something changes, we have no choice but to assume that Amenmosep didn't make it off the Titanic and is trapped in a watery grave on the ocean floor, even as we speak. Hard to kill or not, I don't see how he could survive in such an inhospitable environment." Mina rested a hand on Decker's arm and spoke in a low voice so as not to be overheard on the crowded deck. "We know from history that the Carpathia was the only ship to rescue survivors, so if he is not aboard, then he's gone for good. Besides, what would you propose to do if we actually did find Amenmosep? It's not like we could easily kill him. And even if we tried, the deck of an ocean liner full of traumatized passengers is hardly the place to do it. We would never be able to explain ourselves."

Decker gave a weary sigh. "You're right, of course."

"I know." Mina smiled. She paused a moment and leaned on the rail, gazing out at the faint outline of another ship barely visible through the shroud of fog that had enveloped them for more than a day. This was the USS Chester, sent out to escort the Carpathia on its last leg into New York harbor.

"Amenmosep aside, we have other matters that need our attention. I spoke to the ship's wireless operator this morning after breakfast, hoping to relay a message to Thomas back in London. We are effectively penniless and will need funds if we are to survive and blend in, especially since neither of us is familiar with early twentieth century New York. But the Carpathia's captain has ordered that no messages be sent on behalf of passengers and the radio room is also refusing to answer messages from shore regarding which of Titanic's passengers have survived."

"Which means we're effectively incommunicado until we disembark. Hopefully, we'll be able to send a telegraph to Finch at that point and secure his help." Decker fell silent for a moment. "With any luck, he will be relieved enough to hear from us to forget that I drugged and locked him in my apartment."

"I wouldn't hold your breath." Mina chuckled. "When the pair of you come face to face again, you might want to keep a safe distance from his fist. At least until he calms down."

"Duly noted."

"But I will say that he isn't vindictive by nature and even if his first inclination is to hang you out to dry, he won't do the same to me. He might even be grateful you completed the task for which you boarded the Titanic and rescued me."

"I believe that was all on you," Decker said with a grin. "You rescued yourself. I was nothing but a bystander."

"You were much more than that." Mina looked up at Decker. "You always have been."

THREE

WALLACE ALDEN WATCHED his date step onto the dance floor with Clarence Rothman, throwing him a desperate look to be saved as she did so. But Alden wasn't about to step between Clarence and his desire to dance with the attractive young woman. She didn't mean that much to him. They had only met a few weeks before and he looked upon their relationship as a fling and nothing more, even if she was beguiling and knew how to use her charms both in the bedroom and beyond. But his ties to Clarence Rothman went far deeper, and not just because they both moved in the same elite bohemian Greenwich Village circle that included well-respected artists, writers, actors, and more than one wayward millionaire looking for an alternative to the stuffy lifestyle their old money upbringing provided. He and Rothman had attended the same college and became fast friends.

But he also felt bad for throwing Elise to the figurative wolves. He knew how Clarence treated women. The man had a well-deserved reputation and Alden didn't want to think about where the younger Rothman brother's hands might roam during his spin around the dance floor with Elise. Which was why he turned away and made for one of the wine vaults on either side of the main room, pulling out his silver cigarette case as he went.

He stepped under the arch of a vault lined with thousands of bottles stored on wooden racks twice as tall as himself. Alone now, he made his way deep into the chamber, passing a row of stacked wine casks, and came to another narrow archway at the back that led to what appeared to be a service corridor between the vaults. Alden poked his head through the opening. It stretched away into darkness. A faint, musty smell assaulted his nostrils. He pulled his head back and leaned against the back wall of the vault. Setting his champagne flute down on a nearby upturned barrel, he opened the silver case and slipped a cigarette out. Returning the case to his pocket, Alden put the cigarette to his lips and struck a match, lighting the cigarette. He closed his eyes and pulled the smoke to the back of his throat, then exhaled the long stream.

Music drifted into the vault, rising above the background murmur of voices and laughter.

The waltz would be over soon, and Elise would expect him to save her from a second go around with Clarence, who had surely lived up to his reputation by now and stepped beyond the boundaries of good etiquette. But Alden wasn't ready to return. He wanted to finish the cigarette in peace. He also wanted to avoid being a bad sport and snatching the young woman away from Clarence before he was finished with her. If Elise had to endure a second lap around the dance floor, then so be it. She would forgive him. And even if she didn't, who cared? There were plenty more girls where Elise came from. Girls who were yearning to be at the heart of bohemian New York society.

Alden smiled to himself. Life was good, and only getting better. He took another drag of the cigarette, then strolled to one of the wine racks and pulled a bottle out. It was a Cabernet Sauvignon, caked in dust which he brushed from the label. It was a 1902 vintage from one of the best wineries in France and would be just about aged to perfection by now. The tannins in the wine would have given it a complexity and flavor that couldn't be beat, and a price to match. When this wine finally hit the market, it would provide a nice profit for the Rothman wine cellars, and there were hundreds, if not thousands, more just like it quietly aging in the dark and cool atmosphere under the New York and Brooklyn Bridge, otherwise known as the East River Bridge.

Alden ran a finger over the neck of the bottle and up to the cork. There must be an opener around somewhere. Perhaps near the bar where the servers were collecting glasses of champagne to distribute among the revelers out in the taproom. He could slip from the vault and find a corkscrew, then slink back in here and sample some of Rothman's finest. After all, Clarence himself was dipping into the family stash without permission, so Alden figured he would just be giving the family black sheep a helping hand in needling his elder brother and head of the Rothman business empire. That Clarence derived his money from that very establishment did not seem to bother him, so why should it bother anyone else?

Alden turned the wine bottle over in his hands, relishing the thought of sampling the finely crafted wine within. Hell, with a bit of luck, he might even get away with slipping a bottle out under his jacket when they left to enjoy later with Elise. It would go a long way to making up for abandoning her on the dance floor and she didn't need to know that he hadn't actually paid for it.

Alden was about to slip the bottle back into its nook on the rack while he went in search of a corkscrew, but before he could do so, a faint sound further back in the vault drew his attention. He turned, scanning the darkness between the racks of wine and the stacked casks.

Maybe another guest had stepped away from the main event looking for a quiet place to sneak a cigarette of their own or perhaps fool around with their date.

Except he didn't see anyone.

Alden was still alone in the vault, at least so far as he could tell. He shrugged and was about to turn back to the rack when the sound came again, closer this time. And now he was able to ascertain the direction from which it had originated. The narrow corridor that ran along the back of the vaults.

The hair prickled on Alden's neck.

Nobody was back there. He knew it.

Except that wasn't true anymore. He could hear what sounded like footsteps echoing out of the narrow space. No. Not footsteps. More like feet shuffling on the concrete floor.

Alden's sense of self-preservation kicked in. He forgot about the wine still gripped in one hand and took a step away from the corridor, intending to flee back to the safety of the main room.

Just as a dark shape filled the opening.

Alden gagged as a malodorous scent burned his nostrils, pungent and ripe.

The shape moved from the darkness beyond the vault. Alden could make out no features in the dimly lit wine cave other than a vague sense of heft. It walked in a strange shuffling gait, as if unused to its own legs.

And the smell…

Alden's throat closed even as he backed away from the hulking shape bearing down upon him. He struggled to tear his eyes away, afraid of letting the thing out of his sight.

Then he came to his senses.

Alden turned to flee even as powerful arms reached out and snatched him up, dragging him back toward the dark and fetid tunnel.

The wine bottle slipped from his grasp and shattered on the floor.

He kicked and twisted, reached out and gripped the sides of the tunnel entrance, desperate to avoid being pulled back into its depths. His fingernails scraped across granite, looking for purchase. One bent back and lifted, ripping away from his finger.

Alden didn't even notice the pain.

It was all he could do to let out a single terrified scream as he was yanked back into the darkness, even as the band in the taproom played to a crescendo and drowned out his cry.

He never got the chance to make another sound. A powerful hand restrained his chest. Another gripped the back of his head and twisted. The last thing Alden heard was the sharp crack of his neck snapping.

FOUR

IT WAS EARLY THURSDAY EVENING, almost four days after Titanic slipped beneath the waves, when the RMS Carpathia left the Atlantic Ocean behind and made her way up the Hudson River toward Pier 59. The deck was crowded with passengers eager to escape the confines of the ship, but they would have to wait a little longer, because the Carpathia hadn't quite finished her journey yet. Pier 59 was the Titanic's original destination, and they were stopping only to offload the lifeboats that had been taken in tow. Once that task was completed, the Carpathia headed back down the Hudson to Pier 54, where the Cunard liners docked.

Like everyone else aboard ship, Decker and Mina stood on the deck and watched as the buildings of lower Manhattan slipped past. A skyline that little resembled the 21st-century metropolis they were used to. It would be another eighteen years before the Empire State Building would rise from a plot of land currently occupied by the Waldorf-Astoria Hotel. Right now, the Singer, Woolworth, and Metropolitan buildings dominated the view.

Decker pulled his coat tight against a driving rain that had persisted all day and watched a solitary tugboat full of photographers trailing the ocean liner, the flashes from their cameras lighting the glut of passengers crowding the Carpathia's decks in an unearthly strobing chiaroscuro.

As they approached the pier, an even stranger sight greeted them. Tens of thousands of curious New Yorkers lined the quayside beyond the terminal buildings that lined the wharf.

"Wow. There must be twenty thousand people out there," Decker said, awed by the sight.

"Probably twice that." Mina pressed against the rail to get a better look as the ship slipped up to the vast Cunard terminal that jutted out into the water atop the pier. "We need to be careful after we disembark. There will be journalists everywhere and we can't afford for our photograph to appear in any newspapers."

"Even if they do, I can't imagine anyone would recognize us." Decker hadn't shaved in almost a week. He sported the start of a beard, and his hair was wild because it hadn't been brushed since he boarded the Carpathia. He wore ill-fitting clothes donated by one of the liner's official passengers. There were bags under his eyes from lack of sleep.

"We need to keep it that way for posterity." Mina had fared better. Another woman aboard ship had lent her a hairbrush, and she had snagged a much-coveted opportunity to bathe the day before. A luxury afforded only to a small group of the Titanic's surviving first-class female passengers. She wore a blue silk dress donated to her by one of Carpathia's first-class passengers making the crossing to Europe, and it fit her better than Decker's donated clothing. Not that anyone would mistake the tomboyish waif of her early twenties for the sophisticated woman Mina had become during her years trapped in the past. She might not have aged physically, but she now possessed a grace and maturity that shone through her still youthful countenance.

"You want to take one last go around the decks and see if you sense anything?" Decker asked, watching members of the Carpathia's crew and dockworkers on the pier busy themselves with mooring the ocean liner, a process he figured would buy enough time for one last check of the passengers.

Mina shot him a sideways glance. "You're still worried that Amenmosep might have snuck on board and hidden out of sight somewhere."

"It's a possibility. But unless he wants to end up making the crossing back to Europe as a stowaway, he'll need to disembark with the rest of the survivors."

"Which means he'll have to come out of hiding."

"Exactly." Decker hoped more than anything that they would find no trace of the vampire aboard ship, but he didn't want to leave it to chance. If Amenmosep had somehow survived the sinking and gotten aboard the Carpathia, he would find New York to be a veritable smorgasbord of human offerings ripe for the kill. He could simply disappear into a poverty-stricken neighborhood like the Lower East Side where dirt poor immigrants no one cared about crammed into tenements barely fit for human habitation. Here he could murder at will, picking off the dregs of society just as Abraham Turner, who the world would come to know as Jack the Ripper, had done decades before in the slums of Whitechapel. "It might be our last chance to find him before he escapes into the metropolis."

"I'll take a stroll around the ship if that eases your concerns," Mina said. "But I'm almost certain he is not aboard."

Decker cast another glance down at the men still securing the lines. Soon the gangplanks would be extended, and the surviving Titanic passengers would stream into the Cunard Line's terminal before dispersing to the four corners of the city and beyond. "Good. We don't have much time. Let's go."

FIVE

AN HOUR after the Carpathia pulled up next to the dock, Decker and Mina ascended the gangplank and entered the vast hall that made up the Cunard terminal on Pier 54. The building was packed with not only the surviving passengers and crew of the Titanic but also those of the Carpathia, who had been offloaded so the ship could be prepared to resume its journey to Europe.

The vast throng of onlookers waiting quayside had been denied entry to the terminal. Likewise, there were no reporters or photographers within the building, but there were representatives from several charitable organizations who swiftly went about distributing warm clothing, food, hot coffee, and blankets to the disheveled passengers and crew of the Titanic before steering those without accommodation toward transport waiting on the quayside to take them to shelters in the city.

With nowhere else to go and no means to contact Thomas Finch, at least in the short term, Decker suggested they tag along. "Better to spend the night in a shelter than on the streets with no roof over our heads," he said after accepting a mug of coffee and passing another to Mina.

"And after that?" Mina asked, clutching her mug with both hands to warm them against the insidious chill that wormed its way into her very bones. "We don't have a penny to our names. How are we going to survive, let alone contact Thomas in London?"

"I don't know," Decker admitted. He steered Mina toward a table upon which sandwiches had been laid out by a group who identified themselves as the Women's Relief Committee. He was about to take one and hand it to her when a voice spoke at their rear.

"Helena?"

Decker turned to find a woman in an ankle-length black dress standing there. He recognized her as the passenger who had given Mina a selection of dresses while they were still aboard the Titanic.

A smile spread across Mina's face. "Molly!"

"In the flesh." Molly threw her arms around Mina and hugged her. "I searched aboard the Carpathia but couldn't find you. I had resigned myself to the fact that you must have gone down with the ship. I can't tell you how happy I am to discover otherwise."

"It's good to see you, too." Mina motioned toward Decker. "You remember John?"

"Ah, yes. The man you were traveling with when your jilted lover tried to snatch you off the ship in Queenstown." Molly extended a hand to Decker. "A pleasure to meet you again."

"Likewise." Decker took Molly's hand in a quick embrace, then cast a furtive glance toward Mina. She had escaped the clutches of her captors aboard Titanic by enlisting the help of two passengers, one of whom was Molly. Having given the women a false name, she was forced to keep up the charade later when she and Decker—whom she had introduced as her brother—visited Molly's cabin to borrow a small wardrobe of dresses because Mina had no suitable clothing to blend in with the other first-class passengers. Now she must keep up the pretense once again.

Molly observed them with narrowed eyes. "I don't wish to pry, but do you both have somewhere to stay tonight?"

"We don't," Mina admitted. "We had intended to secure hotel rooms once we arrived in New York, but unfortunately lost all of our possessions during the sinking and have no assets in New York from which to draw."

"We will send a telegram to my London bank when circumstances allow," Decker said. "And arrange for a transfer of funds. In the meantime, we will go to a shelter."

"Absolutely not." Molly shook her head. "I simply cannot allow you to do such a thing. I have already arranged for transportation to the Waldorf-Astoria, where I shall be staying overnight. They know me well and will be more than happy to provide you with a suite of rooms for as long as you need them and bill it to my account along with any sundries. They can also arrange for your telegram to London."

"We couldn't possibly allow you to do such a thing," Mina said.

"Nonsense. What good is there in being rich if one can't help a friend in their hour of need?"

"In that case, we shall accept only under the condition that you allow us to repay you when our funds come through," Decker said.

"How about you donate the money to a good cause instead and we'll call it even." Molly motioned for them to follow her toward the front of the terminal. "Come along, before the press finds their way in here. I fear they will be hungry for news of the sinking."

"Suits me." Decker would rather not linger in the terminal. He had no idea what passed for immigration in the early twentieth century, but would like to avoid answering uncomfortable questions about who he was. Or Mina, for that matter.

He tagged along as Molly led them through the terminal toward the arched front of the building and the white doors that stood open beneath. Beyond these, he could see the surging mass of onlookers pressing against wooden barriers hastily set up by New York's finest, some of whom now stood in a row at the barricades to dissuade the more adventurous among the onlookers. He also noticed several men carrying bulky cameras with large flash units. As they drew closer, he steered Mina behind Molly so that the socialite obscured the photographers' view of them. He knew it wouldn't help once they left the building and ventured beyond the barricades to find Molly's cab, but it was better than nothing.

No sooner had they stepped out onto the quay than a flurry of flashbulbs lit the darkness. Decker turned his head away and pressed forward, blocking Mina with his body. A reporter shouted toward them, no doubt trying for a scoop. His cries were swiftly drowned out by a chorus of other reporters eager to splash first-hand accounts of the tragedy across their front pages.

There was a break in the barriers up ahead and a path of sorts that had been cleared through the milling crowd beyond which a row of horse-drawn carriages waited along with several motorized taxicabs. Molly made a beeline to one of these, pushing her way past the throng and ignoring their attempts to engage her.

Decker and Mina stayed close behind and did likewise. At

least, until Mina faltered and came to a halt. She turned and surveyed the throng of gawkers pressing toward them.

"What's wrong?" Decker whispered, following her gaze. He saw nothing out of the ordinary.

"Vampires," Mina hissed, then she took off into the crowd.

SIX

"WAIT." Decker made a grab for Mina's arm but missed and she was soon swallowed up into the sea of curious onlookers and desperate relatives waiting for news of their loved ones.

Molly was several paces ahead. She stopped and turned, then made her way back to Decker when she saw him standing alone. "Is everything alright?"

"I think so. Helene thought she saw a familiar face," he replied, using the false name that Mina had originally given Molly back on the Titanic. He started toward the spot where Mina had vanished into the crowd. "I'll bring her back."

"Don't waste any time." Molly pointed toward one of the motorized taxicabs. "That's us. I'll tell the driver to wait."

"Thank you." The last thing Decker wanted was to lose Molly and with her their chance of a warm room, hot bath, and soft bed. Not to mention being able to send a telegram back to London. He cursed under his breath and pushed through the jostling crush of bodies, racing to catch up with Mina. Then he saw her up ahead. She had come to a halt, arms at her sides.

At his approach, she tilted her head toward a man and a woman, both in their late twenties. The gentleman was decked out in a black suit and top hat while his companion wore a dark blue silk dress. They appeared oblivious to the rain. "There."

Decker studied the couple with interest. "Which one is the vampire?"

"I don't know. It's..." Mina faltered, furrowing her brow. "I think they both are."

"Can they sense you?"

As if to answer Decker's question, the female vampire turned her head and looked in their direction. Her eyes settled briefly on Mina before flicking away. The male vampire stepped around his companion as if expecting to greet a familiar face, then furrowed his brow in confusion.

"That was close, but I don't think they recognized me as one of their own," Mina said, backing up and almost colliding with a portly gentleman wearing dirt-streaked overalls and a cap.

He mumbled a curse and glared at her until he noticed Decker staring back at him with narrowed eyes. Dropping his head, the man moved off as if deciding it wasn't worth the bother.

When Decker looked forward again, the vampires were on the move, weaving through the crowd toward them. He took Mina's arm. "They're looking for you. Let's go."

"I don't think it's me they're looking for. They can sense another vampire, but they're expecting someone else, probably the two vampires who kidnapped me and killed Faucher's companion aboard the Titanic. They haven't realized who I am yet."

"Then let's not give them the chance." Decker pulled her back through the crowd, jostling elbows and stepping on toes in his haste. He ignored the angry exclamations and curious stares of those around them and kept a grip on Mina's arm to make sure she was still with him. Even though he was sure the vampires had not come to the docks looking for Mina, their curiosity would be peaked if they got close enough to sense she was not the same as them but something new. A merging of human and vampire who possessed the same longevity and healing capabilities as them but lacked their aversion to gold. They would wonder about her. They would want to study her. They would try to become like her and remove the best defense against them. Mina would be in grave danger if the vampires found her again.

"Where's Molly?" Mina asked as they emerged from the jostling throng and back onto the narrow pathway that been cleared to allow the first-class passengers who wished to depart access to their transportation.

"She's already waiting for us in the taxicab," Decker replied, casting a glance over his shoulder.

The vampires were closer now and appeared to have figured out that it was Mina they had sensed. They were pushing startled onlookers out of the way with little regard and closing fast, eyes fixed on their quarry.

Decker broke into a sprint. "Run."

Mina needed no urging. She lifted the hem of her dress up to her knees and fled alongside Decker, their combined footfalls slapping on the wet pavement.

The taxicab was less than fifty feet ahead.

Molly leaned forward and swung the door open, then beckoned for them to hurry when she saw the two vampires on their tail. As they reached the cab, she shuffled over on the backseat to make room as they tumbled inside and slammed the door. Then she banged on the glass between the covered cab and the driver sitting up front in the open air. "Get us out of here. Right now."

The cab lurched forward at a frustratingly slow pace, even as the vampires arrived at the vehicle and tugged at the door handle. Mina lunged forward to secure the door, looking for a lock that wasn't there, even as it flew open, and the male vampire reached inside to grab her.

SEVEN

MINA SCREAMED and pulled back against her attacker.

Decker lunged across the cab to the door and gripped the vampire by his lapels to stop him from dragging her from the automobile.

In the open-air compartment upfront, the driver applied the brakes, sending everyone lurching forward and threatening to throw Decker against the partition separating the driver from his customers.

Molly banged on the partition with her fist. "Don't stop, for heaven's sake. Can't you see this ruffian is attacking us?"

The driver cast a quick glance back at the commotion behind him, then started off again, dragging the vampire along while his companion raced to keep up. She became entangled in the folds of her wet dress and stumbled, allowing the cab to pull away.

The male vampire was not giving up. He snarled and tried to land a punch on Decker with his free hand. "The woman is coming with us."

"Like hell she is." Decker could feel his grip loosening on

the vampire's jacket. In a swift movement he let go and brought his elbow down on the arm still gripping Mina, who twisted away at the last moment, breaking the vampire's grip.

The creature's upper body was inside the cab. Now he tumbled back, clawing for traction and managing to grip the door surround at the last moment. For a second he hung there, flailing as the taxicab gained speed, but then he swung his legs forward and managed to get his feet onto the vehicle's running board and lunged through the doorway again.

Decker was waiting for him. He fell back, brought his legs up, and kicked with all his might, catching the vampire under the chin.

The creature's head snapped back, but he held on.

Decker kicked again, mustering all the force he could.

Mina balled her hands into fists and slammed them against the vampire's fingers that were still curled around the doorframe.

This time, the creature could not hold on. With a howl of frustration, the vampire lost his grip and toppled backward into the rain-soaked night.

Decker poked his head through the door and saw the creature smack against the pavement and roll twice before jumping to his feet.

The female vampire drew level with him and came to a stop, face twisted in frustration. They watched the cab pull away along the docks, hands at their sides and shoulders slumped.

Decker grabbed the door and slammed it closed, then sat back on the bench seat and brushed rain from his face. "That was fun."

"Trouble has a habit of following you," Molly said,

looking at Mina. "Who were those people? What did they want?"

"They were probably associates of the man whose clutches I escaped aboard the Titanic," Mina said, elaborating on her original cover story of a jilted suitor chasing her aboard the ship. "I have no idea if he survived the sinking, but he was very wealthy and undoubtedly had the means to hire ne'er do wells to intercept me upon reaching New York if I evaded him aboard the Titanic. I suspect he sent a telegram to his associates stateside prior to our encounter with the iceberg."

Molly observed Mina with narrowed eyes. "Those two didn't look much like ruffians. Their clothing was expensive despite their ugly manner."

"That is something you would have to ask them about. Either way, their intention was to snatch me from the docks." Mina settled back on the seat and ran a hand through her hair, smoothing it. "I hope you're not having second thoughts about helping us."

"I suspect there is much you haven't told me about your situation," Molly said, her face expressionless. "And my husband might say that helping you is a foolhardy venture. But James is not here and even if he was, I wouldn't listen to him."

"Is your husband back in Europe?" Decker asked, hoping to steer the conversation away from their own situation.

"Dear me, no. He's in Denver tending to his business. We have led mostly separate lives for several years now."

Decker fell silent, sensing that further conversation regarding Molly's domestic situation might prove to be a minefield. He glanced out of the window and noticed that they had left the docks behind and were on W. 14th Street, heading through the Meatpacking District. Darkened warehouses and shops selling produce directly off the boats lined the side of the street. A few automobiles and several horse-drawn carriages moved in the other direction toward the docks.

Decker sat back and forced himself to relax. He felt Mina shift beside him and place her hand atop his, squeezing gently. He wanted to discuss the events on the quay with her, but now was not the right time.

They reached Sixth Avenue and turned left. Decker was surprised how familiar their surroundings looked. Most of the surrounding buildings—stone and brick structures that rose no higher than six stories—would still be there over a hundred years later, at least on this end of the avenue. But as they moved further along the street, toward where the Empire State Building would soon rise high into the heavens, their surroundings became less familiar. In the twenty-first century, this area was dominated by high-rise steel and glass towers crowding the skyline for dominance. In this era, they were surrounded by more brick buildings, many of which appeared to be either offices or retail spaces with apartments above. There was also a smattering of restaurants, only one of which appeared to be open. A twenty-four-hour diner. The streets were mostly empty, and few pedestrians plied the sidewalks. It was also not as bright. There were no neon signs, and the streetlamps gave out only a dim glow. Many of the buildings were unlit, their windows dark.

Decker was fascinated. This was a New York unlike any he had ever seen before. It was serene. Calm. He barely noticed as the taxicab turned on to 33rd Street and came to a stop.

"We have arrived," Molly announced, opening the taxicab door, and stepping out onto the sidewalk. "Let's not linger. After all we've gone through, I could use a soft bed."

Decker motioned for Mina to go next, and then followed

behind. While their host went about paying the cab driver and asking for his discretion regarding the incident at the docks, Decker craned his neck to look up at the magnificent fifteen story building in front of him.

The Waldorf-Astoria.

They had arrived indeed.

EIGHT

ALONE IN THEIR suite and finally able to say what was on his mind, Decker turned to Mina. "Please tell me what you were doing back there, taking off into the crowd like that?"

"You're not my boss and I don't answer to you," Mina retorted. "In fact, if memory serves, I'm technically your boss since you are at present an operative of the Order of St. George."

"That's debatable, since I'm probably not in the Order anymore, given my actions back in London. I'm sure Finch wasted no time in firing me in absentia once he got free from the bedroom I locked him in." Decker prowled to the window and stared out over the New York skyline, and the thousands of twinkling lights spread across the city. "But it's immaterial. We're not in London now and what you did put us both in danger."

"I don't see how."

"Did you ever stop to think what would have happened if your friend Molly decided to continue on without us? We would be homeless and penniless at this very moment." Decker tried to contain his anger but knew it wasn't working. He turned back toward her. "Not only that, but you put yourself in the path of those vampires when there was no good reason to do so. You must have known it wasn't Amenmosep back on that dock because even if he survived and avoided us the entire journey back to New York, he couldn't possibly have gotten off the ship and out of the Cunard terminal so quickly."

"They were vampires, John." Mina folded her arms and glared at Decker. "You understand what that means?"

"It means there are more people like Abraham Turner than we thought. It also means that the two vampires who abducted you aboard the Titanic had a support network here in the United States, and presumably those two we encountered on the quay were there to see if either of their comrades had survived the sinking." Now it was Decker's turn to fold his arms. "But that's no reason to draw attention to yourself and risk stranding us in New York with nowhere to turn."

"For all we know those vampires were waiting for me."

"And there's even more chance that they weren't. I saw the looks on their faces when they sensed you. They were surprised. And if they were looking for you, which is unlikely, then drawing attention to us was just plain foolhardy. Better to disappear into the city and let them think you went down with the ship. Now they know for sure that you're here, and that could be a problem."

"I didn't think they would chase us." Some of the indignation dropped from Mina's face. "I made a mistake. I'm sorry."

"We're lucky that cab driver didn't pull over and throw us

all out. Or worse, report what happened to the police. He probably would have if it wasn't for your friend's influence."

"I said I'm sorry, but I'm used to taking matters into my own hands. I spent decades in the past before you showed up and had no choice but to rely on my instincts to survive."

"None of that is my fault."

"I never said it was." Mina went to a chair and sat down with an exhausted sigh. "Look, I don't want to argue with you. Not now, after we've survived so much. I'll curb my instincts from now on and talk things through with you before acting, if that makes you happy. But please understand that I had to know who those vampires on the dock were. I've spent the last twenty-five years in this era and in all that time have only come across a few others like me, all of which I've kept a safe distance from. Now, ever since Faucher kidnapped me from my room above the pub in Mavendale, it feels like they are everywhere.

"The actions of Faucher and his organization would appear to back that up. There are more vampires hiding in the shadows than I ever imagined. I need to ascertain the danger they pose and what might be coming down the line. Faucher might be dead, but his organization is still out there. They were bringing me to America for a reason and I fear it was not just to escape London. They wanted to continue their experiments where they had access to more funds and better equipment, which means their organization already has a facility, or possibly more than one, in the United States."

Decker paced across the room, trying to release his pent-up energy. "Faucher thought that as a hybrid, neither totally vampire nor human, you might hold the key to wiping out what he perceived to be a vampire scourge. That's why he was experimenting on you. That's also why he wanted to bring Amenmosep here. He just didn't anticipate the creature would free itself from the gold restraints keeping it subdued and escape the ship's hold. But the vampires that kidnapped you, Amenmosep, and Faucher are all gone. His organization, and its vendetta to wipe out the vampires, is no longer our concern. The Order of St. George is more than equipped to deal with the situation, and I propose we let them handle it. We have more immediate concerns."

"You're talking about returning to our own time," Mina said, a peculiar look passing across her face.

"Yes. We need to be on Singer Cay five months from now when Celine Rothman falls forward through time to the twenty-first century and follow her through. It's our only chance. We fail, and we could end up stuck here forever."

"That might be easier said than done. We can't let Celine see us in the past or she will recognize us the moment she arrives in the future. And yet we need to gain access to her private suite of rooms atop the Grand Fairmont Hotel and be there at the exact moment the portal through time opens and swallows her."

"Celine doesn't recognize us when she arrives in the future, so that isn't a concern," said Decker. "Either we managed to get home while keeping a safe distance from Celine—"

"Or she doesn't recognize us because we failed and end up stuck here for the rest of our lives," Mina said, completing Decker's sentence for him.

"My life," Decker reminded her somberly. "If you keep aging at the rate you are, you'll still look like a woman in her early twenties by the time the next century rolls around, and I'll have been dead for decades."

Mina opened her mouth to reply, then hesitated. A tear pushed from the corner of her eye. She wiped it away and stood. "It's late and I'm beyond exhausted. I think I'll retire to my bed now, if you don't mind. We can discuss this in the morning."

With that, she turned and hurried toward the closer of the suite's two bedrooms and disappeared inside, closing the door firmly behind her.

NINE

CHARLES ARCHIBALD FLINT hurried through the darkened streets of Greenwich Village with his coat pulled tight and a cap pulled low over his brow. It had been raining all day in a steady downpour, almost as if the weather were doing its best to match his mood.

Two hours before, the RMS Carpathia had docked at Pier 54 not far away from his current position, carrying the survivors of the ill-fated Titanic. But this was not the cause of his dour mood. In fact, he had gone to the docks and watched the Carpathia arrive to distract himself from the darkness that had recently consumed him, and maybe from a slight sense of morbid curiosity. Once he realized there was nothing much to see since the Cunard Line was not allowing people into the terminal, he made his way back through the Village and found himself at the Liberal Club.

The establishment had only opened a couple of months before, but swiftly became the favorite meeting place of Greenwich Village's bohemian citizenry. Here, they could indulge their love of the arts and engage in a lifestyle frowned upon by the social elites elsewhere in the city. At least once one became accepted as a member, which was no small feat in itself.

It was ironic, Flint thought, that the bohemians of Greenwich Village had created for themselves a class system every bit as elitist and unapproachable as that of the rich bankers and robber barons they so deeply despised. And all the while, didn't see the hypocrisy of their actions. But none of this concerned Flint tonight. He had other matters on his mind. Like, the dreadful slaying at Clarence Rothman's birthday party in the wine vaults under the ramps leading to the Brooklyn Bridge.

He had known Wallace Alden for years. They had attended the same college, then moved in the same circles once they graduated. He was also one of the first to discover the body, drawn by the frantic screams of Alden's girlfriend when she realized her beau had slunk off into one of the side vaults for a smoke and gone looking for him.

Even now, almost forty-eight hours later, Flint still saw the body of his friend every time he closed his eyes... Which was why he lingered in the club for less than an hour, just long enough to put away two large whiskeys, before heading back into the rain-soaked night toward his apartment which took up the second floor of a brick row house on Washington Square Park near Fifth Avenue.

The streets were quiet, with few pedestrians and even fewer automobiles and carriages, thanks to the lousy weather and the spectacle of the Carpathia's arrival down at the docks, which had drawn a good proportion of those who would normally be out and about in the city. Many of them, he guessed, were still there, lingering quayside, hoping to glimpse survivors from the doomed Titanic and witnessing a moment that would surely go down in New York history.

Flint was four blocks from his accommodation. The rain had eased to a steady drizzle. He came to an intersection and waited for a horse and carriage to pass before crossing and continuing his journey. The buildings lining the street were mostly dark at ground level, but on the upper floors, lights burned. He picked up the pace, eager to be home. He didn't see the solitary figure huddling in a doorway until he was right upon him.

The man, who was probably one of the city's myriad homeless, lurched forward, giving Flint a start. He veered to the edge of the sidewalk, barely avoided stepping in front of an automobile in his haste to get around the shambling figure.

The homeless man reached for Flint, grunted something unintelligible, and kept coming.

"Get away from me," Flint said, overcome by a sudden wave of repulsion. He could smell the man's ripe clothing, the body odor that wafted from him even through the rain drenched night.

The man mumbled something else that Flint barely heard as he hurried along down the sidewalk. Three blocks to go until he reached his apartment, which might seem like no big deal, but a New York block could stretch on forever.

"Wait," the homeless man called after him, moving away from the doorway and giving chase. Although the word came out more like *waysh*, probably thanks to whatever was in the brown paper bag shrouded bottle in his hand.

Flint had no intention of waiting. But he also didn't want to show fear, which was why he forced himself to walk at a brisk pace instead of fleeing headlong toward safety. He cast a glance back over his shoulder, hoping the vagrant had given up.

He hadn't. In fact, he was closing in on Flint, making his

way along the sidewalk toward his quarry with a speed and purpose that contradicted his apparent intoxication.

Now Flint decided that discretion was the better part of valor. What good was hiding your fear if you ended up lying bleeding and battered in the gutter at the hands of a vicious ruffian? He ran, fleeing down the sidewalk as fast as his legs would carry him and leaving the homeless man to shout obscenities as he widened the distance between them.

He splashed through a stream of water coursing across the sidewalk from the out spill of a gutter pipe. It doused his trousers, soaking them. But Flint didn't miss a step. He kept going until the door to his row house appeared up ahead, barely even slowing when he reached the cross streets that ran between the blocks.

Flint pulled the door open and hurried through, slamming it behind him with a sigh of relief even though the vagrant had fallen far behind and probably given up the chase before Flint had even made it a full block.

When he reached his apartment, Flint fumbled for the keys in his pocket and pulled them free, then stepped inside and locked the door behind him. He peeled off his wet jacket and hung it on a hook next to the door, then proceeded through the apartment toward the living room, where a bottle of scotch waited with a tumbler sitting next to it.

Then he noticed the muddy footprints on the tiled hallway floor. Footprints that couldn't be his because they were too large, and it almost looked like whoever left them was barefoot. He could see the impression of a heel and five circular smudges that might be toes.

Flint stopped and stared, trying to process the strange sight in front of him. Someone had been here while he was out. Someone with no footwear and filthy feet. Filthy oversized feet. But how had they gotten in? The door was still

locked when Flint arrived home. It made no sense, unless…
The intruder had locked the door behind them. Which meant
he wasn't alone in the apartment.

A prickle ran up Flint's spine. Now the homeless man
didn't seem so bad. It wasn't the mostly empty city streets
that posed a danger. It was his apartment.

He turned and took a step back toward the front door,
reached for the handle, just as he caught a flash of movement
from the corner of his eye.

It had come from the bathroom to his left.

Flint turned to see the bathroom door standing open,
nothing but darkness beyond. Maybe he had imagined the
movement, except… The darkness shifted. A figure separated
itself, too large to be real, and reached toward him.

An odor wafted toward Flint that reminded him of an
open sewer. Or the fetid smell of death.

He recoiled, the start of a scream pressing against his lips,
even as powerful hands yanked him into the darkness
beyond the door and clutched at his head and shoulders. The
last thing Flint saw before his neck snapped was a grotesque
face with barely formed features, looking back at him through
eyes that were as dead as he would soon be.

TEN

AFTER MINA WENT TO BED, Decker sat up a while longer, lost in thought. They had landed on their feet by running into Molly, the woman who had saved Mina from the vampires aboard the Titanic. Even after their run-in on the quay, she had been more than happy to procure the suite that Decker and Mina now occupied at the Waldorf-Astoria. She had also told the desk clerk to put anything they needed on her account, including food and drink from the restaurant and bar. She had also arranged for them to send a telegram to London once the hotel's telegraph office opened the following morning.

They had wasted no time in joining Molly for a late dinner in the Palm Room Restaurant, located in the hotel's Astoria wing, which their host assured them was the most exclusive dining experience in all of New York. As the name suggested, palm trees were spread throughout between tables covered with pristine white tablecloths and glittering silver cutlery. The maître d', who appeared to know Molly personally, wasted no time in arranging their supper. Once the meal was done, Molly informed them that she would be departing early the next morning for Colorado due to a family emergency, which was the reason she had cut her time in Europe short and booked passage from Cherbourg on the Titanic to begin with. She accompanied them to the elevators, shaking Decker's hand and giving Mina a warm hug. She also implored them to be careful and wished them good luck before taking her leave and heading through the lobby toward the Waldorf wing of the hotel where her own accommodation was located.

Decker glanced around the suite. It was sumptuous although old-fashioned by his twenty-first century tastes, but it was warm and safe. Far from the vampires who had tried to snatch Mina and out of their reach. It was also larger than any hotel room Decker had ever stayed in before, with a central lounge area and a pair of amply appointed bedrooms with fourposter beds. One on each side. Even better, they could use it as their base of operations for the immediate future until Thomas Finch wired funds, which Decker was sure he would arrange as soon as they sent a telegram the following morning.

He stood and went to a liquor cabinet against the lounge area's far wall, intending to pour himself a nightcap before bed, but then his eyes fell on a newspaper he had found in the hotel's lobby earlier and picked up out of curiosity. He hadn't paid attention to it before, throwing it down on a side table next to one of the chairs in his eagerness to confront Mina about her actions on the dock.

Most of the front page was taken up with news of the Titanic disaster, and the anticipated arrival of the survivors into New York, but one column on the left side of the page bore a headline that had nothing to do with the sinking.

Grisly Murder at Wine Vault Party for New York Business Tycoon's Younger Brother.

But it was the subhead in smaller lettering underneath that made him stop and stare.

Motive for Crime Lacking in Slaying at Clarence Rothman's Birthday Bash.

Decker could hardly believe that he hadn't noticed the front-page article when he brought the newspaper up to the suite. He picked the newspaper up and read the article. The victim was a man named Wallace Alden, an acquaintance of Clarence Rothman, who's older brother, Howard, had thrown the party. That made him the future brother-in-law of Celine Rothman, the very person they intended to follow back through time to the twenty-first century.

The murder baffled police, being both apparently motiveless and brutal, with no evidence to suggest anyone at the party was involved, although they were all still under suspicion. No mean feat, considering there were over a hundred people in attendance. The murder was grisly. Alden's neck had been snapped, which would have required brute strength. After that, the skin had been torn from his skull, effectively scalping him, and leaving a faceless corpse. If the man hadn't already been dead, he would have bled out in short order. If the police were hoping for a quick resolution —whoever perpetrated the horrific murder would surely have ended up covered in blood—they were not going to find it among Clarence Rothman's guests, none of whom had been touched by even a splash of blood. A set of bloody footprints leading away from the crime and into the tunnels connecting the wine vaults located at the anchors of the East River Bridge

—which Decker knew would later be renamed the Brooklyn Bridge—further exonerated the guests in attendance. Especially since the footprints were—as the paper quoted a police sergeant who attended the scene—of unusual and monstrous size.

Decker read the article again, then placed the newspaper down, an idea forming at the back of his mind. He needed a way into the Rothman family's inner circle in order to reach Singer Cay, where he and Mina could follow Celine Rothman through time to the twenty-first century, and this might be it. A murder perpetrated by a killer who left 'footprints of unusual and monstrous size' sounded exactly like something the Order of St. George might be interested in, giving Decker his opportunity. But there was a problem. The Order was a strictly British institution at this point in time. Classified Universal Special Projects, the international organization born out of the Order of St. George, would not exist for another thirty years or more. Decker and Mina had no authority to involve themselves in the investigation. But that didn't mean he wouldn't try.

Decker paced back to the window and stared out, pushing his hands into his pockets. The New York City skyline looked back at him. Even now, somewhere out in that metropolis, Celine was going about her business completely unaware that five months hence she would vanish on her wedding day only to reappear a hundred and twenty years in the future and kick off the chain of events that led to Decker and Mina becoming stranded in the past. It almost felt like fate had brought them all full circle.

"John?"

Decker turned to find Mina standing in the bedroom doorway with a hotel robe pulled around her body.

"What are you doing?" she asked. "I heard you walking

around out here. Why haven't you gone to bed yet? It's so late. You must be beyond tired."

"I needed some time to let my active mind wind down," he said, eyes shifting briefly to the newspaper. He wondered if he should tell her about the article and link to Celine Rothman but decided it could wait until morning. Mina was right. He was exhausted, and he knew she was, too. "Go back to bed. I'm going to do the same."

Mina hesitated a moment, then she nodded, a wan smile creasing her lips, before she retreated into the bedroom once more and closed the door without another word.

Decker stood near the window a moment longer and stared at the spot Mina had just occupied. The thought that had crossed his mind before she distracted him still lingered there. Was there even such a thing as fate? Because it sure felt like some unseen force was drawing the strands of their lives toward an inexorable convergence like a puppet master pulling the strings of unwitting marionettes.

He didn't have an answer.

Shaking off the strange thought, Decker crossed the lounge to his own bedroom, ignoring the liquor cabinet from which he had intended to make a nightcap only moments before, and stepped inside. Ten minutes later, he was in bed and fast asleep, despite his still chattering mind.

ELEVEN

IT WAS a little after eight when the bright morning sun woke Decker. It streamed into his hotel room through an east-facing window past curtains that didn't quite meet in the middle. He rose and dressed quickly, then made his way to the lounge area but found no sign of Mina. The door leading to the other bedroom was still closed, which meant she had not yet stirred. He almost knocked to wake her, but then thought better of it. She had looked exhausted the night before, and the extra sleep would do her good.

Besides, the task he wanted to accomplish that morning did not require her attention. The first order of business was to contact Thomas Finch in London and let him know they were safe and would need funds. The hotel's telegraph office should be open by now, given New York's standing as one of the world's leading business hubs, even in the first decades of the twentieth century. The millionaire tycoons likely to frequent the Waldorf-Astoria would want to get an early start on the day if they were to conduct international business with

Europe, which was at least five hours ahead of Eastern Standard Time.

Decker rode down in the elevator and quickly found the telegraph office tucked away in a corridor to the right of the main lobby. As he expected, it was already open, and he wasted no time in composing a message to Finch, being careful not to mention anything that would draw unwanted attention on either side of the Atlantic. Unlike the twenty-first century, where international communication was as easy as a phone call, video chat, or email, Decker's message would be sent to another telegraph office in London which would then dispatch a courier to deliver a paper transcription to Finch at the address Decker provided. In this case, the offices of solicitors' *Crosley and Dutton* near Tower Bridge, which served as a front for the Order of St. George, whose subterranean headquarters beneath the solicitors' office occupied a disused underground rail station abandoned years before when the line that ran through it had been rerouted and extended.

The message was simple, not only because Decker dared not fill Finch in on the progression of circumstances leading to their current predicament via such a public means of communication, but also because the telegraph office charged by the word, and he didn't want to waste more of Molly's money than necessary.

Arrived New York. Both safe. Prior situation resolved. Lost all in sinking. Staying Waldorf-Astoria NYC. Suite 504. Need funds. Please respond. John and Mina.

Decker did, however, pay extra for quick service given that it was already early afternoon in London, and he wanted to ensure Finch received the telegram immediately.

With the telegram already on its way to London, Decker returned to the hotel lobby and approached the concierge desk, his mind turning to the newspaper article he had read the previous night.

At his approach, the concierge looked up. "Can I help you, sir?"

"I hope so," Decker replied, thinking fast to come up with a cover story for what he was about to ask. "I've recently arrived in town and hope to catch up with an old acquaintance I haven't seen for a long time. Clarence Rothman. His brother, Howard Rothman, owns an export and import company in the city."

"I'm aware of who he is, sir."

"Fantastic. You wouldn't happen to know where the Rothman family resides, would you?"

"I would, sir, yes. The Rothmans are frequent visitors to the Palm Court Restaurant and have, at times, maintained a suite of rooms in this very hotel. They have a residence on Fifth Avenue overlooking Central Park."

"That's wonderful. I don't suppose you could give me their address?" Decker asked, hopefully. He wasn't yet sure how to approach the Rothmans or how he and Mina would get to Singer Cay. But he was sure of one thing. They had to be there when Celine Rothman met her destiny and accomplish that task while avoiding Celine herself for fear she would recognize them upon her arrival in the future.

The concierge shook his head. "I'm sorry, sir. I can't give out that information. We take the privacy of our patrons seriously."

"Oh. That's inconvenient," Decker said, frustrated. He

decided to play his ace. "Still, I'm sure Clarence wouldn't mind if you made an exception this one time. We were traveling back from Europe aboard the Titanic and I'm sure he would appreciate knowing that my traveling companion and I survived the sinking and arrived safely in New York."

"I'm sorry to hear of your ordeal, sir." The concierge lowered his head. "But I must defer to hotel policy. Besides, you won't find Clarence Rothman anywhere near the Fifth Avenue mansion. His family has practically disowned him. The man has something of a reputation and prefers to spend his time among the artists and poets that reside below 14th Street. Rumor has it he maintains a suite of rooms there which he uses when he is not traveling and squandering the trust fund provided him by his brother."

"He keeps rooms in Greenwich Village?"

"Correct, sir. But before you ask, I still cannot be of any help. Although in this case not because of hotel policy, but rather because I don't know the address of his apartment or even which street it is on."

"Do you know of anyone who would?"

The concierge shook his head. "I'm afraid not, sir, but you might try one of the Greenwich Village establishments popular with the bohemian crowd of which he is so enamored. You might find him there."

"And those establishments would be?"

"The Washington Square Bookshop springs to mind, as does the French Bar of the Hotel Lafayette on 9th Street, Mouquin's, or the Café Boulevard. If all else fails, you might try the Liberal Club, although it maintains a rigorous membership list and you are unlikely to get past the front door." The concierge wrote the names on the pad before ripping the sheet and offering it to Decker.

"Thank you." Decker folded the slip of paper and pushed

it into his pocket. His clothes felt scratchy and uncomfortable. He had been wearing them since arriving on the Carpathia many days before and was aware they were hardly suitable for his surroundings. He and Mina would need to obtain whole new wardrobes if they were to fit in. But they could accomplish nothing until Thomas Finch sent funds. In the meantime, there was nothing Decker could do but wait.

TWELVE

HAVING WRANGLED from the concierge all the information he could, Decker went in search of the last item on his to do list. Caffeine. In the twenty-first century, there would be a coffee maker in the hotel room and probably a Starbucks, or some other coffee stand, in the lobby. In 1912 there was neither. His only option was the café beyond the hotel's ground-floor library and barroom, which was where he went after leaving the concierge desk and ordered two cups of coffee, which he charged to their benefactor's account.

The drinks arrived in fine porcelain cups sitting on dainty saucers and were clearly not meant to be taken from the café, but no one stopped Decker when he left with them and took the elevator back to the fifth-floor suite he shared with Mina.

When he entered, she was awake and sitting in the lounge area, wearing the same robe as the night before.

She looked up as he closed the door behind him. "I wondered where you had gone."

"I sent a telegram to Thomas Finch and then hunted down coffee for us," Decker replied, handing her a cup.

Mina looked at the laughably small cup. "I hope they give free refills. This is barely enough to get me out of bed, let alone wake me up."

"I don't think they give refills," Decker said with a grin. "You'll just have to make do."

Mina stirred the coffee and lifted the cup to her lips, taking a sip. "How long do you think we'll have to wait before Thomas responds?"

"Beats me. It's my first international telegram. I paid extra for speedy delivery though, so hopefully not long." Decker sipped his own coffee. It was strong and bitter. He had tasted better. His gaze fell on the newspaper from the night before. He picked it up and offered it to Mina. "You should see this."

Mina took the paper and studied it with a furrowed brow, clearly unsure what she was supposed to be looking at. Then her eyes widened when she saw the article about the murder in the wine vaults. "Clarence Rothman."

Decker nodded. "Exactly. Celine Rothman's future brother-in-law."

"This could be our way in."

"I thought the same thing. Except we have no authority in the United States. CUSP won't be on the scene for over thirty years. There's no way anyone is going to let us investigate that murder, let alone anything else."

"Then we do what we always do," Mina said. "Achieve the impossible."

"Any ideas on how?"

"Not so much." Mina's shoulders slumped. "We truly are on our own this time. But hey, at least time is on our side. It's only April. We have almost five months to figure out a way onto that island."

Decker nodded in agreement. The odds might be grim, but no more so than at any other time since being thrown into the past. Yet there was an added wrinkle now. One he hadn't been aware of before Thomas Finch told him the truth of his daughter's origins. He hated to bring it up but had to know where Mina's allegiances lay. "Is Singer Cay where you really want to go?"

"What do you mean?" Mina squirmed in her seat.

"You know very well what I mean. Your relationship with Finch. Your daughter, Daisy. You've lived in this era longer than you lived in your own time. You have ties here that you didn't have before. It complicates things."

"I don't want to spend the rest of my life stranded in the past. You must realize that."

"Except that you wouldn't. To anyone else, this would be a life sentence. If we don't reach Singer Cay and follow Celine Rothman through that tunnel in time, I'll end up stuck here. I won't ever see Nancy or Taylor again. I'll be dead and gone long before I reunite with my loved ones. You aren't in that position. You possess a longevity that will carry you beyond your natural born lifespan. Perhaps many centuries beyond. And you've made a life here over the last twenty-five years—"

"Out of necessity," Mina said, interrupting. "It wasn't my choice."

"I know. But it doesn't alter the facts. Even if you've pushed them away, you have a family here. I don't know exactly what happened between yourself and Thomas that led you to walk away, but I saw the look in his eyes when he told me the truth about Daisy. He might have moved on and remarried, but a part of him still loves you. And regardless of your decision to shield Daisy from the truth, she will always be your daughter."

"I don't want to talk about this."

"I know. But you can't ignore it."

"I'm coming with you to Singer Cay. I've been searching for a way home ever since I landed in the past, and that hasn't changed."

"Are you sure about that?"

"I'm not sure about anything anymore." Mina placed her cup down on the side table next to her chair and stood. She lingered a moment, her eyes cast down toward the newspaper, then she turned and hurried back into the bedroom without another word, closing the door behind her.

Decker watched her go with a heavy heart. For him, it was easy. There was no question he would do all in his power to return home. But for Mina, the path forward was far less clear. Adding to that was the knowledge that she wasn't bound by the same constraints of time as those around her. In all likelihood, she would survive through the years to catch up with her original self if she decided to stay, and that would cause issues of its own. Then there was the incident on the docks. The vampires knew of her existence and that she was not like them. They may even realize she was impervious to gold, the one thing that made them vulnerable. They would surely keep coming, which would place her in extreme danger should she remain in the past.

He rose, torn between giving Mina space or comforting her, but then forced himself to sit down again. She would reappear in her own time. But after two hours passed with no sign of her and only silence from the bedroom, he grew worried and stood once more, making his way toward the bedroom. But before he could do anything, there was a sharp knock at the door of the suite. When he opened it, a bellboy stood there with a folded slip of paper clutched in his hand. It was a telegram. Thomas Finch had replied.

THIRTEEN

DECKER TOOK the telegram from the bellboy, closed the door, and retreated into the lounge before reading Finch's curt message.

Relieved both fine. Was worried.
Making arrangements. Stay where you are.
Sending help. Thomas.

He was about to read it again, intrigued by the enigmatic last line, when a voice spoke up to his rear.

"Who was at the door?" It was Mina who had returned from her seclusion in the bedroom. She was dressed now in the blue silk dress given her aboard the Carpathia to replace the garment she had been wearing on Titanic's lifeboat, which had become sodden in the hours while she waited for rescue and had subsequently caught on an oarlock and ripped as she clambered out of the lifeboat.

"Bellboy." Decker held the telegram out to her. "Thomas replied."

Mina took the note and read it, her eyes narrowing. "What do you think he means about sending help?"

"Beats me." Decker had wondered the same thing. "He wasn't exactly chatty. Guess he didn't want to waste money since he was being charged by the word and international telegrams aren't exactly cheap, at least if what I paid this morning in the hotel lobby is anything to go by."

"Not you. Molly," Mina corrected him.

"That's true. And I hope to reimburse her kindness once Thomas provides us with the means to do so."

"Maybe he's sending someone from London," Mina said, a flash of hope crossing her face. "Or maybe he's coming here personally."

"Doubtful." Decker hated to be the voice of reason, but he didn't believe for one moment that Thomas Finch was going to leave the Order of St. George unattended, not to mention his wife, in a frantic effort to reach New York and Mina. It was more likely he would arrange return passage to England for them both, which Decker had no intention of doing since fate had dropped them in the very city Celine Rothman, their potential savior, currently inhabited. "It would take days, maybe even a week or more, for help to arrive from London. Whatever he has planned must be more immediate."

"You're right, of course." Mina's disappointment revealed itself for a split second before she regained her composure. "He could have been more forthcoming. Not that we have much choice in staying where we are since we have no money, nowhere else to go, and only the clothes on our backs."

"That's true. Which means we have no choice but to wait and see." Decker observed Mina, wondering if she had come to terms with whatever emotional demons had driven her away earlier, but he had no intention of asking.

He didn't need to. Mina cleared her throat, raising a hand to her lips and covering her mouth as she did so, then crossed the room and sat down. "I'm sorry about earlier. I know there's more at stake in this than my own future and I shouldn't have let my emotions get the better of me."

"It's an understandable reaction." Decker took a seat opposite Mina and watched her with sympathetic eyes. "You have a foot in two worlds, each of which must hold a place in your heart at this point. If anything, you have more ties here than in the future."

"That's not true." Mina took a deep breath. "Maybe once it was, after I came to terms with my situation and decided to make a life for myself here as best I could. But not anymore. I made the decision long ago not to let emotions rule my head. That I must think of what was best for those around me rather than indulge my own selfish desires."

"I don't understand," Decker said. "Why would you come to such a conclusion if you were resigned to being stuck in the past, possibly forever?"

"I had my reasons."

"I'm sure you did." Decker knew better than to press her on what those reasons might be, and she clearly didn't feel inclined to share them.

"It wasn't a decision I came to lightly. You have to believe that. But it was the right one and there's no going back now." Mina's eyes were cold. Emotionless. It was like a wall had gone up around whatever had driven her to retreat into the bedroom earlier. "I assure you, my motivation for returning to the twenty-first century far outweighs any reason I might once have had to remain in the past. I'm coming to Singer Cay with you, and we'll get home together. That's all there is to it, and you have no reason to think otherwise."

"In that case, I shall put the matter from my mind." Decker wasn't entirely sure that Mina was being honest with him, but there was nothing he could do about it, and he knew how stubborn she could be. Once her mind was made up, there was no changing it. His stomach growled, reminding him it was already early afternoon, and they hadn't yet eaten. "You want to take a stroll down to the lobby and find some food?"

"That sounds like a great idea," Mina replied, rising to her feet. She glanced down at the telegram, still in her hand. "But let's not be too long. I have no idea what Thomas meant when he said help is on the way, but he told us to stay where we are, so we should be ready."

"I couldn't agree more." Decker stood and attempted to smooth the wrinkles in his shirt with the palm of one hand. A futile effort considering how long he'd been wearing the same clothes. "The quicker we remedy our current predicament, the better."

FOURTEEN

NICK SHAW, sole investigator with, and owner of the Shaw Detective Agency, hurried along Mulberry Street toward Columbus Park, weaving through the mid-afternoon city crowds, and staying a safe distance from the woman he had been watching for days, hoping she would reveal her true nature. Which was anything but how she appeared at that moment with her trim figure, softly sculpted face, and flowing red hair that cascaded to her waist. In fact, she looked almost too attractive to be in this area of town, which had until recently been one of New York's most notorious slums known as the five points. An area that was undergoing a steady process of gentrification.

For example, the park that he now saw up ahead on his right had once been a cesspit that went by the name of Bandit's Roost and housed the dregs of humanity. Many of the tenement buildings that had contributed to the neighborhood's unsavory past still surrounded the park, although their own slow gentrification disguised the true nature of what they were, much in the same way that the woman's current appearance masked the truth of what lay beneath those porcelain features. She was, in the literal sense, a monster who preyed upon the hapless men who crossed her path and allowed themselves to be wooed. In his native Ireland, they would have called her a leannán sídhe, or fairy lover. A succubus who took a woman's form to lure men into her deadly trap. But this creature was from a more distant land, having arrived on a boat from Japan many months before. At least if his research was correct. She was a Kitsune. A shape shifter with a voracious and deadly appetite. Although the practical distinction between that and the legendary leannán sídhe of his home country was negligible. Perhaps they both descended from the same ancient creature, or maybe the similarities in their nature were coincidence. Either way, Shaw had no intention of letting this abomination roam free.

The woman had reached the park and hurried along the sidewalk, then crossed over toward the tenement buildings. Here she slowed and cast a furtive glance backward before ducking into a gloomy alleyway and disappearing from sight.

"Dammit." Shaw cursed under his breath, picked up the pace. He couldn't afford to lose her. Not now, after spending so much time tracking the beast.

He approached the alley, slowing as he did so out of an abundance of caution. He didn't think the Kitsune had noticed him trailing her, but even so, his hand fell to the sturdy baton hidden under his coat. If it came to the worst, he didn't want to face this creature unarmed even though she lacked the ability to beguile him, given that he knew her true nature. She was dangerous in other ways. A predator more than capable of defending itself if cornered.

Shaw stopped at the entrance to the alley and gathered his wits. It was confining and dark, the dreary light from a clouded sky barely able to penetrate the narrow slit between the buildings. It was perfect for an ambush. But he couldn't let her escape.

Taking a deep breath, Shaw stepped into the alley and started down, hurrying to catch up with the young woman whom he assumed had reached the other end and turned on to the street beyond. He soon realized his mistake.

A sound to his rear drew Shaw's attention. The slam of a door. He glanced over his shoulder to find two burly men in filthy aprons—laborers who toiled in one of the many slaughterhouses that still prospered in the district—blocking his retreat. When he turned his attention frontward again, he saw another pair blocking his way forward. Behind them, standing with her arms folded near a second door, was the Kitsune. A subtle smile played on her lips.

Shaw tensed and addressed the men. "I got no quarrel with any of you. Step aside."

"You'd like that, wouldn't ya," one of the men retorted in a thick accent that Shaw couldn't identify. "To get yer hands on this defenseless slip of a woman."

"You don't understand," said Shaw, chastising himself for allowing the situation to get out of hand.

"Oh, we understand, all right, don't we, lads?" This was the closer of the men at Shaw's rear.

There was a murmur of agreement.

"I guarantee you don't." Shaw turned so that his back was against the alley wall where he could keep all four men in sight. He needed to diffuse the situation, and quickly. "My motives are not sinister. I'm a private detective and this woman isn't who she seems."

"How about we be the judge of that," said the closest man, as all four started toward Shaw, intentions clear by their clenched fists and determined expressions.

Shaw slipped the baton from under his coat and swung in a wide arc, catching the closest of the men with a vicious blow to his midsection. He grunted and doubled over, but not before the other three had descended upon Shaw in a rain of punches that forced the Irishmen to his knees.

He swung the baton again but there was no room to maneuver and instead he resorted to lifting his arms to shield his face against the vicious barrage. Someone grabbed the baton, twisting until Shaw was forced to let go. He looked up in time to see the man raise it above his head, ready to bring the weapon down on Shaw's skull.

"Stop. That's enough."

The men froze as if she flipped a switch.

Shaw looked up to see the Kitsune standing behind his attackers.

She waved a dismissive hand. "You can all go about your business. He won't give me any more trouble."

The man with the baton opened his mouth as if to protest, but the woman merely smiled and placed a hand on his shoulder. "It's all right. I assure you. I'm safe now."

The man looked at her for a moment, slack jawed. Then he dropped the baton and started back down the alley in silence, with his friends in tow.

Shaw groaned and rubbed his chin where a well-placed fist had made contact moments before. He would have some bruises in the morning, but he was alive, which came as a mild surprise under the circumstances.

The woman kneeled and leaned close, sliding the baton out of reach she did so. "I had pity on you today but let this be a warning. Leave me be."

"Or what?" Shaw said, mustering all the bravado he had left at that moment.

"Or it won't end well for you." The woman barred her

teeth and exhaled a stream of fetid breath. Her soft features fell away to reveal a hideous countenance with mottled, rotten skin stretched over a misshapen skull. Her eyes shone with an unholy fire. Then the nightmare visage melted back into that of an attractive young woman. She climbed to her feet and brushed a crease from her dress before turning and continuing on her way.

Shaw watched her go. There was little point in pursuing the woman. He had lost the element of surprise, if he ever even possessed it. She had known he was behind her all along and had led him into this alley like a lamb to the slaughter. He staggered to his feet, checked himself over until he determined that his injuries were merely superficial, then lurched back toward the alley's entrance.

Twenty minutes later, he arrived at a drab five-story building in the East Village, an area more known for Eastern European immigrants than the Irish. But the location suited Shaw and provided him with a level of anonymity as he went about his work.

He pushed the door open and stepped inside, then headed toward the stairs leading to the second-floor rooms that doubled as both his apartment and office. But before he could get there, a door opened, and a man appeared, clad in a vest that did little to hide the tattoos covering his arms.

He stomped toward Shaw and held out a folded piece of paper. "This arrived while you were out."

"Thanks, Joe." Shaw took the sheet of paper from his neighbor. "What is it?"

"How should I know? Didn't look at it, did I. Know better than to pry into other people's business."

"Right. Of course."

"Yeah. And for your information, just because I live beneath you, that don't make me your secretary."

"Never said it did." Shaw forced a smile and started up the stairs, wincing with each footfall. When he reached the landing and looked back, Joe had disappeared, and his apartment door was closed again.

Shaw made his way into his digs, then looked down at the slip of paper in his hand. It was a telegram, and international at that. When he opened it, a familiar name jumped out. One he didn't expect to see.

Thomas Finch.

FIFTEEN

INSTEAD OF RETURNING to the Palm Room where they had dined the night before, which both of them decided was much too extravagant for lunch since they weren't footing the bill, Decker led Mina to the café in the lobby near the hotel library. They ate a light lunch, bemused by the fact that even though the café was supposed to be casual dining, both lunch and dinner were still full service, unlike earlier in the day when he had gone there for coffee and the establishment had been serving only pastries at the counter. They even had to shoo away a sommelier who approached the table, hoping to provide them with a bottle of wine that would probably have cost more than the rest of their bill.

Once the meal was over, they returned to their suite, eager not to miss whatever help Thomas Finch was sending their way. As they crossed the lobby, Decker grabbed the day's newspaper from a stand near the reception desk and once they were back in their suite, he sank into a chair and wasted no time in perusing it for more articles about the murder in the wine vaults but found only a brief mention on page five that mostly concerned the identity of the victim. There was no mention of Clarence Rothman or his older brother, who would wed Celine at the Grand Fairmont Hotel on Singer Cay five months hence. Instead, the front page and a good portion of the next two carried survivors' accounts of the Titanic sinking, of which Decker needed no reminding.

He threw the newspaper down with a grunt. "I don't like feeling helpless like this. Whatever Thomas has planned, he'd better hurry and get to it."

"Patience." Mina settled opposite him. "I'm sure he's doing his best. Remember the confines of the era. Communication is hardly instantaneous."

"I don't know how you've survived a quarter-century stuck here," Decker said, shaking his head in bewilderment. "No internet. No cell phones. No TV. Hell, they don't even have talking movies."

"It wasn't easy," Mina admitted. "But it's not like I had a choice. Besides, I don't know what you're complaining about. You've only been stuck here for a few months."

"I know. I can't imagine what it's been like for you. But in my defense, I hate sitting around waiting."

As if to punctuate the sentiment, there was a loud knock on the suite door.

Mina looked up, startled. "Maybe you won't need to for much longer. That could be the cavalry."

"Let's find out." Decker rose and crossed to the door. When he opened it, he found a man of modest height and wearing a threadbare tweed jacket looking back at him. There was a cut under the man's eye, and the start of a bruise on his jaw. To say that he looked unsavory was an understatement. Decker took a step back, wondering what kind of trouble was about to ensue. "Can I help you?"

"I certainly hope so," the man replied in an Irish accent

that reminded Decker of Colum O'Shea. "To whom am I speaking?"

"How about you go first?"

"Very well. The name's Nick Shaw." The man paused, looking Decker up and down. "And since this is room 504, you must be John Decker." He peered over Decker's shoulder into the suite. "Which means Mina must be around here somewhere, too."

"Nick?" Mina appeared at Decker's side. "Is that you?"

"Live and kicking." Shaw pushed the door open further and stepped past Decker into the room, then strode toward Mina and gripped her in a tight embrace. "It's been a while."

"Ten years. I didn't know you were in New York."

"I've moved around." Shaw took a step back and studied Mina with keen interest. "I swear, you don't look a day older than the last time I saw you."

"I assure you, that is not true." Mina waved off her old friend's remark, but Decker could tell she was uncomfortable around the subject. Obviously, Nick Shaw did not know of Mina's circumstances. "Dare I ask what happened to your face?" she said, changing the subject. "It looks like you went three rounds with a bareknuckle street fighter."

"Actually, it was four of them, and they worked in a slaughterhouse." Shaw gave a mirthless chuckle. "Goes with the territory in my line of work."

"Which is?" Decker asked.

"I'm a private detective… of sorts. I hunt the dregs of the city, and sometimes they fight back." He reached up and touched the bruises on his face. "It's nothing that won't heal in a few days."

"You always had a knack for getting into trouble," Mina said, a shadow falling across her face briefly. "And I'm not sure I want to know what you've gotten yourself into since we last met. But I have one question. How did you know we were here?"

"How do you think?"

"Thomas. He's kept in touch with you all this time?"

"We don't communicate often, but I keep him informed of my whereabouts. You know, just in case."

"I'm glad that you did." Mina turned and walked deeper into the room, putting some distance between herself and Shaw. Decker wondered if she was uncomfortable with her youthful appearance, which was in stark contrast to Shaw's rugged, middle-aged features. "I assume you're the help of which he spoke in his telegram."

"At your service." Shaw dipped his head in a mock bow and ended it with a flourish of his arm. Then he reached inside his jacket and pulled out a wad of cash. "Speaking of which, this is for you."

"That's a lot of money," said Decker, stepping forward and taking the bundle from Shaw.

"Three hundred dollars in small bills."

Decker whistled. He wasn't sure exactly how much buying power the cash provided them with in 1912 New York City but judging by his rough calculation based on the months he had spent in London he figured it must be worth about nine thousand by twenty-first century standards. That was more than enough to settle their portion of the hotel bill and see them through for a while. But considering that they had arrived in the United States penniless, homeless, and with only the shirts on their backs, it was hardly enough to carry them until Celine's wedding five months hence and their chance of returning home. And if they were to ingratiate themselves with the likes of Clarence Rothman, they would need to project an altogether wealthier façade. He slipped the wad into his trouser pocket. "Without wishing to sound ungrateful, we may need more funds than this."

"Have no fear. Arrangements are being made. This was all I could get on short notice, and believe me, I'm not sure I would want to carry any larger a sum through the streets of New York without protection anyway, and neither should you."

"Fair enough. Where exactly did you get this money?" Decker asked.

"The Order of St. George maintains bank accounts in several cities around Europe and the Americas, for those times when a threat extends beyond the borders of the British Isles. More money is being transferred as we speak, but it takes a while."

Shaw's knowledge of the Order and their operations surprised Decker, although it made sense since he had obviously known both Mina and Thomas Finch for a long time. He wondered if Shaw, who appeared to be around the same age as Finch, had once been an operative of the organization and, if so, why he had spent the last ten years estranged from it.

Shaw must have sensed Decker's curiosity. "Before you ask, it's a long story, and one of which I am not inclined to discuss at present. Suffice to say that I remain loyal to the Order of St. George even in my self-imposed exile."

"And a good thing, too," Mina said, picking up the conversation. "Your presence has made an otherwise trying few weeks a little brighter."

"I appreciate you saying that." Shaw fell silent for a long moment, then cleared his throat. "Thomas seems to think you might not return to London. His telegram was brief and did not go into detail, but he suggested that your stay in the States might be prolonged."

"There is a distinct possibility," Mina said. "The circumstances that brought us here were unexpected, but perhaps fortuitous."

Shaw nodded slowly. He looked at Mina with a furrowed brow. "I remember how much you value privacy, so I won't pry, but I will give you a piece of advice. Don't make the mistake I did in London and run from the place you have come to think of as your home. The world can be cold and harsh when you don't have friends by your side."

"I assure you I'm not running from my home," Mina said. "If anything, it's the opposite."

"I won't pretend to understand what you mean." Shaw pushed his hands into his pockets. "But I will say that Thomas must be missing you."

"Thomas and I went our separate ways a long time ago, at least emotionally. He knows I must follow my destiny, as he must follow his. We have both accepted that."

Shaw shrugged. "Hey. Not my place to get involved. Just offering some friendly advice."

"And I appreciate it. Now, we should get back to business."

"I agree," said Decker. He had a lot of questions for Nick Shaw, but now was not the time to ask them. "We need to settle our bill here and find somewhere less expensive to live. Even with three hundred dollars in our pocket and more money coming from London, we can't afford to make this hotel our permanent base."

"There's an empty apartment on the fourth floor of my building in the East Village," Shaw said. "We could go see the landlord right now. He spends his afternoons in O'Grady's and would be more than happy for the beer money, so he won't ask too many questions."

Decker shook his head. "Thank you, but no. With all due respect, there is somewhere that better serves our purposes."

"Where would that be?" Shaw asked with a raised eyebrow.

"Greenwich Village," Decker said. "I think it's time we embraced our bohemian side."

SIXTEEN

DECKER SETTLED THEIR HOTEL BILL, which came to almost fifty dollars—a good chunk of their newly gained wealth—and proved that their money would not have lasted long had they stayed in the suite beyond one night. Then they headed out into the city in search of somewhere more affordable to lay their heads. But first, they needed some new threads if they were to ingratiate themselves with the wealthy bohemian crowd that hung around the Village.

To this end, Shaw took them several blocks north to an area bounded by Sixth Avenue and Forty-second Street which he said was the best place to purchase clothing at a fraction of what it would cost at one of the city's fancy department stores such as Bloomingdale's or Bergdorf Goodman.

It turned out he was right.

The area was packed with garment factories, many of which were more than willing to sell their wares right off racks sitting in the street outside of the humid and noisy sewing rooms that turned out a staggering quantity of garments destined to be shipped across the United States and beyond. It didn't take long for Decker and Mina to pick out several outfits each, further depleting their funds, before Shaw flagged down a passing motorized taxicab, which was soon on its way to Greenwich Village.

Decker was not sure they should spend their money on such an extravagance. Cabs were not cheap. Molly had paid almost two dollars the previous evening when they had gone to the hotel, which Decker worked out was at least three times what that same journey would cost in the twenty-first century. But Shaw was insistent, saying that asking a cabdriver would be the easiest way to find rooms to rent in Greenwich Village, since they often picked up fares from the docks where the cruise liners came in or the newly completed Penn Station which brought streams of rural Americans into the city looking to make a name for themselves.

He was right. The cabdriver took them straight to a four story row building near Washington Square Park, which ran as a boardinghouse of sorts, presided over by a rotund woman in her forties with an accent that sounded vaguely Eastern European to Decker's ears. She was more than happy to rent them a pair of rooms at a weekly rate for a fraction of what they had paid for one night at the Waldorf-Astoria.

Not that the quality was anywhere near the same. The rooms were small by comparison, and the furniture sturdy but utilitarian. There were no rugs on the bare wood floors and barely a sliver of light made it through the windows thanks to the building's proximity to another, taller structure immediately to the rear. The view from Decker's window was of a blank brick wall with a narrow alley beneath. The rooms contained no facilities. Instead, there was a shared toilet and bathroom down the corridor.

Decker studied Mina's face as they inspected the accommodations, wondering if she would balk and insist upon something a little more salubrious. But she didn't, merely nodding and dropping the bundle of clothes purchased in the garment district onto the bed as if she were happy to be settled.

When the landlady, weekly rent in hand, shuffled off back to her ground floor den, Decker turned to Mina. "I'm sorry our surroundings aren't more inviting."

"It's fine for now and is situated perfectly for our needs." Mina forced a smile.

"The offer of that apartment in my building is still on the table, and it's a leg up from this," Shaw said, glancing around Mina's room with a look of muted disdain on his face. "I'm sure the woman who runs this place will be more than happy to give your money back, with a little gentle persuasion."

"Thank you, but no." Decker appreciated that Shaw was trying to help, and he knew that Mina would have preferred swankier digs, but they needed somewhere in the right location. It also had to be affordable since Decker didn't know how much of their cash it would take to project the necessary image of wealth required to infiltrate the inner circle of prosperous bohemians slumming it in the Village and get close to Clarence Rothman. Maybe when the extra funds Thomas Finch was sending from London became available, they could reassess their situation. In the meantime, he figured that it was more important to look the part in public than live the high life in private.

"If you're sure." Shaw glanced at Mina, then back to Decker. "I promised to keep Thomas appraised of the situation so I'll send a telegram in the morning letting him know where you will be staying. Until then, is there anything else you need?"

"Just one thing," replied Decker. "There was a murder a

few nights ago at a party in a wine vault on the Manhattan side of the East River Bridge."

Shaw nodded. "I heard about that. Grisly affair. What of it?"

"You're a detective, correct?"

"Private detective."

"Right. You must have connections with the local police, given your line of work."

"I have contacts. What of it?"

"Do you have one that could get us inside those wine vaults to look at the scene?"

"I can ask around." Shaw lapsed into silence for several seconds. "Thomas was insistent that I keep an eye on you both while you're in the city. Make sure you don't run afoul of any unpleasantness. Your interest in this murder wouldn't fall into that category now, would it?"

"We're curious, that's all," Decker said, without mentioning their true interest. Clarence Rothman, who happened to be the man throwing the party. "You apparently know about the Order of St. George, in which we are associated, and what it does. The circumstances of this murder fit into that category, at least on the surface."

"Except the Order of St. George doesn't operate outside of the British Isles. At least, not officially, as I'm sure you are aware."

"Doesn't make us any less curious."

Shaw observed them with narrowed eyes, but then he shrugged. "I'll see what I can do, but I'm not making any promises."

"Thank you."

Shaw nodded. "I'll leave the pair of you to settle into your rooms." He turned to Mina. "I would love to catch up at your convenience. Perhaps we could have dinner this evening and talk?"

Mina's eyes shifted from Shaw to Decker. "I'm not sure that I—"

"I meant both of you, naturally. I'm eager to acquaint myself with your new friend, too."

"We'd love to have dinner," Decker said, before Mina could reply. "I would like to know more about you, as well."

"It's settled then." Shaw clapped his hands together. "I shall return at seven. There are several fine dining establishments in this area of the city... and some that are not so fine but still offer a hearty meal and a cold pint."

"Actually, I already have a place in mind," Decker said quickly. "The concierge at the hotel recommended a restaurant that I believe is nearby. Café Boulevard. That is where I would like to dine."

SEVENTEEN

SHAW RETURNED AS PROMISED, dead on the stroke of seven. In the meantime, both Decker and Mina had availed themselves of the meager bathing facilities provided by their landlady and then changed into fresh clothing for the first time since setting foot on the Carpathia.

Shaw led them several blocks east toward the restaurant and gave them a piece of good news as they went.

"I spoke to a contact in the police department," he said. "Someone who can get us into the wine vaults."

"Us?" Decker asked.

"I'm coming with you."

"I don't think that's a good idea." Decker shook his head. They had reached a busy intersection. He waited until they were across before continuing. "I appreciate you getting us in, but we don't need a civilian tagging along."

"Civilian?" Shaw chortled. "That's rich, considering your current situation. The Order of St. George doesn't have any authority here, and it's my contact who's getting you through the door. Besides, I know this city, and the denizens who inhabit it, better than you ever could. If you want to see where that murder took place, you do it along with me."

"John. Let him come," Mina said, placing a calming hand on Decker's arm. "We can trust Shaw. He used to be one of us."

"You sure about that?" Decker asked. Shaw might be an old acquaintance of Mina's, but Decker knew nothing about the man, and given the events of the last several months that had brought them to this point—events precipitated by a trusted member of the Order that neither Mina nor Finch suspected would betray them—he wasn't taking any chances.

"I'm sure." Mina turned her attention to Shaw. "When can we see the wine vaults?"

"Later tonight, after we dine. We're meeting my contact at ten near the entrance to the vaults." The restaurant was up ahead. Shaw quickened his step, perhaps eager to be out of the cold. "If you don't mind me asking, why are you so keen to eat at this establishment in particular?"

"I've heard good things about it," Decker replied, not bothering to elaborate. "The concierge at the hotel said it was a must."

"Sure. I'll pretend I believe that." Shaw approached the restaurant, pulled the door open, and stepped aside for Decker and Mina to enter before following them.

Beyond was a foyer in the shape of a rotunda with an arched ceiling that led into a large dining room surrounded by balconies. An ornate spiral staircase wound up to the second floor, providing a stunning centerpiece to the dining room. An orchestra played a languorous yet haunting melody that rose above the chatter of patrons and clink of glassware.

As the maître d' led them to their table, Shaw leaned close to Decker and spoke in a low voice. "You'll have to level with me, eventually. The two of you are up to something, and it's more than just poking around an unusual crime scene out of simple curiosity."

"I have no idea what you're talking about, Mr. Shaw," Decker said evenly as they reached a table to the left of the orchestra and took their seats. "We have only been in New York for twenty-four hours. Hardly enough time to get our bearings, let alone involve ourselves in any mischief."

"And yet *you are* involving yourselves." Shaw removed a cloth napkin from beneath his cutlery and placed it on his lap. "Sticking your noses into a murder that has nothing to do with you and occurred before you even stepped ashore."

"As I said, merely professional curiosity." Decker leaned forward, elbows on the table. "The unusual circumstances were too much to resist."

"Speaking of unusual circumstances," Mina said with her gaze rooted on Shaw. "You haven't told us how you came to be in New York or what this detective agency of yours actually does. The last I heard you had returned to Ireland."

"That was a long time ago." A shadow fell across Shaw's face. "There was nothing for me there and I moved on. Let's leave it at that. As for the detective agency, I started it to put a roof over my head after I landed on these shores. I was always good at getting to the truth of things."

"I remember," said Mina. "You were one of our best operatives until you walked away."

"I wouldn't go that far, but I appreciate the compliment." Shaw picked up his menu and studied it. He grunted and shot a look at Decker. "Hungarian food. Did the concierge at the hotel bother to mention that fact to you?"

"I can't say that he did," Decker replied in an even tone. He surveyed the dining room packed with patrons and the white shirted waiters flitting around laden with plates of steaming food. "But he was correct in saying that it's a popular place to dine. Do you have an objection to the cuisine?"

Shaw grunted again. "Not as such. I'm just more of a meat and potatoes kind of man."

"I'm sure both those ingredients are on the menu somewhere." Decker continued scanning the restaurant. It was, so he'd been told, a popular hangout of the bohemian crowd, and by extension he hoped, Clarence Rothman. Not that he had a clue how to approach him, assuming he even found the man. This dinner was more of a fact-finding mission than anything else. If it turned out that Clarence Rothman's circle of friends frequented Café Boulevard, then he and Mina would do the same and find a way to make their acquaintance. But it wouldn't be tonight. He saw plenty of diners who clearly belonged to New York's social elite, but none looked like they were yearning to break free of their old money constraints and join the revolution of idealistic poets, artists, and writers who called the Village home.

But just because Clarence Rothman wasn't currently there didn't mean he wasn't a familiar face. Decker forced himself to sit still until a waiter approached their table, deposited a plate of hot and crusty bread, and took their order, then he pushed his chair back and stood. "If you'll excuse me, I need to use the bathroom before the food arrives."

He weaved through the restaurant toward the back and the door marked restrooms, before changing course and skirting around the outside of the dining room and into the foyer where the maître d' was standing at a podium with his hands clasped behind his back.

At Decker's approach, he turned. "Can I help you, sir?"

"I hope so." Decker was pleased to have caught the maître d' during a lull when there was no one waiting to be seated. He would have the man's undivided attention, at least until more patrons came in out of the cold. "I believe an old acquaintance of mine frequents this restaurant with his friends. I was hoping to see him tonight and say hello, but he doesn't appear to be here."

"What would be the name of this acquaintance, sir?"

"Clarence Rothman."

"Ah, yes. You are correct. He does indeed dine here occasionally."

Decker waited for the maître d' to elaborate, but the man merely fixed him with a beady-eyed stare. When it became apparent that no further information was forthcoming, Decker cleared his throat. "Perhaps you could tell me how often he comes here and on what evenings?"

"I could." The maître d' lapsed into silence again.

At first, his unhelpful demeanor baffled Decker, but then he realized what was going on. He reached into his pocket and removed a dollar bill—a sum of money large enough that he hoped it would loosen the man's lips—and placed it on the podium.

"Thank you, sir. Gratuities are always appreciated." The maître d' pocketed the bribe. "Mr. Rothman and his associates can often be found here early in the week where they take up residence near the orchestra and stay the entire evening discussing politics and the arts. You won't be able to miss them if they are here. They can become rather loud and often animated in their discussions."

"Early in the week. Got it." Decker grimaced. It was only Friday evening, which meant the bohemians probably wouldn't be back for several more days.

The maître d', however, was not done. "If you are eager to reacquaint yourself with him immediately, you might try the Liberal Club. His clique is there most weekends so far as I am aware. But it's exclusive. If you aren't a member, you won't get past the front door."

"That's what I've heard." Decker turned to head back into the restaurant.

"Good luck, sir. If you need anything else, I'm at your service."

I bet, Decker mused, thinking about the dollar bill sitting snug in the maître d's pocket. But all he said was, "Thank you." Then he stepped out of the lobby and made his way back to the table.

EIGHTEEN

MINA LOOKED up when Decker retook his seat. "You were gone a while. Everything alright?"

"All good." The food hadn't arrived yet. Decker cut a slice from the small loaf of Hungarian bread sitting in the middle of the table and buttered it. He hadn't realized how hungry he was.

"Nick was about to tell me what his detective agency does."

"Really?" Decker shifted his gaze from Mina to Shaw. "I'd love to hear that."

Shaw glanced around at the surrounding tables, as if checking to make sure no one was eavesdropping. When he spoke, his voice was low. "It's really not much different from what the Order of St. George does. I track and eliminate creatures that shouldn't exist. Nasty creatures that would wreak havoc if left to their own devices."

"You mean supernatural creatures," Mina said.

Shaw nodded. "Just like when I belonged to the Order back in London, except here, I'm on my own." He glanced toward Mina. "No boss to tell me what to do, and no restraints."

"Which means you don't really operate a detective agency," said Decker. "You're just a vigilante monster hunter."

"On the contrary, my agency is genuine. Most of my work comes through clients who have nowhere else to turn. People who can't be helped by regular means. The supernatural is not an affliction unique to England, Mr. Decker, yet there is no official organization tasked with handling such matters on this side of the Atlantic."

"At least, not yet," said Mina, catching Decker's eye before turning her attention back to Shaw. "Your bruises. I assume they weren't from a bunch of angry slaughterhouse workers?"

"Oh, they were. But I could hardly blame those men since they were under the spell of a Kitsune who manipulated them in her attempt to evade me, which was, unfortunately, successful."

"A what?" Decker asked, furrowing his brow.

"Kitsune." Shaw gave the restaurant another furtive glance. "A shape shifting creature that takes the form of a beautiful woman to lull men under her spell and feed off their energy. You might be more familiar with the term succubus."

"Ah." Decker knew exactly what a succubus was. A female entity who preyed on the sexual energy of men, often draining them to the point of death, although he had never encountered one personally. Before working for CUSP, Decker would have dismissed such beings as nothing more than a centuries-old myth born out of superstition and fear. A misinterpretation of lethargy caused by illness or malnutrition at a time in history when they did not understand such afflictions. But now he knew better. While some myths were just that, others had a more frightening factual origin. After all, vampires were not supposed to be real, but yet he had come face-to-face with one in London's Whitechapel district. An encounter that had left Mina forever changed and started the chain of events that led them to become stranded in the past. "Tell me, what would you have done with this Kitsune if you caught her?"

"I would have eliminated her, of course."

"You would have killed her."

"Yes, and I still intend to. She's a dangerous predator who has left a string of dead men in her wake. What other choice has she given me?"

"You haven't looked for another solution?"

"Like what?" Shaw gave a small chuckle. "Ask her nicely to stop murdering people and go back to where she came from?"

"You have a point," Decker said grudgingly. Just because Nick Shaw didn't work for a larger organization that sanctioned his actions, didn't make him any less valid as a monster hunter. But there was one question that still burned in Decker's mind. "I have to ask, if you still believe in ridding the world of monsters, why did you walk away from the Order of St. George?"

Shaw's eyes shifted toward Mina, as if he expected her to provide the answer for him. When she didn't, a faint smile touched his lips. "Because they were better off without me."

"That doesn't answer my question."

"Nevertheless, it's all I intend to say on the matter. And you should be glad that I walked away, otherwise I wouldn't be here in New York to rescue you."

"Fair enough." None of what Nick Shaw had said made him any more trustworthy, in Decker's estimation, but just because he had secrets didn't mean he would betray them. Besides, whatever had driven Shaw from London and the Order all those years ago didn't appear to give either Mina or Finch cause for concern in the present. He took a deep breath and decided to move past the subject. "Your contact in the police force, the man we are meeting tonight. Who is he?"

"A detective in the fourteenth precinct. Known him for years. Saved his life after he cornered a lycanthrope in a dark alley. Creature would have ripped him to shreds if I hadn't shown up and put a couple of silver bullets in the beast. That's how we met back when he was a sergeant in uniform."

"I guess he owes you big time," Decker said.

"He does at that." Shaw leaned back in his chair. "Although he wasn't thanking me when he had to explain the situation in his report without looking like a lunatic."

"I bet." Decker couldn't help thinking of the Lupe Garou that had cost him his job in Wolf Haven. Despite the town mayor being torn to pieces and more than one witness to the creature, he still ended up out of a job and disgraced. At least until Adam Hunt and Classified Universal Special Projects came calling.

"Now he tips me off whenever anything strange occurs in the city. That's how I come by many of my clients."

"There's that many unexplained occurrences?" Decker asked.

"New York is a big city, Mr. Decker. It draws folk from all over the world in search of a better life. And sometimes, they don't come alone." Shaw glanced sideways toward a waiter who was approaching the table, balancing several plates. "But enough shop talk. Our food is here, and I'm starving. Let's eat!"

NINETEEN

THE ENTRANCE to the wine vaults under the East River Bridge didn't look like much. A pair of wooden doors set into an arch under the approach leading to the bridge along a narrow access road on the Manhattan side of the river. Two men were already there, lingering under the arch's shadow and almost invisible in the darkness, when Decker, Mina, and Shaw arrived at a couple of minutes to ten.

The taller of the two, a lean man wearing a black sack coat and derby hat, stepped forward out of the gloom when he saw them and raised a hand to get their attention.

Shaw greeted him and introduced Decker and Mina before nodding toward the man in the sack coat. "This is Detective McCullough."

"Pleased to meet you both," McCullough said, motioning toward his companion. "This is Harry Broadbent. He's a caretaker for the wine vaults and agreed to show them to you."

"Once our business is settled," said Broadbent in a gravelly New York accent.

"Right. Of course." Shaw reached into his pocket and pulled out a wad of dollar bills. He peeled some off and handed four to each man before glancing toward Decker and Mina. "You can settle up with me later."

"This after-hours wine vault tour doesn't come cheap," Decker said, figuring that Shaw had just handed each man the 1912 equivalent of about a hundred bucks. At the rate they were spending it, they would run out of money before Finch replenished the coffers.

"You want to get inside or not?" The detective said, pushing his share of the cash into a pocket inside his coat. "Because I'm only doing this as a favor to an old friend, and I'll happily walk away."

And because you just lined your pocket with a hefty bribe, Decker thought. He smiled and motioned toward the door. "Lead the way."

"That's what I thought." McCullough turned to the caretaker. "You have your money, as promised. Let's go."

Broadbent grunted and turned toward the door, removing a metal ring heavy with keys from his belt and selecting one. "You better not tell anyone about this. Mr. Cutler finds out I let you in here and I'll be out on my ear so fast my rear end won't know what's happening until after it hits the sidewalk."

"Mr. Cutler?" Decker asked.

"Howard Rothman's wine vault manager." Broadbent pushed the key into a heavy padlock and turned it, then removed the lock from the hasp securing the double doors and pushed them open wide enough to step through. "He's a nasty little man with a mean temper and a quick fist. You don't want to get on the wrong side of him, believe me."

"No one's going to say anything," McCullough assured

the caretaker. "And if your boss somehow finds out, which he won't, I'll tell him it was official police business."

"You better. I can't afford to lose this job. Got hungry mouths to feed and another on the way." Broadbent stepped inside and ushered the others through before grabbing an oil lamp from a hook and lighting it. He lit a second lamp and handed it to Decker, before pulling the doors closed again behind them.

Decker studied their surroundings in the flickering yellow glow of the oil lamps. They were in a vaulted chamber at least a hundred feet deep, fifty wide, and just as high. Empty wooden packing crates with the names of French vineyards stenciled on them lined the walls. Straw covered the floor in patches.

"Where's the wine?" he asked.

"Not here. This is just the receiving area." Broadbent led them toward the far end of the space and another wide arch beyond which was nothing but impenetrable darkness. "The vaults are a good sixty feet below us."

"How do they get the wine so deep underground?" Decker asked, surprised.

"Through here." Broadbent stepped under the arch, his oil lamp illuminating a gently sloped tunnel beyond. "When they were building the anchorages for the cables holding up the bridge span, the workers blasted down into the bedrock. Rather than filling in the spaces under and between the cable anchorages when they were done, the bridge's designer built a maze of passageways and arched vaults perfect for wine storage."

"And they bring it all down through this?" Decker asked as they moved deeper underground, following the sloping tunnel as it wound back upon itself.

"There are other ways in and out, but most of the wine

comes through here on trolleys." Broadbent held his lantern high. It swayed as he walked, sending shadows leaping up over the tunnel's walls and vaulted ceiling.

In front of them was another rough-hewn arch that looked like it had been carved from solid granite. To Decker, it had the appearance of a cave entrance. In all his years working as a homicide detective in New York City before returning to Wolf Haven, he had never heard of these vaults. He wondered if they were still there in the twenty-first century.

They reached the arch and stepped through. Decker stopped and gasped. The cathedral-like space in front of them was wide and tall, it's vaulted ceiling at least fifty feet above them. Smaller chambers led off to the left and right through more arches named after French wineries. When they approached the closest of the side chambers, Decker saw hundreds of wine bottles arranged on wooden racks that lined the walls. Given how many other site chambers led off the main vault, he estimated there must be several thousand bottles stored there.

He slipped one from its resting place and looked at the label. It read 1908 Château Filhot Sauternes, which meant nothing to Decker. He returned it to the rack. "Where did the murder take place?"

"Right around here," the detective replied. "The party was taking place in the main vault out there. By the time the victim was discovered, the murderer was long gone."

"How do you know it wasn't someone at the party?"

"We don't for sure, but we questioned the guests before allowing them to leave, and they were all accounted for. Whoever committed the act must have been drenched in blood, given the grisly nature of the crime. Victim's neck was snapped, and then his face was removed. The killer took it with them as some sort of sick souvenir."

"And no one at the party noticed the murderer leaving?" Decker asked. "There were over a hundred people in attendance. Someone should have seen a man drenched in blood and carrying another man's face."

"I'm sure they would, if he had left that way." McCullough motioned for them to follow him through a narrow door at the back of the vault. Beyond was another tunnel that fell away into the darkness. "We think the killer left through here. We found footprints. Big uns' too. Like the brute was eight feet tall. There were twelve of them leading away from the scene before they petered out."

"Where does this tunnel go?" Decker asked.

"Connects up with another tunnel, which leads to the Brooklyn Bridge subway station. That entrance is locked when not in use, but it wasn't on the night in question. Some of the guests arrived that way."

"Meaning the killer could have entered and escaped unseen." Decker peered down the tunnel.

"Unfortunately. We think the victim was selected at random. He ducked into the side vault to smoke a cigarette out of sight and was alone in a location where the killer could do his work undisturbed."

Decker glanced at the ground ahead of them. "The footprints. I don't see them. Where are they?"

"Well, they're gone, of course." The wine vault caretaker, Broadbent, sniffed and wiped his nose with the back of his hand. "No reason to leave 'em and Mr. Cutler doesn't like his vaults being dirty. Says it sets a bad example."

"You destroyed the only evidence left behind by a murderer?" Decker snorted and looked at McCullough. "Did you take photos?"

The detective shuffled from one foot to the other. "Well, not as such. The owner, Mr. Rothman, was adamant that no photos be taken in the vaults or passageways beyond. He wields a lot of influence in this city. Knows the police commissioner personally I'm told. I was only allowed to take a few close-up photos of the victim."

"Why?" Decker asked.

"Mr. Rothman didn't want his competitors using the murder against him. He was concerned the photos would end up in the newspapers and put a stain on his business." McCullough folded his arms. "I'd like to say it doesn't happen, but it does."

"That's just great." Decker stepped back into the vault, not bothering to hide his frustration. "Let's go. There's nothing worth looking at down here."

TWENTY

"YOU WERE KIND OF HARD on that detective back there," Mina said to Decker when they were back at the lodging house.

"I know forensic science is practically nonexistent in this era, but that's no excuse for bad crime scene management. That detective should have insisted on documenting the evidence regardless of what his superior told him," Decker said.

It was midnight and Mina was in Decker's room sitting on the bed, hands resting in her lap. After they left the vault, Shaw had accompanied them back to their accommodation and taken his leave with the promise of returning the following day. Now Decker paced the small bedroom, from the door to the window and back again.

"John. For goodness' sake. Using the murder to get close to Clarence Rothman was always a long shot. You realize that?"

Decker stopped pacing. He looked at Mina. "I'm not just frustrated because the murder scene was a waste of time. It irks me as a former cop that a murder may go unsolved because Howard Rothman doesn't want bad publicity. The murder happened at his own brother's birthday party, in his own wine vault, of all places. He probably knew the man who was murdered, at least in passing. You'd think he would want the murderer brought to justice."

"He's obviously a ruthless businessman intent on protecting his business at all costs." Mina placed a hand over her mouth and yawned before continuing. "And anyway, tonight wasn't a total loss. It still provided us with an opportunity. We saw the wine vaults where Clarence Rothman's birthday party took place. We can use that as a way into his inner circle. Pretend we were there. He couldn't possibly have known all hundred guests in attendance."

"Bond with him over a shared tragedy." Decker rubbed his chin. "I guess it's better than nothing."

"It will work. Human nature. You know what they say... misery loves company."

"Except we have yet to find him." Decker sighed. "Hell, we don't even know what he looks like. We could walk past the guy in the street and never know it. This would be so much easier if we had internet. We could just browse his social media profile and find out everything we need to know, including where he hangs out and when."

"Great. We have a plan." Mina laughed. "We'll just wait around a hundred years and problem solved."

"Not funny. You actually can wait around a hundred years and the problem will solve itself with no need to find a way onto Singer Cay. Me, not so much."

"Hey, I wasn't trying to be insensitive. I just meant that—"

Decker sat down next to Mina and placed a hand on hers. "I know what you meant. I guess the thought of never getting back to Nancy, of dying here alone in the past, terrifies me."

"That isn't going to happen." Mina squeezed Decker's hand. "Even if we can't get to Singer Cay and follow Celine Rothman into the future, we'll find another way. There's *always* another way."

"I admire your optimism, but in this instance, I fear it may be misplaced. The next time we know of a time portal opening up in the Bermuda Triangle is 1942 and that's the one that brought us here. And then what do we do? Steal another plane and follow ourselves into that electrical storm? Apart from the obvious fact that two versions of us running around the base is going to get confusing and might cause a paradox that splits the timeline, or that neither of us knows how to fly, the portal won't open for another thirty years. I'll be in my seventies."

"I never said it was a perfect plan."

"And that's assuming I don't end up killed in one of the two world wars that are about to happen or succumb to the Spanish flu epidemic coming before the end of the decade that's going to kill upwards of fifty million people around the world."

"You're not making this easy."

"Because the future of this century is a minefield I'd rather avoid." Decker lapsed into silence, staring at the far wall of the bedroom as if the answer to their predicament might suddenly appear there.

After a while, Mina slipped her hand from his and stood. "We'll get to Singer Cay, and you'll see Nancy again. I promise."

Decker looked up. "And if not, you've still got that letter I wrote her."

"Safe and sound. But you won't need it, because we're getting home."

"Sure." Decker took a deep breath. "It's late. We should get some sleep."

"Right." Mina walked to the door and opened it. After stepping out, she turned back to Decker. "You going to be all right tonight?"

"I'm fine. Just feeling sorry for myself. You don't need to worry."

Mina smiled thinly. "Good to hear. See you in the morning, Mr. Monster Hunter." Then she pulled the door closed and left Decker alone with his thoughts.

TWENTY-ONE

DECKER AWOKE to someone banging on his bedroom door. He opened his eyes and picked up his watch from the nightstand. Seven in the morning.

The banging came again. Quick and urgent. A voice drifted from the other side of the door. "Mr. Decker, wake up."

It was the private detective, Nick Shaw. Decker swung his legs off the bed and stood, then pulled his pants on. He rubbed the sleep from his eyes and went in search of a shirt.

"John, answer the door." This time, it was Mina. There was an urgency to her voice.

"Hang on." Decker slipped a shirt on and buttoned it, then answered the door.

Mina and Shaw were standing in the corridor. The private detective looked worse than the day before, with ugly yellow bruising on his right cheek and under both eyes.

Decker winced. "You're not getting any prettier."

"Thanks." Shaw forced a grin, which quickly faded. "There's been a development you might be interested in."

"Another murder," Mina said.

"It looks like the same killer," Shaw added. "More muddy footprints."

"Wine vaults again?" Decker asked.

"Not this time. Private residence. An apartment on the other side of Washington Square Park. A conveniently close location. Everything else is the same. Neck snapped, which was at least a quick death, then the perpetrator helped himself to the man's face."

"You get all this from that detective friend of yours?" Decker asked, reaching behind the door to a hook and grabbing his coat.

"He sent a patrolman to rouse me from my bed."

"Does the New York Police Department make a habit of calling on you whenever they find a dead body?" Decker asked.

"I work as an unofficial consultant of sorts whenever something might have a—" Shaw stopped abruptly as if thinking of the best way to phrase what he was about to say. "A supernatural lean. Like the inhumanly large bare footprints and uncommon strength required to rip a man's face from his skull without the use of surgical instruments."

Decker donned his coat and stepped into the corridor. "Detective McCullough's colleagues and superiors are fine with you poking around?"

"They tolerate me, mostly because I can make their problems go away when there is a genuine supernatural cause, even if it doesn't result in an arrest."

"Like the Kitsune you were following yesterday," Mina said.

"Yes. All things being equal, I would have dispatched her and thus brought an end to the destruction she leaves in her wake. Although, in this case, it was not the police who alerted

me to her presence, but a private client who lost a loved one."
Shaw turned and started down the corridor toward the stairs.
"We should make our way to the crime scene before too many
heavy-footed police officers trample over it."

"McCullough mentioned nothing about a supernatural
angle when we were in the vaults yesterday," Decker said,
walking a step behind Shaw with Mina at his side.

"That's because the NYPD doesn't recognize the
paranormal as a valid explanation for the crimes that plague
our fair city, even when it's the correct one. At least, not
officially. But there's a reluctant acceptance among some in
the department that rational explanations don't always get
the job done."

"That's where you come in."

"Yes. In much the same way as the Order of St. George
would take the reins in London."

"And us?" Mina asked. "I assume he knows that we're
tagging along."

"He does. Detective McCullough is the one who
suggested I fetch you both prior to attending the scene."
Shaw glanced over his shoulder toward Decker as they
descended the stairs and stepped out into the street. "I believe
he felt his competence was diminished in your eyes at the
wine vault crime scene yesterday. This is his way of making
amends and redeeming himself."

"And possibly because he's playing nice," Decker said, "to
cover up the fact that he took a bribe to let us into the
aforementioned crime scene. I can't imagine his superiors
would be too happy with that if they found out."

Shaw chuckled. "That might be a part of it, too." He
stepped off the curb and crossed the road, then led them into
the park.

They followed a meandering pathway through the urban

oasis until they reached a large fountain at the center. Beyond this, standing at the park's opposite boundary, was the Washington Square Arch. It was a monument Decker had visited many times during his days as a homicide detective in the city and stirred in him a pang of nostalgia because here in this leafy haven of tranquility amid the bustle of the city, he could almost imagine he was home in his own time and not stranded over hundred years in the past.

But when they stepped under the arch and emerged on the other side, the spell broke. The landscape of early twentieth century Fifth Avenue, which they now faced, looked nothing like he remembered.

"Come on," Shaw said, leading them onto Washington Square North, the road bounding the park's perimeter. "This way."

Shaw crossed the street, stopping to let the horse-drawn carriage trundle past, and took them to a row house in front of which stood a police wagon and a motorized hearse obvious by its ornate decoration, including side panels with carved relief columns and draperies, that gave it the appearance of a tomb on wheels.

A patrolman stood at the door to the building. At Shaw's approach, he stepped aside with a curt nod, obviously recognizing the private detective.

"Detective McCullough is on the second floor. You can go up," the patrolman said, his gaze shifting briefly to Decker and Mina as they stepped past him and into the cool, dark interior of the row house.

Ahead of them was a staircase with an ornate dark oak banister and carved balusters. They climbed to the second floor and encountered another patrolman standing next to an open door through which they could see more police officers. There was also a photographer standing behind a box camera mounted on a tripod. Clearly, Detective McCullough was determined not to appear so inept at this crime scene.

But it was what lay beyond the gaggle of police and the photographer that drew Decker's eye. The body of a man sprawled on the floor and briefly lit in the garish pop of a flashbulb. A man with nothing but raw red flesh where his face should have been.

TWENTY-TWO

"A NASTY BUSINESS, THIS," said a voice to their rear.

Decker turned to see Detective McCullough standing in the corridor, his face drained of color. By way of explanation, he said, "Stepped outside to get some fresh air while the photographer does his work. Figured there was no point in staring at that ghastly corpse any more than necessary."

"When did this happen?" Decker asked.

"Within the last forty-eight hours, but most likely two nights ago."

"How do you know that?" Decker asked, noting the lack of any medical personnel.

"Doctor Edward Goodwin. Lives a couple of doors down in one of the row houses. He spared the time to make a cursory examination and confirm the death."

"What do we know about the victim?" asked Shaw.

"Name's Charles Archibald Flint. Heir to the Flint Industries fortune and apparently rebelling against his blue blood roots, and probably his father, by exploring his bohemian side in Greenwich Village like so many of his peers.

He was last seen at the Liberal Club, where he downed a couple of whiskeys before heading home for the night."

"The Liberal Club." Decker exchanged a glance with Mina before turning his attention back to the detective. "Who found him?"

"A friend. They were supposed to be heading out of town for the weekend. The Hamptons. When he didn't show up, his friend came around here and got the building manager to let him in. That's when they found the body."

Shaw diverted his gaze to the corpse before looking away again. "I guess Charles Flint headed out of town for good instead."

Decker ignored the inappropriate quip. "Where's the friend now?"

"We took a statement and let him go. Couldn't see much point in detaining the man. He obviously wasn't the killer. For a start, his feet are too small to have left the footprints we found."

"You leave those footprints intact this time?" Decker asked.

"What do you think?" The detective jerked his thumb toward the corpse. "Want to see them?"

Decker was momentarily taken aback. In his own era, no police detective would allow civilians to tromp through a crime scene, especially when it was still being processed. But here in 1912, the forensics rulebook hadn't even been written yet. There were no technicians decked out in disposable bodysuits, gloves, and booties. No forensic pathologist on the scene examining the corpse in situ. The police simply found the closest doctor to confirm that the victim was dead—which was already obvious by the condition of the body. He wondered what the homicide solve rate was in this era. He guessed it was low.

"John?" Mina nudged Decker.

"Sorry." Decker's mind snapped back into focus. "Yes, please show us the footprints."

Detective McCullough sidled past them into the apartment and ushered his men aside, then approached the corpse. "Careful stepping around the body."

At first, when he walked into the apartment, Decker didn't see the footprints, but then he saw them on the far side of the body. A trail of distinct muddy impressions leading down the hallway, moving deeper inside the apartment, then another set, some of which overlapped the first, moving in the other direction and ending at a door on the left, which turned out to be a bathroom. Impossibly large footprints that bore the marks of a heel and toes.

Decker kneeled to examine them, then glanced around, peering into the bathroom and toward the front door. "There's no mud anywhere else. The killer didn't track mud in from outside."

"Weird, huh?" Detective McCullough leaned against the wall with folded arms. "A barefooted killer with muddy feet who appears to come out of nowhere and vanish just as quickly."

"The man who discovered the body. You said the building manager let him in, which means when he arrived, the door was locked. Yes?"

The detective nodded. "That's what he and the building manager both say."

Decker turned to look at the corpse, and an object still clutched in the dead man's right hand. "And yet the victim is still holding his front door key. How could the killer have left and locked the door from the outside without a key?"

"Maybe the killer didn't leave that way," Mina said.

"I thought of that," McCullough replied. "We're only on

the second floor, so is not unreasonable to think someone could have climbed out a window and dropped down, or even used the fire escape at the back, except that every window in the apartment is shut and latched from the inside. Our killer might have entered through a window, but they sure as hell didn't leave through one."

"Any other way in or out of the apartment?" Decker straightened up and stood with his hands in his pockets, studying the scene.

"Nope." The detective rubbed his chin. "I figured the killing in the vaults was random. Bad luck on the part of the victim being in the wrong place at the wrong time. That maybe someone went down there taking advantage of the party to steal some of that fancy wine not realizing anyone would be in the side vault. Now I'm not so sure."

"I agree. There was nothing random about this latest killing," Decker said. "The killer was waiting for his victim to return home, which means he was the intended target…"

"Making it likely the killing in the vault wasn't random, either. The killer took advantage of the victim's isolated location for sure but was probably already lying in wait for the perfect opportunity. It wasn't a wine theft gone wrong."

"That's a reasonable assumption." Decker lifted his gaze from the corpse. "You know of any connection between the two victims?"

"They both moved in the same circles and probably knew many of the same people," McCullough said. "But we'll need to do some digging to see if there is—"

A commotion in the corridor outside the apartment cut the detective's sentence short.

Raised voices.

Moments later, a man in a dapper morning suit appeared

in the apartment doorway and stopped short when he saw the body. Two patrolmen appeared behind the newcomer.

Detective McCullough glared at them. "What's the meaning of this?"

"I'm sorry, sir," said one of the patrolmen, a sheepish expression on his face. "He showed up at the front door and insisted on entering. When I told him the building was off-limits, he pushed me aside and barged in."

"We tried to stop him," said the other patrolman. "But he was having none of it."

Detective McCullough waved a dismissive hand. "Get him out of here. If he continues to resist, slap the cuffs on him."

The two patrolmen gripped the stranger's arms and dragged him backwards out of the doorway.

"Release me, this instant." The man did his best to shake them off. "Do you know who I am?"

"If I had to guess," McCullough replied, "you're nothing but a muckraking newsman who got a little too cocky for his own good."

"A reporter?" The man bellowed and blustered as the two cops dragged him away from the door and down the hallway. "I'll have you know I'm no common newshound. Nothing of the sort. I'm Clarence Rothman, second in line to the Rothman shipping fortune, and that gentleman lying dead at your feet is one of my oldest friends."

TWENTY-THREE

"JOHN." Mina had turned toward the commotion in the doorway, but now glanced back at Decker, still standing on the other side of the corpse even as the two patrolmen escorted an unhappy and vocal Clarence Rothman toward the stairs. "This is our chance."

"I realize that." Decker stepped over the body, careful to avoid the dark, wide stain of blood that ringed the corpse's head like a grotesque halo.

He ran to the door, following Mina, who was a couple of steps ahead of him. By the time they traversed the hallway and reached the head of the stairs, the patrolmen were already at the bottom with their charge and bundling him toward the front door.

"Wait. Don't let him leave." Decker sprinted down to the ground floor with Mina at his side and stepped outside.

The sky had been overcast and gray when they entered the building fifteen minutes before. Now a light but steady rain fell. Clarence Rothman stood at the curb with his hands pushed deep into his pockets and shoulders slumped as if he didn't notice the precipitation that slicked his hair and dampened his suit jacket.

"Mr. Rothman?" Decker approached the dejected man and stopped a pace behind him at his right shoulder. "I'm sorry for your loss."

"Thank you." Clarence continued staring at a patch of ground a few feet ahead of him for a moment longer, then lifted his head and turned toward Decker. "It wasn't my intention to make a scene back there. I'm sorry if my actions were ungentlemanly."

"It's understandable," Mina said, coming to a stop next to Decker. "Death is never easy."

"Try losing two friends in the same week." Clarence finally seemed to notice the rain, looking momentarily up at the ashen sky. "Fitting weather under the circumstances, don't you think?"

"Mr. Rothman, is there some place we can talk?" Decker asked. "Somewhere less exposed."

Clarence nodded mutely, then furrowed his brow as if confused. "Sorry, but who are you?"

Decker introduced himself and Mina, noticing for the first time that Shaw had not followed them outside.

"You with the police?" Clarence asked.

"No. We're more like…" Decker struggled to find the right word.

"Consultants." Mina came to his aid. "We help solve crimes that don't have a logical explanation."

"And right now, we'd like to help *you*," Decker said.

"Me? I'm not the one lying dead with my face ripped off."

"No. But you just admitted to knowing both victims personally. I assume that the other dead friend you are talking about was the man murdered at your party." Decker lifted his collar against the rain. "It would seem reasonable to conclude that if this killer is not sated, you will soon lose a third friend."

"Or maybe the killer might strike a little closer to home next time," Mina added.

"You think the killer might come after me?"

"It can't be ruled out." Decker didn't say this just because he wanted to become further acquainted with Clarence Rothman, but also because his years in the homicide division prior to joining CUSP had taught him not to ignore an emerging pattern. Two of Clarence Rothman's friends were dead at the hands of the same murderous and impossibly large footed individual—a perpetrator with a particularly gruesome and distinctive MO—which meant that anyone within his circle was also at risk. The barefooted killer would strike again. Decker was sure of it. The only questions were when and where. "I would suggest that we find somewhere out of the rain, and you tell us everything you know."

Clarence appeared to think upon this for several seconds, then nodded. "Very well. There's a coffeehouse a block from here on the corner. We can go there. It's a discrete establishment and the patrons know to mind their own business."

"That will do fine," said Decker.

"Wait." Mina glanced back toward the building. What about Nick?"

"He seemed good up there. We'll come back for him afterward."

"In that case, I'll leave a message. Let him know we'll return soon." Mina turned back to the row house door where one of the patrolmen who had evicted Clarence Rothman stood on guard. She spoke to him briefly, then returned. "All done."

"Great. Can we go now?"

"Sure."

"Wonderful." Decker turned back to Clarence Rothman and gestured. "The coffeehouse... Please, lead the way."

TWENTY-FOUR

WHEN THEY ENTERED the coffee house, Clarence Rothman led them to a booth in the rear corner of the establishment. After they settled with their coffees in front of them, he leaned forward over the table and looked at Mina, his gaze sweeping her body. "I have to ask, how did a fine-looking woman like yourself end up solving crimes for a living?"

"Are you insinuating that an attractive woman can't have a career, Mr. Rothman?"

"Not at all. I just think you would look better on the arm of a wealthy gentleman like myself, than bothering with such a repugnant pastime. Perhaps when this is all over, we can—"

"I hardly think so," Mina said. "I fear that your intentions might not be pure."

"Where's the fun in being pure?"

"That's enough," Decker said, seeing the look on Mina's face and stepping in before she could respond with a firmer rebuke that might scuttle their chances with Clarence before they even began. "How about we focus on the issue at hand."

"Alright. Fine. You have my attention. Now, what do you wish to know?"

Decker added a splash of milk to his coffee and stirred. "For a start, how did you know to show up at the apartment this morning so soon after the body was discovered?"

"Easy enough to explain. Charles was going on a constitutional for the weekend with a mutual acquaintance, Oliver Bradley. They were heading to the Hamptons, which is a favorite destination among our little group. Several of us own homes there. After he went to the apartment and found Charles dead, he came straight to me. Once the police were done with him, of course. It's the second of our friends to die in the last week and Oliver was rattled."

"The first being Wallace Alden," Decker said. "Who was murdered in much the same fashion during your birthday party in the wine vaults under the East River Bridge."

Clarence nodded. "My brother rents the vaults from the city to store the wine he imports from Europe. It's the perfect location. It's always dark and at a constant ideal temperature of around fifty degrees. He has thousands of dollars-worth down there, which is why I was surprised he let me have it for the party." Rothman snorted. "Although I'm sure he didn't want my friends tromping around the family mansion, so that probably has something to do with it. Still, we made a good dent in his champagne stock. At least until..." Clarence Rothman's voice faltered. He looked away, caught in a sudden moment of emotion. When he looked back, pain etched his face. "Anyway, it doesn't matter what his motives were. When I thought Wallace was the victim of a scoundrel intent on stealing my brother's wine, that was one thing. But with Charles meeting a similar fate... That's why I showed up at the apartment like that. I had to see for myself."

"An understandable reaction," said Mina, a sympathetic

tone in her voice. "You said the victim was one of your oldest friends."

"That's right. We were in school together and have been close ever since."

"And the first victim, Wallace Alden?" Decker asked. "What about him?"

"The same. There were a bunch of us who met in school. We stayed close in the years afterward thanks to our shared ideologies that led us to the Village."

"Bohemian ideologies?"

"I suppose. That's partly why my brother and I don't get along. He despises my values. Thinks I'm lazy because I don't want to join the family business. By extension, he applies those prejudiced beliefs to the rest of my friends. Thinks we're nothing but a bunch of worthless idealists with too much time on our hands. He's even threatened to cut off my trust fund a couple of times, not that he would dare. I know too much about his shady business practices."

"In other words, he's afraid you'll reveal the skeletons in his closet," Decker said.

"Something like that."

Decker nodded slowly. "How many people are in your group of old school friends?"

"There's six of—" Clarence caught himself. "There were six of us. Now I guess it's only four."

"All of whom your brother despises, by your own admission."

"Yes." Clarence was silent for a moment as the implication of Decker's words sunk in. "Wait. You're not suggesting my brother had something to do with those deaths, are you? Because if that's the case, you're wrong. Howard might be a quick-tempered ogre with no time for anyone who doesn't share his capitalistic ambitions, but he is not a criminal, much less a murderer."

"Calm down." Decker gripped his coffee mug with two hands and took a sip before continuing. "I don't think your brother is involved in this. He has too much to lose and not enough motive beyond dislike of the circles you move in. But the violence inflicted on the bodies after death suggests a perpetrator with a personal connection to your group and driven by deep hatred. The killer is sending a message by taking the victim's faces. Think hard now. What might that message be?"

"You think I know?" Clarence threw his hands in the air. "Well, I don't."

"You recall nothing in your past, or the collective past of your group, that would trigger such extreme violence?"

"I don't... I mean..." Clarence stuttered, his eyes shifting between Mina and Decker. "No. If I could, I would have told you." He swallowed. "It could be me next, right?"

"Since two of your friends are dead at the hands of a killer who appears to be targeting your group, I would say it's a distinct possibility," Decker replied. "I'd say you have a one in four chance."

"If this were something less deadly, I'd take those odds. Twenty-five percent. But in this case, it feels a little like playing Russian roulette." Clarence pulled a handkerchief from his pocket and mopped beads of sweat from his brow. "How much do you want?"

"I'm sorry?"

"To keep me safe and stop this killer." Clarence leaned forward. "You claimed to be helping the police. Called yourselves consultants. That means the pair of you must be experts on this kind of thing. The one principal my brother and I agree on is that you should always surround yourself with experts. So, name your price."

"And your friends?" Mina asked. "What of them?"

"When it comes to staying alive, I'm going to think of myself first, thank you very much," Clarence said. "And anyway, if you find whoever's doing this and put an end to their murderous ways, it will benefit them, too. Right?"

"I suppose." Decker pushed his coffee cup away and leaned on the table with his elbows, fingers interwoven. "We'll keep you alive and find the person responsible for killing your friends. But we don't want money."

Clarence looked confused. "Then what *do* you want?"

"A favor."

"Sure. Anything. Name it."

"Not yet. We take care of this, and you'll be in our debt. When the time comes, we'll collect that debt. Do we have a deal?"

Clarence didn't even hesitate with his reply. "Absolutely. Whatever you need." The relief on his face was clear. "What happens now?"

"Now we get you somewhere safe and arrange protection for your remaining friends," Decker said, standing and exiting the booth. When Clarence went to follow, Decker stopped him. "Wait there a moment."

"What are you doing?" Clarence sank back onto the bench.

"A moment, please." Decker went to the counter and asked the young woman behind it for a pencil and paper, which he brought back to the table and put down in front of Clarence. "Here. Write down your friends' names and addresses."

"Sure." Clarence pulled the sheet of paper close and did as requested before handing it to Decker. "Anything else?"

"Not right now." Decker folded the paper into a neat square, then motioned for Mina and Clarence to follow before turning toward the door. "Come on, we have a lot of work to do."

TWENTY-FIVE

OUT ON THE sidewalk once again, Decker turned to Mina and handed her the folded sheet of paper. "I want you to go back to the crime scene and find that detective. Give him this list of names and tell him to assign a police officer to each of them for protection. Tell him that the killer is not done yet and someone on this list is probably the next victim."

"Got it." Mina tucked the sheet of paper into her dress. "What are you going to do?"

"I shall accompany Clarence to his apartment, where he's going to pack enough clothes for at least a week and then arrange a safe place for him to stay until we resolve this situation. I'm thinking a room in the boarding house where we're currently staying should suffice. He'll be under our protection, and the killer won't know where to look for him. Once you're done with Detective McCullough, come straight back to the boarding house and bring Nick with you. We're going to need his help with this, too."

"Understood." Mina turned to walk away, but Decker caught her arm.

"And be careful. Murderers often return to the scene of the crime. Be discreet and make sure you're not followed."

"You don't need to worry about me. I'm a big girl. I can handle myself."

A big girl who got herself abducted not too long ago by carelessly answering the door to a stranger in an unfamiliar location, Decker thought to himself. But he didn't say that. Instead, he merely nodded and agreed with her. "I know you can. Be quick and stay safe."

"Always." Mina hurried away.

Decker watched until she disappeared around the corner, then turned to Clarence. "Let's go."

————

Clarence Rothman kept a suite of rooms at the Hotel Albert on East 11th Street in the Village. It was bigger than the suite he and Mina had shared at the Waldorf-Astoria, but no less fancy, with a chandelier hanging in the tiled entrance lobby, and antique furniture that looked like it had come straight from a French château.

Decker stood in the large, formal living room and looked around with a mixture of awe and disbelief. "I thought you came to the Village to live a simple life and mingle among the artists and poets," he said as Clarence fussed around grabbing items such as a silver hip flask, cigarette case, and several books, which Decker deemed unnecessary but which the aspiring bohemian swore were necessary if he was to be away for any length of time.

Clarence stopped what he was doing and turned to Decker. "Just because I choose to turn my back on the cutthroat landscape of the capitalist world which my brother inhabits doesn't mean I should live like a pauper. Besides, this hotel is popular among the bohemian crowd. Art and comfort can go hand-in-hand, Mr. Decker."

"I suppose that's why you were so keen not to lose that trust fund," Decker replied.

"I have as much right to the family money as my brother does, and my trust fund is meagre compared to the wealth my brother enjoys." Clarence crossed to a bar on the far side of the room, where he found a tumbler and poured himself a large measure of brandy. "Can I offer you a drink?"

"No," Decker replied. "We don't have time for you to have one, either. It isn't safe here."

"Nonsense. Unless I misunderstood our conversation in the coffeehouse, I hired you to protect me, and here you are." Clarence lifted the glass, tilted his head back, and drained it in one go. He smacked his lips and reached for the bottle, pouring another. When he saw the look on Decker's face, he waved a dismissive hand. "Just one more to settle my nerves. After what I've just seen, I need it."

"If we don't get out of here soon, you might end up just like your friend. It isn't safe. Now hurry up and pack a bag."

"All right, already. I'm going." Clarence downed the second drink and put the tumbler on the bar top a little too hard. He stepped away from the bar toward a short hallway with doors on both sides. "You know, I could hire an entire police force to keep me safe."

"Then perhaps you should do that," Decker said, despite himself. He was growing weary of the younger Rothman's blasé attitude in the face of possibly the most serious situation of his life.

Clarence stopped and turned back to Decker. There was a flicker of panic behind his eyes. "Look, I'm sorry. This whole affair has set me on edge, and when I get scared, I tend to hide behind false bravado. I'm sure you'll do a fine job of protecting me, and if I get out of hand, just tell me so."

"You can count on that." Decker watched as Clarence turned back toward the hallway, then a thought occurred to him. "I don't suppose you have a weapon of any type around here, do you?"

Clarence glanced over his shoulder. "You mean like a gun?"

"Yes."

"Sorry, but no. Never liked guns. Our father used to take Howard and I hunting when we were younger, and I despised every second of it. Haven't touched a gun since I was sixteen."

"That's a shame." Decker had been in possession of a gun back on the Titanic when he went into the water, but at some point between then and his rescue by the Carpathia, he had lost it.

"There's a veritable armory at the mansion. Several shotguns and at least a couple of pistols," Clarence said, still lingering in the hallway. "There's even an old rifle-musket my grandfather supposedly used during the Civil War, but I'd rather not have to explain why I need a gun to my brother. Heaven knows, he already thinks I'm useless. I can't imagine what he would make of this current situation."

"He'd probably be worried about you," said Decker.

"I doubt that very much. He views me as a liability. For all I know, he's the one having my friends killed." Clarence fell silent for a moment, then cleared his throat. "Sorry. That was unfair and more than a little inappropriate. My brother loves me, he just doesn't like me. We don't have to visit the mansion, do we?"

"I think we can get a gun from somewhere else." Decker was aware of the minutes slipping away. Two days had elapsed between the first and second murders, which meant that if the killer kept the same timeframe, a third was imminent. He would rather not loiter in the apartment any longer than necessary. "Hurry up and pack. We need to get out of here."

TWENTY-SIX

WHEN THEY ARRIVED BACK at the boarding house, Mina and Shaw were already there. Decker had rented a third room for Clarence Rothman a couple of doors down from his own at the far end of the hallway, meaning that any attacker coming up the stairs would have to pass both Mina and Decker's rooms to get to Clarence. It wasn't ideal but was safer than letting Clarence stay in his own apartment since the last victim had been murdered at home.

But the moment Clarence saw his temporary lodging, he shook his head vigorously. "This won't do. Not at all."

"What's wrong with it?" Decker asked, suspecting he knew the answer.

"It's so... small and average. Cramped. There isn't even a bathroom."

"Bathroom is down the hall," Mina said. "I'm sure you can survive without all the luxuries you're used to for a few days. Unless you'd rather wait in your apartment to meet the same fate as your friends."

"I'm not using a shared bathroom. No way. Bathing in a

tub used by everyone on this floor like some kind of common laborer? There has to be another solution. Maybe we should go to the family mansion, after all. My brother is insufferable, but at least it's clean and comfortable there."

"You would be no safer at your family mansion than your own apartment," Decker said. "While putting your brother and everyone else in the household at risk, too."

"A hotel, then." There was desperation in Clarence's voice. "I'll pay for all of us."

"This is where we're staying. Apart from anything else, if the killer knows you even a little, they won't think to look here." Decker folded his arms and glared at Clarence.

"Some bohemian you are," Nick said with a snort.

"What, you assume that being a bohemian means you have to live in a slum?"

"This isn't a slum." Decker was beginning to see why Howard Rothman disliked his brother. Clarence was a spoiled rotten brat who had clearly never known a moment's hardship in his entire life. "It's a safe place where the killer won't find you. Now quit your complaining and make the best of it."

Clarence opened his mouth to say something else, then obviously thought better and closed it again. He stared sullenly at his surroundings with his arms folded across his chest.

"Speaking of the killer," Mina said, after it became obvious the exchange was over. "Detective McCullough agreed to have officers watch everyone on the list of names Clarence wrote down for us. They'll be given round-the-clock protection."

"Good." Decker couldn't be certain, but his gut told him that the killer wouldn't wait long to strike again. "Since we don't have a patrolman of our own to rely on, we need to arm ourselves." He turned to Shaw. "Given your line of work, you must have weapons."

Shaw glanced at Clarence, who had stepped further into the room and was now surveying the narrow bed and thin sheets with a mixture of disdain and horror. "Wouldn't be much of a—" Shaw paused a moment as if choosing his next words carefully. "A private detective, if I didn't, now would I?" He slipped a hand under his jacket and withdrew a compact pistol. "Webley & Scott model 1905. Lightweight and rugged. This beauty has gotten me out of more than one scrape."

"You have any other weapons?"

"Not with me. Got a pair of rifles and a couple more pistols back at my place."

"We'll need them."

"Sure." Shaw gave Clarence a furtive glance. "Can we talk out in the hallway?"

Decker nodded and followed the private detective out of the bedroom and closed the door so they wouldn't be overheard. "What is it?"

"Mina said you wish to hire me for the duration."

"That's right. So long as it doesn't interfere with your current case."

"The Kitsune?" Shaw shook his head. "I already blew that one. She'll have gone underground by now. Possibly even left the city now she knows I'm on to her. Took me the better part of two months to find her the first time, and she'll be more careful now. Best to let things settle down before I try to pick up her trail again. For the moment, I'm all yours. I'll even give you the friends and family rate. I'd offer my services for gratis, but a man still needs to eat."

"No worries. Take your fee out of whatever money Thomas Finch sends our way."

"In the interest of full transparency, Thomas already said he'd hire me to look out for the pair of you until transportation can be arranged back to London."

"Which means you've been on the payroll ever since you showed up at our hotel room door."

"For your information, I didn't agree to do it for the money. Mina was a good friend to me back in London before…" Shaw fell silent. "Well, it doesn't matter right now. I figured it wouldn't take much of my time to keep an eye on you, but this latest situation changes things." He jerked a thumb toward the closed bedroom door. "I'll charge you the difference between what Thomas Finch pays me and the extra hours it will take to keep that rich brat in there alive. Sound reasonable?"

"Sure. How well do you know Detective McCullough and his men?"

"I know the detective well enough. Our paths have crossed before. As for his men, who can say, but they'll be alert and armed, which will make it more difficult for our killer to find his next victim."

"I hate leaving three other men so exposed," Decker said.

"You have no choice. Even if we split up, there's only three of us, and your interest appears to lie with Clarence Rothman. That's why we went to Café Boulevard yesterday evening, isn't it? You heard the bohemian crowd hang out there and you were looking for him."

"Maybe I just wanted to eat."

"Right. And you were just hankering for an after dinner apéritif when you had me bribe McCullough and that other man to let you into the Rothman wine vaults last night, too. Not to mention how you ran out of the crime scene this morning in pursuit of Clarence Rothman. What business do you and Mina really have with him?"

"I'd rather not say just yet."

"Because you still don't trust me?"

Decker said nothing.

Shaw studied him briefly, face unreadable. "Fair enough I suppose." He clapped his hands together. "You seem to have things covered here for the moment. I think I'll scoot back to my apartment for a while. Someone should stay awake at all times and keep an eye on our ungrateful client in there. I'll get a couple of hours' sleep and come back later this evening with the rest of the guns, ready to take the first overnight shift."

"Thank you," Decker said.

"Don't mention it." Shaw held the pistol out to Decker. "You might want to keep this until I return. It's fully loaded. Try not to shoot someone just because they get on your nerves."

Decker took the gun. "You mean like our unappreciative ward?"

"I never said that, but..." Shaw shrugged and flashed a smile.

"Yeah."

"I'll be back later." Shaw turned, then started down the hallway toward the stairs. He raised a farewell hand without looking back. "Keep your heads down in the meantime."

TWENTY-SEVEN

A COUPLE of hours after Shaw left for his apartment, Clarence finally stopped complaining and settled down on a rickety chair in the corner of his bedroom, nose in a book.

Decker and Mina retreated to Decker's room so they could talk in private. They left the bedroom door ajar so they could see anyone who came and went, including Clarence Rothman himself. Decker figured he might try to flee what he viewed as subpar digs at some point for more comfortable accommodations, like the Waldorf-Astoria where he was known and his family often kept a suite, or even his brother's mansion. Neither place would be safe. But thankfully, the hallway beyond the bedroom door remained empty.

"Clarence is holding back," Mina said, settling into a chair near the window. "When we were in the coffeehouse and you asked if he knew why a killer might target his group of friends, he stumbled over his answer."

"I thought the same thing," said Decker, sitting on the edge of the bed where he could maintain a view of the hallway.

"Whatever he's keeping from us might not be relevant to his current situation, but we can't be sure of that unless he speaks up."

"Maybe he'll be more forthcoming once he's had time to reflect on his predicament."

"I wouldn't hold your breath." Mina sighed. "For a man in the crosshairs of a killer, he doesn't seem to grasp the true gravity of his situation."

"Which is a shame, since we need Clarence Rothman alive and grateful if we stand any chance of getting to Singer Cay."

"I have no intention of letting anything happen to that man," Mina said. "Come hell or high water, I'm getting you home to Nancy."

And you, Decker thought. *Will you be by my side?*

As if sensing what was going through Decker's head, Mina broke eye contact and looked down.

Silence hung between them.

A momentary sense of panic washed over Decker. He didn't want to go back alone. It was his fault she was even in this situation. If he hadn't allowed her to strong-arm her way into the Jack the Ripper situation in Whitechapel, she would never have encountered Abraham Turner and become what she now was. Likewise, when they were in the Lockheed Electra, the pull of Turner's amulet would never have dragged the two of them back in time. Things could have been so different. On the other hand, he knew what Rory would say. The dominoes were destined to fall the way they did. Without Mina, there would be no Order of St. George, which meant that in the future there would be no CUSP. Just thinking about it made Decker's head hurt. He took a deep breath and centered himself. Mina would be there by his side to follow when Celine Rothman was pulled into the future because there was no other acceptable outcome. Better to focus on something else.

"Nick Shaw," he said.

"What about him?" Mina lifted her head.

"How well do you know the man?"

"Well enough. Or at least, I did a long time ago. He and Thomas have been friends for decades."

"And yet he left the Order of St. George and vanished out of your lives."

"Not entirely. You heard what he said. He and Thomas still stay in touch."

"What happened to make him leave his life behind and run all the way to America?"

"There was an incident. He became disillusioned."

"That doesn't tell me anything."

"Because it's not my place to say," Mina replied. "But if you're asking, can you trust him? The answer is yes."

"Considering all that just happened, that we were betrayed from within our own organization, that's a lot to ask when I know nothing about him."

"The circumstances of my abduction have no bearing on what happened with Nick all those years ago. It's not fair to compare them."

"But something did happen back then, right?" Decker said. "Something bad."

"Yes. Something bad. We've all put it behind us and it's no concern of yours. Nick isn't a danger in the present."

"If that's true, then—"

"John. Listen to what I'm saying. You have to trust me on this. Nick is one of the good guys. When he's ready to tell you why he left the Order of St. George, he will. Until then, I won't betray his confidence."

"You're right, of course." Decker might not have a clue

about Nick Shaw's past, but he trusted Mina with his life. She had become like a daughter to him since they first met back in Shackleton, Alaska, even if she was technically older than him now, thanks to the vagaries of time travel. "I'll ease up on the guy."

"That would be appreciated. We need Nick. He's the only friendly face we have in this city right now."

"And he's the only one who can get us that money from Thomas," Decker noted dryly. "Without which we'll be living in the gutter way before Celine's wedding on Singer Cay."

"Which is why you need to start trusting him a little more."

"Message received." Decker picked the gun up and rose, then went to the door and peered out into the hallway. He looked both ways, but it was empty and quiet. So far, so good. Satisfied, he returned to the bed and settled down again. He cradled the gun in his lap. There was nothing they could do now but wait for Nick Shaw to return with more weapons and hope they could stop whoever was intent upon killing Clarence Rothman before it was too late.

TWENTY-EIGHT

OFFICER DOUGLAS SULLIVAN, or Big Doug to his colleagues in the NYPD thanks to his six-foot four height and stocky build, stood in the third-floor hallway of an apartment building a couple of blocks from Washington Square Park, where a grisly murder had recently taken place in a similarly appointed building. One hand rested on the gun in its holster at his hip, while his other hand curled around the baton hanging off his belt on the opposite side.

He shuffled his feet, feeling the faint yield of the plush carpet runner beneath them, and swore under his breath. This was the last thing he wanted to do with his night. It was eight o'clock in the evening already and he should have been across the river in Queens enjoying the company of Rosie Duggan. Instead, he was stuck babysitting some over privileged idiot who would rather hang around the Village and squander his money than do an honest day's work. And all because one of the guy's friends had gone and got himself murdered.

Sullivan leaned against the wall next to the apartment

door and closed his eyes, letting an image of Rosie with her voluptuous hips and ample bosom play against the darkness of his eyelids. He could almost feel her soft, pale skin under the palms of his hands, smell the scent of jasmine from her perfume. It was a pale substitute for the real thing, but it was all he had since his replacement wouldn't show up until midnight. By then, it would be too late to visit Rosie. Not that it mattered. She was sure to be mad at him for standing her up. But what choice did he have? It wasn't like he could argue with Detective McCullough, who had waylaid him in the precinct house earlier that afternoon when he was escorting an overly ambitious daytime drunkard to the tank. His protestations that his shift ended in a couple of hours had fallen on deaf ears, so here he was, miles from Rosie and contenting himself with thoughts of what might have been.

"Officer." A shrill voice blared inches from Sullivan's ear.

He jolted, pushing himself away from the wall, and opened his eyes with a startled cry. The apartment door was open and a waif-thin man who looked like a twig in a flannel shirt and pressed pants filled the space. It was the stuck-up libertine he was protecting. He vaguely recalled that his name was Rufus, or Robert. Something like that. No. It was Rupert. That was it. Rupert Goldman.

"What do you want?" Sullivan barked, irritated.

"Were you sleeping?" Rupert stepped into the hallway. His face twisted into a sneer. "That's so typical of your type."

"Sorry, my type?" Sullivan closed his fingers around the nightstick. If this buffoon wasn't careful, the killer who tore his friend's face clean off his skull would be the last thing the man would need to worry about.

"You know. People of your ilk." Rupert must have sensed Sullivan's annoyance, because no sooner had the words tripped off his tongue, then he took a quick step back toward the safety of the apartment door.

"Was there something you wanted, sir?" Sullivan said through gritted teeth.

"Actually, yes. There's a rather wonderful singer on stage at the Liberal Club tonight and I'm awfully bored just sitting around in there. I thought perhaps we might improve our surroundings. They serve a delightful lobster bisque. I'll treat you."

"No, thank you, sir." Sullivan motioned toward the door. "Go on back inside."

"But I'm bored and hungry. What difference does it make if we are here, or somewhere more pleasant?"

"It makes a difference to me. My orders were very specific. I'm to keep you out of harm's way until this murderer is caught. If you're hungry, find something to eat in your kitchen."

"You're no fun, you know that?" Rupert retreated into the apartment and went to close the door, then stopped at the last moment and peered through the crack. "But I'm glad you're out here. It makes me feel safer."

"I appreciate that." Sullivan tipped his head. "And for the record, I wasn't sleeping."

"Right." Rupert's face disappeared from the gap between the door and the frame.

The door clicked closed.

Sullivan released a long and measured breath. Only four more hours and he could go home, crack open a bottle of Irish, and try to forget the warm spot in Rosie Duggan's bed that wasn't meant to be.

He leaned back against the wall again. It was quiet beyond the apartment door. Sullivan yawned and resisted the urge to close his eyes again. He hadn't been asleep before, but it wouldn't take much. He'd been on duty for eleven hours already. The last stretch to midnight when he will be relieved by another officer felt like an eternity.

Somewhere further along the dimly lit hallway, he heard heavy footsteps. An older man with thin white hair and skin like cracked leather had reached the head of the stairs. Here he paused, resting a hand on the railing while he caught his breath. After a minute, the man pushed off and shuffled toward Sullivan, but soon stopped at an apartment door. He fumbled for a set of keys, pulled them from his pocket. As he did so, his gaze swept along the hallway and alighted on the police officer. Sullivan saw a moment of bewilderment pass across the old man's eyes, but he didn't ask. Instead, he merely nodded a curt silent greeting and pushed his door open, then stepped inside, closing it again softly behind him.

Sullivan rubbed a knot of stiffness in his neck and looked frontward again. He thought about the packet of cigarettes in his breast pocket and briefly considered pulling one out. Except that he wasn't supposed to smoke on the job, and knowing his luck, Detective McCullough would show up the moment he put the cigarette to his lips. The last thing he needed was a reprimand.

Then he heard it.

Another footfall. Heavier this time. More pronounced.

Sullivan turned, expecting to see another tenant returning to their apartment, but something else stood at the top of the stairs, backlit in the glow of a sconce further down the hallway. A freakishly large figure with barely defined features that looked like they were molded from clay.

Sullivan blinked, trying to make sense of what he was seeing.

Then the figure started toward him, leaving a trail of slick muddy footprints in its wake.

TWENTY-NINE

MINA MOVED through the darkened streets heading toward a deli several blocks from the boarding house where she and Decker were currently staying.

Shaw had returned an hour earlier with two more pistols and a rifle, along with several boxes of ammunition. More than enough to stop any intruder who might seek them out with unfriendly intent.

Clarence Rothman had remained in his room and given no further trouble since his initial objections to the accommodation they had provided for him. He had spent his time reading, possibly to distract himself from what he felt were his unsuitable surroundings.

Mina stopped at an intersection and waited for a horse and carriage to pass her by. The streets were busy, but nowhere close to the bustling and hectic crush of locals and tourists, the unrelenting tide of automobiles that would fill them over a hundred years later. Mina preferred New York this way. She had only visited the city a few times during her youth, but always found it claustrophobic and chaotic. Even the skyline felt more sedate, free as it was from the thousands of skyscrapers that would go up over the next century, pushing against each other in a bid for dominance, and each just a little taller than the previous.

The horse and cart were gone now. Mina stepped off the curb, avoiding a puddle of water that sat in the gutter, and continued on her way. As she walked, the pistol concealed in the folds of her dress pressed against her hip. She hadn't intended to take the weapon, but Decker had insisted once the discussion about who should fetch food was over. He had been against her going alone, but that only made Mina more determined. Besides, she said, the real threat was from whoever wanted Clarence Rothman and his chums dead. And it wasn't like she couldn't defend herself. She was not, as she reminded him, an ordinary woman. Any miscreants who crossed her path would regret it soon enough. In the end, Decker had conceded, and so here she was.

The delicatessen was up ahead, the glow of its lights splashing through the windows and onto the rain slicked sidewalk. A steady stream of customers left with brown paper bags in their hands. Mina picked up the pace, eager to be out of the steady drizzle of rain that still fell. She pulled open the door and entered, shaking drops of water from her coat. She approached the counter and waited her turn, then ordered three corned beef sandwiches on rye to go before being handed a ticket with a number on it and stepped aside to await her food.

Only now did she look around to take in her surroundings. The deli had maybe twenty tables, but most of their business appeared to be takeout. Those customers that were seated ate with obvious gusto, heads bent over their sandwiches or bowls of soup. Salami sausages hung from the ceiling, both behind the counter and along the back wall. The atmosphere was redolent with the scents of cooked meats, onions, and garlic. It made Mina's stomach growl.

Which was why she was happy when a rotund middle-aged woman in a stained apron shuffled down the counter carrying sandwiches wrapped in grease paper and called her number. After placing the food in a brown paper bag, she handed it to Mina and shuffled off again with barely a word.

Mina checked the sandwiches to make sure she had everything, then turned toward the door to leave.

And that was when she felt it.

A tingling sensation that started at her extremities and worked its way toward the center of her body. She froze, one hand reaching for the delicatessen door, even as the tiny pinpricks of electricity coursing through her coalesced to a single point that felt almost like a gut punch. A prickle of dread ran up her spine.

There was a vampire here.

Mina withdrew her hand from the door handle and looked around, studying the delicatessen dining room, hoping to find the cause of her discomfort. No one was paying her any attention. If the vampire was aware of her presence, which was almost certain, they were doing a good job of hiding the fact.

An elderly gentleman in a raincoat and cap grumbled as he weaved his way around her, casting an annoyed look backwards as he stepped through the door. Before it could bang shut, another customer pushed past her, almost knocking the brown paper bag from her hands, and disappeared into the darkness.

The strange sensation sat in her stomach like a lead weight. She sucked in a frantic breath, studying the faces of the customers waiting at the counter and diners sitting at the tables, but still no one gave her a second glance.

That didn't mean she was safe. Mina reached for the door again, snapping into action. She yanked it open and rushed through, almost colliding with a young woman about to enter the delicatessen. She mumbled a brief apology and hurried away, holding the brown paper bag to her chest with one hand while she reached for the pistol with the other. Not that bullets would do much against a vampire, but it made her feel better to curl fingers around the grip.

The sensation was still there, less intense but stubbornly persistent. It pulsed deep within her, refusing to ebb away. Had the vampire slipped out of the delicatessen to follow her? Mina cast a furtive glance back over her shoulder, but it was impossible to identify a threat among the pedestrians that crowded the sidewalks heading for any of a dozen restaurants or disappearing underground through one of the subway entrances thereabouts.

The rain was getting heavier again now; the drizzle turning into a downpour, but Mina hardly noticed. She hurried back toward the boardinghouse, taking a circuitous route that made her journey longer than she would have liked by crossing from one street to another and doubling back again. But it was necessary. She had to know if a vampire was following her... Could not lead it back to her destination.

The sensation finally began to dissipate, and soon it was nothing more than a vague flicker that she might not have ordinarily noticed. Mina breathed a sigh of relief and pushed ahead, reaching the boardinghouse, and paused to look around one last time, just to be safe, before stepping inside and heading up to the second floor. Only then did she relax her grip on the gun.

THIRTY

OFFICER DOUGLAS SULLIVAN observed the silhouetted figure advance along the hallway toward him with a mixture of horror and fascination. His hand reached for the gun at his hip, pulled it from the holster, raised the weapon, and aimed center mass at the strangely inhuman shape.

"Stop right where you are, or I'll shoot," he sputtered, voice cracking as he gave the command.

If the figure heard him, it paid no heed, advancing with singular intent even as Sullivan took a step back toward the closed apartment door.

"Don't come any closer, I tell you." Sullivan gripped his .38 caliber police-issue revolver with both hands, fighting against the tremble that threatened to derail his aim.

The figure was less than twenty feet away now. It plodded along with ponderous yet precise steps, and now Sullivan fully understood the breadth of what he was dealing with. The man, if you could call him that, wasn't just large, he was enormous. His head barely cleared the eight-foot hallway ceiling, and his girth took up almost the entire width, especially with his meaty arms hanging at the sides.

Sullivan had never seen anything like it.

He took a deep breath, willed his shaking hands to still themselves, and made one last effort to avoid what was swiftly becoming inevitable.

"Take one more step and I'll shoot," he said with all the authority he could muster. "This is your last warning."

There was still no reaction from the creature. Because Sullivan was now certain that whatever he faced was not human. Far from it. The figure wore no clothes. Its skin appeared to ooze and shift as if it were struggling to hold itself together. The creature's face, briefly illuminated by a wall sconce, looked more like a crudely made clay mask than anything else. The creature was completely hairless. And then there was the smell... A rancid, pungent odor that reminded Sullivan of rotten meat... No, it was worse than that. It was more like human excrement.

He gagged, resisting the urge to put a hand to his face and cover his nose. Instead, he gave up all hope of talking his way out of the situation. He pulled the trigger.

The boom in the narrow hallway was deafening. But if Sullivan was expecting the creature to drop, he was disappointed. Instead, it kept on coming, leaving that trail of muddy footprints in its wake.

How could he have missed at such short range? It wasn't possible, and yet... He pulled the trigger a second time, the subsequent crack of the revolver leaving his ears ringing. And this time, he saw the bullet hit its mark. Saw it drill through the creature's chest right where his heart should be.

He didn't have time for a third shot.

Two things happened at once.

The apartment door opened. Rupert appeared, a startled expression on his face. His lips moved, no doubt asking what the commotion was, but Sullivan heard nothing over the roar in his ears from the pair of gun blasts.

At the same time, the creature closed the last few feet between itself and Sullivan. It raised a thick arm and swiped sideways, its open palm catching Sullivan about the torso and sending him reeling sideways. He smashed into the wall. His shoulder smacked hard, sending tendrils of fiery hot pain down his arm, and causing him to release his grip on the gun, which fell harmlessly to the ground, robbing him of his only defense.

The creature raised its hand again, this time closing it into a fist.

Sullivan spun sideways, trying to avoid the blow he knew was coming. He caught a fleeting glimpse of Rupert, standing in the doorway, mouth agape. He wanted to shout out, tell the fool to run. To get as far away as possible.

And then the blow landed… a vicious uppercut that lifted Sullivan off his feet and sent him flying down the hallway.

He hit the floor and slid, then came to rest in a heap twenty feet from the apartment door. His lower jaw felt like it had been hit by a sledgehammer. His leg lay twisted at an unnatural angle beneath him and even though he couldn't see it, he could feel the shattered bone sticking out through his skin.

His eyes watered.

He gasped for breath.

When he lifted his head to look back, Rupert had vanished back into the apartment, slamming the door as if the flimsy piece of wood could protect him.

Now he noticed the creature, standing like a statue, head

turned in his direction, possibly assessing the remaining threat. Then it lost interest in Sullivan and stepped up to the apartment door, drew its arm back, and took the flimsy barrier clean off its hinges with one fast punch.

A shriek of terror wafted from inside the apartment.

The creature lowered its fist and stepped through the doorway.

Sullivan could see his gun lying out of reach down the hall. He was in no shape to stop what he knew was about to happen, but he was still a police officer.

Then he noticed the old man who had returned earlier peering out through his cracked open door. Their eyes met and for a moment Sullivan thought help was at hand. He looked at the gun and then back up, silently communicating what he needed, but now he saw the fear in the old man's eyes. At least, until the face vanished from the crack and the door clicked closed.

Sullivan was on his own.

With a grunt, he flipped over onto his front and dragged himself along, arm over arm, fingernails digging into the carpet runner for purchase as he inched slowly toward the gun.

But it was too late.

From somewhere beyond the shattered apartment door, Rupert uttered the last sound of his privileged life. A high-pitched warbling squeal, abruptly silenced. And then Sullivan heard something worse. A squelching, sucking, tearing noise, like... He tried not to think about the cause.

He was halfway to the gun. The pain in his leg was excruciating, but if he didn't get the weapon, it would be him next. But before he could close the gap and reach for the revolver, the figure stepped out of the apartment, holding what looked like a bloodied dish rag in one hand. Except the rag had eyeholes, and a slit where a mouth should have been.

The figure loomed over Sullivan, observing him with cold indifference. He pressed his eyes closed and waited for the end to come, but instead heard the thud of heavy footfalls retreating down the hallway. When he opened his eyes again, Sullivan was alone.

THIRTY-ONE

SHAW TOOK the first shift guarding Clarence Rothman. He dragged a hardback wooden chair from one of the bedrooms and settled in the hallway with a revolver cradled in his lap. It was eleven o'clock at night and he would remain there for at least another four hours until Decker took over allowing him to catch a few winks of sleep.

The boardinghouse was quiet. There were only four rooms on the second floor, three of which had already been rented by Decker and Mina, while the remaining room sat empty. Earlier that evening, after they had eaten, Decker went down to the landlady's apartment on the first floor and rented the last room for Shaw so he wouldn't have to go back and forth between the boardinghouse and his own apartment. It also guaranteed they wouldn't be disturbed should another renter come calling, looking for accommodation.

Mina had retired to her room an hour before, having been unusually silent through dinner. Now, Decker decided to find out why. He stepped into the hallway and cast a sideways glance at Shaw. The private detective's eyes were closed, his head resting against the wall, but he wasn't sleeping. At the sound of Decker's door closing, he opened them and gave a curt nod.

Decker returned the gesture and made his way to the room next door, knocking twice. When Mina answered, he stepped inside without waiting to be invited and pushed the door closed behind him.

She was wearing a flannel nightgown. Her hair flowed unrestrained over her shoulders. Decker glanced toward the bed and saw that it hadn't yet been slept in.

"I was about to turn in for the night," Mina said, as if in answer. "What do you want?"

"To know why you've been so quiet since returning with the sandwiches." Decker stepped into the middle of the room. "I know you too well. What's going on?"

Mina hesitated, as if deciding whether she wanted to speak, then appeared to make up her mind. "I didn't want to say anything in front of Nick, but I sensed a vampire in the delicatessen. I'm sure they sensed me, too."

"Did you see who it was?"

Mina shook her head. "No one exhibited any visible reaction to my presence outside of the ordinary. Whoever it was kept a good poker face. Much better than I did."

"Does this happen often?" Decker asked. Until now, he had assumed that vampires were a fairly rare breed, but he was beginning to wonder.

"I've come across them once in a while. Mostly, I'm able to back off and make an escape before they pay too much attention to me. I feel like it's different now. Those two on the dock. They knew about me and what I am, I'm sure of it."

"The two vampires on the Titanic," Decker said. "It's

possible they had the wireless operator send a message letting their accomplices in New York know what they had stumbled across."

"You mean me."

"Yes. They weren't expecting to find you in Faucher's cabin. They were looking for a clue to Amenmosep's location in the hold and hoping to find his amulet."

"And in doing so, came across me by accident." Mina sighed. "I've spent the better part of two and a half decades trying to steer clear of the vampires for fear of what they would do if they knew someone like me existed. In his zeal to defeat them, Faucher might have ended up doing the opposite. I'm neither fully vampire nor human. I might not have all of their abilities, but I'm also not prone to their greatest weakness."

"Gold."

"Yes. Now that they're aware of my existence, I fear they won't stop until they have me in their clutches."

"That's possible," Decker said. "But we don't know how well organized these vampires are. Just because you sensed one in the deli doesn't mean they recognized what you are. They might just have assumed you were another random vampire. Maybe that's why they didn't react to your presence any more than I would react to seeing another human."

"I'd like to believe that, but I must be careful." Mina crossed to the window and drew the curtains. "I could still sense the vampire for a while after I left the delicatessen. It was faint but definitely still there, like they were trailing me from a distance. That's why it took me so long to return with the sandwiches."

"Why didn't you mention this earlier?"

"I didn't want to say anything in front of Nick."

"I thought you trusted him?"

"I do. But he doesn't know about my situation. At least, not all of it. Thomas and I made the decision right at the beginning to keep what I am a secret, even from most of those within the Order of St. George."

"That must have been difficult," Decker said. "You barely aged in a quarter of a century. How have you explained that?"

"A rare genetic disorder that affects my outward ability to age. It's a ridiculous pretense, I know, and it wouldn't work in the twenty-first century. But at the end of the nineteenth, such things were not so well understood. Thankfully, very few people have been around me long enough to require such a cover story."

"Is Nick among those people?"

"We told him I had a condition that affected the way I aged." Mina was silent for a moment. "But I'm not sure how far my credibility has been stretched since I don't look like I've gotten a day older since the last time he saw me ten years ago."

"Have you considered telling him the truth?" Decker asked. "It might make things easier, especially if you're still in danger from the vampires."

"I thought you didn't trust him?"

"I don't. But you trust him, so I've decided to defer to your instincts."

Mina went to a chair and sat down. "I'm not ready yet."

"Because you're scared of how he'll react?"

"Maybe."

"The man tracks monsters for a living. He might already know about vampires, which could prove useful to us."

"Let me do this in my own time, okay?"

Decker was about to answer, but at that moment there was a knock on the door. He opened it to find Detective McCullough standing in the hallway next to Shaw.

The detective cleared his throat. "There's been another murder."

THIRTY-TWO

THE NEXT MORNING AT EIGHT, Decker strode into the lobby of St. Vincent's Hospital with Mina at his side and quickly found someone to give them the whereabouts of Officer Douglas Sullivan, who had been brought there the night before.

Decker would have preferred to visit the injured officer the moment they found out about the latest murder, but Detective McCullough informed them in no uncertain terms that it wasn't going to happen. Sullivan was in no shape to answer their questions, having been given a large dose of morphine, and would also be undergoing treatment for his injuries. Better to wait until the next day. Which is what Decker had done, albeit grudgingly. He had retired to his room at the boarding house and forced himself to get some sleep until it was time for his shift guarding Clarence Rothman. Shaw had retreated to his room only to reappear at seven a.m. at which point Decker decided he had waited long enough.

Decker disliked hospitals. The smell of them. The general aura of sickness and death. It was in the mortuary of a building such as this that he had last seen his mother laying cold and lifeless on a slab when he was ten years old. He ignored the faint stir of anxiety as they were led through halls painted an off-white hue, passing the doors to wards beyond which came the various sounds of sickness. Wheezing. Coughing. The occasional distressed wail.

They passed a woman and child, heads bent low as they walked in the other direction. The child's face was ashen, his expression stony. The mother's cheeks were streaked with tears, her eyes puffy and red. Decker's gaze fell to the boy, and he wondered if that was how he had looked all that time ago, except it was his father, the original Sheriff Decker, leading him away from his first taste of death.

Then, thankfully, they reached their destination. The nurse who was escorting them indicated which bed they wanted, then took her leave, but not before warning them to be brief.

Officer Sullivan was lying in a partially raised bed toward the back of the ward and looked like he was sleeping, but as they drew closer, his eyes opened.

"Officer Sullivan, would you mind answering some questions?" Decker said, after introducing himself and Mina.

Sullivan reached for a glass of water on a narrow table next to the bed before answering. He took a few sips, then placed it back down with obvious discomfort. "I can't imagine there's anything I can tell you that I didn't already tell the detective," he said. "But fire away."

"How about we start easy," Decker said. "Why don't you give us an account, in your words, of what exactly transpired last night."

"Sure." Sullivan hesitated, as if compiling his thoughts,

then went through the events of the previous evening in an emotionless, flat voice, almost as if he was relaying them to a courtroom. He stopped a couple of times to take further drinks of water to soothe his scratchy voice. When he was done, Sullivan looked up with a wide-eyed expression as if he expected them to contradict his account… or maybe call for the nurse to fetch a straitjacket.

Decker said nothing for a long minute, letting the details of what he had been told sink in, then he took a step closer to the bed and spoke in a soft voice. "The assailant. You said it looked like they were covered with mud?"

Sullivan nodded. "I know it sounds crazy, but that's what I saw. The thing was inhumanly large, too. Like over seven feet. Honestly, I'm not even sure it was human. I put two bullets into it at point-blank range. There's no way I missed, but it kept coming. It was like the bullets just passed right through it."

"Did your attacker say anything?" Decker asked.

"Not a word. I'm not even sure… I mean the face… It was like crudely sculpted clay. I didn't even see a mouth. There's something else too. It had a tattoo on its forehead. Some kind of word, but I couldn't make it out. Everything happened so fast." Sullivan drew in a long, quivering breath. "Rupert Goldman. He's dead, isn't he?"

"Has Detective McCullough not told you?" Decker asked, surprised.

Sullivan shook his head slowly. "I was in no state to be told anything last night. Not after they gave me the morphine."

"Yes. He's dead. Killed the same way as the other two victims. Neck snapped and…" Decker trailed off, figuring there was no need to go into gory detail.

"And his face torn off and taken by the killer," Sullivan said, finishing Decker's sentence anyway. "That's what the creature was carrying when it left the apartment. I hoped it was a trauma-induced hallucination. You know... From a concussion. I took a wicked crack to the head when the thing knocked me off my feet. I let that man die."

"I'm sure you did everything possible," Decker said.

"You shouldn't dwell on it," Mina added, stepping up to the bed and placing a gentle hand on the officer's shoulder.

"What about the others?" Sullivan tried to sit up further, winced, and sank back down. "Nothing is going to stop that creature. Not bullets. Nothing. If it comes for another victim, the next man who tries to stop it might not be so lucky as me. I'm still not sure why it didn't kill me when it had the chance."

"Maybe the killer got what they came for." Decker could see Sullivan's strength waning. The nurse's warning to keep it brief rang in his head. He turned to Mina. "We should leave this man to get some rest, unless you have any other questions."

"I don't." Mina withdrew her hand and stepped away from the bed.

Sullivan's eyes fluttered closed. It had obviously been a great effort for him to talk with them, since he was clearly still under the influence of the morphine he had been given to numb his pain.

Decker headed for the exit, leaving the ward and leading Mina back through the hospital corridors until they were outside once again under a dreary New York late April Sky.

Finally, he turned to her. "What do you make of it?"

"We're not dealing with a regular human. At least, not if we believe Officer Sullivan's description."

"Which leaves us with one logical alternative," Decker said.

Mina nodded. "Our killer is a supernatural entity."

"Yes," replied Decker. "The only question is, what?"

"That isn't the only question." Mina paused for a moment. "We also need to find out why."

THIRTY-THREE

"HAVE EITHER of you ever come across a creature that matches officer Sullivan's description?" Decker asked. They were back at the boardinghouse and had requested that Shaw join them in Decker's room. "A supernatural being with crudely defined features that looks like it's made of mud, has a foul stench, possesses incredible strength, and is impervious to bullets."

"That's a new one on me," Shaw said.

"Me too," Mina agreed.

"Which leaves us about as close to stopping this killer as we were before." Decker rose and went to the door, which was cracked open a few inches, and peered out into the hallway to make sure that Clarence Rothman's door was still closed, and he hadn't tried to leave. The last thing they needed was to lose the person they were supposed to be protecting, especially since Clarence had been vocal about the poor quality of his surroundings and lack of freedom to visit the Liberal Club or other such establishments. There were, he reminded himself, two other potential victims still out there, not counting their own charge since the entity was targeting Clarence Rothman's circle of old school friends. And if the current timeline of murders remained the same, one of the three would be marked for death in less than thirty-six hours. It gave them some breathing room, but also a tight deadline, and Decker had no intention of letting a fourth person die. "We need to speak with Detective McCullough. His men are guarding two of the remaining three potential victims at their places of residence. That won't do, given what we now know. We need to move them out of the city and to a safe location where they can't easily be found. We also need to make sure that a story detailing their hasty departure from New York, but not their destination, goes into the newspapers."

"You want to publicize what we're doing to keep Clarence Rothman and his friends alive?" The incredulity in Mina's voice was hard to miss. "Why on earth would you do that?"

"Because we need to lure the killer out. It's the only way to find out what we're up against. There are still three potential victims, and we don't know which will be next. Clarence Rothman is, hopefully, safe since we moved him to a place where he cannot be traced. Once we've done the same with his friends, we can set a trap. Force the killer to go after the victim of our choice."

"And we will be waiting."

"Precisely," Decker replied.

Mina leaned back in her chair. "Alright. Tell me more. I'm listening."

THIRTY-FOUR

TWO HOURS LATER, Decker and Shaw sat in a cramped office inside the New York Police Department's 17th precinct station house, whose jurisdiction covered both Greenwich Village and the West Village, and told Detective McCullough of their plan, which hinged upon his cooperation. Mina was back at the boardinghouse, entertaining Clarence Rothman with a game of cards—a French game called Bezique that had become something of a hit—since he had already devoured the books he brought from his apartment and was getting more restless by the hour. Which was why Decker and Shaw's current task was of such importance.

"I'm sorry, you want me to do what?" McCullough observed Decker and Shaw from across his office desk. "Do you have any idea how much that will cost?"

"Less than the cost of two lives," Decker said, meeting McCullough's gaze. "It's also a win for your department. You move the two men you're still protecting out of the city to somewhere beyond the reach of this killer, while still providing them with police protection, of course. We'll continue to take responsibility for Clarence Rothman, and then we will lure the killer to us and eliminate him or her. You can take the credit, of course."

"And the blame if this goes wrong, no doubt."

"I hardly think you can be in a worse situation than you are right now," Decker pointed out. "Another victim killed under your supervision and one of your own men in the infirmary."

"You don't need to state the obvious." McCullough's displeasure with Decker's blunt observation was clear. His shoulders slumped. "Run me through the details of this harebrained scheme again. I want to make sure I have it straight in my head."

"Very well," said Shaw. "We shall remove two of the three remaining potential victims from the killer's reach by spiriting them out of New York to an undisclosed location far away. That part will be on you. We will keep Clarence Rothman sequestered safely where he is. You will then speak to the press and tell them that you have everything under control and you have taken additional steps to protect any future targets of the killer's wrath. You will mention that they have all been moved out of the city, but not where they have gone. You will then arrange for an unauthorized leak to the press, mentioning that one of the three remaining potential victims, Clarence Rothman, refused to be relocated and has returned to his apartment in the city saying that he no longer trusts the police to protect him since the last murder."

"Hold on a gosh-darned minute." McCullough's cheeks flared. "You want me to throw my own men to the wolves by admitting that we failed to protect the last victim, even though he was under police supervision?"

"No," Decker said, chiming in. "Nothing of the sort. I want to create the narrative that Clarence Rothman recklessly returned to his apartment at the expense of his own safety. You will, of course, issue a statement after the leak saying that your officers are more than capable of protecting victims of crime in this city and that you take no responsibility for Clarence Rothman's ill-advised decision to fend for himself."

"Well, that's something, at least. What next?"

"Simple," Shaw replied. "If our killer follows the same timeline as before, he will look for another victim tomorrow evening. We will lay in wait at Clarence Rothman's apartment, which will be empty, of course, since that will be our killer's only remaining option. When he shows up, we neutralize him."

"Just like that?"

"Yes." Decker sat back in his chair and folded his arms.

"How many of my men do you want for this little flytrap?"

"None. We'll handle this ourselves. Feel free to put a few extra patrolmen on the streets around Rothman's apartment, but don't overdo it. An unusually heavy police presence may scare the killer off, which would defeat the purpose of what we have planned."

"In other words, you want me to let a pair of civilians run a stakeout to catch a dangerous murderer." McCullough didn't look convinced.

"It really isn't any different from other times we've worked together," Shaw said. "Having heard the account from your injured officer, you surely realize that our adversary is unusual."

"That's putting it mildly." McCullough leaned his elbows on the desk, then rubbed his forehead with the palm of one hand. "Barely formed features and covered in mud? Seven feet tall? I'm not sure what to make of it."

"Which is why this is best left to us."

"Except that unlike the previous times I've used you, I'm up to my neck in it. I have no plausible deniability. I can't even claim ignorance of your involvement since the pair of you are currently sitting in my office, and it was at your suggestion that I provided official protection for the potential victims."

"You still have deniability," Decker said. "None of your officers will be involved in this particular endeavor, and we are already responsible for Clarence Rothman's safety."

"If the worst happens," Shaw said, "and tragedy befalls us, you can just say we kept our intentions from you."

"Are you sure this will work?" McCullough asked, sounding skeptical. "My officer couldn't stop the brute, so what makes you think it will go any better for you?"

"Because this isn't the first time I've dealt with such threats," Decker said. "And besides, your own statement just validated us. If you decline to go along with our plan, *that brute* will return tomorrow evening to claim another life and there is no reason to believe it would go any better than the last time and will probably put another of your men in the hospital."

"Since you put it like that..." McCullough didn't look happy, but then again, in the short time he'd known the man, McCullough had never looked happy. "I'll make the arrangements. Just try not to get yourselves killed and make even more work for me."

"We'll do our best," Decker said with a mirthless chuckle. "We'd hate to be a burden."

THIRTY-FIVE

DESPITE HIS OBVIOUS RESERVATIONS, Detective McCullough arranged for an impromptu press briefing to be held at three p.m., where he would address the issue of the Greenwich Village Butcher, as the press had christened what they believed to be a burgeoning serial killer with a grisly MO.

Since Clarence was under Mina's watchful gaze, and Decker wasn't expecting the killer to make a move until the following evening, given the time that elapsed between the previous attacks, he suggested to Shaw that they stick around and observe the proceedings.

The briefing took place in a drab room off the main lobby of the precinct house. They had obviously used it for previous such events, since a sign on the door read 'Press Relations'. There was a podium set up at one end on a raised platform that looked like someone had cobbled it together from spare wood then painted black.

Rows of folding wooden chairs had been arranged facing

the podium—at least twenty—but the turnout was underwhelming. Instead of a clamoring throng of eager newsmen looking for a scoop, only a handful of reporters bothered to show up and now sat about as far away from each other as the chairs would allow.

Decker surmised this turnout was due not only to the short notice but also because the newspapers were still consumed with news of the Titanic and its survivors. There was already speculation that inquests would be held on both sides of the Atlantic, and survivors' accounts—the more harrowing the better—were running daily on the front pages of every major publication.

Still, writers from both the Herald and Tribune were in attendance, so Decker was sure the killer would get the message. In his experience, murderers found it impossible not to scour the papers for coverage of their crimes, and he hoped that this one, even if there was a supernatural angle, would be no different.

Detective McCullough was brief, keeping strictly to the details they had discussed earlier, and refusing to give any hint regarding where they were going to take the men who might be next on the killer's list. But he also made sure one of his more loose-lipped patrolmen was waiting on the steps of the precinct house and knew exactly what to say—off the record of course—when the disgruntled reporters filed from the room with little more to show for their time than they already knew.

After the room emptied, McCullough stepped down from the podium and approached Decker and Shaw with an expectant look on his face. "How was that?"

"Not bad," said Decker. "You should consider a career on the Broadway stage."

"I hardly think my performance was that good."

"Yeah, maybe it wasn't worthy of The Great White Way," Shaw said. "But it was believable enough for an audience of barely awake newsies already thinking about how their few column inches will fit around the biggest story of the year."

"Titanic," McCullough said with a shudder. "You wouldn't catch me on one of those ocean liners. No, sir."

"Me either," said Shaw, glancing at Decker with a wry smile.

"Let's hope your man out on the steps gives an equally convincing performance," Decker said. "All this will be for nothing if the killer doesn't think that Clarence Rothman is the only target left available."

"And a sitting duck," added Shaw.

"He'll do his job. Don't you worry about that," McCullough replied, a faint smirk creasing his lips. "Those newspaper boys think they have a chatty cop with no sense of when to shut his trap, but the reality is that they've been hearing exactly what I want them to hear for nigh on three years. All nice and unofficial, of course."

"You're a devious man, Detective McCullough," Shaw said.

"Don't you forget it." McCullough slapped Shaw on the back. "Now I think you owe me a finger or two of whiskey for my troubles over at McCluskey's Alehouse."

"I think we can swing that." Shaw glanced at Decker. "Any objections?"

"I'm sure Mina can handle things a while longer back at the boardinghouse," Decker said, even though he would rather have gone straight back. But he also saw the value in forging useful relationships, and once all this was over, he and Mina might be stuck in the city for several more months. "So long as we're not too long."

"Excellent." Shaw started toward the door with Detective McCullough right behind.

Decker glanced back toward the empty podium, then hurried to catch up. With any luck, the seed was sown. Now it was out of their hands. Either the killer would take the bait, or they wouldn't.

THIRTY-SIX

DECKER DRAINED the last dregs of whiskey and put the tumbler down on the pitted bar top at McCluskey's Alehouse with a grimace. The liquor was not particularly good. All burn with very little complexity of flavor.

Detective McCullough, however, didn't seem to notice and readily ordered a second, slamming the neat liquid back with a smack of his lips before dropping the tumbler to the bar just a little too heavily and proclaiming his satisfaction. Soon after, he thanked them for the drinks and took his leave, weaving through the smoky and dimly lit bar room toward the exit. When he opened the door, a rectangle of bright light spilled in from outside, and soon swallowed him up as he stepped through.

Decker expected that Shaw, who had been quietly sipping his own drink and only now polished it off, would be ready to leave now that McCullough was gone, but instead he hailed the bartender. "Give me two more whiskeys. Make it Irish this time. The Comaraugh fifteen year."

"You sure about that?" Decker said. "I don't want to leave Mina alone with Clarence Rothman for too much longer."

"She'll be fine, and we need to have a chat." Shaw tapped his fingers on the bar while the server went about pouring their drinks.

"Okay. But that whiskey had better be a notch above the last one."

"It will be. Don't you worry about that. Couldn't see the point in wasting the good stuff on Detective McCullough. For a man who claims his ancestors hailed from Scotland, he has suspiciously poor appreciation of its most famous export."

"He did appear to enjoy his drinks despite the taste," Decker said, before getting to the point. "What's on your mind?"

Shaw waited for the whiskeys to arrive, then lifted his glass and took a sip before answering. "You and me, we're going to be standing shoulder to shoulder against an unknown enemy sooner rather than later if all this goes to plan. Before that happens, I thought we should clear the air."

"Does it need clearing?" Decker asked.

"You tell me. Ever since we met, you've looked at me like I was about to steal the family silver. You don't trust me, despite whatever assurances you're giving Mina, and I don't blame you. Truthfully, I haven't been inclined to trust you, either. But Thomas says you're a good man. Says I should trust you as I would him. That's good enough for me. But I don't feel like you've come to terms with your own mistrust. I also think there are things you and Mina haven't told me."

"Ah." Decker lowered his head and stared into his drink. When he looked back up, Shaw's gaze was firmly fixed upon him. "You figure we can bond over a couple shots of Irish and tell each other the hard truths."

"Something like that." Shaw took another sip of his drink.

"The three of us… me, you, and Mina, will be relying on each other to stay safe. This creature we're about to lure our way, whatever the hell it is, took two bullets from a patrolman's gun, incapacitated him, and committed a cold-blooded murder with impunity. Then it sauntered off as if it had not a care in the world. I need to know you've got my back, and you need to know the same from me, because if not, one or all of us could end up like that patrolman, or worse."

"I can't argue with that. Which of us goes first?"

"I'll take the first leap." Shaw finished his drink and ordered another. He looked down into the amber liquid for a moment before continuing. "In the interest of full disclosure, I heard you and Mina talking last night. Hard not to, since I was sitting in the hallway. The walls of that boardinghouse are paper-thin, just so you know."

"I'll keep that in mind for next time," Decker said. "Your point?"

"I know what she is. Have done for years. I grew suspicious while I was still at the Order and approached Thomas. He tried to rehash the genetic disorder excuse, but I didn't believe it any more back then than I had previously. In the end, he swore me to secrecy, even from Mina, and told me the truth. She's a vampire. Or at least, something akin to one. That's why she doesn't age."

"What else did Thomas Finch tell you?" Decker asked, wondering just how much Shaw really knew. "Did he mention how she got that way?"

"Are you asking because *you* want to know, or because you want to know *how much I know?*" Shaw leaned on the bar top with one elbow.

"Answer the question."

"No, he didn't tell me how she got that way. Or anything else about her past, for that matter." Shaw observed Decker with narrowed eyes. "All he said was that her affliction was forced upon her. That she was a victim of circumstance and had no choice. He asked me to leave it at that and not to probe further."

"And you were good with that?"

"Not really. But what choice did I have?" Shaw picked up his drink. Sipped. Placed it back on the bar. "You know how she got that way, though. I'm sure of it. Want to share?"

"What do you think?"

"Yeah." Shaw shrugged. "Honestly, it's none of my business, anyway."

"Why did you resign from the Order?" Decker asked. He wondered if Shaw's feelings for Mina had been more than platonic. Did he leave to put distance between them? Or maybe Thomas Finch banished him in an attempt to protect her. "Was it because of Mina?"

"If you're thinking I had romantic designs on Mina, you're wrong." Shaw shook his head. "Nothing of the sort. Thomas was the one who fell for her, not me. I left for entirely different reasons."

"Care to tell me?"

"Not really, but it was my idea to have this tête-à-tête," Shaw said. "There was an incident. People died. It was my fault."

"What type of incident?"

"The kind where I let myself fall under the influence of a supernatural creature. A siren, to be precise. She manipulated me into releasing another one of her kind from a facility we maintain called the Menagerie."

"I know all about the Menagerie," Decker said. He had seen the 1942 version of that same facility on Singer Cay. Likewise, CUSP ran a more modern and humane version known as the Zoo underneath its Maine island headquarters. "And the deaths?"

Shaw looked uncomfortable. "Two of the facility staff were killed by the sirens in their attempt to escape."

"That's hardly your fault."

"Except that I'm the one who facilitated the escape. If I hadn't let that siren control me, those two men would be alive to this day. I failed the Order of St. George. There was no other choice but to leave, both as a punishment and for the safety of those around me."

"Did Thomas Finch ask you to go?"

"No. In fact, just the opposite. He said I should stay. That what happened was a hazard of the job and that no one blamed me. But I blamed myself. I should have been stronger. Resisted the siren. I couldn't trust myself if a similar situation arose in the future."

"And yet you still track and eliminate monsters," Decker said.

"It's different. I work alone. If I make another mistake, the only life on the line is mine."

"You're not working alone right now." Decker lifted his glass and drank from his whiskey for the first time. Shaw was correct. It was better than the previous one. Markedly so. "You have me and Mina."

Shaw was silent for a moment before answering. "Maybe I'm going soft in my old age."

"Or maybe you're getting fed up with being a lone wolf. Ten years is a long time to punish yourself."

"Never thought about it like that." Shaw downed the last of his whiskey. "I've been bending your ear long enough. Let's get back to Mina."

"Sounds good to me." Decker swallowed his whiskey and put the empty glass on the bar.

Shaw settled their bill, then jumped down off his stool before turning to Decker. "Do me a favor, okay? Don't tell Mina that I know her secret."

"I'll keep your confidence for now," Decker said. "But you should consider telling her yourself."

"I don't think that would be a good idea." Shaw started toward the door. "Mina values her privacy, and I would hate her to feel awkward around me. Not only that, but it might cause friction between her and Thomas. I know they're not together anymore, but that doesn't mean they feel any differently about each other, and I'd rather not get in the way of that. Do you understand?"

"Sure." Decker followed Shaw to the door and stepped out onto the busy street beyond. He felt better about working with the private detective now he knew the truth of his circumstances. And their talk couldn't have come at a better time, because if all went to plan, they would soon be face-to-face with a killer the likes of which Decker suspected he had never seen before.

THIRTY-SEVEN

NINE HOURS after Decker and Shaw returned from Detective McCullough's press conference, Mina lay in the darkness of her room at the boarding house. She slept fitfully, dreaming of an endless hallway down which she and Clarence Rothman were being pursued by a featureless dark shape that left muddy footprints in its wake.

Except that she wasn't really running because her legs were impossibly heavy, as if they were made of lead. Which was why Clarence Rothman had pulled away, not even bothering to look back and see if she was alright.

Mina glanced over her shoulder and saw that the creature had closed the gap between them. There was no way she could outrun it. Not unless her legs suddenly decided to respond. She drew in a sharp breath, waited for the inevitable...

'Mina.' A voice she didn't recognize spoke inside her head, soft and menacing. Sibilant. It drifted through the barrier of her sleeping mind just as her dark and featureless pursuer lunged toward her, thick arms extended.

"Mina." The voice said a second time.

The dream shattered into a million pieces.

She sat bolt upright in her bed, a silent scream on her lips, and looked around, frantic. Her bedroom was silent and dark. A faint sliver of moonlight inched its way between the boarding house and the building across the alley. It cast a narrow splash of white light over the floorboards under the window.

'Mina!' The voice spoke again, with more urgency this time. It came from inside her head but somehow also from the other side of her bedroom door.

She swung her legs off the bed, went to the door, and opened it a few inches. Peered through into the dimly lit hallway beyond. Empty.

She pushed the door wider, stepped out into the hallway. Decker's room was to her right, and beyond that the one where Clarence Rothman now slept. The wooden chair outside his door was unoccupied. Either Shaw or Decker should have been there, keeping guard with a gun in their lap. Making sure they were safe.

Had they heard the voice, too?

Maybe They had gone to investigate.

'Mina.' The voice sounded more urgent this time.

Now she was sure it was inside her head and not coming from elsewhere in the building. She knew something else, too… What it wanted.

As if to confirm that she was right, the voice spoke again. 'Let us in, Mina.'

The hairs on the back of her neck stood up.

Where *was* everyone?

She glanced toward Decker's door, hovering between rushing back into her bedroom and barricading herself in or waking him so she wasn't alone. But even as she weighed both options, she found herself walking down the hallway toward the stairs instead.

She descended to the bottom floor, padded quietly past the landlady's apartment, and stopped at the front door. She reached out, hand gripping the knob, and then she forced herself to stop.

'Let us in, Mina.' The voice was urgent now. 'Let us in.'

"I don't want to let you in," she said, attempting to pull her hand from the doorknob. Couldn't. It was like her arm would not obey the messages she was sending it.

'Open the door, Mina.' The voice rose in pitch. 'Open it, right now.'

"Please, don't make me do this," she begged, making one last effort to pull her hand from the doorknob. But to her horror, she turned it instead.

The door swung outward to reveal a street shrouded in fog. A lone streetlamp flickered in the darkness. Thick tendrils of mist curled around the doorframe. From somewhere out in the darkness, a church bell tolled, melancholy and hollow.

Mina's breath caught in her throat. She backed away from the door.

And then she saw it. A figure that separated itself from the darkness beyond the door. It walked down the street toward her; the fog falling away as it went.

Mina wanted to run with every fiber of her being, desperately wanted to escape, but she couldn't. Her legs refused to work. Instead, she stood rooted to the spot as the figure drew ever closer. But this was not the same creature from her nightmare. This was a woman. She could see the billowing folds of her dress as they caught a spectral wind and whipped around her.

Mina recognized this woman because she had seen her

once before. It was the female vampire from the docks. One of the pair who had tried to pull her from the cab as they made their escape.

"Please, don't come any closer," Mina begged, because she could do nothing else.

The woman smiled, revealing rows of stained yellow teeth.

"Mina." The voice was different this time. It was deeper. More resonant. And it didn't come from inside her head.

The woman was at the door now, reaching out with fingers that looked more like talons. Reaching for—

"Mina, wake up!"

For the second time in as many minutes, the dream shattered and crumbled around Mina. She staggered backward, suddenly aware that she wasn't in her bed. Instead, she was standing in the boarding house entrance hall facing the open front door, through which she could see the dark and empty street beyond.

"Mina, are you all right?"

She dragged her eyes away from the door and saw Decker standing at the bottom of the stairs. "How did I... What's going on?"

"You tell me." Decker stepped toward her, placed a calming hand on her shoulder. "I was sitting outside Clarence Rothman's room, guarding him. You left your bedroom and came down here. It looked like you were in some sort of trance. You didn't answer when I spoke to you. Were you even awake?"

At first, Mina wasn't sure. But then the awful truth descended upon her. "It wasn't a trance. I was sleep-walking."

"Have you ever done that before?" Decker asked. His voice was laced with concern... or maybe it was fear.

"No. Not that I'm aware of."

"Then why did you do it tonight?"

"It wasn't me." Mina looked back at the open door, remembering the voice that weaved its way into her dreams, and the figure that stepped from the fog. She shuddered. "It was the vampires. They reached out, touched my mind."

"Why would they do that?"

"Because they were looking for me," Mina said, her voice small and quiet.

"Did they find you?" Decker stepped around Mina and closed the front door, cutting off her view of the street.

"I don't know." Mina folded her arms across her chest, suddenly aware that she was wearing nothing but a thin cotton night dress. She was freezing. "I hope not, otherwise the next visit won't be in my head."

THIRTY-EIGHT

"ARE you sure it was the vampire from the docks?" Decker asked, standing in Mina's room at the boarding house, hands pushed into his pockets. It was the next morning, and he had taken the opportunity to talk while Shaw was out picking up bagels for breakfast from a bakery two blocks to the east.

"Sure as I can be," Mina replied. "Maybe it was all inside my head and I'm overreacting, but I sensed the vampire inside my mind. Heard her as clear as I hear you right now. I was in the middle of a nightmare, and she woke me up. Or at least, I thought she did. I realize now that I was still dreaming."

"And sleepwalking, apparently. You're sure this has never happened to you before?"

"No. Which is why I don't think this was just my overactive imagination creating dreams within dreams. It was more like a psychic connection, as if the vampire was reaching out and touching my mind with hers."

"Is that something they can do?"

"If it is, I wasn't aware of it." In the hours since finding herself standing at the front door of the boarding house in nothing but her nightgown, Mina had thought of nothing else. Returning to her bed, she had laid awake, partly because she was afraid of what would happen if she fell asleep again, and also because her feverishly racing mind refused to shut down. During that time, she had attempted to reason the incident away as nothing more than her own subconscious regurgitating the anxiety that had accompanied her ever since she escaped her kidnappers aboard the Titanic and feeding off it. But deep down, she knew it wasn't merely the primitive parts of her brain working through the irrational fears that lingered there. She hadn't been dreaming... Not exactly. It was more of a trancelike state between the dreamworld and the waking world where both collided. And the vampire invading Mina's mind was firmly in the driver's seat, trying to discover her location. "This is bad. How can I ever trust myself to sleep if the vampires can get inside my head at will any time they feel like it?"

"It's not a choice. You can't stay awake forever."

"And I can't risk giving the vampires our location, assuming I haven't done so already."

"Maybe there's a way you can block their influence."

Mina yawned. "I'm not sure it's that simple. I wouldn't know where to begin. This is all new to me, and frankly, a little bit nuts."

"On the contrary, it makes sense," Decker said. "After all, vampires have the ability to sense others of their own kind within a certain distance, just like you did on the docks. That has to be a form of telepathy. It's not a stretch to think they could also use a similar power to seek out other vampires at greater distances if they know where to concentrate their power. You were sleeping. Your defenses were down. It might have been as easy for that vampire as turning the proverbial tuning knob on a radio until they found you."

"If you're trying to make me feel better, it's not working."

"I'm just saying that we shouldn't be surprised at this newly discovered ability. Let's face it, we know next to nothing about vampires except what we've learned from your own situation, and the few other creatures we've encountered since Abraham Turner. For all we know, they can turn into bats and fly."

"I'm pretty sure they can't turn into bats and fly," Mina said, smiling finally. "At least, if they can, that's one ability I don't want to experience first-hand."

"I'm just pointing out that there's a lot we don't understand yet. But if the vampires have the ability to get inside each other's minds, they must also possess the ability to block those intrusions when they are unwelcome. It's only logical. Perhaps you have that same ability."

"Maybe. But I wouldn't know where to begin unlocking it." Mina agreed with Decker, but it wasn't like she had a user manual listing how to be a good vampire. And up until a few months ago, she hadn't needed one. In the quarter-century she had been stuck in the past, Mina had done a good job of avoiding the vampires, only crossing paths with them infrequently and making sure to beat a hasty retreat the moment she sensed one. Now, though, ever since being kidnapped by the late Ignatius Faucher, she felt like they were everywhere. And worse, they were actively pursuing her. She took a deep breath and forced herself to relax. There was nothing she could do about the situation, and they had bigger worries. Like defeating whoever or whatever was hellbent on killing Clarence Rothman and his friends, because without him, they might not make it back home to their own time. To that end, she said, "Do you think the killer will take the bait tonight?"

Decker observed Mina for a moment, as if he wasn't quite finished with their previous conversation. Then he shrugged. "Hard to say. If he sticks to his previous MO, there's a good chance."

Mina's eyes fell to the newspaper lying on a table near the window. It was the previous evening's edition. The story that Decker and Shaw had so carefully planted thanks to Detective McCullough occupied a whole column on the front page, and two more on page three, with a headline that read **'Police Move Potential Victims of the Greenwich Village Butcher to Undisclosed Location'**. A subhead underneath baited their trap. **'Clarence Rothman Refuses to Cooperate and Stays Home'**. There was also a grainy photograph of a patrolman guarding the entrance to the previous crime scene. They had gotten lucky, tricking at least one major newspaper into running their false story at short notice. If they hadn't, who knew where the killer would have struck next.

Not that it would have resulted in another death. McCullough really had moved the two remaining potential victims to a safe location, which was where they would stay until the situation was resolved. But instead of Clarence Rothman, the killer would find Decker and Shaw waiting at Rothman's apartment later that evening. With any luck, the murder spree would come to an end before midnight.

Yet Mina couldn't shake a sense of foreboding that had settled over her from the moment Decker and Shaw returned from their meeting with Detective McCullough the previous day. A nagging unease that had gotten lost in the bigger picture of her psychic encounter with the vampire in the early hours of the morning.

There was something they were all missing. Mina was sure of it. She just didn't know what...

THIRTY-NINE

CLARENCE ROTHMAN'S suite of rooms at the Albert Hotel was about as opulent and comfortable as Decker's room at the boarding house was spare and small.

Nick Shaw stood in the doorway and whistled appreciatively. "Man, what I wouldn't give to live in a place like this. It's no wonder Clarence has done nothing but complain about that dingy room we put him in."

"It might be dingy, but it's safe," Decker said. "And it just might keep him alive."

"Not arguing with you there." Shaw stepped into the apartment and placed a long, slender bag on the floor. He kneeled and opened it, taking out a Winchester Model 1907 semiautomatic rifle and handing it to Decker. He removed a second rifle, which he kept for himself, and stood up. "There are ten rounds in the box magazine of each weapon, but I sincerely hope we won't need anywhere near that amount of firepower. It's not the hardest hitting weapon, but I wouldn't want to be on the receiving end of it. You ever fired one of these before?"

"Nope. But I've fired plenty of other rifles." Decker inspected the gun. It was five in the evening, and while Decker and Shaw were setting up their trap to catch a killer, Detective McCullough's men were quietly ushering the other residents out of the building to a line of carriages waiting to take them to different lodgings several blocks north for the night. It was an expense McCullough would rather not have incurred, and the hotel's management were none too pleased, but it was preferable to a civilian getting caught in the crossfire when and if the murderer showed up.

Now, Decker glanced at his watch, frustrated that the evacuation was taking too long. For all they knew, the murderer was already watching the hotel, biding their time. He was about to voice his complaint to Shaw when there was a light knock at the apartment door.

A young patrolman stood there, his gaze flitting nervously between Decker, Shaw, and the two rifles. "Detective McCullough asked me to tell you that all the residents are safely out of the hotel. We're pulling back, too. In a few minutes, the building will be empty except for the two of you."

"Good." Decker nodded. "I need you to relay a message to Detective McCullough. Tell him to keep his men at a safe distance and out of sight. Under no circumstances is anyone to reenter the building until morning unless specifically asked to do so by myself or my colleague. Is that understood?"

"Yes, sir. He's already said as much. You'll be left alone tonight."

"Thank you." The patrolman turned to leave, then looked back at Decker and Shaw. "Good luck tonight, sirs. I'm glad you're tackling this monster, and not me."

"I've got a third gun if you want some excitement," Shaw said, slipping his Webley & Scott model 1905 pistol from its holster at his hip and holding it out. "Better than that service revolver you're sporting."

"That's quite alright, sir." The patrolman almost bumped into the door surround in his haste to retreat.

Shaw chuckled and slipped the gun back into its holster. "That's what I thought."

"There was no need to do that," Decker said, even though he couldn't help grinning. "The poor lad couldn't have been more than twenty years old."

"Hey, I'm putting my life on the line here. At least let me have some fun."

"Fair enough." Decker returned to his study of the rifle. "You sure this has the stopping power we need? That cop at the last crime scene claimed he put two bullets into the killer with no effect."

"For all I know that cop was just a lousy shot." Shaw patted his rifle. "Or too terrified to aim straight. Plus, he was using a revolver. Hardly the same thing. Trust me, nothing is going to get past these rifles unless it's already a ghost."

"I wouldn't discount that theory," Decker said, and he was only partly joking.

"Neither would I." Shaw gave his rifle a cursory once over to make sure everything was in order, including checking the magazine. "And hey, if our killer does turn out to be of a more supernatural variety than we expected, at least we'll know for next time."

"I'm hoping for good old flesh and blood," Decker said. "Because if we can't stop this thing, we might end up dead before we get another chance."

"That's cheery."

"Just stating a fact," Decker said. He thought about Mina back at the boarding house guarding Clarence Rothman and felt a prickle of concern. He hated leaving her alone while they took care of the killer, because there was another concern now. The vampires. What had seemed like a chance encounter on the docks had swiftly morphed into something more dangerous. They were actively looking for her and every moment he was staking out Clarence Rothman's apartment for the Greenwich Village Butcher, she was vulnerable. He had briefly considered insisting that Shaw stay behind with Rothman while Mina accompanied him to the apartment, but that would only have put her in even more danger. And even though he hated to admit it, Mina was more important than the private investigator. Who knew what the repercussions would be if she died in the past, or how it would affect Decker's quest to return home to the future and Nancy. It was, he felt, a no-win situation and all he could do was hope that nothing untoward happened at the boarding house while he and Shaw were taking care of business at Clarence Rothman's apartment.

"Decker. You ready?" Shaw asked, cutting through his reverie.

"Ready." Decker hitched the rifle over his shoulder and stepped toward the apartment door. "The killer will expect there to be a guard posted in the hallway on Rothman's door. That will be me. If the last killing is any indication, it won't give them pause. There's only one way up to this floor and we know the killer isn't already in the building because the entire place has been searched top to bottom, so it should be easy enough to spot our target when they arrive."

"Agreed," said Shaw. "I'll hunker down in here and lie in wait. Should be a nice surprise for our killer when they enter the apartment. The last thing they will expect is to be staring down the muzzle of my rifle. And remember, take one shot when the killer arrives to let me know the game is on, and then retreat. You don't need to be a hero. Remember what happened to that cop at the last crime scene."

"I know what I'm doing," said Decker. "Once the killer enters the apartment, I'll step into the doorway to block his escape. We'll have the bastard trapped. Just remember to stay out of my line of fire."

"Trust me, I intend to." Shaw was gripping his rifle so tight that his knuckles turned white. "You ready to do this?"

"Ready as I'll ever be," said Decker, then he stepped into the hallway, closed the suite's door, and took up a position nearby. They had set the trap. Now all they could do was wait and hope the killer had taken their bait.

FORTY

FIVE HOURS PASSED with no sign of movement in the empty hotel. Decker sat in the hallway on a chair dragged from Clarence Rothman's rooms with the rifle resting on the floor and tucked at his side. Stifling a yawn, he wondered how Shaw was doing inside the apartment. He briefly considered poking his head inside to break the monotony, but decided against it and leaned his head back. He stared absently at a small black spider that scurried along the wall near the ceiling until it reached a crack in the plaster and pushed its way inside.

The wait was interminable.

It was past ten, and Decker was beginning to think the killer had not fallen for their ruse. Or maybe the forty-eight-hour span between the previous killings was not a pattern, but merely coincidence. The killer might show up a day from now, or even a week. Or they might not show up at all. Hell, maybe the killer was in another apartment building entirely, stalking some random stranger even now, and there was no actual connection to Clarence Rothman and his circle of friends.

Then a nasty thought occurred to him. What if the perpetrator was one step ahead of them all along and knew exactly where Clarence Rothman was at that moment? What if they were sitting here in the hotel, waiting for an adversary that would never show up, while Mina was back at the boarding house facing the killer all by herself? For all he knew, Clarence Rothman might already be dead, and Mina could be next. She was tough, thanks to her altered physiology, but not invincible.

Decker's gut clenched.

He tried to tell himself that he was being ridiculous. The killer could not possibly know where Clarence Rothman was hiding. But the irrational thought lingered. It exploded in his head until all he could think about was Mina facing off with a murderer too clever to fall for their trap.

Damn. How could he have been so naïve.

Decker stood and turned toward the suite's door, intending to call out to Shaw. Say he had a bad feeling about the situation... that they should return to the boarding house right now.

And then he heard it.

A sound, faint and distant, like shuffling feet.

Decker froze. He stared down the hallway toward the stairs, scanning the gloom. Holding his breath. Straining to listen.

The sound came again, closer this time. A footfall, heavy and ponderous. Then another. The darkness at the top of the stairs shifted and morphed. It coalesced into the shape of a figure. An impossibly enormous figure with a wide, thickset body and heavy arms dangling at his sides.

And the smell. It wafted along the hallway, foul and cloying. Rank.

Decker suppressed a gag and fumbled for the rifle, unwilling to tear his gaze away from the figure at the top of the stairs. His fingers closed over the barrel. He lifted it. Aimed.

The figure advanced on him, making its way down the hallway with singular intent.

The odor was so strong that Decker's eyes watered.

He blinked to clear his vision, finger curling on the trigger. Aiming high, he let off a shot that slammed into the ceiling above the intruder's head. Not just a warning shot, but also a signal to Shaw inside the suite to be ready.

A cascade of broken plaster tumbled down, but his shot did nothing to slow the figure down.

"Stop, or next time I won't miss," Decker said, taking an instinctive step backward as the hulking figure drew ever closer.

The intruder kept coming, stepping into a pool of light cast by a flickering wall sconce, and Decker got a good look at his adversary for the first time.

It was no man, but more like a crude representation of one, with a roughly hewn face that looked like it had been created by a sculptor with a fevered mind. There was no discernable mouth. The nose was nothing more than a misshapen lump. The eyes were hollow sockets, as if they had been created by poking a finger into soft clay. They stared ahead with dead indifference.

"I said stop." Decker retreated further, backing down the hallway away from the apartment door. He aimed. Fired again.

The sound was deafening in the confined space. If Shaw

hadn't gotten the message already, there would have been no mistaking this second shot. The trap had been sprung.

Not that Decker's bullet had much effect. It slammed into the creature's chest, opening a gaping hole that quickly reformed and closed upon itself as if the creature were made of molten lead.

Decker halted his retreat, set his feet, and fired again, aiming at the creature's head. He might as well have been shooting into a pile of mud. The bullet cleaved the creature's skull, momentarily splitting it. But there was no sign of bone, or any other underlying structure to the face. Even as he watched, the two halves flowed toward each other and meshed back together. And all the while, the creature kept coming.

Relentless. Unstoppable.

It reached the suite, lowered its shoulder, and barged forward with barely a missed step, sending the door slamming back on its hinges with the crack of splintered wood.

Decker had time to fire one more round before the creature disappeared inside the suite.

There was a moment of terrible silence.

Decker raced forward, reaching the shattered door just as Shaw opened fire. Three quick pops from his rifle that had about as much effect as the shots Decker taken in the hallway.

The creature whirled around, looking for the source of its aggravation, and found Shaw standing to one side, rifle raised.

Then it lunged forward, faster than anything of such a large size should have been able to move.

It barreled into Shaw, lifting him from his feet before he could even react, and sending the surprised man flying across the room. He hit the floor with a sickening thud and slid a few feet. The rifle fell from his hands.

Shaw didn't get back up.

Decker held his breath, expecting the creature to finish the job. Instead, it turned and lumbered toward the back of the apartment, disappearing into the bedroom. A moment later, it reappeared and headed toward the kitchen, searching for a victim that Decker knew it would not find. Then, as if realizing it had been lured into a trap, the creature turned and started back toward Decker, who stood blocking the doorway.

He lifted the gun, fired two more quick rounds even though he knew it was pointless. The bullets only seemed to enrage the creature. It barreled forward, slammed into Decker before he could even react. It was like being hit in the gut with a sledgehammer. The air whooshed from his lungs. His feet left the ground. There was a moment of weightlessness. Then he crashed into the far wall, head slamming back into the brickwork hard enough that his vision blurred.

Decker struggled to stay conscious, lost the fight.

Darkness rushed in.

But not before he glimpsed something strange. A single word gouged into the creature's forehead.

Emet.

FORTY-ONE

DECKER SWAM BACK TO CONSCIOUSNESS, forced himself to focus. He must have been out for only a few seconds, merely stunned, because the creature was still there. Except it was paying him no heed. Instead, it had turned and was stomping back down the hallway, leaving huge muddy footprints in its wake. The putrescent odor wafted behind it, growing fainter as the creature reached the stairs, but still strong enough that Decker held his breath.

He struggled to his feet, grabbed the rifle, and staggered after their attacker. As he passed the suite, Decker glanced inside, saw Shaw sprawled unmoving on the floor. Was he dead? There was no time to check.

Decker limped along the hallway, ignoring the throbbing headache that flared with each footfall. His ankle hurt, too. He must have twisted it when the creature swiped at him.

By the time Decker reached the stairs, the creature was at the bottom. He raised the rifle, pinned the beast in his sights, then lowered it. What was the point? Both he and Shaw had already shot the creature several times to no avail. No point in wasting another bullet.

He started down the stairs, had to stop when he was hit by a wave of dizziness. He gripped the stair rail, held on to stop himself from pitching forward. By the time the feeling subsided, the creature was on its way across the lobby and out the door.

Decker took several long breaths, continued down. He reached the bottom and limped across the lobby. When he reached the open front door, the creature was about twenty feet ahead on the sidewalk.

A horse and carriage appeared, clacking down the road. It slowed, almost stopped, the driver distracted by the strange figure loping down the sidewalk. Then it veered away from the lumbering creature, toward the center of the road and into the path of a carriage moving in the other direction. There was a brief unpleasant exchange of words between the drivers that Decker could not fully hear, then the carriage corrected course, barely avoiding a collision. With a crack of his whip, the closer driver sped up and raced away into the darkness even as the other carriage continued on, seemingly oblivious to the reason behind the other driver's consternation.

The figure paid the near miss no heed. It kept on walking for thirty feet more and stepped into the street, coming to a stop above a cast iron sewer grate. Here it paused for a moment, turned its head toward Decker as if mocking him. A faint glint sparked in the creature's dead eye sockets. Then it appeared to melt right in front of his eyes.

The figure lost cohesion. It undulated and rippled, the human form collapsing upon itself and becoming like liquid. It remained that way for a few seconds—a column of squirming, writhing mud—before it flowed down through the grate and into the sewer below.

FORTY-TWO

BY THE TIME Decker arrived back at Clarence Rothman's suite of rooms, Shaw was climbing to his feet on shaky legs. He picked up his rifle and made his way to the door, almost bumping into Decker coming in the other direction.

"Did we get the blighter?" Shaw asked, hopefully.

"More like the other way around," Decker replied, probing a spot at the back of his head where his skull had impacted the wall. The skin wasn't broken, but it was tender. He winced. "Damned thing nearly knocked me into next week after it discovered that Clarence Rothman was not here and took off."

"I suppose tonight was a waste of time, then. Other than getting well and truly trounced." There was a note of annoyance in Shaw's voice.

"On the contrary, we learned a great deal. We know that the murderer is not mortal flesh and bone, just as we suspected. We also learned that it isn't a man, but rather a supernatural creature. And it doesn't appear to be thinking independently. It showed no emotion, angry or otherwise, upon discovering that Clarence Rothman is not here. It had no interest in killing us, much like the last murder scene when it left the patrolman alive. That leads me to believe that it is merely a puppet being controlled by some external force. Probably someone who doesn't wish to get their hands dirty by participating in the murders directly."

"Great way of doing it," Shaw said. "Kind of hard to catch a murderer when they stay far away from the crime scene and the instrument of the crime is made of clay."

"Not clay." Decker shook his head. "More like mud. A supernatural entity created from inanimate mud. That's why our bullets had no effect on the creature. There was literally nothing to damage and any wound we did inflict simply flowed back together as if it had never been there."

"Well, that's just fantastic." Shaw flexed his shoulders and rubbed the back of his neck. "Where's the damned thing now?"

"It escaped into the sewer system," Decker replied. "Literally deconstructed itself in front of me and flowed through the sewer grate. That's how a creature with such a startling appearance is able to move around so easily."

A look of disgust flashed across Shaw's face. "That would explain the foul smell. I guess it's not completely made of mud. There must at least be a small portion of human excre—"

"I don't think we need to dwell on the exact composition of the creature," Decker said, cutting Shaw off before he could voice what they were both thinking. It was bad enough to contemplate in silence, let alone speak aloud.

"Of course. You're right. Have you ever come across such a supernatural creature before?"

"No, I haven't. The closest match I've encountered is a tulpa."

"An entity created through the power of the mind," Shaw said.

"Yes. But I don't believe that this creature is a thought form, although I suspect it bears some similarities in that it is given life where none previously existed."

"If you can call that creature alive."

"It isn't, at least in the true sense of the word. But then, neither is a tulpa. The life force is merely a projection of the person who created it."

"So, if it isn't a tulpa, then what?"

"I don't know. But there's more. The creature had a word carved into its forehead. It was crudely rendered as if made by a finger, or maybe a stick, but easily readable."

"This just keeps getting weirder," Shaw said, crossing to the sofa and sitting down with an audible sigh. "What did the word say?"

"Emet. Mean anything to you?" Decker lowered himself into a chair opposite Shaw, happy to take the weight off his feet.

"Not a thing, but it's not English. I can tell you that much."

"Obviously. Which leads me to the next question. What language is it?"

"We find that out, and it might give us a clue regarding who is responsible for this mud creature."

"Perhaps." Decker wasn't convinced. New York was a melting pot of cultures and with no obvious motive for the killings, the best they could hope for was to narrow it down to one ethnic group or another. Even that was a long shot. For all they knew, the word meant nothing in particular and was just a name, or even a random collection of letters with no meaning beyond what the person controlling the creature had ascribed to them.

"Maybe Clarence Rothman will be able to enlighten us," Shaw said. "After all, he appears to be up to his neck in this."

"I thought the same thing," Decker replied. When they first spoke, Decker had suspected that Clarence Rothman was holding back. He claimed to be ignorant of any reason for the murders, but his body language said otherwise. Now, with concrete proof that he was a target, Clarence might rethink his recalcitrant attitude. Of course, that didn't mean the word would mean anything more to him than it did to Decker and Shaw. But it was a place to start.

Decker pushed himself out of the chair and stood, fighting a moment of dizziness as he did so. He wondered if he had a concussion. "There's nothing more we can do here. I suggest we secure the suite as best we can, inform Detective McCullough that he can let the other residents of this building return to their accommodation, and head back to the boarding house."

"You think it's safe to let people back in here?" Shaw was slower standing than Decker. It was obvious that he was in some measure of pain.

"I don't see why not. The creature was obviously interested in only one person and made itself scarce when it realized that the object of its wrath was not here. It could easily have killed both of us, but it didn't."

"It sure gave us a good hiding."

"That was only because we got in its way. Even after being shot several times, the creature was not inclined to finish me off. It merely wanted to continue with this task uninterrupted. The same goes for its attack on you. And besides, it's already gone, and I doubt it will return unless Clarence Rothman does. The occupants of this building have nothing to worry about. I am, however, concerned about Mina guarding Rothman on her own back at the boarding house. I would like to return there as quickly as possible and regroup."

"Suits me." Shaw was already moving toward the door, albeit with less of a spring in his step than when they arrived. "Let's get out of here."

FORTY-THREE

MINA WAS WAITING when they returned to the boarding house. As soon as she heard their footsteps coming down the hallway, she flung open the door to Clarence Rothman's room, where she had been keeping him company, and raced to meet them.

"Did it work?" She asked breathlessly. "Did you figure out what we are dealing with?"

"We confirmed the murderer isn't human, if that's what you mean." Decker opened the door to his room and stepped inside. "It's supernatural, just as we suspected."

Mina followed behind him.

"And impervious to bullets, unfortunately, just like that patrolman claimed." Shaw entered the room and leaned against the wall with his arms folded.

"That's because it's made of mud." Decker sank down onto the bed and leaned back. His whole body ached. All he wanted to do was get a good night of sleep. "There is no inherent intelligence within the creature. I'm not even sure if it's sentient."

"Someone must be controlling it," Shaw said. "But we have no idea who or why."

"And it gets weirder." Decker propped a pillow behind his head and fought back a yawn. Then he told Mina what had happened at Clarence Rothman's apartment, including the strange word carved into the creature's forehead, and the way it vanished into the sewer system.

When he was done, there was a moment of silence as Mina absorbed the information. She sat on the edge of the bed and looked at Decker. "Emet. I've never heard that word before."

"Me either, but there must be a reason why it's there."

"Maybe it has something to do with controlling the creature?" Shaw hypothesized.

"It's possible," Decker said. "But until we have more information, there's simply no way to be sure."

"And it doesn't help us to figure out who the real murderer is," Mina said. "The person behind the creature."

"Not yet. But it's a clue, and the only one we have." This time, Decker failed to suppress his yawn. He could barely keep his eyes open. "After it attacked us, I hoped to trail the creature back to its point of origin, but that was not feasible considering how it escaped. Even if I could have gotten into the sewer, there would be no way to follow a formless ribbon of mud."

"So where do we go from here?" Mina asked.

"We figure out what that word means and the connection it might have to the creature," Decker said. "And I think it's time we had another chat with Clarence Rothman. He knows more than he's saying. I'm sure of it."

"Maybe he knows what the word means," Mina said.

"What word?" asked a voice from the doorway.

When they looked around, Clarence Rothman was standing there, a quizzical look on his face.

"Emet," Decker replied, watching Clarence closely as he answered. And he was rewarded. A flicker of recognition passed across the other man's face.

"Where did you hear that word?"

"It doesn't matter." Decker swung his legs off the bed, stood up, and approached the younger Rothman brother. "Tell us what you know."

"Nothing, really." The color had drained from Clarence Rothman's face. He retreated into the hallway and turned back toward his room.

Decker followed and caught up with him at the door. "You know what *emet* means. I saw it on your face."

Clarence stopped and turned back to Decker. "I don't know what it means. I swear. But I have heard it before. A long time ago, back when I was in college. It's a Hebrew word."

"I think it's time you leveled with us," Decker said, steering Clarence back toward the room where the others were waiting.

Clarence hesitated a moment, looking between the three of them, then his shoulders slumped. "Look, I'll tell you what I know, but I wasn't holding back on you. I didn't think there could possibly be any connection to what happened back in college, but then I heard you mention the mud creature."

"You were listening in on our conversation?" Mina said.

"No. I wasn't snooping. I wanted to know if you had caught the killer... If I could go back to my apartment. I came out of my room and heard you talking when I was in the hallway."

"You've seen the mud creature before?" Decker asked.

"In a sense, yes." Clarence fell silent for a few seconds, as if trying to decide if he should say anything else, then he cleared his throat and continued. "My friends and I were joined to a club of sorts in college. That's how I met them."

"You mean like a fraternity?" Shaw asked.

"No. More like a secret society. A lot of prominent colleges have them."

"What was the name of this secret society?" Decker asked.

Clarence hesitated. "I can't tell you."

"What?" Decker could hardly believe what he was hearing. The man's life was in danger, and he was still trying to hold out on them. "Why on earth not?"

"Because the whole point of a secret society is that it's... well, secret."

"And you're willing to go to an early grave in a horrendous fashion to keep that secret?"

"Well... I..."

"If you don't want our help, just say so and you can take your chances without us." Decker infused just enough annoyance into his voice that Clarence took a step back. "But if you would rather stay in the land of the living, I suggest you do what's necessary. That includes telling us everything you know."

Clarence opened his mouth then shut it again. Finally, he appeared to come to a decision. "You'll hold what I tell you in the strictest confidence?"

"We'll be discreet, you have my word."

"I suppose that will have to do," Clarence said, sounding resigned. "I'd rather be shunned than dead."

"A wise choice. Now, the name of this group, if you please."

Clarence hesitated a moment longer, then he sighed. "The Servants of Cratus." He held his hands up. "I know. It sounds ridiculous. But it was incredibly exclusive. Invitation only."

"Cratus. The god of strength in Greek mythology," Mina said.

"Yes." Clarence nodded. "My father and grandfather were both members in their day, as was my brother Howard. I was what they called a legacy."

"Because multiple generations of your family were members."

"Right. Not that I knew anything about that before they invited me to join. It's incredibly exclusive and you never stop being a member, even after college." Clarence glanced toward the door as if he expected someone to come barging through and stop him from talking. "Of course, they could expel me for even confirming the society's existence to nonmembers."

"We already agreed to keep your secret," Decker said. "What does the mud creature have to do with this secret society?"

"I'm getting to that." Clarence stepped further into the room. "There was a place on campus. A hidden chamber beneath one of the buildings, accessible only by those who knew how to find it. The man who donated the money for the building's construction was one of us and had his architect include the room because he wanted somewhere for the society to meet. The college is aware of the room's existence, of course, but never pry into what goes on there or try to access it. They leave us alone. The Servants of Cratus have a lot of influence. The membership includes a lot of powerful men and the favors they do for the college carry a lot of weight. Not to mention the sizable cash donations. We would meet once a week in the chamber to drink wine and mingle with others of the same social standing."

"Sounds harmless enough," Shaw said. "If a little pretentious."

"Except that wasn't all we did in the chamber back then. The Servants of Cratus has built up an extensive occult library since their inception in the 1830s. I don't know how the tradition began, but chapters in colleges across the country hold rare volumes on the subject in their temples."

"The temple?" Shaw asked. "I assume that's what you call your secret meeting room?"

"Yes. Our temple on the campus of Rathmore College has hundreds of such books. It was a tradition to end every meeting by performing a ritual selected from one of the books. No one really believed any of it, of course. After a night of carousing, we were all pretty drunk. I barely remember most of the rituals, and none of them ever actually worked."

"How can you be sure of that?" Shaw asked.

Clarence looked at Shaw like he was unhinged. "Because it was a fun tradition. That's all."

"In other words, it was a bunch of inebriated and entitled brats who were messing with the occult for no other reason than to relieve their boredom."

"I suppose you could put it that way."

Shaw snorted. "You were playing with fire."

Clarence stared at Shaw. "You actually believe in this stuff?"

"Just because something can't be explained by science doesn't mean—"

"Okay." Decker stepped between the two men. "We're getting off topic." He turned to Clarence. "I assume you performed a ritual involving this mud creature?"

Clarence nodded. "At the end of each meeting, we nominated a member to pick the ritual for the following week. We chose some rituals because they were supposed to provide a benefit, like money or power—"

"Didn't you already have enough of that?" Shaw asked, interrupting.

"You can never have too much of those things," Clarence replied. "At least, that was what we believed back then, growing up surrounded by family members eager for wealth and influence. It was only later that some of us came to realize differently and adopted a more bohemian lifestyle."

"But not all the rituals were about personal gain?" Decker suspected where this was going, but he wanted to hear it.

"No." Clarence paused, perhaps wondering if he had said too much. Then he took a deep breath. "Sometimes the rituals had a darker purpose. That's how I first heard that word. And honestly, considering the circumstances surrounding it, I truly wish I hadn't."

FORTY-FOUR

CLARENCE FELL SILENT.

Decker folded his arms. "You've come this far. Let's hear the rest of it."

"Right." Clarence shuffled from one foot to the other, obviously uncomfortable with what he was about to say. "This happened a long time ago, so my memory is a little hazy on the exact details, but I'll do my best. One of our members, Francis Kingsley, was seeing a young woman. I forget her name. She worked at her father's deli in town. They had the best bagels as I recall. She was Jewish, just like him, and Kingsley was madly in love even though they came from wildly different backgrounds. He was from a wealthy family, while hers was decidedly working class."

"That must have been awkward," Shaw said.

"It was. His parents did not approve of the relationship and made their disdain for the poor girl abundantly clear. They viewed her as nothing more than a classless gold-digger. Especially when Kingsley told them he had asked her to marry him and that they were planning to tie the knot after he graduated the following year. His parents were furious. Especially his father. But Kingsley believed he could win their approval during the summer, when he accompanied them on the family's annual trip to Europe. They went every year, and he thought the grand tour would be a great opportunity to get their blessing. But they were having none of it, and the trip became a tense affair full of argument. Which was why he stayed less than a month in Europe and returned home on the first available steamer a full two weeks early."

"He must have loved her very much," said Mina.

"He did. She was his world. But when he went to the deli to surprise her, she was with another man. They were clearly together. Huddled in a booth, holding hands and leaning close to each other as they talked. Kingsley never went in. He was too hurt and angry. Refused to even tell her he was back or speak to her after that. All he could think about was how she betrayed him. That's when he found the ritual for the mud creature in one of the old books in our society's occult library. A volume written entirely in Hebrew. I don't think anyone else had ever even opened it, but Kingsley said the creature was part of his folklore. That it would exact revenge on his behalf."

"Your circle of friends helped him summon the creature, I assume," Decker said.

"Yes. A few weeks later when school reconvened after the summer break. There were around thirty members in the Rathmore College chapter of the society back then but only the seven of us were involved in that particular ritual. Kingsley wanted it that way. He was ashamed and only confided in his closest friends. I guess he couldn't stand the thought of everyone knowing what that girl had done to him."

"What happened next?" Mina asked.

"We went to the society's regular Friday evening meeting as usual. I remember we drank a lot of booze, generally partied, then performed some lame ritual meant to make us irresistible to the opposite sex, which was kind of ironic. Afterward, when everyone else had left and staggered back to their rooms, we stayed behind. Kingsley found the book and copied the incantation because we couldn't risk removing the book. The rest of us had no idea how to read any of it, but that didn't matter. Then we went into the woods behind the college and piled mud into a mound forming the rough shape of a person. It was raining pretty hard all that day as I remember so there was plenty to work with. We weren't too happy to be sloshing around out there in the cold and the dark, I'll tell you. It was miserable. But he was our friend, so we endured it."

"You performed the ritual."

Clarence nodded. "Kingsley told us what to say and we all recited the incantation. Then he carved that word into the mud figure's forehead using a stick. Emet. After that, he gave the figure its instructions."

"Which were?"

"To make sure his fiancé's suitor would never come near her again. Scare him off. It was supposed to be the last step of the ritual. But nothing happened. The pile of mud just stayed exactly that. A lifeless pile of wet dirt in the shape of a man. None of us expected it to work, except perhaps for Kingsley himself. The rituals never worked. We went along with it because we believed it was a harmless way for Kingsley to work through his jealousy."

"And did he?"

"Yes. He was in high spirits after that. The alcohol helped, too, I suppose. We were all more than a little intoxicated. We didn't see him the next day, nor the one after that. He never showed up for class. Didn't meet us for dinner. Eventually, we got worried and went to find him. He had a room in Coulter Hall, and we checked there first."

"He lived on campus?" Shaw asked.

"Yes. We all did. Coulter was the best hall of residence. All the rooms were single occupancy and furnished to the highest standards."

"Did you find him there?" Decker asked.

"Unfortunately, yes. He was dead. Murdered in a horrible fashion. It must have happened not long after we parted ways the night of the ritual. He was wearing the same clothes from that night, still caked in mud."

"And you're sure he was murdered?" Decker asked.

"A hundred percent. His neck was snapped, head turned at an impossible angle. And the look on his face. I'll never forget it as long as I live. It was a look of pure terror." Clarence steadied his trembling voice. He took a long breath. "But the weirdest thing was the mud…"

"There was mud in the room?" Decker asked.

"Yes. A pile of it, just heaped there next to the body, all cracked and dried up. It was so strange."

Mina exchanged a glance with Decker. "What happened after that?"

"There was a police investigation, of course. They never found the culprit despite grilling everyone who came into contact with Kingsley since his return from Europe. They looked into his past, his finances, those of his family. They were really hard on his fiancée when they heard about her dalliance with another man."

"I bet." Shaw shook his head.

"But nothing ever came of it. I don't know what she told the police, but they dropped her as a suspect pretty quickly."

"You never asked her?"

"No. It didn't seem appropriate. We only met her the once after Kingsley's death. He'd told us about the relationship of course, several months earlier when he decided to marry her, but never introduced us. I don't know why. Maybe she was embarrassed considering her lowly status, or maybe she thought we would react the same as his family."

"How did you meet her, then?" Shaw asked. "I can't imagine she would be eager to meet under those circumstances if she hadn't been before."

"It was about a week after Kingsley's death. We were in his room on campus packing up his belongings to ship back to his parents. We thought it was the least we could do under the circumstances. Anyway, she showed up there all tearful and distraught. She wanted some mementos to remember him by. Said there were some items that meant a lot to her. She stayed a few minutes, grabbed an old sweater of his... a few other trinkets. Earlier that afternoon I'd found a journal Kingsley must have been keeping. There were some letters tucked inside it. I didn't look inside or read any of it, of course, but I knew what they were. Love letters. When she was about to leave I fetched the journal and letters from a box and gave them to her. Figured they would mean more to her than his parents, who didn't even approve of the relationship. None of us ever saw her again after that. She wasn't really part of our crowd, and with Kingsley dead..."

"Right." Decker nodded. "Is there anything else you want to tell us?"

"No. That's all of it." Clarence glanced toward the doorway. "Can I go back to my room now? It's late and I'm tired."

"Sure." Decker waited for Clarence to depart before turning to Mina and Shaw. "What do you make of it all?"

Shaw was silent for a few seconds. He rubbed his chin.

"Summoning a creature to exact revenge? A creature that sounds an awful lot like what we encountered tonight. Mud at the murder scene? That can't be coincidence."

"Exactly what I was thinking." Decker looked at Mina. "Have you ever come across anything like this before?"

"No." Mina shook her head. "But if that word is Hebrew, that's a good place to start. We should find someone who knows what it means."

"I can help with that," Shaw said. "I know a man."

"Perfect." Decker went to the door and poked his head out. The hallway was empty. Clarence Rothman's door was now closed. Satisfied all was in order, he turned back to the others. "Make it happen."

"Sooner would be better than later," Mina said. "The killer failed this evening and will surely want to try again. We can't assume they will stick to their previous timeline."

"I agree," Decker said. "The remaining potential victims are all hidden and out of harm's way for now, but we can't guarantee it will stay that way. Our killer is employing the supernatural to achieve their goals, which leaves us vulnerable in ways we can't anticipate."

"We'll go there first thing in the morning. I'm sure he'll see us," Shaw said.

Decker nodded. "In the meantime, we should all get some rest. It's been a long day."

"Works for me." Shaw started toward the door with Mina following behind.

Decker reached out a hand and stopped her.

After Shaw departed, he leaned close and spoke in a low voice. "Are you alright?"

"Yes." Mina narrowed eyes. "Why?"

"Last night. What happened with the vampires and the

sleepwalking. Have you sensed them trying to reach out again since?"

"No." Mina shook her head. "And now that I know what they can do, I'll be better prepared if they try again."

"Good." Decker paused, wondering how to phrase what he wanted to say next. Then he took a deep breath. "I think we should lock you inside your room tonight. Just to be safe. Either Shaw or I will be out in the hallway at all times keeping watch."

A gulf of silence hung between them for a while, then Mina nodded and reached into her pocket, handing Decker her room key. "Perhaps that would be for the best."

FORTY-FIVE

AT QUARTER TO ten the next morning, Decker sat in the back of a carriage with Shaw at his side. They had left Mina back at the boarding house, even though Decker suspected it annoyed her to be sidelined once again and left on babysitting duty with Clarence Rothman. But there was nothing he could do about that. Someone had to stay and keep an eye on their over-privileged ward and since they were going to see Shaw's contact, it made sense for that person to be Mina.

It was a dreary morning, with fine rain misting the air and a chill breeze whipping through the streets. It leached the city of color, rendering the landscape beyond the carriage in shades of muted gray.

After a twenty-minute ride into the lower East Side that took them through densely packed streets lined with tenements, synagogues, and factories, they pulled up in front of a dreary three-story building that looked about as likely to collapse as to remain standing. The windows on the top floor were boarded up with planks that looked like they had been there for a decade or longer. Those on the second floor were flung wide open despite the inclement weather, and Decker could hear what sounded like sewing machines running from somewhere within. A lone woman with a shawl around her shoulders peered out from one window, meeting his gaze as he climbed from the carriage and looked up, before quickly disappearing back into the gloom beyond.

In front of them, on the ground floor, stood a bookshop. A weathered sign that stretched across the front above the windows read 'Weinberg's Rare Volumes' in peeling gold lettering.

Shaw came around the side of the carriage and met Decker, then made his way toward the shop's front door as their ride clattered away along the congested street, choked with pushcart vendors and open top horse-drawn carriages laden with barrels and crates. Children in ragged clothing darted between the traffic and raced along packed sidewalks with cries that ranged from excitement to hungry desperation. But it was the stench hanging in the air that Decker noticed most. A putrescent scent of decay mixed with excrement. He resisted looking toward the gutter and what he suspected it would contain, as they crossed the sidewalk and entered the store.

Decker stepped inside to find himself amid stacks of volumes jammed into tall bookcases with nary a space to be found. The air inside the store was better. Instead of the rotten odor permeating the streets, the atmosphere was laced with the scents of old paper and aged leather. It reminded him of the bookshop in Mayfair, where he had purchased a Charles Dickens first edition for Nancy. That particular book still sat on a shelf in his sitting room back in London. It was meant to be a Christmas present for her when he returned to the twenty-first century, but now it was an ocean away and out of reach.

"Can I help you, gentlemen?" said a voice from somewhere toward the back of the store. Moments later, a man appeared from the darkness beyond the stacks. He looked to be in his sixties and walked with the aid of a cane. His hair was graying, and stubble darkened his jawline.

"Jacob, it's so good to see you again," Shaw said, hurrying forward and extending a hand in greeting. "How the devil are you?"

"Nicholas, my boy. Better perhaps before you stepped inside my humble business." Jacob cleared his throat with a phlegmy rattle. "Where you go, trouble is often not far behind."

"Don't be so ill-disposed. That poltergeist would still be rattling around in here throwing books, banging on the walls, and making a general nuisance of itself if it wasn't for me."

"Which I appreciate wholeheartedly. Dodging Poe and Bronte as they literally fly off the shelf gets tiresome, I'll admit, but I've helped you plenty in return for that favor."

"And you can help me one more time," Shaw said. "A small favor, I promise. Information, that's all."

"Business is slow. I suppose I can make the time," Jacob replied, his attention shifting from Shaw to Decker. "Who's this?"

Decker stepped forward and introduced himself, shaking hands with the curmudgeonly shop owner. "Pleased to meet you, sir."

"Just call me Jacob. Everyone does."

"Very well." Decker glanced around. Many of the books sitting on the shelves looked old. Some were leather bound, while others were finished with cloth. He recognized several titles from authors such as Jules Verne, Alexander Dumas, and Mark Twain, along with others he didn't recognize. "You have an extraordinary collection of books in your shop."

"I do indeed." Jacob smiled thinly. "Perhaps you could unburden me of a few volumes once our business is completed, by way of thanks."

"It would be my pleasure," Decker said, as a slim woman wearing an ankle length dress entered the store and disappeared between the bookcases. "Is there somewhere we can go to talk in private?"

"Come with me." Jacob turned and shuffled back between the stacks toward the rear of the store.

Decker and Shaw followed along behind.

They stepped into a narrow corridor with doors off to both sides. One of these was open. Jacob stopped and poked his head inside, barking the terse command for someone to go watch the store while he was gone.

As they passed, Decker glanced into the room. It was windowless and gloomy, lit only by an oil lamp sitting on a table. There were cots on both sides. At least six people of varying ages huddled in the semi-darkness. He guessed they were relatives of the bookstore owner. A girl no older than sixteen stood and slipped past them, heading toward the store without so much as a word.

Jacob ushered them along until they reached another room at the rear of the building. They entered to find themselves in a chaotic office with a desk and chairs in the center and more bookshelves stacked with piles of papers, and what Decker assumed to be rare volumes.

Rounding the desk, Jacob sat down and motioned for Shaw and Decker to do the same. Then he fixed them with a steely gaze. "Tell me, what is it that brings you to my store?"

Shaw leaned forward. He found a sheet of paper on the desk and picked up a pen, then wrote a single word on it in bold block letters. Then he turned the sheet and slid it toward Jacob. "Tell us what that means."

The bookstore owner stared at the sheet of paper for a short while. Then he raised his head and looked at Decker and Shaw, eyes glinting in the pale light that filled the room. "My dear Nicholas, whatever have you and your friend gotten yourselves into?"

FORTY-SIX

"I TAKE it you know what the word means and why we are here," Decker said, leaning forward and looking at the sheet of paper with 'EMET' written in large letters.

"I know the word." Jacob picked up the sheet of paper and studied it for a moment, then set it back down again. "It means truth in Hebrew. But knowing Nicholas and what he does for a living, I suspect the word itself is not what you are concerned with. Your real interest is how it relates to Jewish folklore and the supernatural entity associated with the word. Am I right?"

"You mean a creature about seven feet tall that appears to be made of mud?" Decker replied. "Because if that's what you're referring to, then yes, we are very interested."

"Ah. It is as I suspected." Jacob leaned his elbows on the desk. "In Jewish folklore, the creature is called a golem. It is an entity created entirely from inanimate matter, like mud or clay. An anthropomorphic being animated through ritual incantations to serve the purpose of its creator. It has no capability for independent thought but is, rather, a blunt instrument that will follow the tasks assigned to it blindly and literally."

"That sounds a lot like our mud creature," Shaw said, glancing at Decker before turning his attention back to Jacob. "How easy is it to create one of these creatures and bring it to life?"

"Well, gentlemen, that would depend upon who you listen to. The golem has been a part of Jewish folklore for hundreds of years. Ancient texts going back at least ten centuries mention the golem. The instructions for creating such a creature has changed countless times. For example, one text from the Middle Ages requires the creator of a golem to animate it by having what the text describes as an ecstatic experience, although I could not tell you what counts as an ecstatic experience or how to achieve it. Other texts talk of placing certain holy words upon the creature, either around its neck, by inserting slips of paper into its mouth, or inscribing the word onto its forehead. Even the word itself varies, but *emet* is one such word."

"Let's say, for the sake of argument, that we have encountered a golem," Decker said. "How would you suggest we deal with it?"

"Carefully. As I said, the golem is a mindless instrument following the instructions of its creator. The creature will pursue the task assigned to it with relentless determination. If the desires of its creator are benign, or even benevolent, then you have little to worry about. But if the person who created the golem has darker motives, then the creature will be very dangerous indeed. Stand in its way and you could lose your life."

"How are we supposed to stop it, then?" Shaw asked.

"The ancient texts are contradictory. Sometimes even vague." Jacob tapped the sheet of paper. "But since you asked about that word, I shall tell you what I know of it. Emet means 'truth', but if you remove the E to form the Hebrew word met, it now means 'death'."

"Are you saying that removing an E from the word inscribed on the creature's forehead will kill it?" Decker asked.

Jacob nodded. "At least according to folklore."

"That sounds too easy."

"Because it is." Jacob settled back in his chair. "The trouble with folklore is that you can't take it literally. Stories change over time. The creature was, I suspect, created with incantations. You will need to not only change the meaning of the word on the creature's forehead from truth to death by removing a letter, but you will also need the incantation used to breathe life into the golem in the first place. There should be a further incantation to render it inanimate once more."

"And there's no other way to stop this thing?" Shaw asked.

"There is one way. Let the golem complete the tasks assigned to it, and the creature will have no further purpose. It will return to a lifeless pile of inorganic matter all by itself."

"Yeah. That's not an option," Decker said.

"Then I'm afraid, gentlemen, that you have no other choice but to find the incantation used to animate the golem and hope that there is a similar incantation to render it inanimate once more."

"I don't suppose you have a book with that incantation lying around here somewhere, do you?" Shaw asked, hopefully.

Jacob shook his head. "I'm afraid not. Such volumes are rare. I have only ever seen one, and that was many years ago during my travels in Europe. Even if I could provide you with such a book, there's no guarantee that the incantations within it would work. The occult is not an exact science."

"It was worth a try," Shaw said.

Jacob pushed his chair back and climbed to his feet. "Now, if you have no more questions, I have much to do."

Decker and Shaw both stood up.

"No more questions. You've been very helpful," Decker said, thanking the bookstore owner. He stepped out of the office and made his way back to the bookstore, with Shaw at his side.

"I believe you forgot something," Jacob said, as Decker reached to open the front door. "The books you promised to purchase. I'm sure you don't want to leave empty-handed."

"Of course. I almost forgot." Decker turned around. He looked at Shaw. "Any suggestions?"

Shaw shrugged. "Not much of a reader, I'm afraid."

"If I might be so bold," Jacob said, crossing to a shelf containing leather-bound volumes. "These are some of the finest books in my shop. Rare editions. Hard to find. Perhaps you would like to take a couple of those."

"Sounds expensive," Decker replied.

"No more so than the value of my knowledge," Jacob said. "Would you care to make your selections?"

"How about you just pick a couple, and we'll settle up," Decker said, reaching for the cash in his pocket. He had a feeling the price would be the same regardless of which books he took.

"It would be my pleasure," Jacob replied. Then he slipped two volumes from the shelf and turned toward the counter, motioning for Decker to follow.

FORTY-SEVEN

OUTSIDE ON THE SIDEWALK, with two volumes under his arm that had cost him more than he considered any book to be worth, Decker turned to Shaw. "Your friend in there. Does he always drive such a hard bargain?"

Shaw laughed. "He's never made me purchase a book, let alone a pair of rare first editions. He must know a sucker when he sees one."

"Thanks. Let's hope we don't have to go back and see your friend again, or I might not be able to pay rent at the boardinghouse when it comes due."

"I wouldn't worry. Your funds from Thomas Finch in London should be available soon enough." Shaw stepped into the road and flagged down a carriage.

After they climbed in and rode the carriage back toward the boardinghouse, Decker spoke again. "Clarence Rothman claimed that the incantation used to create the golem was from a book in the secret chamber used by the Servants of Cratus."

"Which would be on his old college campus. I assume you want to pay a visit?"

"I don't see any other way to get our hands on the book, and your friend Jacob said we can't neutralize the golem without it."

"Then we're in luck," Shaw said. "We have our very own Servant of Cratus waiting for us back at the boardinghouse. I can't imagine he's forgotten how to access the secret chamber. Are you going to tell Detective McCullough what we've found out?"

"Not yet. I realize he's consulted with you in the past about his more unusual cases, but the man is still a police officer. He relies on empirical evidence. Even if we tell him about the golem, his first instinct will be to dismiss our findings as hokum."

"Except that one of his own men has already had a run-in with the creature and made a report of the encounter from his hospital bed."

"That doesn't mean Detective McCullough will take that report at face value. He's more likely to believe the murderer is a large but mundanely human man covered in mud than a supernatural creature born out of superstition and folklore. Besides, the two men under police protection are out of harm's way for now and informing Detective McCullough of the golem will give him no advantage in dealing with it since bullets don't work and we don't currently have any other way of stopping it."

"But it will allow his men to make an informed decision if they end up face-to-face with the golem."

"And do what?" Decker asked. "Beat a hasty retreat and simply let it kill the men they are guarding unopposed? Those policemen are as likely to do that as the golem is to let them arrest it."

"Fair point. It just feels wrong to let Detective McCullough continue operating in the dark."

"The detective's own training and experience will ensure that he continues to do that, regardless. Better to focus on finding a way to stop this creature, than waste our time trying to convince a man who holds hard evidence on a pedestal that a creature made solely of mud and brought to life by supernatural means is the killer."

"Technically, the golem is more like a walking murder weapon," Shaw said. "The real killer is the person behind this diabolical plot to kill Clarence and his friends. The question is, how do we find them?"

"We don't, without a direction in which to look." The carriage clattered over a pothole, the wheel bumping down and causing Decker to fall silent momentarily. "But I think it's fair to say that whoever is doing this has a grudge against the Servants of Cratus, or at least those who were in the secret society alongside Clarence Rothman."

"And we already have a connection," Shaw said. "That word, *emet*, and the creature associated with it."

"I agree. It can't be coincidence that Clarence and his associates tried to create a golem back then, and the same creature is hunting them down now."

"The question is, how do we find the link?"

"I think we already have," said Decker. "The man who died while Clarence Rothman was in college, Francis Kingsley. He instigated the plot to create a golem for revenge all those years ago."

"Right," Shaw said. "But don't forget, their attempt to animate the golem didn't work. Rothman said so himself. They didn't even expect it to work. It was just a bunch of rich kids playing around with the supernatural out of boredom."

"Except that against their expectations, it did work,

although they never realized it at the time," Decker replied. "At least if my theory is correct. They found Francis Kingsley dead in his room on campus. Murdered with his neck snapped."

"Just like the current killings."

"Precisely. And when he was discovered, there was a pile of dried mud next to him."

"You think it was what remained of the golem?"

"It would make sense. They went into the woods that night and fashioned a golem out of wet earth. They inscribed the necessary word into its forehead and recited the incantation to animate the creature, then gave the creature its instructions."

"To make sure his fiancé's suitor could never come near her again."

"Yes. But not really believing their ritual would work, they lost interest when nothing happened and returned to their rooms on campus for the night."

"I see where this is going," Shaw said. "You think the golem came to life after they left, then went about its business?"

"Yes."

"So why did it kill the person who created it?"

"I don't know. But that appears to be precisely what happened. Then, thinking its task was complete, the golem returned to an inanimate state."

"The pile of mud on the floor."

"Yes." Decker glanced absently out the carriage window. They had left the lower East Side and its squalor behind and were almost back at the boardinghouse. "Of course, it's all speculation, and there is still much to be answered. Like why the creature turned on its creator, and what relevance Kingsley's death has to the present situation."

"It sounds like we have our work cut out," said Shaw as the carriage pulled up in front of their accommodation.

"Yes. And we had better find the answers quickly, because the person behind the golem failed in their last attempt at murder and will be all the more eager to succeed with their next." Decker pulled his door open and stepped out. After paying the carriage driver, he turned to Shaw. "I suggest we collect the others, then leave right away for Clarence Rothman's old college and the secret chamber belonging to the Servants of Cratus."

FORTY-EIGHT

"ABSOLUTELY NOT." Clarence folded his arms, a defiant look on his face. "It's simply impossible."

"We don't have a choice." Everyone was gathered in Decker's room at the boardinghouse while Decker explained what had happened when they spoke with Shaw's contact. Then he appraised them of his plan to retrieve the book from the hidden occult library at Clarence's old college. This had been met with a less than enthusiastic reaction, but Decker persisted anyway. "The incantation in the book you used to create the golem all those years ago might be the only way to defeat it now."

"We didn't create a golem," Clarence protested. "Although not for lack of trying, I'll admit. But nothing happened, just like every time we used a book from that library. We were a bunch of naïve college students, not serious occult practitioners making pacts with the devil. We had no idea what we were doing."

"That's the problem," said Shaw. "If our theory is correct, the incantation worked and you actually created a true to life golem, but you didn't wait around long enough to see if it became animated. The creature then went in search of its creator—the person who gave it purpose—and killed him."

"You're trying to tell me that a monster made of mud killed Francis Kingsley?" Clarence laughed, the sound shrill and nervous. "A monster we supposedly summoned using a pile of dirt, a few verses from a moldy old book, and a stick to write that word on its forehead. The whole thing is preposterous."

"No more preposterous than the murderous creature we ran into last night," Decker said. "Which I am now a hundred percent certain was a golem."

"All right. Fine. Let's assume you're right and there was a golem at my apartment last evening. What does that have to do with the book in the occult library at Rathmore College?" Clarence turned to Shaw. "Your friend said that only the exact incantation used to summon it could ultimately defeat the creature. There isn't one shred of evidence to suggest that anyone used that particular book to create another golem. How could they? It's locked safely away in a secret library."

"I don't know." Shaw paced across the room. "But given the circumstances, it's only logical to assume that the current killings have a connection to the events back then. If that's the case, it's also logical to conclude that book you used to create your golem is the same one used to create the creature that attacked us and killed your friends. We have no choice but to get our hands on that book if we are to stop the creature."

"He's right," said Mina. "I know you don't want to hear this, but there is simply no other way. If we're wrong, then our situation is no worse than before, but if we are correct, the book will save your life and that of your remaining friends. I don't see how you can refuse to even entertain the idea."

"Because if the Servants of Cratus discover I broke my

oath of secrecy and told you of their existence, they could expel me from the organization, and there's no way of explaining why I need the book without revealing your involvement, which makes this entire conversation moot. They won't let us into the room, let alone give us the book."

"You don't know that. They might just as easily be aghast that someone is trying to kill members of their organization and decide to help."

"While I concede that they are likely alarmed at the recent murders, that doesn't mean they will believe the killer is a creature composed entirely of mud." Clarence looked miserable. "This all sounds crazy, even to me. In all probability they will just think I'm unhinged."

"Surely it's worth the risk." Mina went to him and took his hand in hers. "If we don't do this, you might not live to see next week. The same goes for your friends. I know it's hard, but sometimes you have to think of the greater good."

"You mean throw myself on my proverbial sword?"

"If that's how you want to look at it."

"Maybe you don't need to tell them anything," Decker said, looking at Clarence. "You know where the room is and how to access it. You can go in there on your own at any time and get the book for us with the Servants of Cratus being none the wiser."

"It's not that simple. The chamber can only be accessed by pressing six buttons hidden within a carved molding next to the chamber door in the correct order. They change the sequence every semester. I would need that sequence, known only to the current Rathmore membership."

"Then ask them for the sequence. Surely they let alumni into the chamber."

"They do. But not unaccompanied. There is always a current campus member present. And I wouldn't be allowed to remove the book from the chamber, which brings us right back to where we started."

"Why don't you just open the book in the chamber, find the incantation, and write it down," Mina said. "That way, you won't need to remove the book."

"With any other book in the library that would be an option. But this particular volume is written in Hebrew. I would never be able to transcribe the page correctly even if I could identify the right incantation in the first place. We would need someone who reads the language."

"Like the bookstore owner we saw earlier today," said Decker. "But if we can't get in, we sure as hell aren't going to get some crotchety old bookstore owner inside that chamber."

"We're wasting valuable time." Shaw ceased his pacing. "If you won't help us retrieve the book, we'll be forced to do it on our own."

"Impossible. You don't know where the chamber is or the sequence to gain access," said Clarence, but he looked nervous, nonetheless.

"Would you care to place a wager on that?" Shaw asked.

Clarence fell silent. He bit his lip, a pained expression on his face.

Decker waited a moment then said, "Look, the Servants of Cratus are going to find out that you told us about their secret meeting chamber whether you help us or not. Wouldn't you rather they hear it from your lips instead of ours?"

"Are you blackmailing me?" Clarence's expression turned to thunder.

"Not in the slightest. But these things have a way of coming out. I can't imagine our presence on that college campus will go unnoticed, especially when we start asking discrete questions about the Servants of Cratus."

Clarence appeared to contemplate this, then his head drooped. "I don't have much choice, do I?"

"Not if you want to stay alive," said Shaw.

Clarence walked to the window with his back to the room and stared out at the wall of the building opposite. After a while, he turned back to face them. "Very well. We'll go to Rathmore College, and I'll see what I can do. But I make no promises. And I warn you, they are just as likely to censure me and revoke my privileges within the society as they are to help us."

"In that case, you had better make a convincing argument in favor of letting us take that book," Decker said. He glanced at the clock sitting on the side table next to his bed. It was already midday. "We should leave sooner rather than later. Every hour of delay brings us closer to another encounter with the golem."

"The college is all the way up in Connecticut," Shaw said. "We won't make it there and back in one day."

"Then I suggest everyone pack the necessities for an overnight trip."

Shaw nodded, then turned toward the door and stepped out into the hallway with Mina right behind.

Clarence lingered. "You really think this is the only way?"

"I do," said Decker. "Unless you would rather the golem snap your neck and remove your face."

"When you put it like that, a trip to Connecticut would be preferable."

Decker walked him to the door. "I could not agree more."

FORTY-NINE

THEY LEFT by train from Penn Station in the early afternoon to make the two-hour trip north to Clarence Rothman's old alma mater of Rathmore College in Connecticut. Decker would have preferred to take private transportation, but that simply wasn't possible given the state of the roads—most of which were unpaved—between New York and their destination. At best, Clarence assured him, it would take the better part of a day to make the journey by horse and carriage, or even automobile, which would get constantly mired down by mud. The train was, therefore, their fastest option, even though it meant staying overnight and returning the next morning.

But the train proved a welcome respite, even though conversation was minimal. Decker, Mina, and Shaw found it hard to keep their eyes open, lulled by the rhythmic clatter of wheels on rails. None of them had gotten much rest at the boardinghouse, between guarding Clarence, and Mina's concern that the vampires would reach into her head again when she slept. Clarence brought a book and spent most of the trip with his head down, reading, or staring through the window at the landscape rolling past beyond.

After arriving at their destination, a small town nestled on the water between Stamford and New Haven, they wasted no time in securing rooms at a local inn near the docks and then completed the last three miles of their journey to the college riding in the back of a carriage.

Rathmore was one of those old-money schools that looked like it might have been around forever. It boasted a small campus comprising several stone buildings clustered around a central quad and smaller buildings, including the residence halls, beyond. All of this was nestled in a swath of pristine woodlands that must have been glorious in the fall but were now barely starting to leaf as winter gave way to spring. Despite the drab weather, gaggles of students had settled on benches in the quad, while others wandered back and forth between the buildings.

"I guess it's down to you now," Shaw said as they stood under the shadow of Rathmore's main building.

"I'll need to speak with the Guardian of the Temple. It's my only hope of getting the correct sequence to access the chamber. And it won't be easy, I assure you."

"Who?" Decker raised an eyebrow.

"The Guardian of the Temple. Each year, the Servants of Cratus selects one student member to be responsible for the temple."

"You mean the secret chamber?"

"Yes. The guardian defends the temple's secrets."

"Let's hope he or she is in a receptive state of mind, then," Decker said.

"He," Clarence said, correcting Decker. "There are no women allowed in the Servants of Cratus."

"Figures," Mina snorted. "You probably wouldn't be in

this situation if there were a woman or two around to talk sense into you all."

"Perhaps." Clarence turned to Mina. "I didn't make the rules."

"No, but you could try changing them."

Clarence stared at Mina as if she had suggested he jump off a tall building, then he shifted his attention back to Decker. "You should all stay here while I find the guardian and explain our situation."

"You think he'll believe you?" Decker asked.

"There's only one way to find out." Clarence turned and started toward the largest of the buildings surrounding the quad. "Wish me luck. I'll be back soon."

———

Almost an hour later, Decker, Mina, and Shaw sat on a low wall surrounding a water fountain in the quad. Despite promising to be quick, Clarence had not yet returned. Decker was beginning to think the Servants of Cratus had done something nefarious to him for revealing the existence of their secret society, but then he saw a familiar figure exit the building and descend the steps, walking in their direction.

As Clarence approached from the other side of the quad, his shoulders were slumped. Decker guessed it would not be good news. He was right.

"It's a no go, I'm afraid," Clarence said as he reached the wall and sat next to them. "The Guardian of the Temple was most emphatic. No one outside of the society is allowed to step foot in the temple."

"What about you?" Shaw asked. "You're a member and you've seen the book before. Surely you can go in there and get it for us."

"Not that easy. The guardian was concerned because I breached our sacred vow of secrecy by revealing our existence and that of the temple. He has forbade me from entering and will be referring my conduct to the elders."

"I assume the elders are your governing body?" Decker asked.

"Yes. The Council of Elders comprises some of the most distinguished and long-serving members of our group. The Servants of Cratus maintain a presence on many elite college campuses and our members can be found among the most powerful men on the planet. World leaders. Captains of industry. Renowned entertainers and artists. Individual chapters might number only a small handful of members on campus at any one time, but the greater organization is large, and membership is for life. I broke our code of secrecy when I revealed my affiliation to you."

"In other words," Mina said, "they have suspended you from the organization."

"Something like that. And I fear it will not go well for me. The chances are that I will be expelled just as I warned you could happen."

"Did you impress upon him the urgency of our situation?"

"I did, and he said that if the police ask to see the book in question he would be more than happy to provide it to them but until that time comes, it stays right where it is."

"Maybe I should speak to this guardian," Decker said. "Convince him of our plight."

"Not an option. Even if I could arrange such a meeting, which I cannot, it would do no good. I assure you of that. He would not budge, or even admit to the book's existence to a non-member such as yourself. Likewise, if they granted me permission to enter the temple and locate the book, I would not be allowed to remove it from the chamber. The guardian was most emphatic on that point. I'm afraid we will need to find another way to defeat the golem."

"Not so fast," Decker said, addressing Clarence. "We came all this way, and I refuse to leave without that book. It's simply too important. You know where the secret chamber is and how to gain access. If the Servants of Cratus won't help us, then we shall find another way to gain access."

"I don't see how," said Clarence. "We don't know the door's access sequence and if the guardian won't give it to us, none of the other members will."

"You're not much of an optimist, are you?" Shaw said, shaking his head.

"I'm a realist." Clarence replied glumly.

"Let's go. There's no point in lingering here. We'll return to our accommodation and figure out what to do next." Decker went to stand up, but at that moment a freckle-faced student with sandy blond hair appeared and sat a few feet away on the wall.

The student kept his gaze fixed forward and spoke under his breath. "Be at the covered bridge over Clary Creek after sunset. Eight p.m."

"Are you talking to us?" Decker asked, turning to look at the newcomer.

"Who else would I be talking to? Be there at dusk and don't be late," said the student. "Not all of you. Just Rothman."

"Not going to happen," Decker said quietly, looking frontward once more. "There's a killer on the loose. We're responsible for Clarence Rothman's safety."

"Fine, then one of you may accompany him. But only one. Any more than that, and the meeting doesn't take place. Understand?"

"We understand."

"You know the bridge?"

"I know where it is," said Clarence.

"Good. Don't be late. And tell no one of this conversation." With that, the messenger stood and walked quickly away, soon to be lost among the throng of other students strolling through the quad.

FIFTY

ALONE IN ONE of the rooms back at the inn with the door firmly closed, Decker addressed the rest of the group. "Does anyone have any thoughts about our clandestine meeting this evening?"

"Either we are about to get the help we need, or it's an attempt to finish what the golem couldn't accomplish at the apartment last night," said Shaw.

"I agree," said Mina. "We need to be careful. The killer could be anyone, even a person on the campus of Rathmore College. It might even be the Guardian of the Temple himself for all we know. There's a high probability this is a trap."

"You can't be serious," Clarence said. "The Guardian of the Temple? Why would he do such a thing?"

"I don't know." Mina settled in a chair on the far side of the bed. "But we can't assume you are safe on the college campus or anywhere else. There is a cunning and as yet unidentified killer at large with unknown motivations. That in itself is enough reason not to trust anyone. Present company excepted, of course."

"On the other hand, we can't afford to ignore an opportunity such as this when it presents itself," Decker said. He had been mulling over their encounter on the quad all the way back to the inn and had arrived at the conclusion that there was no option but to be waiting at the covered bridge over Clary Creek when dusk came. He agreed with Mina that there was risk involved. It could easily be a trap, especially since their mysterious messenger had requested that Clarence Rothman come alone. The person behind the murders could be drawing him out, separating Rothman from the rest of the group for an easy kill. But on the other hand, the killer had no way of knowing when or if they would come to Rathmore College in search of the book. Either the killer was already on campus and their arrival presented an unexpected opportunity, or someone at the college wanted to help them, albeit surreptitiously. "I say that Clarence and I go to that meeting but keep our wits about us. At the first sign of trouble, we get the hell out there."

"You don't need to go alone," Shaw said. "Mina and I can accompany you most of the way and then hold back out of sight. That way, if this is a trap, you stand a better chance of escaping unharmed."

"I agree," said Mina. "I'm not letting you walk into a dangerous situation without backup."

"No." Decker shook his head. "We do exactly as the messenger told us. I don't want to risk scaring off a potential ally."

Mina jumped to her feet. "Unacceptable. Thomas would never agree to such a reckless plan. That's not how we do it at the Order of St. George."

"We're not in England now," Decker reminded her. "We are on our own and those rules don't apply."

"What's the Order of St. George?" Clarence asked.

"That's not your concern," Mina said, perhaps a little too sharply. Then her demeanor softened. "I'm sorry. That was unfair."

"Apology accepted." Clarence looked at her as if waiting for further explanation.

Mina folded her arms. "I'm still not telling you about the Order of St. George."

"I don't see why not. I told you about the Servants of Cratus, after all. At great personal expense, I might add. Seems only fair."

"That's enough," Decker said. "We have bigger issues at hand than tit for tat. Clarence and I will go to the meeting and we're going alone."

"But—" Mina started to protest.

"No buts. Thomas Finch isn't here, and if he was, he would agree with me. The risk is substantial, but the rewards are greater. We need to stop this killer before they strike again, and we can't do that by being timid."

"And what if this meeting turns out to be the killer striking again?" Mina wasn't backing down.

"Then our adversary will have revealed themselves, since only a couple of people know we are here. Either way, we come away more knowledgeable than before."

"Unless you're dead," Mina said. "I don't like this. While I agree with your reasoning for going to the meeting, the risk of spooking a potential ally is less than the risk of keeping Shaw and I sidelined should things go south."

Decker met Mina's gaze. "If this turns out to be a trap and we come face-to-face with the golem without a way to kill the creature, it won't matter whether you're there or not. Trust me on that."

"Then at least agree to take a gun," Mina said.

"I thought you didn't like guns."

"I don't," Mina replied. "But I'd rather you be armed with one of Nick's pistols than be completely defenseless."

"I'm not sure that will be much help," Shaw said. "My rifles had no effect on the creature last night, so I can't imagine a pistol will fare any better."

"It's better than nothing." Mina's jaw clenched. She clearly did not want to concede the last shred of argument available to her.

"Hey, I'll take a gun," Decker said. "But you don't need to worry. We'll be careful. Nothing bad is going to happen this evening."

"You've said that before," Mina replied. "And it didn't stop you from getting into trouble."

"I'm still alive, aren't I?" Decker grinned.

Mina glared at him. "Just make sure it stays that way."

FIFTY-ONE

AS THE SUN sank below the horizon and darkness spread across the sky, Decker followed Clarence Rothman along a dirt road that wound through the woods behind Rathmore College. Both men carried lanterns borrowed from the inn. And a good job too, because without them, they would not have been able to see a foot ahead of them.

"I wouldn't want to be out in these woods alone," Decker said, swinging his lantern around to take in their surroundings. Tall trees pressed close against the primitive road on both sides, the space between them nothing but a dark void ready to be filled by whatever nightmare creatures his imagination could summon. A canopy of branches arched overhead, blocking the moonlight that had aided their progress as they traversed the college campus minutes before. "Is this where you came to create the golem all those years ago?"

"Not here, but close by." Clarence kept his attention on the road ahead, wary of the deep ruts and potholes created by the wheels of carriages and hoofs of trotting horses. "There's a path that branches off somewhere up ahead. I can't remember the exact location we tried to make the golem—it's been a long time—but it was somewhere down that path in a small clearing near the creek."

"I can see why you weren't pleased to come out here back then," Decker said, stepping over a muddy puddle full of brackish brown water. The sodden earth underfoot sucked at the soles of his shoes with each step, making it hard to walk. "It's not exactly a pleasant stroll, especially in the dark."

"Maybe if we'd said no to Kingsley and hadn't indulged his need to let off steam, there wouldn't be a killer stalking me now," Clarence said, a bitter tone in his voice.

"There's no point in dwelling on things that can't be changed," Decker said. "Trust me, I know. There's plenty in my own past that I would do differently given another chance."

"Like getting involved with the Order of St. George?"

"Nice try." Decker chuckled. "How far away is this bridge?"

"Straight ahead, just around the next bend." Clarence picked up the pace.

"Good. We can't afford to be late." Decker hurried along beside Clarence as they approached the curve in the road. His hand fell to the pistol concealed at his waist under the flap of his coat. He wasn't sure how much use it would be if the killer was waiting for them up ahead, but he felt better for having it. Still, there was no reason to walk blindly into an ambush, which was why he reached out and brought Clarence to a halt as the bridge came into view around the bend.

Decker stepped sideways toward the edge of the road, pulling Clarence along with him, so they were concealed by foliage. He peered up the road, eyes scanning the darkness for any sign of trouble. The bridge was empty and silent, at least so far as he could tell. If there was a golem waiting up ahead, it wasn't about to show itself.

"We only have a few minutes," Clarence whispered.

"I'm aware of the time," Decker replied quietly. It was now or never. They either continued to the bridge and took their chances, or they retreated with nothing to show for their efforts. It wasn't even close. Decker tapped Clarence on the shoulder and motioned toward the bridge, then he stepped out of concealment. "Come on."

FIFTY-TWO

DECKER APPROACHED the covered bridge with caution, his gaze sweeping the woods ahead of them for any sign that they were walking into trouble.

Clarence walked beside him, his gait stiff and hesitant. If there was any doubt he was nervous, it was dispelled when he fell back and took up a position to Decker's rear as they stepped onto the bridge.

Old boards creaked under their feet. Further beneath them the creek flowed in a gushing torrent, its banks swollen by snowmelt. Their lanterns pushed at the gloom inside the old wooden structure, splashing flickering yellow light across the bridge's walls and up to the beams that supported its roof. Shadows jerked and danced, causing Decker's heart to leap more than once as his eyes picked out vague movements in the darkness.

"There's no one here," Clarence whispered as they approached the middle of the bridge and stopped.

"So far as we can tell," Decker replied. He went to the rail and leaned on it, looking out through one of the wide oblong gaps in the bridge's side wall, designed to allow the wind to flow through and ease stress on the structure. The trees on both sides of the brook were nothing but dark outlines against the sky above. He could barely discern where the woods ended, and the heavens began. If it hadn't been for the moon hanging low in the cloudless sky, he might have seen nothing at all beyond the bridge, save for swirling blackness.

"Maybe they decided not to come," Clarence said, clasping his arms around his chest and hugging himself against the chill.

"Let's give it a little longer." Decker turned away from the rail and glanced along the bridge in both directions. There was no sign of movement. He checked his watch in the glow from his lantern. The person they were here to meet, whoever that might be, was now officially ten minutes late. A person whose messenger had made it very clear that they should not be late themselves. Despite what he had just said, Decker was starting to think they should leave while they still could. He was about to say as much when a twig snapped somewhere in the darkness beyond the bridge.

Decker whirled in the direction of the noise.

He brought the lantern up and held it at arm's length.

Clarence whimpered, pressing so close that Decker could feel the man's breath against the nape of his neck.

Then a figure separated itself from the blackness, stepping onto the bridge and approaching at a cautious pace.

The man drew closer, the lantern finally illuminating his features to reveal a youthful face with a chiseled jawline and narrow, angular nose.

Clarence gave a small sigh and stepped out from behind Decker. "Thank goodness. It's the Warden of the Temple."

"The two of you came alone, as I requested?" The warden asked, closing the distance between them. His gaze roamed briefly beyond Decker and Clarence to the other side of the bridge.

"There's no one else here," replied Decker, as the man came to a halt a few feet away. Decker noticed he was also carrying a lantern, but it had been extinguished, possibly as he approached the bridge for fear of detection before he was ready to reveal himself. "How about you introduce yourself. I like to know who I'm dealing with."

"I'd rather not, if it's all the same with you. As Clarence already informed you, I'm the Warden of the Temple. Our business doesn't require further familiarity."

"Fair enough." Decker figured the young man before him couldn't be any older than twenty-one, yet he carried himself with an air of authority that belied his youth. "You already refused us access to the book we need. Why did you ask that we come here tonight?"

"Please understand, I can't allow you access to that book in my role as Guardian of the Temple. Likewise, I could not let Clarence's indiscretions in revealing our society to outsiders go unpunished."

"Even though someone is out there killing members of your organization in a grisly fashion," Decker said, not bothering to hide his disdain. "Snapping their necks and removing their faces."

"You don't need to try and shock me. I couldn't agree to let you take the book in my official capacity as a member of the Servants of Cratus, but I am concerned about the recent spate of killings, just as you are. The perpetrator of these heinous acts must be stopped and brought to justice."

"Is that your way of saying you'll help us?" Decker asked.

"It is. Unofficially, of course."

"As long as it gets the job done," Decker said. "What changed your mind?"

"It wasn't a question of changing my mind. I have a duty to ensure that the secrets of our society are not revealed to outsiders such as yourself. But I also have a duty to protect the membership from external threats."

"Such as a murderer picking off your members," Decker said.

"Precisely. In this case, those two edicts require contradictory action."

"In other words, you can't be seen helping us, but you can't ignore the situation either."

"Something like that."

"Does that mean you brought the book?" Decker asked.

"No. I can't risk having a book such as that on my person around campus. If I were caught, my punishment would be much worse than censure and suspension, believe me. That is a risk I'm not willing to take. But if the book were to be stolen by persons unknown, that would be beyond my control. Not that I would ever suggest such a thing."

"Naturally."

"Even if someone did break into the building and find the hidden door leading to your temple, there's still the small matter of opening it," said Decker.

The Guardian of the Temple hesitated a moment, as if deciding if he really wanted to violate the rules of his organization, then he withdrew a folded slip of paper upon which were written six digits which he offered to Clarence. "Memorize the sequence, them burn this."

Clarence took the slip of paper.

A look passed between them, as if each man realized a line

had been crossed. Then the Guardian of the Temple cleared his throat. "Make sure no one else dies."

"We'll do our best," Decker said.

The guardian stood there a moment longer, then he nodded wordlessly and turned, heading back along the bridge, before being swallowed up by the darkness beyond.

FIFTY-THREE

THE CAMPUS of Rathmore College took on a whole other personality after midnight. The previous afternoon, it had been a bright and bustling place with students roaming in all directions and an air of academic dignity. Now it was dark and empty, the buildings surrounding the quad standing like ghostly sentinels, their windows dead and black. It was, Decker thought with a shudder, like they had stepped into a soulless shadow of the real world, devoid of all life but their own.

"I don't like this," Clarence said for the fourth time since they left their rooms at the inn they had booked into for the night. "Are you sure we can get into the building without anyone seeing?"

"Would you relax," Shaw said, walking alongside Decker and looking back over his shoulder at Clarence. "This isn't a big deal. What's the worst that can happen?"

"We could get arrested for burglary and go to jail."

"No one is going to jail," said Mina as they approached the three-story brick building concealing the secret chamber used by the Servants of Cratus. "We know what we're doing."

"This isn't your first time breaking and entering?" Clarence asked, his voice rising in pitch.

"Not even close." Decker reached the steps leading to the building's main doors and started up. As expected, the door was locked.

"Leave this to me." Shaw stepped around Decker and removed a small leather wallet from his pocket. When he opened it, instead of bank notes, there were six slim silver picks with various hooked and notched ends.

"You carry those all the time?" Clarence asked in a hoarse whisper.

"In my line of work, one never knows when a locked door might get in one's way." Shaw selected a pick and went to work on the door lock.

"Aren't they illegal?"

"Nothing illegal about carrying lock picks. What you do with them, now that's another matter." Shaw twisted the pick in the keyhole, working it back and forth until the lock disengaged with a gratifying click. He turned the door handle and pushed the door inward. "Voilà."

"Good job." Decker stepped across the threshold into the darkened lobby beyond. He waited for the others to join him and watched Shaw close the door again before addressing Clarence. "It's all down to you now. Show us the secret chamber."

"This way." Clarence took the lead and started across the lobby to a large room filled with rows of tall bookcases fashioned from oak that held thousands of volumes. The room encompassed the full height of the building with two levels of bookcase lined balconies circling the outer walls and accessible via wrought-iron spiral staircases. Above them, a glass atrium ceiling allowed pale moonlight to slant down into the enormous space.

Clarence made a sweeping gesture with his hands. "This is the Clarington Library, paid for by Ernest Ross Clarington, a past member of the Servants of Cratus and one of Rathmore college's most generous benefactors before his death. He paid for the construction of at least three buildings on campus and made more than one sizable cash donation."

"Sounds like he was a generous man," Decker said, as they made their way through the library.

"With an ulterior motive, apparently," Shaw added.

"Where is this secret room?" Mina asked.

"It's back here," Clarence replied, leading them down a narrow aisle between two looming bookcases.

The library was so dark that Decker could not make out the subjects of the books lining the shelves. If it hadn't been for the moonlight bathing everything in a faint glow, the library would have been impossible to navigate.

They reached the end of the aisle, and an alcove that contained a Romanesque plaster bust. There was nowhere else to go, or so it seemed. But Clarence didn't stop. Instead, he walked through the alcove, and Decker realized that there was another small chamber beyond the alcove that had been built in such a way that even from the end of the bookcases, it was impossible to detect. The entrance had been concealed in plain sight by a clever use of perspective that presented the illusion of a solid wall at the end of the narrow aisle when in reality they were looking at another wall containing the bust set further back beyond the outer rim of the alcove. Unless someone actually tried to touch the bust, they would never know the entrance was there.

"We're here," Clarence said, turning back to the rest of the group. "What are you waiting for?"

Decker shook off his amazement and stepped through the alcove, noting that the bust was actually larger than it first appeared, to account for the added space between the back wall of the library and the real wall set eight feet further away. The room was wider than it looked as well, with several feet of space concealed behind the library walls to his left and right. And if anyone did inadvertently stumble across the small anti-chamber, they would find more bookcases, framed by intricately carved wooden panels about six inches wide, on both side walls.

This was how members of the Servants of Cratus could come and go without being observed, especially since Decker doubted many students ever ventured down the aisle leading to the concealed space.

Clarence stepped to the left and approached one of the bookcases where he studied the carvings on the left-hand side panel framing the shelves. A scrolling vertical grape design with bulbous fruits intertwined with curling leaves. He focused on one particular section with six grapes. Then he reached out pressed them, his fingers pressing the carved fruits in the order that matched the sequence given them by the Guardian of the Temple and Decker realized that the grapes were, in fact, cleverly concealed buttons.

There was a click, and the bookcase swung inward on hidden hinges to reveal a short corridor that ended at a set of stone steps. He stepped through, motioning for Decker and the others to follow.

The corridor beyond the concealed door was only wide enough to be traversed in single file. Clarence led them down the steps, which spiraled around a central column constructed of round stone blocks, to a large rectangular room that was lit with flickering gas sconces inset into notches around the walls at intervals. Between these hung oil paintings in ornate gold frames. Portraits of stern looking gentlemen who stared out at them as if resentful of the interlopers entering their sanctuary. Decker assumed the portraits to be important members of the secret society, although he didn't stop to read the brass plaques mounted to each frame.

The center of the room was sparsely furnished with several high-backed leather chairs arranged in an oval around a central stone dais that had the appearance of a sacrificial altar. A dark wood bar, well-stocked with liquor, lined one wall, creating an incongruous juxtaposition to the furnishings in the rest of the room.

"Welcome to the Temple," Clarence said, pausing momentarily and looking around with a wistful expression, before leading them across the chamber to an archway set into the wall opposite the bar. Beyond this was a smaller room lined with more bookcases packed with volumes of a less scholarly persuasion than those in the space above.

The occult library.

Clarence wasted no time in examining the shelves, going from row to row and running his fingers across the spines of books, some of which looked old enough that they should be on display in a museum. With a tut, he abandoned one bookcase and moved on to the next, then another. After twenty minutes of searching, during which he made several more noises of frustration, each slightly louder than the last, he turned back to Decker, Mina, and Shaw.

"I can't find it," he said. "It should be here, but it's not."

"How do you know?" asked Decker, his gaze roaming over the shelves packed with tomes of varying thicknesses. Hundreds of them.

"Because I remember what the book looked like," Clarence said. "It was very distinctive. The text on the spine was written in Hebrew. In fact, it's the only Hebrew language book in the library. That's how I know it isn't here."

"Then what could have happened to it?" Mina asked.

"I don't know. We returned the book to the library after using it all those years ago. I know that for sure because I was the one who returned it." Clarence turned toward a shelf and pointed to a space between two volumes. "It should be in this section. Right here. The book hasn't been misfiled either, because I've gone through every other shelf in the library. It's simply gone."

"Maybe the book was removed from the library after you left college," Mina said.

"No. Books are never permanently withdrawn from the library, and no one is allowed to take them out of the temple. We broke the rules when we took that book into the woods to create the golem. It was a huge risk. If we had been caught, we would have been kicked out of the society."

"Maybe someone else broke the rules, too," said Mina.

"And just so happened to smuggle the same book out right when we need it? That's too much of a coincidence."

"Unless the Guardian of the Temple took it," said Shaw.

"Why would he, after going out of his way to help us?" Decker asked. "There would be no reason."

"Fair point."

"Which means whoever took the book did so without permission," Decker said.

"In other words, someone already came down here and stole the book," Shaw said. "And there's only one reason for that. To summon the golem."

"A golem that we can't stop without those incantations," Mina said.

"Which means we have a problem," Decker said. "A huge problem."

FIFTY-FOUR

THEY ARRIVED BACK at their overnight accommodation in the early hours of the morning dejected and at a loss for how to continue. They barely said a word as they entered through a side door and trudged up a set of narrow stairs to the second floor. The inn was small, and they had only managed to secure two rooms at such short notice. Luckily, each came with a pair of narrow beds, so Mina agreed to share with Decker while Shaw and Clarence Rothman took the other room. The arrangement was uncomfortable but had the upside that no one would need to stand guard over Clarence during the night, which they were all grateful for given their exhaustion.

Once they got to their room, Mina grabbed her overnight bag and padded along the hall to the shared bathroom where she got ready for bed. When she returned, Decker did the same. They barely spoke, except to say goodnight, and once Decker turned the lights off, he was asleep in under ten minutes.

The next morning, as they were preparing to meet the

others in the lobby and head to the train station for the journey back to New York, Mina finally found her voice.

"I've been thinking," she said, returning from the bathroom and closing the bedroom door. "We're going to have to tell Nick the truth about us at some point."

"You think that's wise?" Decker asked, surprised.

"I don't see that we have any other choice. Although I can't imagine how he's going to handle learning not only that I am part vampire but also that we are from the future and looking for a way home."

"I wasn't going to tell you this," Decker said, "but Nick Shaw isn't as clueless as you think. He knows what you are and why you haven't aged."

"That's not possible," Mina said, growing pale. "I've been very careful not to reveal my true nature to anyone other than Thomas."

Decker said nothing. He didn't need to, because he saw the realization dawn upon her.

"Of course. Thomas told him. They were always thick as thieves, at least until Nick ran from his troubles. I should have suspected as much." She picked up a silk slip and threw it into her overnight bag, then followed suit with the blouse she had been wearing the night before. "He had no right."

"Take it easy. I'm sure he had no choice. Nick confronted him when he realized you weren't aging at a normal pace."

"He should at least have conferred with me before breaking my confidence." Mina's bottom lip trembled. "I loved Thomas. I trusted him." She zipped up her bag. "How did you find out that Nick knows?"

"He admitted it to me the day of the press conference," Decker replied. "Detective McCullough demanded a couple of whiskeys at an alehouse for his cooperation, and after he left, Nick cornered me, wanting to clear the air between us.

He was concerned that I didn't trust him and decided to open up."

Mina turned on Decker, her eyes blazing. "And you kept it to yourself?"

"He asked me not to tell you. Thought it would make you uncomfortable."

"Not as uncomfortable as everyone keeping me in the dark. What else aren't you and Nick telling me since you appear to be best buddies now?"

"Nothing, I swear. He doesn't know how you became a vampire or that we're from the future. Thomas didn't share any of that." Decker crossed to Mina and looked her in the eyes. "I'm sorry. I should have told you that he knows about your condition, regardless of what Nick wanted me to do. It was a mistake. I would never deliberately hurt you."

Mina was silent for a while, then she nodded. "I know. In a way, it's a relief. I've spent decades finding ways around explaining why I never age. It makes long-term relationships, romantic or otherwise, difficult to say the least. Which brings me back to the original point. Nick thinks we will be returning to London and the Order of St. George. He fully expects us to book passage back on an ocean liner when the opportunity presents itself. We both know that isn't going to happen. Furthermore, we will have to enlist Clarence Rothman's help once this is over to make sure that we are on Singer Cay for Celine and Howard's marriage so we can follow her through that portal and back to the twenty-first century. I don't see any way around taking Nick into our confidence."

"You really want to tell him everything?"

"I think we have to tell him the bare-bones truth without revealing our knowledge of the future to him, yes."

"You think he'll believe us?"

"I don't see why not. He already believes that I'm part vampire, and he was chasing a Japanese succubus through the streets of New York right before we met up with him. And don't forget, he was a valued member of the Order of St. George back in London. It's not like he hasn't seen and heard strange things before."

"Very well. If that's how you want to handle it."

"I do. He could be a valuable ally and we might need all the help we can get over the next four months."

"Let's not tell him just yet, though," Decker said. "I'd like to take care of this golem situation before we fill his head with more fantastic stories."

"I was going to suggest the same thing," Mina replied. She picked up her overnight bag and moved toward the door. "If you're ready, we should probably get down to the lobby. The others will be waiting."

Decker grabbed his bag and followed. This time they took the front stairs because the inn was open. When they reached the lobby, Nick Shaw and Clarence Rothman had arrived ahead of them. But they weren't alone. The Guardian of the Temple was there, too. Standing with his arms folded and a somber look on his face.

FIFTY-FIVE

"WHAT ARE YOU DOING HERE?" Decker asked, descending the last of the stairs and crossing the lobby toward the group, his gaze firmly fixed on the Guardian of the Temple.

"I guessed you might be leaving this morning and thought I should drop by and say farewell," the guardian said. "I assume you had a productive visit to our little college?"

"We didn't," Decker replied. "And I think you might know why."

"Really? I'm sorry to hear that your visit was not as you hoped, but what makes you say that?"

"The book. It wasn't there. Someone had already removed it. You wouldn't know anything about that, would you?"

The Guardian of the Temple stepped forward so that his mouth was close to Decker's ear. "If the book you were looking for was not there, it had nothing to do with me, I promise you."

"John, it's fine," Clarence said, stepping forward. "I'm

sure no one at the college had anything to do with the book not being there."

"He's right," said the Guardian of the Temple. "I assisted you as best I could out of concern for the horrendous acts being perpetrated upon some of our members. If I didn't want to help, I would not resort to subterfuge. I would simply not do so."

"Then why are you here?" Decker asked.

"I simply wanted to say goodbye to a valued member of our organization."

"Really?" Decker wasn't convinced. "Yesterday you wanted to throw him out of your little club for revealing its existence to us."

"I know. But now that I've slept on it, I don't think that will be necessary. After all, I broke the rules myself in aiding you. I think it would be better for everyone if we agree that this whole incident never took place."

"Hey, you're off the hook," Shaw said, punching Clarence lightly on the arm. "Good going."

"Not quite," Clarence said. "There's still the small matter of someone trying to kill me."

"Which I hope your friends can thwart even without the book," said the Guardian of the Temple. "After all, that same killer murdered the last alumni who visited the college."

"What did you say?" Decker could hardly believe what he was hearing. "One of the three victims came here recently?"

"Yes. Wallace Alden."

Decker exchanged a glance with Mina. "The man killed at the wine vaults."

"When did he come here?" Shaw asked.

"About two weeks ago."

"And you didn't think to mention this when Clarence

confided to you about what we were doing here?" Decker asked.

"I didn't think of it. He was in town for the weekend. Wanted to show his new girlfriend where he went to college. Nice girl. He introduced me to her. I don't see how his death would be connected to coming here."

Decker felt a vein throb in his neck. "I hate to ask this, but did you give him the sequence to access the Temple while he was here?"

"He asked to see the temple, yes. We've had alumni drop by before and want to go back there. It's not unusual. But we don't just let them come and go as they please. One of our current members accompanies them and opens the door."

"But he could have seen the sequence when it was being entered… Memorized it."

The Guardian of the Temple shrugged. "I suppose. If he really wanted to."

Decker cursed. "That's why the book isn't there. I'd lay odds on it."

"You think an alumni member stole it from the library?" The Guardian looked shocked. "Surely not."

"Either Wallace Alden took it, or his girlfriend did," Decker said. "Can anyone think of another reason that book wouldn't be there?"

There was a brief silence.

Decker nodded. "That's what I thought."

"I can't imagine Wallace Alden took the book since he ended up dead at the hands of a creature brought to life using one of the incantations within its pages," Shaw pointed out.

"So that leaves the girlfriend," Decker said.

Clarence raised a hand. "Her name's Elise. I danced with her at the party. Pretty young thing."

"You know where she lives?"

Clarence shook his head. "No. I only met her the once."

"Then we need to find out," Decker said. "She's just jumped to the top of a very short suspect list."

"How are we going to do that?" Mina asked.

"I know how." Shaw stepped forward. "Detective McCullough surely questioned her at the scene of the crime. He must have taken her address."

"Then we need to get back to the city and have a word with our friendly detective." Decker picked up his travel bag. "And the longer we wait, the more chance there is that someone else will die."

FIFTY-SIX

FOUR HOURS after they left Clarence Rothman's old college in Connecticut, they arrived back at the boardinghouse in New York. Decker was eager to speak with Detective McCullough sooner rather than later and track down the mystery girlfriend who had accompanied Wallace Alden to Rathmore College several days before his untimely death down in the wine vaults under the New York and Brooklyn Bridge. There had been plenty of time on the train journey back to reflect on the situation, and while a motive for the attacks remained elusive, everyone agreed that Alden's visit to the college appeared more than coincidence.

That was why, as they climbed the stairs to their rooms on the second floor of the boardinghouse, Shaw volunteered to head back out and find the detective just as soon as he dropped his bag and freshened up.

But when they reached the top of the stairs, Decker stopped. The door to Mina's room was ajar. A thin sliver of daylight shone through the gap between the door and frame.

Somewhere over his left shoulder, Decker heard a sharp

intake of breath that he recognized as Mina. He reached inside his jacket and withdrew the Webley & Scott pistol hidden beneath.

Shaw had his gun out, too. He tapped Decker on the shoulder and motioned silently for them to proceed, leaving Mina near the top of the stairs with Clarence Rothman.

They made their way along the hallway, moving with stealthy coordination. Shaw held his gun out in front with both hands, fingers curled around the grip. Decker kept his own gun in the low ready position, just as he would have done when he was a homicide cop in the city years before.

Decker risked a quick glance sideways at Shaw, a silent exchange that confirmed what they were both thinking. The killer had somehow found where they were staying, and in all likelihood there was a golem waiting for them on the other side of Mina's door, even as they crept ever closer to it.

From somewhere behind them came a nervous cough. Clarence and Mina were still standing at the head of the stairs. Decker resisted the urge to turn and tell them to get the hell out of the building, which would seem to be the logical course of action. But the cracked open door could be a double bluff meant to separate them. Instead of waiting in the room beyond, the golem might be somewhere else in the building entirely, looking for an opportunity to kill Clarence with as few witnesses as possible. Better to stick together.

They arrived at the door.

Decker motioned for Shaw to go left when they entered and make sure the golem wasn't waiting out of sight behind the wall. Once they confirmed that the room ahead of them was clear, which would only take a split second, he would swing right and check behind the door. After that, anything could happen.

With a deep breath, Decker lifted a hand from his gun and

swung the door inward. He dropped the hand quickly back to the gun, bringing it up. At the same time, he stepped across the threshold, moving far enough into the room so that Shaw had space to follow tight behind.

The room appeared to be empty. Mina's bed was still made, the pillows plumped and the blankets unruffled. Nothing had been moved so far as he could tell. Behind him, Shaw swiveled to the right to cover their rear. Decker followed suit to the left.

Nothing. The room was indeed empty.

Then Decker noticed something else. He directed Shaw's gaze to the wide oak planks beneath their feet. "Whoever came in here, it wasn't a golem."

"How can you tell?" Shaw asked.

"Because the golem always leaves muddy footprints, and this floor is clean."

Shaw pondered that observation, then nodded. "There were no footprints in the hallway, either. Maybe the landlady came in for some reason and forgot to close the door all the way."

"Or maybe it was an attempt to distract us." Decker was already turning back to the door, gun at the ready again. He raced into the hallway and was relieved to find Clarence and Mina still lingering unharmed near the stairs.

As he approached them, Mina stepped forward to meet him. "Nothing?"

Decker shook his head. "Other than the door being open, there's no sign of an intruder."

"This doesn't feel right," Mina said. "The house is too quiet. There are two more floors above us with guestrooms and we haven't heard a single cough, footstep, or voice since we stepped inside the building."

"I agree." Decker hadn't noticed it before, but now he

realized that for the first time since renting rooms several days before, the boardinghouse was silent.

"Maybe the guests in the rooms above us checked out," said Shaw, hopefully, although the look on his face told Decker that he didn't really believe that.

"There's only one way to find out." Decker walked past Mina and started down the stairs. "We ask the woman who rented the rooms to us."

The landlady occupied an apartment on the ground floor. The only other space, apart from a rudimentary laundry facility, was a communal dining room at the rear of the building where a meager evening meal was prepared and served by a pair of spinster sisters employed by the woman who ran the boardinghouse.

Decker checked the dining room first but found it empty. He had expected as much, since the sisters lived elsewhere and arrived in the late afternoon to begin their work.

When he returned to the lobby, Shaw was knocking on the apartment door. They waited, but received no answer. Shaw knocked again with the same result, then he reached down and tried the handle.

The door opened inward to reveal an over furnished living room with plush chairs, a threadbare sofa, and ottoman. A grandfather clock stood against a wall opposite the window. A bureau desk and banker's chair occupied another wall.

"Mrs. Krantz?" Shaw called out. "Are you in here?"

His only answer was the steady tick of the grandfather clock.

"Hello?" Shaw waited for a reply but got none. He turned to Decker. "She's not here and her door was unlocked. I don't like this."

"Me either." Decker was already heading back toward the stairs. "We should check the upper floors."

They ascended in single file, moving slowly and on high alert. They were the only occupants of the second floor, and they had already been there, so they continued on up to the third. There were six rooms, including the bathroom. They checked them one by one and found the bathroom and four of the bedrooms to be empty. The other two rooms were inaccessible, their doors locked, but they received no answer when they knocked.

Retreating along the hallway, they climbed to the fourth and final floor with the same result. In one room, they found a small table with a half-eaten meal of bread, cheese, and salami.

Decker touched the food and found the bread still soft, with only a stale crust where it was exposed to the air. The cheese was warm but still pliable.

"Like the Mary Celeste," Mina breathed with a shudder.

"There's one place we haven't looked," said Shaw, heading back into the hallway.

"The attic." Decker followed him toward the one door they hadn't yet checked at the end of the hallway.

Clarence held back. "I don't think that's a good idea. We should get out of here right now."

"We've come this far. Might as well see it through." Shaw pushed the door open to reveal a set of rough wooden steps. He pointed his gun upward as if expecting someone, or something, to appear above them. When it didn't, he started up.

"Everyone stay together," Decker said, following behind.

The stairs creaked underfoot as they climbed to the attic. Shaw was already at the top, several feet distant, when

Decker got there. He had lowered the gun, and was standing with his arms at his sides, transfixed.

At first, Decker didn't understand what had stopped the private detective in his tracks, but then, as his eyes adjusted to the gloom, he saw it.

A shaft of weak daylight lanced downward from a filthy skylight window so dirty it was amazing any light penetrated at all. And there, piled on the attic floor in a haphazard heap, were the occupants of the boardinghouse.

FIFTY-SEVEN

CLARENCE LET OUT a strangled cry of alarm. He backed up quickly toward the attic stairs, almost bumping into Mina, who sidestepped the last moment.

Decker approached the pile of corpses, instantly noticing the brutal manner in which they had been killed. Their throats were cut. Blood had pooled around them like a viscous lake. Halfway down the stack was the landlady, her head turned at an angle, dead eyes staring into the gloom. The terror etched on her face told Decker all he needed to know about what those eyes had witnessed in their last moments.

"This doesn't look like the work of a golem," Shaw said. "What could have done this?"

Mina stepped past Shaw and observed the mutilated corpses. "Vampires."

"We have to go right now." Decker gripped Mina's arm and pulled her back toward the stairs.

Clarence needed no urging. He was already on his way down. Shaw stood there a moment longer, transfixed by the ghastly tableau in front of him, then he snapped out of his fugue and followed.

They descended the attic steps and raced back along the hallway toward the main staircase. But before they got there, a figure climbed into view and stood at the head of the stairs, facing them. A woman in a black dress with long flowing hair the color of night cascading over her shoulders. Two more figures appeared, also dressed in black. Decker recognized the closest of the three instantly. It was the woman from the docks who had tried to drag Mina from the carriage.

"We're not here to cause trouble," said the woman, stepping forward as Decker came to a halt with the rest of his group behind him. "We just want the girl. Give her to us and will let you live."

"Just like you let the occupants of this boardinghouse live?" Decker said with a sneer.

The female vampire's mouth curved up into a half smile, revealing gleaming white teeth. She dragged her tongue slowly across her lips, leaving them glistening. "Everyone has to eat."

"You're not taking Mina," Shaw said, stepping in front of her.

"I beg to differ." The vampire took another step forward. Her companions followed dutifully behind. "Make it easy on yourselves. Give her to us before you end up in the attic, along with the rest of the pathetic creatures who inhabited this hovel. It really is your only option."

"I don't think so." Shaw lunged forward.

Decker tried to grab him, realizing the futility of the private detective's actions, but it was too late. Shaw sidestepped Decker and threw himself at the woman, letting off two shots from his gun in rapid succession as he went.

The vampire made no attempt to evade his assault.

Instead, her arm shot out so fast that it was nothing but a blur. Her hand closed over Shaw's throat, bringing him to an abrupt halt. She lifted him from the floor. He sputtered and pawed at her arm, his feet treading air. Then she turned and tossed him along the hallway toward the stairs as if he weighed nothing.

Shaw crashed into the railing, splintering several spindles. His gun clattered to the floor and disappeared into the stairwell. A moment later, there was a faint thud as it landed several floors below.

The vampire wasn't done yet. In the blink of an eye, she shot forward with the other vampires at her side.

Decker realized what was happening a moment before he tumbled backwards, the air rushing from his lungs. It felt like a sledgehammer had hit him in the chest. He hit the floor hard and slid for a second before coming to rest.

To his left, he heard a pained grunt as one of the other vampires knocked Clarence from his feet.

Mina screamed.

Decker pushed himself up on his elbows in time to see her being dragged back toward the stairs, with one vampire gripping each arm. She fought furiously against them, twisting and bucking, but it was no use. They were too strong.

The female vampire stood in the middle of the hallway with a smug expression on her face as her companions took Mina. Then she advanced on Decker and Clarence, removing a silver pendant from her pocket that Decker knew would contain the amulet that played a part in letting her steal the remaining years of her victims and adding them to her own.

Then, two things happened in rapid succession.

He scrambled to his feet, desperate to evade the assault he

knew was imminent. Beside him, Clarence was scuttling backward, making small whimpering sounds.

The vampires who had Mina in their grip were almost at the stairs. Decker risked a glance beyond his own assailant. At that moment, the dynamics changed. Mina lowered her head, face contorted with rage, and caught Decker's eye. At the same time, she flung her arms wide, defying the vampires' powerful grip, and sent them crashing into the walls on each side of the hallway.

But Mina wasn't done yet.

The vampire to her left staggered forward, trying to rein her back in, at least until Mina's hand shot out and gripped his face, her fingers digging into the pallid flesh of his cheeks and jaw. The vampire to her right fared no better.

She stood for a second, arms straight out, holding the vampires against the wall. Then she tilted her head back, drew a breath, and let forth with a guttural roar loud enough to halt the female vampire's pursuit of Decker and Clarence and cause her to turn toward the commotion.

Electricity crackled in the air, a blue sparking halo that danced around Mina' head, then worked its way down over her shoulders and wound up her arms until it enveloped the stricken vampires in crackling tendrils of energy.

They jerked in unison, bodies wracked by spasms that sent their arms smacking against the walls, and heels kicking the baseboards.

The female vampire looked on, frozen to the spot in disbelief, as her companions succumbed to Mina's unexpected assault upon them. She had likely never seen anything like it across the long centuries of her life.

The dancing fingers of lightning flowed back the other way now. It twisted around the vampires one last time before weaving back along Mina's arms and coiling around her momentarily before ebbing away as if it had never been there.

For a long moment, no one moved.

Mina's head drooped. Her breath came in ragged, quick gasps. Then she dropped her arms, releasing her grip on the vampires' faces and letting them slide to the floor.

They were clearly dead, their faces withered, limbs twisted and deformed.

Mina stood like an avenging angel, unmoving. Then she lifted her head and fixed the remaining vampire with a bone-chilling stare. When she spoke, her voice had a peculiar timbre, almost as if more than one person were speaking at once. "Go. Tell the rest of your kind to stay away from me and my friends from now on or they will meet the same fate as your companions."

The female vampire glanced at the withered corpses on each side of Mina. Her face twisted into a mask of rage. "This isn't over."

Yes, it is," Mina said, taking a step toward her. "You've got one minute before you end up like them."

The female vampire lingered a second longer, then she strode toward the stairs without another word and started down, soon disappearing from sight.

Mina watched her go, then turned back toward Decker.

He saw a brief flash of energy dance behind her eyes, and then, before he could say anything, her legs gave out and Mina crumpled to the floor.

FIFTY-EIGHT

"MINA!" Decker raced forward and dropped down next to her on the floor. For a terrible second he thought that she was dead, but then she groaned, and her eyes fluttered open.

She looked up at him. "What happened?"

"You tell me," Decker replied, glancing toward the pair of corpses sprawled beside them. "You just killed two vampires."

Disbelief flashed across her face. "That's not... How could I..." She sat up, rubbing her temples with one hand. "I feel like someone is trying to hammer their way out of my skull."

"After what I just saw, I'm not surprised." Decker stood, then eased Mina to her feet.

She tottered for a moment, unsteady, then regained her balance. Her gaze shifted to the dead vampires. "I remember now."

"Have you ever done anything like that before?" Decker asked.

"Never." Mina shook her head. "I'm not even sure how I did it. When they grabbed me, tried to take me away, I got so angry. I didn't want to be abducted all over again. I could feel the anger building inside of me, rising up like a wall of blackness. Then… I stole their life force. Took the years they had left. Their memories too. I can feel it inside of me."

"How is that even possible?" Decker asked. "You need an amulet to do that."

"I know."

"And can vampires even kill other vampires?"

"I didn't think so, but Amenmosep killed those two on the Titanic. I put it down to his extreme age and power. He must have been one of the first of their kind and who knows how much they've changed and their bloodline has become diluted in the thousands of years since the last time he walked the earth. But now I'm not so sure."

"Whatever just happened was a complete surprise to that bitch who wanted to kill us," said a voice from the rear. It was Shaw, who stood rubbing his neck with a grimace. "If she wasn't aware that vampires could be killed by their own kind, I'm guessing it doesn't happen too often."

"If at all," Decker added. "I guess you've just discovered a new power."

"Great." Now it was Mina's turn to grimace. "I'll throw it on the pile, along with all the other powers I don't want."

"Hey, it just saved our hides," Shaw said. "If you hadn't done what you did, none of us—" he stopped mid-sentence as a new thought dawned on him. "You don't look surprised that I know what you are."

"John already told me that Thomas confided in you years ago while you were still in the Order of St. George."

"You're not angry?" Shaw took a step back.

"I wasn't happy about it at first, but I'm fine now."

"Glad to hear it." Now it was Shaw's turn to glance at the

vampire corpses. "Because I really don't want to get on your bad side right now."

Clarence had picked himself up. "Um, don't you think we should leave before that woman comes back with reinforcements?"

"I don't think she's coming back anytime soon," Decker said. He had witnessed something on the woman's face he had never seen in his previous encounters with the vampires. Fear. Mina had swiftly gone from a curiosity to be hunted and absorbed into the vampire collective for her unique abilities to something else. An apex predator. Still, Clarence made a good point. Their accommodation had become a charnel house and they had enough to deal with, without trying to explain how the residents of an entire building ended up slaughtered.

Shaw had come to the same conclusion. "Regardless of whether that woman comes back, we can't stay here. There will be too many questions. We need to collect the rest of our belongings and get as far away from this place as possible."

"And go where?" Mina asked.

"My place. Like I said before, there's an empty apartment on the floor above mine. You don't need to be in the Village anymore and it's about as safe as we're likely to get. I'll take you there and make the arrangements, then go and see Detective McCullough to get that address."

"Right." Decker turned to Mina. "Are you feeling okay?"

"A little shaky, and I still have a headache, but it's passing. I'll be fine."

"Good." Decker started toward the stairs. "Let's grab our stuff and make it quick. I'm sure some of the residents who live in this building were not at home when the vampires went on their killing spree, and I'd rather not be around when they find the bodies."

"This unexpected diversion aside, the golem is still out there and looking for his next victim," Shaw said, waiting for Mina and Clarence to follow Decker, then dropping into a position at their rear. "The quicker we find Wallace Alden's girlfriend, the sooner we'll get some answers and put an end to this madness. I don't know about the rest of you, but I've had just about enough of people trying to kill me for one week."

FIFTY-NINE

IT TOOK LESS than fifteen minutes to rent the apartment above Shaw's. While they settled in, the Irishman took his leave and went in search of Detective McCullough.

The accommodation was small but serviceable, and best of all, it came furnished. There were two bedrooms, neither of which was big enough for more than one twin bed pushed up against the wall and a nightstand. Between these was a small bathroom. A kitchen/living room combination furnished with nothing except a ripped sofa and two mismatched chairs completed the floor plan.

Mina took the bedroom closest to the door, while Clarence got the other one. Decker would sleep on the couch, uncomfortable as it looked, and he was happy to do so. Not only did it allow him to protect Clarence Rothman, but he could keep an eye on Mina lest the vampires try to reach into her mind again and manipulate her into revealing their new location. He didn't think that was likely, though. Her actions back at the boardinghouse would no doubt give them pause for thought. As creatures at the top of the food chain, they were not used to people fighting back and winning.

Still, there was another reason he wanted to keep a watchful eye on her. It appeared that she had absorbed the life force of the two vampires that had tried to abduct her. That meant she would not only extend her own life by the combined years both vampires had accumulated, but would also incorporate their memories, and those of their victims, into her own psyche. Neither of them could predict how that would affect her in the short term, and the last thing he needed was Mina going off the rails.

He had hoped she would want to talk about it after they settled in, but Mina retreated into her bedroom, saying she needed to lie down and closed the door. Instead, it was Clarence who eventually appeared with a puzzled look on his face.

"Can we talk about what happened earlier?" he asked, approaching Decker and settling into one of the chairs. "Were those people back at the boardinghouse really vampires?"

Decker was sitting on the sofa with his head resting against the wall and his eyes closed. He opened them and looked at Clarence. "Yes, they were. Or at least the closest thing to vampires that there is in the real world."

"They killed all those people." Clarence looked sick to his stomach. "Just cut their throats and piled them up in that attic like they were nothing. Why would they do that? I thought vampires used their teeth, not knives."

"Not these vampires," Decker replied wearily. "They don't have fangs, have no aversion to sunlight, although they prefer the darkness, and I'm pretty sure that sharpened stakes won't have much effect beyond annoying them. Maybe they aren't vampires in the true sense of the word, but it doesn't alter the fact that they are ruthless and deadly."

"And Mina is one of them?" Clarence asked, glancing toward the closed bedroom door.

"Not entirely. She's something in between."

Clarence thought about this for a while. "Is she safe to be around?"

Decker's first instinct was to reply in the affirmative. Mina had never posed a threat despite her unique physiology. But that was before she eviscerated two vampires with the same ease that he might squash a cockroach underfoot. In the end, Decker just said, "I think so."

Clarence leaned back in the chair with a sigh. "I liked my life better when I thought the supernatural was just a fun diversion after a night of drinking. I don't care if I never see that occult library in the bowels of Rathmore ever again. I'm not even sure if I still want to be in the Servants of Cratus. I guess it's true what they say. Ignorance is bliss."

"I can't argue with you there," Decker said. Sometimes he missed the life he had before his encounter with Annie Doucet in Wolf Haven. It had been simple. Uncomplicated. But on the other hand, he might never have reignited his relationship with Nancy if it wasn't for those terrible events, and that was worth more to him than anything. Decker felt his throat tighten. He tried to push the thoughts of Nancy from his mind but failed. Luckily, Shaw returned at that moment and provided a welcome distraction.

Decker jumped to his feet. "Did you get it?"

Shaw held up a page that looked like it had been torn from a notepad. "Elise Felder. Lives with her brother and his wife in the Lower East Side on Orchard Street."

"Good job. Did the detective ask why you wanted her address?"

"Naturally." Shaw tucked the page back into his pocket.

"What did you tell him?"

"That we wished to express our condolences for the loss of her boyfriend."

"And he believed that?"

"I can't imagine. But the man wasn't really in a position to pry since he lined his pocket with our money at the wine vault. I'm sure the police commissioner would be none too pleased if he found out that one of his officers was taking bribes." Shaw chuckled. "Besides, he was more interested in the five dollars I slipped him for the address than knowing why we wanted it. Speaking of which, how do you think we should approach this?"

"Carefully. If we're correct, the woman has a golem stashed somewhere and I would rather not run into it again until we're ready," Decker said. He turned to Clarence. "You met Elise Felder at your party in the wine vaults, correct?"

"Yes. I danced with her right before the body was discovered."

"That will be our reason for the visit. You will claim to have dropped by to see how she's doing since the murder. Pretend to be concerned for her welfare. Offer your condolences."

"Me?" Clarence shook his head. "If she's the killer, I don't want to go anywhere near that woman. What if she sets the golem on me?"

"She won't. Not in her own home with her brother and sister-in-law nearby," Decker said.

"Are you sure about that?"

"Sure as I can be."

"That's hardly comforting. And how is offering my condolences going to help us find out if she killed Wallace and the others?"

"Because while you keep her talking, I'll take a look around. If she took the book, it must be there somewhere."

"And the golem, too."

"Perhaps."

"When do you want to do this?" Clarence asked.

"No time like the present." Decker replied.

Shaw glanced around. "Where's Mina?"

"Sleeping, and I think we should leave it like that. She's been through enough for one day."

"Someone should stay behind, then. Keep an eye on her." Shaw glanced toward the closed bedroom door. "What do you think?"

Before Decker could answer, the bedroom door flung open, and Mina appeared.

"Not a chance," she said, striding into the room. She looked nothing like she had two hours before when she retreated into the bedroom. The color had returned to her face, and her eyes were bright and clear. She stepped past Decker toward the apartment door. "I'm perfectly fine. Let's go."

SIXTY

THEY ARRIVED at the Orchard Street address provided by Detective McCullough a little after six in the evening. It turned out to be a narrow six-story red brick tenement with a men's clothing shop on the ground floor. A fire escape snaked down the front of the building like an iron skeleton, stopping short of the ground-floor above the store's awning. As they approached the building, Decker glanced at the clothing in the windows. Suit jackets on wooden manikins stood behind a display of pressed and folded shirts, trousers, and waistcoats. A sign hanging in one window offered 'low factory pricing' while another read 'shirts and pants tailored while you wait'.

"Elise lives on the second floor above the shop," Shaw said, heading for a door to the right of the store. Behind it was a set of narrow stairs that led to the upper floors.

They made their way up to a dimly lit hallway with two doors on each side and another open door at the end that appeared to be a bathroom. A faint odor of mildew hung in the air. The carpet beneath their feet was worn through in places with nothing left but the backing threads. The walls were grimy, and Decker noticed a couple of sooty, child-sized handprints.

Clarence wrinkled his nose. "This place is awful. I can't believe people live like this. It's abominable."

"You've never been in a tenement before?" Shaw asked.

"Heavens, no. And after this, I hope never to step foot in one again."

"Spoken like a truly caring human being." Shaw took the slip of paper from his pocket and double-checked the address, squinting to make it out in the weak light, before going to the closest door. He motioned for Clarence to join him. "Come on, then. Make yourself useful and get us in the door."

Clarence raised his hand to knock, then hesitated, as if loath to touch the door.

"Oh, for heaven's sake." Shaw closed his hand into a fist and banged twice on the door, then stepped back.

"Who is it?" said a gruff male voice from the other side.

Clarence cleared his throat and introduced himself.

"If you're a rent collector, you'll be disappointed. I told the last one, business is slow, I won't have the money until next week."

"I'm not here to collect rent," Clarence said. "I'm looking for a friend. Elise Felder."

There was a brief silence, followed by the sound of a latch being drawn back. The door opened to reveal a clean-shaven man in his mid-thirties with short, dark hair combed back slick over his head. He observed the four strangers standing before him with obvious distrust. "Elise is my sister. What do you want with her?"

Clarence shifted his weight from one foot to the other. "Like I said before, she's a friend."

"And who are these people?" The man asked, his gaze drifting from Decker to Shaw, and finally settling on Mina before snapping back to Clarence. "More friends?"

"They are associates of mine," Clarence replied, his voice cracking.

Decker sensed he was about to get the door slammed in his face. He stepped forward and intervened. "We were passing through the neighborhood and Clarence asked if we minded stopping so he could pay a brief visit to Elise. I understand she suffered a loss recently."

"I wouldn't know anything about that," the man replied. "Elise keeps her private life to herself. Has done ever since... you know what? That isn't relevant. So long as she does her work and stays out of trouble, she can do as she pleases as far as I'm concerned."

"Elise works for you?"

"Needs to earn her keep somehow," said the man.

"Where is she now?" Decker asked, shifting position to get a better view of the apartment beyond the door. It was small, but tidy. He saw a wood table with four chairs, and a sitting room with a sofa, and side tables beyond. An archway led into a kitchen with a coal-burning stove.

"She's down in the sewing room behind the shop."

"You own the business on the floor below?" Mina asked.

The man nodded. "My wife and I inherited it last year after her father passed away, though we've been running it for several years. He was not in good health."

"You mind if we go down there?" Decker asked.

"Suit yourselves." Elise's brother shrugged. He jerked his thumb toward one of the other doors. "You can take the back staircase."

"Thank you."

The man grunted an acknowledgment and stepped back into the apartment, closing the door on them.

Shaw was already leading the way to the stairs. They descended through a narrow stairwell with bare lath walls to find another door at the bottom. It was standing open, and Decker saw bolts of fabric piled on shelving constructed from rough wood. Beyond this, he heard the steady clack of a sewing machine.

The room was cramped and packed with all the sewing supplies needed to make the wares on display in the tailor's shop at the front. A slim woman with shoulder-length blonde hair was crouched over a desk at the back of the space feeding fabric through the sewing machine. Elise Felder. She didn't notice them, but when Decker cleared his throat, she looked up, her eyes widening with surprise.

"Clarence?" She pushed her chair back and stood. "What are you doing here, and who are these people?"

Decker stepped forward and introduced himself, then did the same for Shaw and Mina.

"I came to see how you've been coping," Clarence said. "You know, since Wallace…"

"Yes, I know." Elise bowed her head. "Not so well."

"We were hoping you might answer a few questions," Decker said, getting straight to the point.

"What kind of questions?" Elise glanced from Decker to Clarence. "What's going on?"

"About your relationship with Wallace Alden," Decker replied. "I understand he took you on a trip several days before he died."

"I wanted to see where he went to college. He was always talking about it. He offered to take me, and I said yes." Elise shook her head. She motioned toward the bolts of fabric stacked almost to the ceiling. "As you can imagine, my life isn't exactly a bed of roses. I wasn't about to turn down a weekend away. I don't see what this has to do with anything."

"I'm not trying to be insensitive," Decker said. "Three men are dead, including your boyfriend, and I want to know—"

Clarence stepped in front of Decker, interrupting him. He was staring at a heart-shaped silver locket with an intricate filigree design hanging around Elise's neck on a slim chain. "Where did you get that?"

Elise raised her hand and touched the locket. "This? I don't know. I've had it for years."

"Can I see it?" Clarence moved closer still. He couldn't take his eyes off the piece of jewelry.

"I don't think so." Elise took a step back. Her eyes flew wide again, but now Decker saw something other than surprise in them. He saw fear.

"Clarence, what are you doing?" Mina asked. "Why are you so concerned with that locket?"

"Because I've seen it before. Years ago, back when I was in college."

"What are you talking about?" Elise said, a slight tremor in her voice.

"Francis Kingsley." Clarence almost spat the words.

"Who?" Elise recovered quickly, but Decker saw a flash of recognition on her face.

"You know who." Clarence stalked toward her. "Francis purchased that locket for his fiancée before he went to Europe for the summer the year he died. He wanted her to have something to remember him by until he came back. I know, because I was with him when he bought it."

"This is ridiculous." Elise had backed up about as far as she could go and now stood with her legs pressed against the sewing machine table. "There must be thousands of lockets around like this. You've made a mistake, that's all."

"I don't think so. Not exactly like that one."

"Clarence, you sound crazy."

"But I'm not. You've dyed your hair blonde, and you've aged, of course, but it was you who came to the halls of residence that day after Francis died. You took his journal and a stack of love letters."

"I swear, I have no idea what you're talking about." Elise glanced around, frantic, as if looking for a way to escape.

"Then prove it and give me the locket." Clarence lunged forward with lightning speed and swiped at the jewelry around Elise's neck before she had time to react. His fingers closed over the locket. There was a moment of resistance, then the chain broke.

Clarence let out a small cry of victory and retreated. He held the locket up for all to see and pried it open with a fingernail to reveal a tiny black-and-white photo within of a young man with dark combed-back hair and a thin, angular face. "I knew it. That's Francis."

Elise stood transfixed for a moment, her face a picture of anguish. Then, in a flash, she turned and fled toward a narrow door tucked away at the back of the sewing room. She tugged at the handle, flung it open, and disappeared into the gloom beyond.

SIXTY-ONE

FOR A SPLIT SECOND, Decker was caught off guard, then he raced after her, arriving at the door in time to see Elise descending a set of rickety wooden steps into a basement underneath the building.

He sensed Shaw at his rear.

Clarence and Mina were not far behind.

"Stay up here with Clarence," Decker said to her quickly, glancing over his shoulder. He pulled the gun from beneath his jacket and started down, taking the steps as fast as he dared. They groaned and trembled under his feet and, more than once, Decker thought it would give way and send him crashing onto the floor below. But thankfully, the stairs held, even with Shaw right behind him.

He reached the bottom and looked around quickly, half expecting to see Elise come screeching out of the darkness waving an ax or some other sharp implement, but then his eyes grew accustomed to the gloom, and he saw her standing on the other side of the underground chamber illuminated by a shaft of light that angled in through narrow hopper windows caked with grime set into the wall to his left near the ceiling.

Elise wasn't trying to run anymore. She stood with her feet spread slightly apart and a defiant look on her face. She was holding an old leather-bound book that Decker assumed to be the one stolen from the occult library maintained by the Servants of Cratus. It was opened to a page somewhere in the middle.

Decker lifted his gun. "Elise, put the book down and step away from it."

"That isn't going to happen," she replied, glancing briefly down at the open book.

Decker took a step forward. "No one's going to hurt you, but we need that book."

"Don't come any closer," Elise said.

Her gaze drifted toward the floor, and Decker noticed a large mound of dirt sitting near her feet. At first he was unsure what he was looking at, but then realization dawned. At the same moment, Elise lowered her head and spoke quickly in a language he didn't understand. The words were almost lyrical. They tripped off her tongue so fast that by the time Decker's finger curled on the trigger of his gun, it was too late.

The mound of earth undulated and rippled as if something deep inside it were alive. The dirt rose up, spiraling into the air and coalesced into the rough shape of a man.

"We need to get out of here," Decker said, retreating toward the stairs while keeping his gun trained on Elise. He briefly considered shooting her but realized it would do no good. "She's summoning the golem."

"You don't need to tell me twice," Shaw said. He turned toward the steps leading up to the cellar but came to an abrupt halt.

Mina and Clarence were already making their way tentatively down. Standing in the doorway above them, a rifle angled down at their backs, was Elise Felder's brother.

Decker turned back to her, eyes flashing in anger. "Why are you doing this?"

"Ask him," Elise said, nodding toward Clarence Rothman, who had reached the bottom of the cellar stairs with Mina right behind.

Decker risked a quick glance toward them. "What's she talking about?"

"I don't know. I swear." Clarence was staring at the creature standing next to Elise. It was fully formed now, towering almost seven feet high.

The golem took a step toward Clarence.

"Not yet," Elise said, closing the book. "Wait until I'm done with them."

The golem froze.

Elise turned her attention back to Clarence. "You know exactly why I'm doing this."

"I don't." Clarence said the words so quickly that they tumbled into each other. His voice cracked. "Decker. For the love of God. Shoot her before she sets that thing loose on me."

"I wouldn't do that if I were you," Elise replied with a thin smile. "I'm the only thing holding this creature back from ripping Clarence limb from limb right now. And don't forget, my brother is at the top of the stairs with a rifle. He'll drop the rest of you before I even hit the ground."

"Are you going to tell us why you're doing this or not?" Decker asked, hoping to stall long enough to think of a plan. "Because three innocent people are dead, thanks to you."

"Innocent?" Elise laughed, the sound hollow and chilling. "None of those men were innocent. They're the reason why the love of my life is dead." A tear pushed at the corner of her eye. She wiped it away with the back of one hand. "We were engaged to be married, Francis and me. We were in love. Then he was ripped away from me."

"You didn't love him," Clarence said. "You cheated on him. The whole time he was in Europe, you were seeing another man."

"That's not true."

"Yes, it is. He came home early from Europe because he couldn't bear to be parted with you. He went to your parents' deli and saw the two of you together holding hands. He told us everything."

"I know what he thought. I read it all in that journal you gave me when I came to his room." The tears were flowing freely down Elise's cheeks now. "But it wasn't true. I wasn't seeing another man. He was my cousin, and he was going through a rough time. His parents had died. Typhoid. I was comforting him."

"What?" Clarence looked shocked.

"Francis didn't even bother to tell me he was back. Didn't talk to me about it. If he had, none of this would've happened." Elise held the book up. "Instead, he made a golem to exact revenge for a transgression that never took place. And all of you helped him. Encouraged him."

Clarence shook his head. "We never thought it would work. I swear. We thought it was just a way for him to work through his anger. I mean, come on. A golem? How can that even be real?"

"You didn't know what you were meddling with. The golem turned on him. Killed him. You have blood on your hands, every last one of you."

Finally, Decker understood the whole tragic affair. He took a step forward. "Clarence and his friends aren't responsible for your fiancé's death. Francis brought it all upon himself when he gave the golem its instructions. He told it to make sure your suitor would never come near you again. But there was no other suitor. Only him. The golem is a blunt instrument, incapable of thinking for itself. It follows instructions blindly."

"Which is exactly what it did," Shaw said. "When Francis and his friends made the golem in the woods that fateful night, they believed the incantation had failed because nothing happened. But it hadn't. After they left, the golem came to life and tracked Francis down in his room at the college. It did exactly as it was told and made sure he could never come near you again. It killed him."

"Then, it's task finished, the golem returned to its inanimate state," Decker said. "That's why there was a pile of mud on the floor in his room." He looked at Elise. "What I don't understand is how you knew about the golem."

Elise was shaking. "The journal. He wrote everything in the journal. The last pages were nothing but a scribbled rant about how he was going to exact his revenge using the book in that library underneath the college. My family is Jewish. We know all about the legend of the golem. I decided right there to get my own revenge on the men who took him from me using the same creature. Somehow it felt... poetic."

"Then why did you wait so long?" Decker asked.

"Because I didn't have the book. It was hidden away in that stupid library. I tried to get in there several times over the years but failed. When I had to move from Connecticut to help my brother and his wife with the tailor shop, I almost gave up hope of ever having an opportunity to avenge my darling Francis. Then I crossed paths with Wallace Alden, and I saw my chance. I knew exactly who he was, but he didn't recognize me. And why would he? We only met once when you were all cleaning out that room after Francis died. Just to be sure, I dyed my hair blonde and made myself a wardrobe appropriate for his social circle. Then I orchestrated a chance meeting at a coffee shop he frequents. After that, it was easy. All I needed to do was flirt a little and convince him to show me where he went to college. He told me all about that ridiculous secret society he was in one night when he was drunk. I knew he'd want to pay them a visit again while we were there. It only took getting him drunk a second time to get the sequence that opened that door. Then, while he was passed out, I went down there and took the book. After that, everything I needed was in place to put things right."

"You became a murderer," Decker said.

"I became an avenging angel." Elise moved to an old cabinet standing against the cellar wall. She opened it with a flourish to reveal what looked like three limp and bloody rags hanging from nails. Except they weren't rags. She looked back at Clarence. "Would you like to say hello to your friends one last time?"

The color drained from Clarence Rothman's face. "Is that…"

"Justice?" Elise stepped away from the cabinet. She motioned toward the guns Decker and Shaw were holding. "I'm walking out of here now, and you're not going to stop me."

"I wouldn't count on that," Decker said, trying not to look at the grisly display in the cabinet.

"You make one move toward my sister, and I'll put a bullet in each of your heads, starting with the girl," said the man at the top of the stairs.

"I understand why Elise wants revenge," Decker said, looking up at the man. "But why are you willing to commit murder?"

"Simple. If Elise had married Francis, our family would be living the good life now instead of mucking by, working our fingers to the bone just to survive. You and your friends ruined all our lives. Now put the guns on the floor and kick them away."

They were in a no-win situation. Elise and her brother had the upper hand. He possessed the high ground, and they would never be able to take him out before he shot one or more of them. And even if Mina could survive a bullet, being part vampire, he and Shaw could not. What's more, the golem would likely attack regardless, and they couldn't protect Clarence if they were dead.

Decker exchanged a glance with Shaw and knew that the private detective was thinking the same thing. Reluctantly, they laid their guns on the ground and kicked them away.

"That's better." Elise stepped around Decker and started up the stairs, still carrying the book. At the top, she turned and looked down at the golem. "Kill them all."

SIXTY-TWO

THE DOOR at the top of the cellar stairs slammed shut, followed by the sound of a bolt being drawn.

They were locked in.

"This is bad," Shaw said, scrabbling to find his gun in the gloomy half-light.

"Decker, the golem," Mina said, pointing.

The creature, which had stood like a statue throughout the exchange with Elise, now took a step toward them.

"I see it." Decker looked around for his own gun but couldn't find it in the darkness. And there was no time to hunt for it.

"Get out of the way," Shaw said, waving for the others to step back and give him a clear shot at the creature. When they did, he fired three shots in quick succession, each bullet slamming into the golem's chest. A tightly packed cluster of shots that would have put any mortal man on the ground. But the bullets simply passed through the golem as if it wasn't even there and slammed into the brickwork at the back of the cellar.

"It's pointless," Decker said, hustling Clarence and Mina back toward the stairs even though he knew the door above was locked.

"We can't get out that way." Shaw looked around frantically, his eyes finally settling on the narrow windows near the ceiling. "Maybe we can get through one of those."

"Not a chance. Even if we could reach the windows, they aren't wide enough for us to climb through," said Decker, backing away as the golem took another ponderous step forward. He ushered Clarence and Mina sideways toward Shaw, realizing that the stairs were a trap. Narrow and steep, they would become a bottleneck with no escape if the door at the top of the stairs couldn't be opened.

"We can't just keep circling around and trying to stay out of reach," Shaw said. "At some point, this creature is going to get fed up toying with us and attack."

"There," Mina pointed toward the back wall near the open cabinet and its macabre contents. "It looks like the brickwork has been punched out."

Decker turned to look at where Mina was pointing and saw what she meant. It was barely perceptible in the darkness beyond the faint light filtering in from the windows, but there was a definite hole in the brickwork... And it looked big enough for them to get through.

"It's worth a try." Decker made a move toward the back wall, but then he sensed a rush of movement.

"Too late," Shaw cried out, firing two more shots as the golem launched itself toward them with surprising agility.

Clarence stumbled away in a blind panic. The back of his leg struck a steamer chest, and he lost his balance, pitching backwards. He landed heavily and grunted. Before he could scramble to his feet again, the golem kicked the steamer chest out of the way and loomed over him, ready for the kill.

"Stop." Mina barreled forward, hitting the golem's midsection. She wrapped her arms around it and drove the creature back even as it reached down and wrapped her in its thick arms.

She gasped as the air rushed from her lungs.

"Mina!" Decker saw a plank of wood leaning against the wall under the window. He grabbed the makeshift weapon and swung it in a wide arc toward the creature's head. But before he could land a blow, the golem released Mina with one arm, still holding her with the other, and swiped him away.

Decker went airborne for a split second before landing on the rough dirt floor and rolling. The board clattered harmlessly to the ground.

Now it was Shaw's turn. He leaped toward it, scooping the plank up and turning to mount a second attack even as Decker climbed to his feet.

"No." Mina's voice was ragged, breathless. "I've got this."

Decker couldn't imagine what she meant. Mina was still caught in the golem's viselike grip as it tried to crush the life from her. But then he saw the look on her face. The same look that had come over her right before she dispatched the vampires back at the boarding house.

Except this wasn't a vampire. It was a seven foot tall mound of mud in the shape of a man with no life beyond what Elise Felder had endowed it.

But that wasn't going to stop her.

Mina twisted back and forth in the creature's deadly grip, somehow making enough room to bring her arms around to her front. Then she clenched her hands into fists and punched forward, penetrating the creature's torso just below the chest and bringing her arms quickly up to cleave the creature in half. Then she spread them wide, obliterating the creature's head and scattering mud across the cellar floor.

The golem's arm fell away, releasing her, as what remained of its torso swayed a couple of times before toppling backwards and disintegrating into several large chunks of mud.

"You saved me," Clarence said, heaving himself up. "You killed the golem."

"I didn't kill it," Mina said. "We need to go right now. We don't have much time."

"She's right," said Shaw, discarding the plank. He was staring at the scattered pieces—all that was left of the golem. Somehow, incredibly, they were inching across the floor, squirming toward each other and coalescing.

Decker climbed to his feet. "It's reforming."

"How can it do that?" Clarence asked, a visible shudder running through him.

"Who cares?" Decker was already heading toward the back wall. Now that he was closer, he saw that the brickwork had been removed to create an entrance into a dark space beyond. A foul odor wafted out, causing him to gag. But it didn't matter. "This is our only way out."

"It's pitch black in there. We won't be able to see our hands in front of our faces," Shaw said, guiding Clarence toward the opening anyway.

"Here." Mina rushed to the cabinet containing the limp faces of the three dead men. A ghastly cabinet of curiosities. Nearby, hanging on a hook, was an oil lantern. She snatched it and sprinted back to the hole in the wall. "How about this?"

"Better than nothing." Decker cast a glance back toward the golem. It was almost fully formed now, the mud rising from the floor and compacting itself into a familiar human shape. Another moment, and the creature would be upon them again. "Does anyone have a match?"

"I do." Shaw produced a box of matches from his pocket. He took one out, lit it, and held it close to the wick. The lamp flared. Mina replaced the globe and adjusted the flame, then took a deep breath and stepped through the hole into the darkness beyond.

"You're next," Shaw said to Clarence, bundling him through before following behind.

Decker cast one more look around the cellar, his eyes briefly alighting on the mostly recovered golem, then he stepped over the threshold into the darkness beyond the opening, and the unknown.

SIXTY-THREE

"THIS IS A SEWER," Clarence said as soon as they stepped beyond the hole in the wall, his voice laced with disgust. "We're in a sewer."

"It's how the creature has been moving back and forth around the city," Decker said. He wrinkled his nose against the foul stench. They were standing on a narrow platform made of bricks next to what looked like a slow flowing canal. Except this man-made river wasn't built to carry boats. The water was brown with sludge and thick with clumps of all shapes and sizes that Decker didn't want to think too hard about. "Elise and her brother must've discovered the sewer running on the other side of the center wall and broke through."

"Those two are certifiable," Shaw said, taking the lead and starting off down the narrow platform, away from the opening with the lantern held high to light their way. He glanced back at Clarence, who was walking behind. "Still, you have to admire her tenacity. Seducing Wallace Alden and convincing him to show her his old alma mater."

"Then manipulating him into telling her how to access the secret chamber and get the book," Decker said. He wondered how different things would have turned out if Wallace Alden had recognized Elise for what she was. It almost certainly would have saved his life and those of his friends. She was clearly a sociopath, driven mad by the loss of her fiancé all those years ago and striking out at the only people she could find to shoulder the blame. Francis Kingsley's college buddies.

"Speaking of the book," Mina said. "She took it with her. What I did back there was only a temporary solution. We can't defeat the golem without it."

"I'm aware of that." Decker glanced back along the sewer tunnel toward the hole in the wall. The golem hadn't appeared yet, but he knew it would soon give chase. They needed to escape the sewer, and quickly. "We need to move faster. Find a way out."

"What do you think I'm trying to do?" Shaw replied from up front. "It's disgusting down here. The smell is so bad it's actually burning the back of my throat. I'm trying not to think about what I'm breathing."

"There's a ladder up ahead," Mina said. "Maybe that's our way out."

Decker looked past the group and saw what she was talking about. An iron ladder was attached to the tunnel wall about a hundred feet distant. It disappeared up into a circular shaft.

"Thank goodness for that." Shaw picked up the pace and hurried toward the ladder. Reaching it, he peered upward. "I can see what looks like a manhole cover up there, but who knows where it comes out."

"Probably in the middle of the road," Decker said. "Who wants to go up and take a look?"

"I'll do it." Shaw handed the lantern to Decker and put a foot on the bottom rung of the ladder. He started climbing. A moment later he was the top and lifting the round iron cover with obvious effort. He grunted and gave it one last heave, finally pushing the cover aside.

Decker saw a circular patch of dark sky appear.

Shaw poked his head up out of the hole, then drew it quickly back with a startled cry.

"What's going on up there?" Decker asked.

"You were right. It's in the middle of the road. A horse and cart almost took my head off." He risked a second look, lifting his head back up. Then he called back down the shaft. "It might be okay. The street isn't too busy."

"Good, because we're out of time." Decker glanced back along the tunnel and was dismayed to see the golem lumbering toward them. He prodded Clarence. "You're up next. Climb. Fast as you can."

Clarence needed no urging. He had also seen the golem. Another minute or two, and it would be upon them, and this time there wasn't enough room to fight back. He scrambled up the ladder, feet slipping on the rungs as he went.

Mina went next, barely waiting for Clarence to climb before she was following him up.

Above them, Shaw heaved himself up and out of the shaft. He vanished for a moment as he clambered out onto the road, then his face reappeared in the hold. He reached down to Clarence. "Take my hand. Quickly."

Decker was the only one left. He set the lantern on the ground, placed a foot on the ladder's bottom rung, and looked back down the tunnel one last time.

The golem was too close.

It was moving faster now, determined not to let them escape.

Decker started climbing. He pulled himself up, hand over hand until he entered the narrow shaft leading to the manhole above. Then, just when he thought he was going to make it, a powerful hand gripped his ankle and yanked him down.

Decker lost his grip on the ladder. He dropped several rungs, frantically grasping for another handhold. Finally, he found one and arrested his downward trajectory.

Above him, Mina was climbing out of the shaft. She turned and looked back down, eyes wide with fright. "Keep climbing. Fight back."

"That's what I'm trying to do," Decker said through gritted teeth. He kicked at the golem, frantic to break its grip. But it was no use. The creature had no intention of letting go. It gave another mighty tug on his ankle, and Decker felt his fingers slip from the rungs. He paddled at empty air for a second, trying to find another handhold, but this time there was none. The golem dragged him back down out of the shaft. He felt himself toppling backwards, his momentum finally breaking the golem's grip. But it was too late.

"John!" Mina screeched.

He caught a brief glimpse of her looking down through the shaft from the street above as he fell back into the sewer. Then he landed hard on the narrow platform beside the flowing river of filth. A moment later, the manhole cover slid back into place, and he was left alone with the golem.

SIXTY-FOUR

"NO. WAIT." Mina cried, jumping away as Shaw heaved the manhole cover back into place dropped it down into the opening with a dull clunk. She stared at him in disbelief. "What are you doing?"

"What do you think I'm doing?" Shaw snapped back. "Keeping you and Clarence safe."

"But John's still down there." Mina tried to lift the manhole cover. "We have to help him."

"It's too late for that. The golem has him." Shaw pulled Mina away from the manhole. "I know he's your friend, but the best thing we can do now is retreat and find another way to defeat that creature."

Mina whirled on Shaw. "I'm not leaving him down there."

"You don't have any choice." Shaw replied in a flat voice. They were in the middle of the street. Traffic passed in both directions. Horse and carriages whose drivers gave the bedraggled group strange looks as they passed. He pushed her toward the sidewalk, then turned to her. "We're about two blocks from the tailor shop. I'm going back to get that book. Stay here with Clarence and don't move until I return. And whatever you do, don't try to enter that sewer again. Chances are, John's dead already."

"He's not dead." Mina replied, with less conviction than she intended. After everything they had gone through, she desperately wanted to believe he was still alive. After all, they were so close to finding a way home.

"Mina, you have to be realistic. The golem had him in its grip."

"And you just abandoned him down there." Mina glared at Shaw. "Still, I suppose it's not the first time you've abandoned a friend."

"That's not fair." Shaw clenched his jaw. "You know why I left London. How could I stay after what happened?"

"You could at least have tried."

"We don't have time for this right now." Shaw checked to make sure his gun was still tucked inside his jacket where he'd put it when they entered the sewer. "I'm going back to get the book. Don't move from this spot until I return."

"Not a chance. I'm going with you," Mina said. "We both are."

"What?" Clarence's eyes narrowed. "We shouldn't go anywhere near that place again. Those people are insane."

"Insane or not, they have the only thing that can stop the golem."

"And you won't be able to get your hands on it alone. Not two against one," said Mina. "It's not up for discussion. I'm not some helpless woman, as you well know."

Shaw sighed. "If you want to come, I can't stop you."

"Now you're learning." Mina stepped past Shaw and started back toward the tailor shop. Her mind was still on Decker. She wanted to help him, but knew it was already too late. He hadn't made it up the ladder and out through the manhole, which meant that he had either escaped the golem and was still trapped in the sewers looking for another way out, or... Mina didn't even want to think about the alternative but knew there was no choice. John Decker might very well be dead already. The best way they could help him now was to find the book Elise Felder used to create the golem and turn it against the creature. Stop it from killing anyone else. But that would be easier said than done. Elise would never give up the book without a fight. And even if she did, there was another problem. None of them spoke Hebrew. This was looking more and more like a fool's errand, she thought, as they rounded a corner and walked the last block to the tenement building and the apartment Elise shared with her equally crazy brother.

At the entrance, Shaw brought them to a stop. "I don't want Clarence anywhere near that woman again. I'm going in there alone and this time I mean it."

"I thought the whole point of us coming was that you couldn't deal with this on your own," Mina said, taken aback.

"No. I let you come along because I could tell you wouldn't take no for an answer. And even if you stayed behind with Clarence, I'd be worried the whole time, in case you went back down into the sewer looking for John Decker. Besides, I need someone out here. If Elise and her brother see me coming and try to run, we need to stop them."

"Fine. I'll stay here with Clarence." Mina folded her arms and watched silently as Shaw approached the building, stepped inside, and started up to the second floor.

Clarence glanced around nervously, as if he expected Elise and her brother to appear at any moment. Or perhaps he was worried that the golem had backtracked and was even now close at hand, ready to finish what he had started.

But when the door to the tenement building opened ten

minutes later, it wasn't some monster dredged from the darkest corners of hell that came through. It was Shaw.

"No luck?" Mina asked.

He shook his head as he approached them. "The apartment was empty. So was the sewing room and tailor shop. They're gone and they must have taken the book with them."

"And the cellar?" Mina asked, hoping that Decker might have made his way back there.

"I unlocked the door and took a quick peek down there. That was empty, too. No sign of John or the golem."

Mina's heart sank. "What are we going to do now?"

"We get Clarence back to my place, where he might be safe. After that, I have no idea."

SIXTY-FIVE

DECKER ROLLED SIDEWAYS AS the golem slammed its fist into the sewer platform inches from his head. He saw the lantern he had set down before starting to climb the ladder and reached for it, snatching it up seconds before the golem made a second attempt to crush his head.

Scrambling back, he swung the lantern at the creature before it could land a third blow. The flame within flickered, and for a moment Decker thought it would go out, but then it flared back up even as the golem flinched back.

Wary of fire, Decker thought as he took the opportunity to scramble to his feet. *That's good to know.* Although he didn't think the puny flame inside the lantern would help him much. Which was why he turned before the golem could regain its composure and fled along the sewer tunnel. When he looked back, the golem was already giving chase, lumbering along behind him at a surprisingly fast pace, given its bulk.

He was outrunning it, but not by much. And as his legs grew tired, he would be forced to slow down. Worse, the narrow platform upon which he ran was wet and slippery. More than once, he lost his footing and almost tumbled into the foul river of raw sewage flowing to his right.

There was a cross tunnel up ahead. Decker figured he could take the corner faster than his much heavier pursuer. He forced a spurt of speed and reached the tunnel, barely slowing down as he took the corner. His feet slipped from under him and once again Decker felt himself losing his battle with the slimy bricks that made up the platform beneath his feet. He reached out and placed a hand against the side wall, which was enough to steady him. And now he saw something that made him almost cry out with joy.

The tunnel ended several hundred feet ahead. But it wasn't a dead end. Not entirely. There was an iron grill blocking his path. Beyond that, he saw a dim glimmer of faraway lights beneath the dying embers of a glorious sunset that still tinged the sky a fiery red. There was something else, too. A faint briny smell that told Decker he was close to a large body of saltwater. Most likely the East River. That made sense since the sewer system discharged into the tidal estuary. Even in the twenty-first-century, sewage often overflowed into the local waterways. Billions of gallons of untreated water. He always hated how dirty the rivers were when he lived in New York. Now, for the first time, he was glad for the discharge tunnel. It provided him with an escape route.

But he didn't have long.

Decker glanced over his shoulder. The tunnel behind him was empty. For a moment he wondered if the golem had given up, but then it came into view at the intersection between the tunnels.

Decker flattened himself against the wall, covering the lantern's globe with the palm of his hand and merging into the darkness.

The golem came to a halt. It looked left and right, as if trying to decide which way Decker had gone. Then it started off again, turning in the other direction.

Decker held his breath, watched the creature step down into the filthy sewer water and wade through it to the other side of the cross tunnel. But then, just when he thought it would keep going in the wrong direction, the golem stopped again. It stood in the water, ignoring the brown sludge that flowed around it, and lifted its head.

Then it sniffed the air.

Decker's blood ran cold. Incredibly, even though the creature was made of nothing but mud, it was doing more than just giving chase. It was *tracking him.*

The golem sniffed the air one more time, as if picking out Decker's scent from the foul odors given off by the raw sewage it was standing in, then it turned and looked straight at him.

Decker didn't wait to see more. He dropped his hand from the lantern and fled toward the grill, praying there would be a way through. Because if there wasn't, he would be trapped. Then, as he drew close, his prayers were answered.

There was an iron access gate set into the bars.

Decker willed himself to move faster despite the treacherous conditions underfoot. More than once, he slipped, almost falling, but each time he was able to save himself and keep going. He was spurred on by hope. Maybe he would survive this ordeal after all.

But when he drew close to the gate, his heart fell. It was secured by a rusty padlock that didn't look like it had been opened in years. He reached through the bars and grabbed it, gave it a hard tug, then another. The lock didn't budge. He gripped the bars of the gate and pushed, hoping the latch was rusty enough to snap. It held firm.

Decker swore.

He glanced to his right where sewage flowed freely out into the river. Here the grill descended beneath the water, although he had no idea if it went all the way to the bottom of the tunnel.

If he couldn't open the gate, this might be the only way out, but the bars were not wide enough to slip through. That meant he would have to dive into the effluent and hope there was a gap beneath the water line big enough for him to squeeze through. He didn't relish that thought. Which was why he turned back to the lock and gave it another hard tug. Flakes of rust crumbled on his fingers, but the shackle held solid.

He glanced over his shoulder again. The golem was halfway along the tunnel, but obviously having as much problem staying upright on the slippery brick pathway as Decker had. It was moving slower than before, taking careful steps, but that would only buy Decker a few extra seconds. Half a minute at the most.

He looked around for anything that might help him break the lock, but he saw nothing. He didn't even have his gun, which he'd lost back in the cellar. But he had the lantern. Not perfect, but it was better than nothing.

Decker slipped the lantern through the bars and brought it down as hard as he could on the body of the padlock.

The lantern's flame flickered and went out, but the padlock remained stubbornly closed. He lifted the light again, aware that if he failed this time, it would be over. He could practically feel the golem advancing on him.

He brought it down, delivering a perfect blow to the body of the padlock right next to the shackle.

At first, he thought the lock had held yet again, but when he snaked an arm through and tugged, the entire body of the padlock came away in his hand, leaving the shackle orphaned and hanging loose.

Decker breathed a sigh of relief, quickly discarding the shattered padlock body and slipping the shackle from the latch holding the gate closed, then he opened it and slipped through, closing the gate quickly behind him.

And in the nick of time.

The golem was less than twenty feet away and closing fast.

Decker looked around and saw that he was standing on a narrow gravel path next to the sewer discharge. On one side was a high wall and on the other, the fast-flowing East River. He recognized it because of a towering structure that loomed over him, spanning the waterway. He recognized it instantly. The Williamsburg Bridge. The lights he had seen twinkling beyond the grill while he was still in the tunnel had come from Brooklyn, sitting across the river. Not only had he escaped the sewer system, but he knew exactly where he was. But none of that would matter if he couldn't slow the golem down.

Decker scanned the ground around him for something to secure the gate but found nothing useful. Then his eyes fell on the lantern handle—a loop of thick wire secured by an eyelet on each side of the lantern's frame.

It just might work.

Decker took hold of the wire, twisting and working back and forth to free it from the body of the lantern. At first the handle didn't give, but then the metal snapped on one side. It only took him a moment to work it free on the other. He discarded the body of the lantern and slammed the hasp over the latch on the gate, then slipped the thick wire handle down through and bent it back upon itself, pulling tight and twisting it underneath and back through a second time.

When he looked up, the golem was right there, mere inches from his face. He stared into the dead countenance, noting the crude holes where eyes should have been, and the word scrawled across the creature's forehead. Emet.

For a moment, he couldn't tear his gaze away. They stood looking at each other. Deadly foes separated by nothing more than a piece of rusting iron grillwork. Then the golem raised a heavy fist and brought it down on the gate, causing it to shudder in its frame.

That was enough to break the spell. Decker turned on his heel, then raced away from the sewer grill as fast as his legs would carry him. He followed the gravel path until it ended at a set of steps leading to the city above and started climbing. While behind him came a heavy thud, then another. It wouldn't take long for the golem to escape its temporary prison. By that time, Decker intended to be far away.

SIXTY-SIX

MINA REMAINED silent on the trip back to Shaw's apartment. They rode in a carriage the private detective had flagged down. She kept her head bowed for the entire journey, staring at the floor between her feet. No matter how much she dwelled on it, Mina couldn't think of a way Decker could have survived the golem. She had witnessed the creature drag him back into the sewer. Then Shaw had sealed Decker's fate by replacing the manhole cover and cutting off his only viable escape route.

She fought a simmering rage that bubbled within her and for a moment Mina actually sympathized with Elise Felder. Losing someone you loved hurt. It stung more than anything she had experienced before. Cutting Thomas Finch out of her life, at least romantically, had been hard. Watching him find solace in the arms of another was worse. Walking away from her daughter had left a psychological wound she feared would never heal. But she accepted these things because she understood it was the only way to protect her loved ones from the forces that swirled around her. It was harder to justify what had just happened. She should never have let Shaw replace that manhole cover. She should have gone back down and fought the golem. At least tried to save Decker. But instead, she walked away. And then she realized. Her anger wasn't just directed toward Shaw, but also inward. She was as much to blame as him.

One day, over a hundred years from now, she would face Nancy. And what would she say? That Decker suffered a needless death because she was protecting the person they thought would get them home instead of standing at his side? Her pit of despair grew deeper. She didn't even notice when the carriage pulled up and came to a stop.

"Hey. We're here." Shaw put a hand on her knee.

Mina brushed the hand away and pulled the carriage door open, stepping out and waiting silently for Clarence and Shaw to join her.

As they approached the steps leading to Shaw's building, he spoke again. "Stewing over what happened isn't going to help anything."

"I'm not stewing," Mina replied, climbing the steps toward the front door. "I'm angry."

"I can see that." Shaw held the door open and let her step inside. He waited for Clarence to follow, then brought up the rear.

Before Shaw could say anything else, a door opened to the right of the stairs and a man with tattoos on both arms and greasy, slicked back hair emerged. There was an envelope in his hand. He stomped toward them with a scowl. "There was someone here looking for you earlier. Said his name was Jacob."

"What did he want?" Shaw asked.

"Beats me. I've told you before, I'm not your damn message service." The man thrust the envelope toward

Shaw. "Not that you ever listen. He told me to give you this."

Shaw took the envelope. "Thanks, Joe. I owe you one."

"You owe me a bushel." Joe turned and strode back into his apartment, slamming the door.

"Who's Jacob?" Clarence asked, peering over Shaw's shoulder at the envelope.

"Isn't he the bookstore owner?" Mina said. "The one you went to see with John?"

"Yes." Shaw ripped the top of the envelope open and took out a folded sheet of writing paper. He unfolded it and read the message, then handed it to Mina. "Looks like things aren't as hopeless as they seemed."

Mina took the sheet and looked down. The note was written in spidery handwriting, and it took her a moment to realize what it said.

Nicholas,

I have what you asked me about. Found it in an old manuscript in my personal collection. I've translated the relevant passages. Didn't want to leave it with your neighbor. He looked unsavory. Come to the store.

Your friend

Jacob

Mina folded the letter and gave it back to Shaw. "Does this mean what I think it does? He found an incantation to stop the golem?"

"That would appear to be the case." Shaw slipped the letter into his pocket. "But we won't know for sure until I go to the bookstore."

"We should all go," Mina said. "The next time I see that golem, I want it to be the last."

Shaw shook his head. "No. I'll go alone. It would be best for Clarence to stay out of sight. Not only is the golem still on the loose, but Elise and her brother are out there somewhere. It's not safe."

"It's no less safe than sitting around here and waiting."

"This isn't up for discussion. I'm going by myself. I can be there and back in an hour."

"No." Mina had already lost Decker thanks to Shaw's dubious decision to abandon him in the sewers. She didn't trust his judgment anymore. "Splitting up is a mistake."

"Then it's my mistake to make." Shaw was already walking back toward the door. "Take Clarence up to the apartment, lock yourselves inside, and don't let anyone in but myself."

"You're leaving us defenseless?" Clarence asked, his face a picture of alarm.

"Not defenseless." Shaw glanced back over his shoulder. "You have the rifles. Use them."

"You know I don't like guns," said Mina.

"Then start liking them," Shaw said, stepping through the door. "They might just save your lives."

"Wait." Mina wasn't done with the conversation, but it didn't matter. Shaw was gone, the door already swinging closed behind him. She and Clarence were on their own.

SIXTY-SEVEN

WHEN SHAW STEPPED OUTSIDE, the horse and carriage that had brought them back to the apartment was still there, the driver sitting up front with his eyes closed and head resting against the back of the cab. He didn't appear to notice the private detective until Shaw opened the rear door to the carriage.

"Whoa. What do you think you're doing?" The driver asked, looking down with a scowl.

"I need you to take me somewhere," Shaw replied, giving him the address of the bookstore.

"Sorry. I finish at eight. Done for the evening. Go find someone else to take you."

"I don't have time," Shaw snapped. "Double the fare if you take me there right now. It's not that far."

The driver considered this for a moment, then he nodded. "Alright. Hop in."

Shaw climbed into the passenger compartment and pulled the door closed, settling on the bench seat. A minute later, they were on their way through the dark streets. Fifteen minutes after that, they arrived in the lower East Side and were soon pulling up outside of Weinberg's Rare Volumes.

Climbing from the cab, Shaw handed the driver a dollar. He removed two more from his pocket and waved them in front of the man. "Stay here and wait. I'll need a ride back."

The driver eyed the cash with interest. He licked his lips. "How long are you going to be?"

"I don't know. Fifteen minutes, maybe more."

The driver wavered; his gaze still fixed on the cash. "That might not be enough."

Shaw reached into his pocket. "Fine. I'll add another dollar. Do we have a deal?"

"Three bucks if I wait and take you back?"

"Yes." Shaw swallowed a wave of frustration. "The longer we stand here talking, the more time this will take."

"You have a deal. But if you're not back within thirty minutes, I'm leaving. Understand?"

"Yeah. I understand." Shaw pushed the money back into his pocket, then turned and strode toward the bookstore. The door was unlocked. When he entered, a bell hanging from a small chain above tinkled. The store's interior was swathed in darkness. He made his way between the stacks, expecting to see the store's owner appear at any moment. When he didn't, Shaw called out. "Jacob?"

Silence.

Shaw continued toward the back of the store. An aroma of old paper and antique leather mixed with a faint odor of decay assaulted his nostrils. He called out again, the hairs on the back of his neck prickling. It was too quiet. Had Elise and her brother somehow found out about Jacob's message and already paid him a visit? Was the golem even now standing in the darkness, waiting to strike?

But then, just when Shaw was about to retreat back to the

safety of the sidewalk, a pale and ghostly figure leaning on a cane separated itself from the darkness up ahead.

Shaw recognized the faux apparition with a flood of relief. "Jacob. I was starting to think you weren't here."

"I was upstairs in my private library. Left that message hours ago. Took you long enough to get here."

"It's been a hectic day," Shaw replied. "I'm here now. What do you have for me?"

Jacob turned and beckoned Shaw to follow him with two crooked fingers. They stepped into his cluttered office, which was lit by the warm orange glow of gas sconces.

Moving behind his desk and leaning the cane against it, Jacob touched a large leather-bound volume that looked like it had been around much longer than he had. He opened it to a page saved by a silver bookmark to reveal writing that Shaw recognized as Hebrew, even though he could not read it.

Jacob cleared his throat. "I forgot this was in my collection. My father brought it over from Central Europe when he came here as a young man, but it's much older than that."

"The incantation to make a golem is in that book?" Shaw asked, stepping closer to the desk for a better view.

"Maybe not your golem. Like I said, there are many different texts, but if you believe the stories, then yes, this will do the job."

"And there's an incantation to render the creature inanimate again?"

Jacob nodded. He indicated a passage toward the bottom of the right-hand page, touching it lightly with his finger. "This incantation, if said in conjunction with altering the word carved on the golem's forehead from truth to death by removing the E in *emet* to form the Hebrew word *met*, will strip the creature of its power to exist, and turn it back to whatever base material it was made from. It will, in effect, kill the golem."

"But only if that incantation is compatible with the one that created it?" Shaw asked.

"Yes."

"How will I know that?"

"You won't, until you try to use it on the golem." Jacob opened the drawer in his desk and removed a sheet of paper upon which was written a paragraph of text in the same shaky handwriting as the note that had summoned Shaw to the bookstore. Jacob held it out for the private detective. "I translated this from the Hebrew. If the text in the book used to create the creature matches the text in my book, it will reduce the golem to dirt. If not…"

"This will be the last thing I ever read," said Shaw, taking the sheet of paper and studying it. "What are the odds this will match the other incantation?"

Jacob shrugged. He closed the book, not bothering with the bookmark. "Volumes like this are rare. Uncommon enough that I have never had the opportunity to compare texts. But I do know that stories of the golem have been around since the early days of Judaism. Early writings claim that Adam, from the Garden of Eden, was first created as a golem kneaded from dust into a shapeless mass until he received a soul. Since that time, through the Middle Ages and beyond, the stories have changed and expanded, as have the ritual texts required to create one."

"Which tells me nothing."

"I can't tell you what I don't know. Maybe the incantation will work, and maybe it won't. But I will impart one piece of advice. If you don't believe the words you are speaking—if you don't have faith in their ability to render the golem harmless—then you are doomed before you even start."

"You're not filling me with confidence here, Jacob."

Jacob settled into a chair behind the desk and looked up at Shaw. "If you don't want the truth, then don't ask for my help."

"Point taken." Shaw folded the sheet of paper and put it in his pocket. "I have to go."

Jacob smiled, but there was sadness in his eyes. "Good luck, Nicholas. If this is the last time we see each other, I want you to know that I've enjoyed our friendship."

Shaw looked at Jacob for a moment, unsure how to respond, then he turned and walked out of the office without another word.

SIXTY-EIGHT

MINA PACED BACK and forth in the apartment while Clarence looked on from a chair near the window. Thirty minutes had passed since Shaw left for the bookstore and she was no less frustrated now than she had been then.

Everything was falling apart.

They had only been in New York for a week and already their plan to get home was crumbling. Decker was missing and presumed dead in the sewers beneath the city. Shaw had raced across town on his own with no regard for her opinion and had yet to return. The golem was still out there, harboring deadly intentions toward all of them. And they had let the creature's creators, a pair of psychotic maniacs hellbent on revenge, slip away into the night. And on top of everything else, she had discovered a new and disturbing fact about her vampire side she wasn't sure how to deal with.

Mina swore under her breath.

"Hey, calm down." Clarence said, watching her clench and unclench her fists for the tenth time in as many minutes. "We're safe here and Nick will be back soon."

Mina stopped pacing and turned to face him. "You don't understand. There's more at stake than just the golem. I had a responsibility to keep John safe. It's my fault that he was even here. Everything is my fault. I should have let Decker and Colum deal with Abraham Turner on their own instead of forcing my way into the situation. I wish I'd never even gone to London in the first place. I've been nothing but trouble ever since John first met me."

"I don't have a clue what you're talking about," Clarence said. "But it can't be as bad as you make out."

"Believe me, it is." Mina turned away, blinking back tears.

Clarence stood up. "Hey, you can't go through life regretting the stuff you did in the past. We've all made mistakes. Look at me. I'm being hunted by a creature from Jewish folklore simply because I got drunk one night with my friends and performed in a ritual none of us really thought would work in a million years. It's easy to look back on your mistakes and think you should have acted differently. But you don't have the benefit of hindsight when you're in the moment. The future isn't ours to know. All we can do is our best when it arrives."

Mina couldn't help but laugh despite herself. She probably knew more about the future than anyone else on the planet except John Decker, and that knowledge hadn't helped her one bit. She wiped the tears away and took a deep breath, then turned back to Clarence. "Thank you for trying to help."

"It's the least I can do. I'd have a snapped neck and no face right now if it wasn't for all of you."

"I wouldn't thank us yet," Mina said. She went to the window and looked out across the city. A crescent moon hung in the sky, partly obscured by clouds. She was about to look down at the street, wondering how much longer it would be before Shaw returned, when there were three heavy thuds on the apartment door.

A small whimper escaped Clarence's lips. "It's the golem."

Mina swiveled and rushed across the room, snatching up one of Shaw's rifles despite her aversion to guns. She motioned to Clarence. "Get in the bedroom and close the door. Whatever you do, don't come out."

Clarence ignored her. He stood fixed to the spot staring at the door, eyes bugged out.

Mina was about to repeat her command when there were two more thuds. A familiar voice called out from the other side of the door.

"Hey, is anyone in there? Open up."

Mina almost fainted with relief. She discarded the rifle and ran to the door, flinging it open and wrapping her arms around the figure that stood on the other side. "John. You're alive."

"Hey, easy there." Decker extricated himself from Mina and stepped into the apartment.

"I was so worried," she said. "I thought the golem had killed you."

"It almost did." Decker closed the door and locked it. "I barely escaped the sewer in one piece." He looked around, puzzled. "Where's Nick?"

"There was a message waiting when we got back here from that bookseller you went to see. Said he'd found what we were looking for in an old manuscript."

"The incantation to kill the golem?"

"I think so," Mina said. "Nick left to go get it. I thought he would be back by now."

"Let's hope he doesn't take too much longer," Decker said. "I trapped the golem in the sewer, at least temporarily, but

I'm sure it's broken out by now and I'm sure it's looking for us."

"It can't find us here, though, right?" Clarence said, glancing nervously at the door.

"I don't know," Decker replied. "It found your friends easily enough."

"Because Elise knew where they lived, thanks to Wallace Alden," Mina said. "She manipulated him, used him, then let the golem kill him in the wine vaults before sending it after the others. And don't forget, we lured it to Clarence's apartment because Elise must have seen the newspaper article and thought he was there."

"Except something's changed," Decker said. "I thought I'd lost it down in the sewers, but I hadn't. The golem almost went in the other direction, but then it stopped and sniffed the air like it was tracking me. It was like the golem had my scent."

"You're not serious." Mina went to the window again. She looked down into the street before turning back to Decker. "Do you think it could track you here?"

"I don't know. I almost didn't come back here because of that. But I figured that if it had my scent, it probably has yours, too. We were all down in that cellar with it. I had to warn you. This apartment isn't safe anymore. We need to leave right away."

"And go where?" Mina asked. "Because if the golem can track us here, it can follow our scent anywhere."

"The bookstore." Decker crossed the room and picked up the rifle Mina had discarded. "It's our only chance. That's where Nick went. With any luck, He'll still be there, and he'll have the incantation to stop the creature."

"And if he's not?"

"We'll leave a message. Tell him where we've gone. It's

not a great plan, but it's better than staying here where we're completely defenseless."

Mina hesitated a moment. In all likelihood, Nick had made it to the bookstore, got the incantation from Jacob, and was already on his way back. But Decker was right. They couldn't defend themselves in the apartment. Even if Nick had already left the bookstore, Jacob would still be there and could give them another copy of the incantation. As long as the golem followed them and didn't go after Nick instead, he would be fine. In the end, she relented. "Fine. I'll leave a message for Nick and then we'll go."

The relief on Decker's face was clear. He slung the rifle over his shoulder. "Make it quick."

Mina turned to look for a sheet of paper and a pen, but at that moment, there was another loud bang on the apartment door. It didn't sound like Nick. It was more like—

Before she could finish the thought, there was a second heavy thud, and the door flew off its hinges and crashed inward. They weren't going anywhere. The golem had found them.

SIXTY-NINE

THE DOOR CRASHED to the floor in a hail of splintered wood. The golem lowered its enormous head and pushed itself through the shattered doorframe, stepping into the room and leaving muddy footprints in its wake.

Clarence let forth a high-pitched squeal and backpedaled until he bumped into the sofa and almost lost his balance. He saved himself at the last moment and scrambled behind the sofa as if the flimsy piece of furniture could protect him.

Decker slipped the rifle from his shoulder and lowered it, aiming at the creature, even though he knew it would do no good. He pressed the trigger, feeling the recoil slam into his shoulder a split second before his bullet found its mark, opening up a hole in the golem's chest that quickly flowed back together and closed.

If the golem felt even the slightest discomfort, it didn't show it. Instead, the creature stomped into the room, flinging a small table aside with a quick swipe of its arm. An empty vase sitting on the table crashed to the floor and shattered, sending shards of ceramic in all directions.

Decker adjusted his aim, even as the golem set its sights on Clarence. It lunged forward, throwing the sofa out of the way with the same ease that it had dispatched the table, and made a grab for the terrified man just as Decker fired again.

This time, the bullet sailed wide and smacked into the opposite wall, leaving a gaping hole in the plaster.

Clarence ducked as the golem tried to grab him but wasn't fast enough. The creature's arm coiled around Clarence's chest and lifted him from the floor in a one-armed bearhug.

Mina raced forward with a shriek, bringing her hands up, fists clenched, to punch into the creature's soft torso. But the golem anticipated her attack and swung around, catching her on the shoulder with his free arm and sending her tumbling over the upended sofa.

Decker aimed for a third shot, then thought better of it. The golem would only shrug the assault off just like it had before, and he couldn't risk hitting either Mina or Clarence. Instead, he turned the gun around like a club, hands gripping the barrel, and leaped toward the creature, swinging the butt end of the gun at the golem's head, hoping to decapitate it and give Clarence an opportunity to free himself.

The heavy weapon made contact, meeting a moment of satisfying resistance before it sliced through the golem's neck a few inches below the jaw and came out on the other side, trailing a thin spatter of mud. The unexpected ease with which the weapon cut through the golem left Decker momentarily unbalanced, and he struggled to rein in the wild swing before the rifle's momentum tore him from his feet. He twisted around in a stumbling dance, almost losing his grip on the rifle's barrel. When he regained his balance, Decker was disappointed to see that his efforts were for naught. It was impossible to inflict any meaningful damage on the creature. It might as well have been made of water.

But Clarence was not so lucky. He opened and closed his mouth, gasping for air as the golem increased its grip upon him. He paddled at the creature's thick arms, his fingers gouging the mud and unable to get a grip on anything solid enough to make a difference.

Mina was struggling to her feet. She looked at Decker, a helpless expression on her face, and he knew what she was thinking. There was nothing they could do. The golem would kill Clarence in short order, then it would turn its wrath upon them. And even if they ran, it would hunt them down and finish the job. Because the creature was a mindless killer, incapable of reason and unburdened by emotion. It would follow them to the ends of the earth to fulfill the task Elise Felder had given it. She was the only person who could stop the slaughter, and she was almost as heartless as the creature she had created. Unless something changed in the next few seconds, they were all dead.

And then, as if he'd been waiting for the right moment to make his entrance, Nick Shaw appeared at the door.

SEVENTY

SHAW TOOK a moment to take in the scene unfolding in front of him, then he reached into his pocket and pulled out a sheet of paper. He waved it at Decker. "I have the incantation."

"Great. Now would be a perfect time to use it." Decker swung the gun around again, so the business end was facing away from him.

Clarence was losing his battle to stay alive. His face had turned a bright shade of purple. His Eyes bulged out of their sockets as the golem crushed the air from his lungs. Sooner rather than later, Decker knew, the creature would snap his neck and finish the job. He was surprised it hadn't done so already. The constant assaults he and Mina had mounted were probably the only reason Clarence was still breathing.

Decker raised the gun and aimed, keeping his gaze on the creature. It glared back at him from eyeless sockets, black as coal. From the corner of his eye, he saw Shaw open the piece of paper and study it for a moment, then look up.

"I don't know how any of this works, or even if it will work at all. Just giving you fair warning," Shaw said.

"Who cares," Decker hissed. "Just get on with it."

"Don't forget, the incantation won't work on its own. We need to remove the first E from that word on the golem's forehead."

"Leave that to me," Decker said, aiming the rifle and praying the creature wouldn't turn away from them before the time came to take the shot. "Now start reading before it's too late."

"Here goes nothing." Shaw looked back down at the sheet of paper in his hand. He began to recite the words as loud as he could, talking in a fast cadence that made the incantation sound almost lyrical.

The golem turned to look at him, clearly unaffected.

Shaw faltered, lost his rhythm.

Decker glanced at him. "Keep reading. Try again."

Shaw nodded and started again, reading from the beginning, slower this time. This time, he didn't lose his way.

The golem stomped a foot. Shook its head from side to side. A shudder ran through it, like a ripple across the surface of the pond.

"It's working," said Mina. "Don't stop."

Decker curled his finger on the trigger and aimed at the writing scrawled across the creature's head, anticipating the creature's jerking movements. He had no idea when he should take the shot, but he knew one thing: if he missed, there wouldn't be a second chance.

Shaw kept reading, taking care with each word, taking it slower than Decker would have liked.

The golem twisted one way, then the other. It threw its head back, momentarily depriving Decker of his shot.

Then it released Clarence, who sank to his knees gasping for breath.

Shaw spoke the last words of the incantation, his voice booming in a deep bass.

The golem thrashed and clawed at the air. It took a faltering step toward the private detective. Decker steeled himself—waited for the creature to lift its head. Then, when he saw his chance, he took the shot.

For a second, time stood still.

A horrible thought rumbled through Decker's mind. He had missed. But then the bullet slammed into the creature, hitting just above its thick brow, and opening up a hole right on target. The first E of emet. *Truth* had become *death*.

The golem stopped mid-stride. It froze as if a switch had been flipped. Then it started to crumble from the top down. The enormous head with those hollow eye sockets fell apart, disintegrating into a cascade of dirt that rained to the floor. The rest of the creature swiftly followed until it was nothing but a heaped mound of inanimate earth.

Decker lowered the rifle and exhaled, releasing a long breath. "The incantation worked."

The sheet of paper slipped from Shaw's hand and fluttered to the ground. "For a moment there, I thought it wouldn't."

Mina ran to Clarence, still kneeling hunched over. "Are you alright?"

"I think so." His face had returned to its normal color. Mostly. He looked sideways toward the pile of dirt. "It's over. You did it."

"Not quite," Shaw said. "Elise and her brother are still out there."

"And they have the book," Decker said. "They can make another golem whenever they want."

Shaw turned toward the door. "Not if I can help it."

"Where are you going?" Clarence climbed to his feet with Mina's help.

"To see Detective McCullough. I think it's time he caught some killers." Shaw tipped his head toward Decker, then stepped into the hallway beyond the shattered door, and started down the stairs, ignoring the curious looks from the building's other residents drawn from their homes by the commotion above.

SEVENTY-ONE

DECKER GOT A BETTER night's sleep than he had in days. He and Mina were back at the Waldorf-Astoria occupying another two-bedroom suite, this time paid for by a grateful Clarence Rothman who told them to stay there for as long as they wanted. And it was a good thing too, because they couldn't return to the boarding house and the apartment in Shaw's building was unlivable. With Elise and her brother on the run and the golem dead, Clarence returned to his rooms at the Hotel Albert, which was where Decker and Mina were heading now. The open-ended accommodation at the swanky hotel was a welcome respite from the less salubrious digs they had recently inhabited, but they still intended to collect on Clarence's promise of help in exchange for keeping him alive. It was now time to explain everything to Clarence and call in the favor. But when they got to his apartment, Shaw was already there, along with Detective McCullough.

"Is there a problem?" Decker asked, stepping into the apartment and spotting the detective.

"No problem." McCullough stood with his hands in his

pockets. "I dropped by to give you an update. We arrested Elise Felder and her brother early this morning at Penn Station, trying to leave the city. We've booked them both on murder charges thanks to Nick's tip about the grisly keepsakes Elise was storing in the cellar under her brother's tailor shop. They confessed to everything, although the story they told was more than a little fantastical. Chances are they'll end up in an asylum rather than serving time in a prison. I mean, monsters made of mud... Who the hell is going to believe that?"

Decker and Mina exchanged glances.

McCullough sighed. "I tell you; it's been the strangest week between that and the mass murder over at Bailey's boardinghouse. A pile of corpses stacked in the attic with their throats cut and two more that looked like they'd been dead for a hundred years, just sitting in a hallway a couple of floors below, all withered and dried up. To top it all, we found a survivor hiding in a wardrobe. A fourteen-year-old girl who wouldn't stop babbling about vampires."

"That's certainly strange," Shaw said, a deadpan look on his face.

"Isn't it, though?" McCullough fixed the private investigator with a curious stare. "You wouldn't happen to know anything about those deaths at the boardinghouse, would you?"

Shaw feigned innocence. "I'm sorry, Detective. I know nothing about any of that."

The detective nodded. His gaze swept the room, taking in Mina and Decker before returning to Shaw. "I suppose I'll have to take your word for that. But if your memory suddenly improves, feel free to pay me a visit at the precinct house."

"You can be sure of that." Shaw smiled.

"Oh, I almost forgot." The detective reached under his coat and withdrew an old leather-bound volume. Decker recognized as the book used to create the golem. "Elise Felder had this when we arrested her." He held it out to Clarence. "I believe you know who's missing it."

"I'll make sure it gets back where it belongs," Clarence said, taking the book.

"Don't you need it for evidence?" Shaw asked.

"Not on your life." The detective shook his head. "This whole mess is crazy enough without trying to explain that. We'll get a conviction easily enough, between the damning evidence we found at the tailor shop and Elise Felder's rantings. Crazy as she is, her fevered babblings will do nicely as a confession."

"Then everything appears to be settled," Shaw said.

"That it does." The detective turned toward the door. "I'll leave you good people to your day." As he stepped out into the hallway, he glanced back over his shoulder. "Do me a favor, all of you. Try not to get yourselves involved in any more weirdness. I'm looking forward to a quiet couple of weeks."

"We'll do our best," Decker said, stepping toward the door and closing it behind the detective. When he was sure McCullough was gone, he turned toward Clarence and Shaw. "Now, I think it's time we tell you the truth about who we are and how we came to be here, because we're going to need your help. Both of you."

"To do what?" Clarence asked.

"To get home." Decker looked at Mina, making sure they were still in agreement on what was going to happen next. Then he took a deep breath and told them everything.

SEVENTY-TWO

FOUR MONTHS later

John Decker walked across the ballroom of the Grand Fairmont Hotel on the Bahamian island of Singer Cay, weaving through the crowd of wedding guests and approaching a bar at the back of the room where Mina stood waiting with Clarence Rothman at her side.

"You look smart," she said, giving his black tuxedo and starched white dress shirt the once over.

"You don't look so bad yourself," Decker replied, taking in her beaded V-neck dress that shimmered under the lights.

"Thank you." Mina looked away, a slight blush touching her cheeks. When she looked back, it was gone. "Have you seen the bride to be?"

"Yes. Celine is near the dance floor being congratulated by a group of society women." Decker and Mina had stayed mostly on the periphery of the room until now, keeping out of Celine's way. They couldn't risk her seeing them in case she recognized them when she arrived in the future. Soon, they would put the trickiest part of their plan into action, with Clarence's help. Decker checked his watch. "It can't be long now before she goes upstairs to change out of her wedding dress and encounters the rift in time. We should get into position."

"Are you sure this is the only way?" Clarence asked, a pained look on his face. "When he loses Celine, my brother will be devastated, and while I don't hold him in high regard, I can't help but love him."

"We can't interfere," Decker said. "If we stop Celine from going upstairs and meeting her destiny, it could have unintended consequences. This was always meant to happen. We are not causing it, but just taking advantage of an event that was already preordained."

"It just feels so wrong, not helping her."

"If we hadn't told you that we were from the future, confided in you what is about to happen here tonight, you would be none the wiser."

"But you did." Clarence looked down at the bar, and the martini sitting there next to a silver cigarette case. When he looked up again, his eyes were moist. "You say that she's alive and well in the twenty-first century?"

"Yes," Mina said. "If a little confused."

"And there's no way for her to return here?"

"No. The historical record states that Celine Rothman vanished on her wedding night during a terrible storm," Decker said. "She was presumed to have toppled from the balcony of her private suite atop the hotel into the ocean below and drowned. Her body is never recovered."

"That's because she was never in the water," Clarence said. "At least, if your strange tale is to be believed."

"Everything that we've told you is true," Mina said. "You

343

should take some consolation in the fact that your brother's new wife does not die tonight."

"Even if I can't breathe a word of this to Howard."

"Yes. We've been over this. He can never know the truth." Decker felt sorry for Clarence. The events that were about to happen would tear his family apart and leave Howard a broken man. But there was no way to change them.

Clarence gave a resigned nod. He slipped an envelope from his pocket. He offered it to Decker. "I have one small favor. Can you give this to Celine when you see her in the future? I wrote it last night in my room."

"I'll make sure she gets it." Decker took the envelope. He studied it for a moment, then slipped it into his pocket next to another item he was carrying to the future. A Dickens first edition. The same book he had purchased from a London bookseller months before as a present for Nancy if he ever found a way back to the twenty-first century. When he boarded the Titanic, Decker had left it behind, believing he was going to disembark in Queenstown. After realizing that he and Mina were not returning to London, Thomas Finch had sent it to him. Now, just minutes away from his only chance to get home, Decker closed his hand over the book and said a silent prayer.

Clarence nudged him. "Celine is making her way across the ballroom. I think she's about to go up to her suite."

Decker felt the coil of anxiety that had been sitting in his gut since they arrived on Singer Cay twist into a tight ball. "This is it."

"You know what to do," Mina said to Clarence. "Just buy us enough time to get to the elevator and go up ahead of her."

Clarence nodded. He opened the silver cigarette case and withdrew a cigarette, then picked up his martini. He took a step toward Celine, then turned and looked back at Mina and Decker. "Good luck. I hope you get home. And thank you for saving my life."

"You're welcome," Decker said.

Clarence lingered a moment longer, then made his way through the throng of wedding guests to intercept Celine. He positioned himself near a marble pillar, waited for her to walk past, and drew her into conversation.

"She's distracted. Let's go." Decker grabbed Mina's hand and led her across the ballroom, skirting the dance floor and staying far away from Celine and Clarence. They reached the grand staircase and started up, exchanging pleasantries with another couple going in the other direction. On the second floor, they hurried to the elevator that Clarence had pointed out earlier. A private elevator that only went to Howard Rothman's suite at the top of the hotel.

Glancing around to make sure they weren't observed, Decker pulled the grill open and waited for Mina to step inside, then followed. During the hotel's normal operations, the elevator grill would be locked to prevent guests accessing the private suite above, but all the guests at the hotel tonight were there for the wedding, and Howard Rothman didn't want the inconvenience of having to remove a padlock every time he retired to his suite. For that, Decker was grateful. He pulled the grill closed, then hit one of the only two buttons inside the elevator.

The car shuddered and clanked, then rose. For a while Decker could see the ballroom below through the elevator's outer cage, but then it slipped from view as they went higher, passing through five floors of guestrooms before coming to a jolting stop.

This was the penthouse suite.

Decker stepped out of the elevator and waited for Mina,

then reached in and pressed the button to send the elevator back down.

Now he took in his surroundings. A storm was raging outside. He could see it through a pair of French doors on the other side of the suite's living room. It was a violent tempest that lashed the panes of glass with driving rain. Lightning forked across the sky and stabbed at the earth. Somewhere out there, far below, would be the Atlantic Ocean, whipped into a roiling frenzy.

From the elevator shaft came a familiar clanking sound. Clarence Rothman had delayed Celine long enough for them to slip up to the second floor and take the elevator. Now she was on her way up to meet her fate.

"We have to hide." Decker looked around frantically.

"In here," Mina said, guiding him toward the bedroom. She opened the double doors, stepped inside, and pulled them almost closed, leaving a slim gap through which they could observe the living room.

Decker glanced around, curious. His gaze fell to a ballgown draped over a chair near the bed. It was a stunning dress that had probably cost Howard more than he paid one of his employees in an entire year. And Celine Rothman would never get to wear it.

The elevator came to a clunking halt. The sound of the cage being drawn back reached their ears. He peeked through the gap between the doors just in time to see Celine Rothman cross the living room toward the French doors and the balcony beyond. She pulled them open and stood staring into the heart of the storm. The wind whipped her hair and tugged at her dress. Rain lashed through the opening.

A flash of lightning cracked the sky in half.

Celine stepped back, alarmed. She reached for the doors, intending to close them again. She never got the chance. A second bolt of lightning erupted from the heavens and forked down, hitting the side of the hotel and enveloping her in a flash of blinding light.

Decker turned away instinctively, shielding his eyes. When he looked back, the storm beyond the French doors was gone, replaced by a swirling vortex that emitted a faint greenish light.

"This is it." Decker flung the bedroom doors wide and raced across the living room toward the vortex, grabbing Mina's hand and dragging her along behind. He could already see it collapsing in upon itself. Another few seconds and it would be too late. He lunged forward, diving toward the strange tunnel.

But at that moment, Mina pulled her hand from his.

"I'm sorry," she said. "I can't go."

"Mina. Don't be ridiculous." Decker teetered at the edge of the vortex. He could feel it sucking him in. He resisted with all his might, unwilling to leave Mina stranded alone in the past. "You have to come. It's your only way home."

She shook her head. "I have unfinished business here. My daughter needs me. I'll take the long way around."

"Mina, you can't—" Decker never got to finish the sentence. At that moment, he lost his battle with the vortex and tumbled backwards, falling head over heels as it sucked him inexorably in. He caught a brief glimpse of Mina standing with her arms at her sides in the penthouse suite, an anguished look on her face, and then the tunnel folded closed and left him falling through an expanse of impenetrable blackness that he feared would never end.

SEVENTY-THREE

MINA WATCHED Decker fall into the swirling vortex even as he reached out, desperate not to leave her behind. There was so much she wanted to say to him in that moment, but no time to do so. She had made the decision to stay behind weeks before but hadn't possessed the heart to tell Decker. Now she wished the opportunity had not been wasted. Her daughter was here. She wanted to see Daisy grow up and blossom into a confident young woman. Decker would have understood. Instead, she had taken the coward's way out and went along with his plan until the bitter end, then given him no choice but to leave her behind.

Mina choked back a sob and took a step toward the vortex, hoping to catch one last glimpse of John Decker. But at that moment, the tunnel shimmered, contracted, and closed in upon itself, then blinked from existence.

A sudden and terrible loneliness descended upon her.

It would be over a hundred years before she would see Decker again. That immense gulf of time stretched ahead of her, a seemingly impossible obstacle to surmount even though she knew there was enough stored up in life coursing through her veins to make it there. Thanks to her vampire side, she would probably live a thousand years. Maybe even ten thousand, thanks to Abraham Turner, and the combined life forces of the two vampires she had killed at the guesthouse. By the time her journey looped back to the point where it had begun, she would probably not look any older than she did right now. That was little consolation.

Mina glanced around one more time, taking in the evening gown that Celine Rothman would never get to wear and the raging storm beyond the French doors. Then she turned and made her way back to the elevator and rode it down.

When she entered the ballroom, Clarence Rothman was standing at the bar once again, smoking a cigarette.

He looked up, surprised, at her approach. "It didn't work?"

Mina didn't trust herself to speak, so she merely nodded.

"Then why are you still here?"

Mina finally found her voice. "I decided not to go."

"And John... Did he get back?"

Mina shrugged. "I don't know. I hope so, but I won't have that answer for a very long time."

Clarence observed her for a few seconds. He picked up his martini and took a sip. "What will you do now?"

"Go back to New York and say goodbye to Nick all over again, then I suppose I'll book passage on a steamer to London."

"Or you could stay with me," Clarence said, a wry smile touching his lips. "I've grown quite fond of you over the last few months."

Mina placed a gentle hand on his arm. "That's sweet, but I

don't think you're ready to settle down, and I know you're not ready for a woman like me. No offense."

"None taken." Clarence wrapped an arm around Mina's shoulder and pulled her close. "But if you ever need anything, I'm always here."

"I appreciate that," Mina replied. Then she rested her head on Clarence Rothman's shoulder and wept softly, because at that moment, she felt herself to be the loneliest woman in the world.

SEVENTY-FOUR

PRESENT DAY—PORTLAND, MAINE

NANCY WAS in the kitchen at the back of the bakery when she heard a knock at the front door. It was late, after nine, and they had been closed for several hours, but she had decided to stay behind and prepare dough for the next day's bread and batter for the Beignet's that had become a signature of the business she had started the previous January in the old Port District of the city. The bakery had been something to do while Decker was away on assignments but had become something even more valuable since his disappearance the previous April on what should have been her wedding day... A lifeline.

She had spent over a month on Singer Cay, hoping and praying that Decker and Mina would reappear, but with each day that passed, it became less likely. Eventually, she was forced to accept the inevitable and return home. It was now September. Five months had passed. Five long and dreadful months. And in that time the bakery had become her refuge.

She worked seven days a week and often stayed late, just like she had done today, because filling her hours with work was better than facing an empty house night after night.

Not that the house was completely empty. Her daughter Taylor, attending college in Massachusetts, dropped by regularly to see how she was doing, and then there was Celine. Stranded eleven decades from her own time and with no way to get back, Celine Rothman had struggled at first. Which was why, after her return from Singer Cay, Nancy had taken her in and even given her a job in the bakery. The arrangement was mutually beneficial. It provided company for Nancy while allowing Celine to adjust at her own pace. But now, even that was coming to an end. Celine wanted to have her own space and move out, and Nancy understood, albeit with a tinge of sadness.

The knock came again.

Nancy left the kitchen, hurried around the counter, and weaved between the tables she had set up in what had once been a hardware store to create a space where her patrons could sit and sip coffee while they ate their fresh croissants, and hot Beignets.

When she opened the door, Adam Hunt was standing on the other side. "Celine said I'd find you here."

"Adam. Please, come in." Nancy held the door wide and waited for him to step inside before closing it again. "What brings you out so late?"

"I was on the mainland and wanted to check in on things before returning to the island," he said, referencing CUSP's headquarters on a small island off the Maine coast. "I stopped by the house and Celine said you hadn't come home yet."

"You don't need to keep checking on me," Nancy replied. "I'm doing just fine."

"I wasn't just checking on you. I also wanted to stop by

and talk to Celine, make sure she's ready for the big move into her own place next month."

"I'm sure she is," Nancy said. "And if she needs any help, I'm sure Colum will be more than happy to provide it. He's been paying her regular visits of late and has even taken her out a few times."

"I warned him not to pressure her," Adam said, clenching his jaw. "I'll have another chat with him."

"There's no need. Celine likes his company. She needs to move on with her life. We both do."

"Speaking of which…" Adam looked awkward.

"I'm moving on, too." Nancy pulled a chair out and sat down, then motioned for Hunt to do the same. "I've accepted what happened to John. He thrived working for CUSP. Loved every minute even if he wouldn't say as much. If he had to leave—" Nancy's throat tightened. She looked away, took a deep breath. "Sorry. Just because I've come to terms with his death doesn't mean I don't miss him."

"There's no need to apologize. I know how much you miss John, and I also know you've accepted his fate. That's why I want to give you this." Hunt reached inside his coat and withdrew a yellowed envelope. He placed it on the table and slid it toward her.

"What is it?" Nancy reached out and touched the envelope, feeling the brittle paper under her fingers. Then she saw the name written on it. Nancy. Her heart leaped into her mouth because she recognized the handwriting. "Where did you get this?"

"I think you know the answer to that," Hunt replied. "From John, in a roundabout way. But more important is the how. CUSP has been holding onto this letter for a long time, and before that, the Order of St. George."

"What?" Nancy could hardly believe her ears. "The Order

353

of St. George hasn't existed since before the Second World War and they were an English organization. How could they possibly have been in possession of this letter?"

"Because that's where John ended up." Hunt shifted in his seat, refusing to meet Nancy's gaze. "London in the year 1911, to be exact."

There was a moment of stunned silence as Nancy absorbed this new information. She glared at Hunt. "And you're only telling me this now."

"Yes. Because I only found out a few days ago, myself. The information was withheld from me, as was the letter."

"By who?"

"My superiors. That's all I'm at liberty to divulge. But I can tell you something of John's time in the past, although not a lot."

"Then what are you waiting for?" Nancy resisted the urge to open the letter there and then. She wanted to hear what Hunt had to say first. Then she would open it in private.

Hunt cleared his throat. "When we all flew up into that storm over Singer Cay in 1942, hoping to travel forward in time and get home, most of us did just that. But John and Mina somehow ended up going the other way. He landed in London around November 1911."

"How is that possible?"

"How is any of this possible?" Hunt countered.

"And Mina... What about her?"

Hunt remained silent for a moment, perhaps weighing his answer. "I can't say."

"What does that mean?" Nancy wondered how much Hunt was still holding back. "You don't know, or you won't tell me?"

"How about we get back to John?"

This time it was Nancy who remained silent. She was desperately trying to process all this new information.

Hunt apparently took her silence as agreement. "John stayed in London until April 1912, when he boarded an ocean liner bound for the United States. He was on that ship when he wrote the letter you have in front of you... because he didn't think he would survive the crossing."

"Why would he think that?"

"Because the ship was the RMS Titanic."

Nancy was overcome by a sudden chill. She fought back a sob. "Are you telling me John died on the Titanic?"

"No." Hunt shook his head. "He made it to New York on the rescue ship Carpathia. What happened after that, I don't know."

In the months after John's disappearance, Nancy had clung to a slim hope that he would get back. Decker always made it back. But with this news, that hope crumbled. "It doesn't take a genius to figure out what happened. He was stranded at the beginning of the twentieth century. He grew old and died before he'd even been born."

Hunt tapped his fingers on the table. He glanced down at the envelope, then he pushed his chair back and stood up. "I'll leave you to read that in private."

Nancy still couldn't speak. She didn't trust herself.

Hunt backtracked toward the door. "If you need anything, you know where I am."

Nancy watched him step outside and pull the door closed, then she sat there for what felt like an eternity, staring at the yellowed envelope. Eventually, she picked the envelope up and reached for a knife to slice it open, but then she hesitated. Whatever was inside that envelope had laid undisturbed since John Decker put it there over a century before. She felt like opening it was the culmination of a journey that ended with her knowing unequivocally that the man she had almost married was gone forever. But refusing to read it wasn't going to bring him back.

She slipped the knife under the flap and ran it along the envelope's top edge, careful to do the least damage possible. Then she plucked out the folded sheet of paper within. When she opened it, she understood why Adam Hunt had told her about Decker's appearance in 1911, and his presence on the Titanic, even though she was sure he knew a lot more that he was keeping to himself for whatever reason.

The letter, in Decker's unmistakable hand, was written on three sheets of notepaper with the White Star Line name and logo on top.

She almost folded the pages and slipped them back into the envelope, not sure she could face the last words he would ever say to her at that moment, but then she took a deep breath, bowed her head, and began to read.

SEVENTY-FIVE

ANOTHER TIME AND PLACE

THE FIRST THING Decker noticed was the heat. It pressed down on him like a smothering blanket. The second thing he noticed were the trees reaching toward the night sky above. Gumbo-limbo, lancewood, and mahogany. Fauna not native to colder climes like the countryside around London, or New York State. He was lying on his back atop a cushion of earthy detritus that felt spongy under his back when he moved.

Decker pushed himself up to a sitting position, then climbed to his feet and took in the tropical forest surrounding him. A spark of hope flickered in his soul. Was it possible that he was still on Singer Cay? And if so, in what decade?

There was only one way to find out.

Walk until he spotted a familiar landmark.

But which way to go? He was, apparently, deep in the forest and could see no trail to guide him. Worse, it was night, and he had no lantern or other source of light to guide his way. But what he did notice was the faint sound of waves crashing somewhere off in the distance to his left. If he was still on CUSP's tropical island, there would be a coast road that ran in a loop. Assuming, of course, that he had arrived at a point in time after that road had been built. Either way, heading toward the water made sense. It was his only fixed point of reference, and the alternative was wandering aimlessly in the forest.

Decker was still wearing the heavy tuxedo. He removed the jacket and draped it over his arm, then took off the bow tie and undid the top button of his shirt. Then he took a moment to pin down exactly where the sound of waves was coming from and set off.

He moved slowly, picking his way through the underbrush with caution. Thankfully, there were no venomous snakes and very few other dangerous forms of wildlife on the islands that comprised the Bahamas. The biggest threats were black widow spiders, a particularly nasty centipede, and the Cuban tree frog. But none of these creatures posed much threat unless antagonized. But even so, there could be unseen obstacles laying in the darkness waiting to trip him up. Fallen logs and thick branches, holes in the ground, and even man-made clutter that had built up thanks to centuries of human habitation going all the way back to the late fifteenth century when Christopher Columbus first sailed these waters, and colonization by native peoples before that.

After thirty minutes he reached the edge of the forest where an encouraging sight greeted him. A thin strip of asphalt following the curve of the coastline in both directions. The road. Not only did it provide him with a direction in which to travel and confirm that he was, in fact, on Singer Cay, but it also narrowed down the decade he was in. The road was not there when Howard Rothman built his island paradise hotel, the Grand Fairmont. It was constructed years later during World War II when the newly formed organization called Classified Universal Special Projects took possession of the island. Even so, he could as easily be in the 1940s as the twenty-first century.

Decker emerged from the forest and stood in the middle of the road. He looked left and right, trying to find a familiar landmark, but saw none. He could be anywhere on the island since the road circled the entire perimeter. The only way to find out was to pick a direction and walk. If he was lucky and was indeed back in his own time, he would eventually come across CUSP's island retreat, La Casa de Playa. Except one direction would be a longer walk than the other. Deciding it was nothing but a tossup, Decker picked a direction, turned to his left, and followed the road.

He walked for another hour, listening to the roar of waves crashing ashore as he went. His thoughts turned to Mina, still trapped in the past by her own choice. His last glimpse of her had come as he tumbled helplessly into the vortex. She was standing with her arms at her sides in Howard and Celine Rothman's penthouse suite, watching him vanish from her life.

Decker's throat tightened. Was she even still alive? Mina had an advantage, for sure. It wasn't like she would age and die like a mortal woman. She was, after all, not totally human. But there were so many unknowns between then and now. World wars. Famine. Civil unrest.

And there were the vampires.

They had tried to capture her at the boardinghouse and failed. Mina dispatched them with frightening ease. She had killed two and sent the third back with a message for the rest of their kind. But was it enough? That question, like so many others, remained unanswered.

The moon came out from behind scudding clouds and lit the landscape ahead of him in a silvery glow. Decker wondered how far he had walked. It felt like miles. In all that distance, he hadn't seen a single building or come across any other roads. But he knew that would change, eventually. Either he would find what he was looking for, or he would reach the road that cut through the middle of the island on its way to the military base hidden deep within the island's interior.

He wiped sweat from his forehead with the palm of his hand and kept going. His shirt clung to him, damp and sticky. Perspiration ran down his neck and under his collar. He needed to find water, and soon. He wasn't sure how much longer he could press on without hydrating.

Then, just when he was starting to lose hope, he rounded a bend and saw a set of gates ahead on the left. Beyond them was a driveway that wound through a manicured tropical landscape. Decker's heart leaped when he recognized where he was.

He almost ran the last several hundred feet to the gates, which opened silently inward as he reached them, as if inviting him to enter. And perhaps they were, given the small security cameras mounted on each gatepost.

He made his way up the driveway, pressing on with renewed hope, and soon the building came into view.

La Casa de Playa.

The last time he had been here, the luxury resort was bustling with activity. It glowed with light from every window. Wedding guests enjoyed the amenities and excited conversation mixed with hearty laughter filled the air. Now, the resort looked dark and abandoned. There were no vehicles outside. No staff to greet him. He could see nothing but blackness beyond the building's windowpanes.

He almost fell to his knees in despair. Had he arrived months, years, or even decades before his wedding? Or maybe he was a century too late. There was no way to tell.

But then, as he drew close, a door opened underneath the building's front portico, and a figure stepped out to greet him.

The despair faded in an instant, because he recognized the person standing at the top of the steps leading up to the resort's main entrance.

Mina.

But there was someone else, too. Another figure had appeared behind her, and now Decker wasn't sure what to think. Because he also recognized the second young woman. It was Mina's daughter, Daisy.

SEVENTY-SIX

THEY COULD HAVE BEEN SISTERS. Mina and Daisy looked so close in age that no one would ever have believed they were mother and daughter.

Decker followed the two women through La Casa de Playa's grand and expansive lobby in silence, despite the thousand questions that swirled in his head. He had tried to ask at least a few of those questions already, but after embracing him in a tight and lingering hug at the top of the steps, Mina told him to follow her, then refused to say anything more except that he would have his answers soon enough.

They approached a bank of four elevators. Three of these had spent the week of Decker's wedding carrying guests to and from their rooms on the higher floors of the building. The fourth had never worked, its doors remaining stubbornly closed and call button dark. Decker had assumed it was out of service. Now he learned differently.

They entered the elevator, and Mina pressed an unmarked

button on a panel to the right of the doors. The elevator started moving, but it didn't go up. It went down.

They descended for about twenty seconds. Decker felt the familiar lurch of his stomach that he always experienced on high-speed elevators. Wherever they were going, it was taking them there quickly... and going deep.

The elevator came to a stop.

The doors opened to reveal a windowless corridor lit in a faint bluish-white light, although Decker could not see the source of the illumination.

Mina led them along the corridor until they arrived at a set of smooth metal doors that slid back to reveal a square and featureless room beyond. On the far wall was an identical set of doors. Above these was a small semi-sphere set into the wall that looked like it was made of smoked glass. At Mina's approach, a beam of red light appeared, fanning out, and dropped to scan them. After a moment, the red light turned green, and the beam retracted. The doors ahead of them slid silently open.

When they stepped through, Decker found himself on a raised platform that ran around the periphery of a much larger, circular room. In the center of the space, resting about eight feet lower than the platform, was what looked like sleek computer servers in silver enclosures. The only sign anything was happening within the servers was the occasional blink of a light, either red or green, on one or the other of the units. The platform itself contained several workstations that faced large, curved monitors mounted to the equally curved walls. None of the workstations were manned, even though streams of data flashed across the screens.

Mina and Daisy came to a stop and waited for Decker to absorb the scene in front of him.

Then Mina finally spoke again. "John, welcome to Monitoring Station Alpha."

Decker studied his surroundings, overawed by the amount of technology in front of him. He was perturbed by Mina's so far stilted response to his arrival back at La Casa de Playa—since she hugged him on the front steps, Mina had shown no other sign of emotion—but couldn't help asking the obvious question. "What are you monitoring?"

Now Mina's façade crumbled, just a little. She smiled. "For you. I always hoped you would arrive back minutes or hours after you left, but there was simply no way of knowing, and given the inaccuracy of our previous time travels, I couldn't risk you turning up somewhere else in time entirely. That's why I set up the monitoring stations. This was the first one because Singer Cay is where our journey began, but there are others. Over thirty of them spread across the globe. And they all do the same thing."

"Which is?"

"Look for anomalies in space-time. Ripples in the fabric of this dimension. Disturbances that might indicate your arrival."

"How is that possible?" Decker's head was spinning.

"I assembled a team of scientists. Quantum physicists. Astrophysicists. Theoretical physicists. The best our world has to offer. They built all of this in secret, operating outside of and unknown to the rest of CUSP. Only a few other people in the entire organization are aware of the truth."

"Adam Hunt?"

Mina nodded. "Adam has been vital to everything. At least, over the last decade or two."

Decker took a moment to absorb this. "And the truth you speak of, I assume it's bigger than just these monitoring stations?"

"Yes. Much bigger. And I will explain everything, I promise."

"Great," said Decker. "Then do it, because if you built all of this for me, then I deserve answers."

"Not yet. There's plenty of time for that." Mina laid a hand on Decker's arm. She touched the fabric of his shirt, looked into his eyes. "I remember you wearing this in the ballroom of the Fairmont Grand. You looked so handsome. I wish Nancy could have seen you then. It's so strange, touching it. Knowing that for you, Celine's wedding was only a few hours ago."

Decker's throat tightened. "About Nancy... Is she here?"

"No." Mina shook her head.

Decker almost didn't want to ask the next question. "When is this? I mean, the month and year."

"It's October. Six months after your wedding day."

Six months? He had been gone for that long? Decker could only imagine the hell Nancy had gone through. Was still going through. Up until now, he had been bursting with questions about Mina, and what had happened since they last saw each other. About her daughter, Daisy, and how she could even be alive in the twenty-first century and looking like she hadn't aged a day, just like her mother. But now, all of those questions took a backseat to the only one that mattered. "When can I see her?"

Mina's smile widened. "Soon. There's a boat on standby to take you to the mainland first thing in the morning. From there, a private jet will fly you up to Maine."

Decker was confused. "If you didn't know when I would arrive back, or even if I would, how can you have a jet ready to fly me home?"

Mina glanced at her daughter, then back to Decker. "Because there's always a jet ready to fly. Has been ever since

I had the power to do so, just like these monitoring stations." She placed a hand on Decker's shoulder and started walking again, steering him around the raised platform toward the door on the other side. "I'm sure you could use a hot shower and a change of clothes."

"I'd rather you tell me what you've been doing in the years since Celine's wedding." Decker glanced at Daisy. "Like how your daughter can even be here."

Mina reached the door and stopped before turning to him. "Like I said, there will be plenty of time for that. Freshen up, clear your head, and then I'll tell you everything."

SEVENTY-SEVEN

DECKER WAS NOT PREPARED for what lay beyond the door. It was nothing like the cold and clinical facility that had come before. It bore a startling resemblance to the opulent resort above them. He was greeted by a wide central hallway with a polished parquet wood floor, masterful French impressionist oil paintings hanging on the walls, and a fine crystal chandelier. This lavish entryway provided access to a suite of rooms every bit as comfortable as those he and Mina had occupied at the Waldorf Astoria, except more modern. There was a library replete with shelves of volumes that stretched from floor to ceiling, a spacious living room, and a dining room with enough seating for at least ten people. Beyond this, Mina told him, was a chef's kitchen to rival that of the best five-star restaurants. Lastly, there were four bed chambers, one of which had been set aside for him.

Decker was curious to know the purpose of such a lavish apartment hidden beneath the resort—after all, the occupants could just as easily stay in one of the equally appointed suits in the resort above—but he held his tongue as Mina showed him his room and requested that they meet an hour later in the library. That done, she and Daisy departed, leaving him alone to freshen up.

A clock sitting on a nightstand next to the bed told him it was ten p.m. On the other side of the room was a cabinet built around a small beverage fridge with a glass front. Inside, he found bottles of water, soda, iced tea, and a small selection of craft beers. He grabbed a water, twisted the top off and quickly drank it, then did the same with another. His thirst quenched for now, Decker stripped off his sweat-drenched clothes and placed them over a nearby chair. Carefully, he reached into his jacket pocket and removed two items. The Dickens first edition that had accompanied him from the past, and the letter Clarence Rothman had given him to pass on to Celine. Then he went to the ensuite and took a long hot shower, washing away the grime from the forest and stale sweat.

Back in the bedroom, he discovered a small wardrobe of casual clothing in the walk-in closet. Polo shirts, shorts, khakis, and more. There were several sizes of each available, and Decker soon found a selection to fit him. Then he stepped back into the hallway and started toward the library to meet Mina.

SEVENTY-EIGHT

MINA WAS WAITING when Decker entered the library, sitting next to a round table with an inlaid checkerboard pattern top made of both light and dark wood, her head buried in a book. On the table sat a bottle of wine and two glasses.

When he entered, Mina closed the book and placed it on the table. She stood and met him then wrapped her arms around him in a tight embrace, holding on longer than her previous hug, then released him with a wide smile on her face. "I've missed you so much."

"I wish I could say the same," said Decker. "But the way I remember it, I last saw you a few hours ago in the ballroom of the Fairmont Grand." He looked around. "Where's Daisy?"

"She's giving us space to talk," Mina said, motioning toward the table. "Please, sit down. We have so much to discuss."

Decker settled in a wingback chair next to the table and waited for Mina to sit back down in a similar chair. He had so many questions but didn't know where to begin. Then, just when he was about to say as much, he glimpsed movement near the door from the corner of his eye. He looked around to see a distinguished gentleman in a casual white polo shirt and crisp, khaki pants. He carried a silver tray, upon which Decker saw an arrangement of cold cuts, cheeses, and fruit.

Mina motioned for the man to enter and directed him to set the tray down on the table next to the wine. Then she turned to Decker. "This is Lucas."

"Pleased to meet you, sir," Lucas said, bowing his head ever so slightly. He turned to Mina. "Will there be anything else?"

"No. I'm done for the night."

"Very good." Lucas made his way back out of the room, walking with the graceful stealth of one who wants to remain in the background, unseen. Like an assassin, Decker thought, surprising himself. Yet the analogy wasn't entirely false. There was something about the way Lucas carried himself that made the hairs on Decker's neck stand up. The man felt... dangerous. Like a coiled snake waiting to strike.

"You have a butler?" Decker asked finally, raising an eyebrow.

"Lucas is more than just a butler. He acts as my personal chef and also a bodyguard of sorts. The cabal of vampires who tried to snatch me at the boardinghouse in 1912 would still very much like to get their hands on me. They just don't have the nerve, but that could change at any time. Lucas is more than equipped to defend me, or even stand at my side and fight, should it become necessary."

"He's a vampire?" Decker asked, surprised.

"No. But he has his skills. Let's leave it at that. There are more important things to talk about, like the events of the last century. You have a lot of catching up to do."

"Apparently." Decker glanced at the food on the table. He was starving.

"Please, feel free to pick while we talk," Mina said, noticing his interest. She removed the stopper from the wine bottle and poured two ample glasses. "You should appreciate this wine. It's from a certain set of cellars under the Brooklyn Bridge."

"Howard Rothman's wine vaults?" Decker glanced toward the bottle, noting the fine layer of dust adhering to the glass, and the year on the label. 1908. "Are you sure we should drink this? It must be worth a fortune."

"I'm sure it is. But there's plenty more. I procured a sizeable collection when Howard Rothman's business empire faltered. With Clarence's help, of course. We stayed in touch for many years after the affair with the golem." Mina glanced toward the cork, lying next to the bottle. "Besides, it's open now and we might as well enjoy it. What I have to say may take a while."

"Then you had better get to it." Decker plucked a wedge of Stilton from the platter.

Mina was silent for a moment as if composing her thoughts, then she nodded. "After we got separated in Celine's penthouse suite on Singer Cay I returned to New York and spent the next several months there—"

"We didn't get separated," Decker interrupted. "You chose not to come with me."

"Very well. After I decided to stay behind in 1912, I returned to New York. But I didn't stay for long. When the opportunity presented itself, I traveled back to London to be close to Thomas and my daughter. Of course, at that time, Daisy didn't know who her real mother was. I returned to my duties at the Order of St. George, running it alongside Thomas for several more years until he decided to step back for personal reasons, at which time I assumed full control on my own. By then, two things had become clear. The first concerned Daisy. She wasn't aging anymore. I had, apparently, passed my vampire genes to her. At that point, I had no choice but to reveal myself as her mother."

"That couldn't have been easy for either of you," Decker said.

"It wasn't. I had walked away from her years before, precisely to protect her from the dangers presented by my unique nature. Now I discovered that she was more like me than I ever could have imagined. She was angry at first. Bitter. She didn't want to know me. Wanted even less to accept what she was. But eventually we resolved our differences and, as you can see, we are now about as close as any mother and daughter could be. She even helps me run CUSP."

"Wait, hang on a minute." Decker could hardly believe what he was hearing. "You run CUSP?"

Mina nodded. "That's the second thing that became obvious to me after I took the reins at the Order of St. George. It could not stay an organization confined to one country. We had to expand or succumb to the growing threats from a world becoming more global by the year. At the onset of World War II, all the pieces were in place to create Classified Universal Special Projects."

"CUSP is here because of you." Decker returned the wedge of cheese to the tray without even taking a bite. A horrible thought had dawned on him. "Everything that's happened to me since Wolf Haven was because of you."

"John, we're getting ahead of ourselves."

"I don't think we are. You helped establish the Order of St. George and dealt with Abraham Turner, otherwise known as Jack the Ripper. I already knew that. But then you took full control of the Order and steered it to become CUSP... The organization Adam Hunt recruited me into. All the way back to the nineteenth century, you've been the force behind both the Order of St. George and its successor. Guiding them. Crafting them to be what you wanted. Tell me I'm wrong."

Mina said nothing. She picked up her glass of wine, gave it a swirl, and stared into the crimson liquid.

Decker had his answer. "That's what I thought."

Now Mina looked up. "You still don't understand. I wasn't steering the destiny of CUSP with Machiavellian intent. The decisions I made grew organically out of circumstance. Don't forget, I knew very little about the history of CUSP before I lived it, so I had no blueprint to follow beyond a few fixed points in time that I knew had to happen such as Singer Cay in the 1940's. I did what I thought was best."

"And how do I fit into all of this?" Decker asked. He was beginning to feel like a pawn in a very big game. "Were you behind me getting fired as sheriff of Wolf Haven?"

Mina recoiled. "Absolutely not. That had nothing to do with me. I swear."

"And Shackleton?"

This time, Mina looked less offended. "I might have used my influence to make sure the town manager hired you to deal with their problem. I also asked Adam Hunt to go there and monitor the developing situation. Make sure everything fell into place. That's why he spent so long in Alaska."

Decker was almost speechless. Almost. "Which means the only reason I ever met your younger self was because the older version of you made sure it would happen. You schemed to set in motion the events that would eventually bring us to this point."

"Don't you see? I had to preserve the timeline," Mina said. "John, please don't be mad at me."

"How could I not be mad?" Decker stood up to leave, although he wasn't quite sure where he would go. Instead, he turned on Mina. "Nothing in my life since Wolf Haven has been my choice. You've been hiding out of sight, pulling the strings to make sure I went exactly where you wanted me to go. All this time, I blamed myself for what happened with Abraham Turner in London. I thought you almost died because of me. Instead, you arranged the whole thing. That's why Adam Hunt didn't protest more when you wanted to join the investigation. He was working for the older, less idealistic version of that girl."

"That's not fair." Mina leaped to her feet. There were tears in her eyes. "I could have stopped all of this from happening simply by telling Adam Hunt not to let my younger self get involved. Then I would never have become a vampire, gone back in time, or founded the Order of St. George and CUSP. I was tempted, believe me. Then I realized that it would change nothing. You heard what Rory said about time travel when we were trapped in the 1940s. Any change to the timeline creates an alternate reality and allows the original reality to keep going unaltered. I wouldn't have achieved anything by stopping myself from helping defeat Jack the Ripper. All I would have done was create one reality that continued as preordained to lead us right where we find ourselves now, and another that split and took a different path. Hell, for all I know, I tried to change the future and the timelines *did* split. We just don't remember it because we're stuck in the original unaltered timeline."

Decker thought about this for a minute and realized she was right. Nothing Mina tried to do differently in the past would alter the future. At least, not *their future*. It had to happen this way, because it had already happened and always would happen. It made his head hurt. The anger drained away, and he sat down again. "I can't believe you were there all the time, working in the shadows to make sure everything happened the way it needed to. I'm not even sure which event precipitated the others. Did all this happen because of the encounter with Abraham Turner, or did the encounter with Jack the Ripper, and everything that came after, happen because you were there to steer destiny?"

"I'm not sure we'll ever know the answer to that. It's the classic chicken and egg causality dilemma," Mina said. She retook her seat and looked at Decker across the table. "It wasn't easy, keeping myself and Daisy hidden from sight all these years. There was barely anyone I could confide in except Adam Hunt, and I only took him into my confidence out of necessity. I ached for the day when the events of the last fourteen decades would catch up to themselves and you would be back. I missed you dreadfully. But I didn't know when and if you would reappear. That's why I had to create the monitoring stations. It would have ruined everything if you'd ended up returning to the twenty-first century days, weeks, or even months early and not realized exactly when and where you had ended up. The potential to split the timeline was too great."

"And the apartment?" Decker asked. "Why build such lavish quarters down here?"

"Because I needed to be here when you returned. I moved into these quarters over a year ago along with Daisy. We brought only Lucas to tend our needs. We've been here ever since, waiting for you to reappear, hoping you weren't lost forever in the void."

"You were down here when we were at the resort above for the wedding?"

"Yes. It took all my willpower not to pay you a visit. For all I knew, it would be my last chance."

"But you didn't, and that's probably for the best," Decker said. "Timelines and all that."

"I suppose. I saw you though. I snuck up and watched from afar the day of the wedding. Kept out of sight. I came back down here in such a black mood. Consoled myself that you would arrive back from the past sometime soon after and my long wait would be over. But you didn't, and I started to think it might take decades for you to get here, just like it did back in London, if at all." Mina slumped back in the chair. "I'm so glad all of this is over. It hasn't been easy going through life knowing the future. For the first time in almost a century and a half, I don't have a clue what's going to happen next. Can you imagine how liberating that feels?"

"Yes, I can," Decker said, reaching for his wine at last. He was exhausted, but happy to be in Mina's company, even though he wasn't sure if she was the same young woman he'd left behind in 1912. And as he took a sip, his thoughts turned to an even more exciting prospect. Being reunited, finally, with the woman he loved.

SEVENTY-NINE

NANCY ARRIVED home a little after five in the evening, which was unusual for her. Any other night, she would have still been at the bakery and might even have stayed there working until ten or even eleven. But Adam Hunt had called earlier in the day and requested that she meet him at the house. There were papers that needed to be signed. Papers to do with John that he claimed to have put off until now because he didn't want to upset her. But he could wait no longer. It was, he said, vital that they take care of this business right away. Which was why Nancy had agreed to meet him at the house even though she thought the bakery would be as good a place to sign a bunch of mundane paperwork as anywhere else. To be honest, she didn't even know why there was paperwork in the first place. Hunt had never asked her to sign anything before, like waivers of liability, or confidentiality agreements relating to John's work, so why would he decide to start now? It didn't make sense. But regardless, she was home promptly at five.

Going to the kitchen, Nancy opened the fridge and found a bottle of white wine, then poured herself a glass. She stood and listened to the silence. The house felt big. Empty. Celine had lived with her for over five months while she adjusted to life in a new century, but she couldn't stay forever, and had moved out a couple of weeks before into her own place. A small apartment overlooking the docks. It was perfect, because Celine refused to drive a car, and her new accommodation was close to Nancy's bakery and coffee shop where she still worked. At least when she wasn't spending time with Colum O'Shea, whose interest was obviously more than platonic, even if Celine wasn't yet ready for such a step. But in all fairness, the Irishman had been nothing but a gentleman, which came as a mild surprise to Nancy, given his reputation.

She took the wineglass and went back to the living room, then settled down on the sofa and pulled a blanket toward her, covering her feet. She took a sip and picked up a book she'd been reading, opening it to a page near the middle and removing the bookmark. But before she could begin reading, there was a knock at the door.

Nancy replaced the bookmark and closed the book, set it aside and put down the wine, then stood and went to the door, expecting to find Adam Hunt on the other side with those urgent papers in his hands. But when she opened it, there was someone else entirely waiting there.

Nancy gasped. Her hands flew to her mouth. For what seemed an eternity, she was frozen to the spot not even daring to breathe, afraid that the man on her doorstep was merely an illusion spawned by grief. Then, when she realized it wasn't a dream, she flung her arms around John Decker, buried her head against his chest, and cried tears of joy.

FINAL DESTINY

The next John Decker Thriller
Night Wraith

New Decker Universe Novella Series - The CUSP Files
Book 1 - **Deadly Truth**

ABOUT THE AUTHOR

Anthony M. Strong is a British-born writer living and working in the United States. He is the author of the popular John Decker series of supernatural adventure thrillers.

Anthony has worked as a graphic designer, newspaper writer, artist, and actor. When he was a young boy, he dreamed of becoming an Egyptologist and spent hours reading about pyramids and tombs. Until he discovered dinosaurs and decided to be a paleontologist instead. Neither career panned out, but he was left with a fascination for monsters and archaeology that serve him well in the John Decker books.

Anthony has traveled extensively across Europe and the United States, and weaves his love of travel into his novels, setting them both close to home and in far-off places.

Anthony currently resides most of the year on Florida's Space Coast where he can watch rockets launch from his balcony, and part of the year on an island in Maine, with his wife Sonya, and two furry bosses, Izzie and Hayden.

Connect with Anthony, find out about new releases, and get free books at www.anthonymstrong.com

Made in United States
North Haven, CT
13 December 2023

45645949R00236